CHASING ANTIGONE

Chasing Antigone

Stephen Hirst

Chasing Antigone
Stephen Hirst
Copyright 2015 Stephen Hirst
Revised Edition 2026
http://stephenmhirst.com

All Rights Reserved
No portion of this book may be published
without permission of the author

ISBN-13: 978-0692370254
ISBN-10: 0692370250

Cover and text design by Stephen Hirst
Cover art:
Almaisa, l'Algerina, Amadeo Modigliani 1916
Detail on *ca.* 550 BC Grecian urn, Frist Center for the Visual Arts, Nashville TN

The individuals and events depicted in this work are fictional.

Muuso Press

Flagstaff AZ

*Native peoples across the west speak widely
disparate languages; yet from the Great
Basin to Mexico they call the exotic house cat
"muuso." Linguists do not offer an explanation
for this odd singularity.*

CONTENTS

Heartfelt thanks to the accomplished writers of PlateauAuthors for their input, though they bear no responsibility for the final result. You know who you are Martha Blue, Marty Crump, Nancy Flood, Warren Perkins, and Kay Porter.

To the Vietnam vets who shared your stories in country and in the aftermath, words cannot do you justice.

To EMT extraordinaire Pete Walka, many thanks for guidance on emergency care.

The generosity of the Michigan Council for the Arts supported writing this story.

For her fine eye and attunement to period detail, consistency, and personal interaction I am completely indebted and in thrall to my most exacting editor, Lois Loesch Hirst.

Ἀντιγόνη:
τίς οἶδεν εἰ κάτωθεν εὐαγῆ τάδε;
οὔτοι συνέχθειν, ἀλλὰ συμφιλεῖν ἔφυν.

Antigone:
Who's to say our warring's sanctified?
I came here to love and not divide.

OHIO
March 9, 1970

Miamisburg, Ohio spreads east under darkness from its paired iron bridges across the Great Miami River. Two days of rain have flooded the bottomlands and inched the current halfway up the levee. Rafts of brush and driftwood rock against the bridge piers. A promise of spring scents the sleeping town with wild onion and river mud.

On the south edge of town, Monsanto's Mound Laboratory overlooks the Miami Valley from a limestone ridge split by the New York Central railroad. One side of the vast compound runs along the brink of the railway cut. A mile back from the cut, a 2,000-year-old Adena mound rises above the countryside. Come daylight, a few season-pushers will tee up on the golf course that surrounds it.

One-thirty in the morning: The week clicks into Monday. Soon, people will rise to another workday, but for now only a glare of floodlights traces the scatter of labs inside the concertina-topped chain link. A security guard moves among the buildings, crossing pools of illumination.

Art Montgomery's breath steams as he checks doors and tests enclosure gates. Stopping to check his watch, he lights a Camel and looks out over the valley.

Street lights flicker lines through the budding trees. Here and there a house winks from the darkness. A locomotive rumbling a coal train into the railway cut emits reverberant blasts as it approaches the town's dozen street crossings, some still paved in brick.

•

At the Miamisburg Municipal Building, Ethel Gebhardt reads the latest *Life* at the police station switchboard. Her week has already started, but she has not taken a night call since the Thanksgiving barn fire on Maue Road.

She turns to a photo story about the fighting in Indochina, thinking *What if it had a picture of Bob's outfit?*

The phone rings. Bother.

"Miamisburg Police," she answers.

A woman's voice jerks Ethel to attention.

"THERE'S A BOMB AT MONSANTO! YOU'VE GOT FIFTEEN MINUTES! Get everybody out!"

"Wait! What? Please, slow down! *What* now?"

1

"A bomb! At Monsanto! In Building T! It'll go off in fifteen minutes!"

"Monsanto?"

"Yes! And no one answers. Please, please, please, get someone out there to warn them!"

Ethel buzzes Mike Hoerner, the officer on night duty.

"All right. Calm down," she says, "Where are you calling from?"

"There is someone *in* Building T. You have to get him out before it's too late. Please! Move!"

The woman is screaming now. Mike appears at the door, and Ethel shields the mouthpiece to tell him, "Saddle up, Mike. I've got a woman on the line claims there's a bomb out at the atomic lab." She uncovers the receiver again.

"You say someone's inside. Do you know who?"

"Oh for Christ's sake! Montgomery I think."

"Art?"

"I don't know. Yes."

"Give me your name, please."

The woman says something incoherent. Ethel begs her to speak more slowly.

"It doesn't matter," the woman replies. "Just get someone out there."

"We are, but I need your name."

The woman says something that Ethel makes out as, "Ann Tiggany."

"What? Ann what? Spell that."

"God! *Antigone,* A-N-T-I-G-O-N-E. Now hurry, hurry, hurry! You have fourteen minutes. Do you understand? Fourteen minutes!"

"Got it. An officer is on the way, but stay on the line; I need your location."

The phone goes dead.

Keys in hand, Hoerner waits at the door for details.

Ethel tells him, "There's supposed to be a bomb in Building T, wherever that is. They'll know at the gate. Mike, doesn't Art Montgomery work out there?"

"Yeah. Security guard. Why?"

"According to this woman, he's in the building, and it's supposed to go off in—" She checks her watch. "thirteen or fourteen minutes."

Hoerner clucks his tongue. "I'm on the way. I bet it's kids."

"This didn't sound like a kid or anybody playing around."

"You'd be surprised."

"I'm telling you, Mike, I don't think she was joking. I'll get hold of somebody out there and have them keep an eye out for you. And, Mike, be careful; if she's serious, this thing could go off any minute."

•

Art Montgomery checks his watch again. One fifty. He reaches down and shuts off his two-way. Sweeping his flashlight, he walks directly to a brick building in the center of the laboratory complex. He gives a low whiste and then reels

2

out a master and lets himself in, making sure to leave the door unlocked behind him. A sign over the entrance reads simply "Building T."

Montgomery pockets his flashlight and proceeds to the guidance lab, where he punches in the admission code.

•

Ethel Gebhardt tries the main Monsanto number without much hope at this hour. As she expects, no one answers. None of the numbers listed raise anyone, and her directory lists nothing specific for the guardhouse or the gate. Wracking her brain for someone who works there, Ethel finally thinks of Marilyn: Her husband works the night shift. Marilyn answers half asleep after eight rings, and Ethel identifies herself apologetically to ask if she knows the front gate number for Monsanto. Her watch reads one fifty-one.

•

Officer Hoerner switches on his flasher but leaves the siren off. The streets are too quiet to need it.

Ethel needs to chase down a few of these pranks. Bombs are always pranks.

Rounding the corner at Mound, he steps on it until his headlights pick out a freight rumbling north across the street ahead, and he comes to a stop at the crossing gate. Slow-moving hopper cars creak around the long, banked curve from the railway cut into the street light and trundle away into the dark. Hoerner rolls down his window and listens. Far up the tracks, the locomotive horn drones monotonously. It must be across Kercher by now, blocking every crossing in town. He will have to turn back and head south under the railroad bridge and up Benner Road the back way. He swings around and smokes the tires. What if? The time is one fifty-two.

•

Ethel gets through, and a man answers, "Yo. Gate. Dick here."

"Dick!"

"Yeah, what's up?"

"This is Ethel. At police dispatch? We just had a bomb threat called in for Building T out there. It could be real. Mike Hoerner's on his way; should be there any minute."

"All right; we'll check it out."

"Listen, be careful. Just get everyone out. The caller said it's supposed to go off around two o'clock. That's only five minutes."

"Okay, will do. Thanks."

Dick sees no sign of any police cars coming up Mound and punches the two-way to let Art, who should be out making the rounds, know the situation. Probably some of these long-hairs trying to scare people about the war, but he is not taking chances.

3

"Art, 23-11, Art, come in. This is Dick, 23-10. Over."

Static. He shakes the radio. Is his battery dead?

"Art, 23-11, come in. Emergency. Dick here, 23-10. Over."

Still no answer. Peculiar. Sonofagun must be sleeping. Dick gets out the plant directory and looks up the guidance lab to be on the safe side.

•

Art Montgomery grows irritated. His watch reads two o'clock. Still no show. He picks up the phone on the unit director's desk to see what the holdup is but gets no tone. Lifting the phone, he discovers the modular cord missing. Typical.

•

Officer Hoerner screams up Benner Road. Still a mile to the lab. He glances at his dash clock, which now reads two. It clicks over to two-oh-one. Nothing happens. He relaxes a little and lets up on the gas. Thank God. A hoax after all. Still, better a wild goose chase than the real thing.

•

Dick lets the guidance project ring twenty times before he breathes relief. Art would hear it if he were in the building, so he must not be. He would go look, but that would leave the gate unmanned. The police should have been here by now. Switching batteries in the two-way, Dick tries one more time and shakes his head. They will give him shit and fifteen reports to fill out, but he's going to sound a general alarm. He wants Art in here now. There is no excuse for this.

•

Feeling with his feet, Art tries to locate the phone cord. No luck. Bastard should have been here with the money five minutes ago. Art just hopes he has not been suckered, or he is definitely going to kick some butt.

The general emergency sounds. Art jumps to his feet. The dumbass probably set it off at the door.

•

Hoerner wheels onto Mound Road, cruising now. Just as the Monsanto fence comes into view alongside, sirens start whooping from all the buildings. When Hoerner steps on it and turns to look, a huge, blinding flash goes up right in his line of sight. A second later, the impact hits his patrol car with such force that Hoerner jams on the brakes and kills the engine. Brick rattles across the pavement as he stares out the window in disbelief, his ears still ringing. A chunk of masonry clanks off the cartop, and then another.

4

MICHIGAN
November 1992

The hitchhiker emerged ghostlike from the snow crossing Graham's headlights. Miles from nowhere, he waited with half-raised thumb as if the appearance of a car made no difference.

Graham slid to a stop in the snow along the road. He needed company.

After jolting awake halfway across a bridge with the speedometer pegged on sixty about ten miles back, Graham had tried pinching and slapping himself, finally resorting to musical caffeine, the honky-tonkin' done-me-wrong of WJPD, to stay awake. Driving with the window rolled down, he had been wailing into the frigid blast with Loretta Lynn and Willie Nelson, all to no avail. Twice more he had nodded off.

Graham watched the man scuff up in the rear-view mirror dragging an olive-drab duffel. God knew what he was doing way out here in the wilds of Michigan's Upper Peninsula. He had on faded jeans and what looked like an embroidered red bowling jacket straight from St. Vinnie's. The man pulled open the door and hoisted his duffel.

In the dome light, his dirty blonde hair—thin on top and pulled over to maximize the coverage—hung almost to his collar. Stubble undid whatever impression the man's half-neat goatee might have made. His gray-tinted aviator glasses looked incongruously expensive.

Graham reached across and popped the seatback so the man could toss his duffel onto the truck's jumpseat. As the man slid in and turned to pull the door shut, Graham glimpsed the legend on his jacket before the dome light went off: "THE LORD IS COMING." Some kind of x-shaped emblem below it.

"Good of you to stop, pal. Dave Meachum," the man said, extending his hand across the seat. He smelled like patchouli and dirty socks.

"Graham Bell." Graham half offered a hand, waiting for the man's inevitable "related to the telephone?" before easing his Toyota pickup out of the snow and back onto the road. Instead, Meachum pumped his hand like a politician until Graham finally had to pull it away so he could back up for a better run at the pavement.

Meachum said, "You spell 'Graham' like the cracker?"

Graham looked over to see him jotting something in a small spiral pad.

5

"Like to keep track of the people I meet." The man tucked the notepad back into his jacket. He continued talking as the truck achieved the roadway, but Graham was not listening.

"Where are you headed?" Graham finally asked.

"St. Ignace, then Detroit."

"I can give you an hour down the road to Marquette."

"Maybe I'll lay over. Been on the road three days from Boise."

Graham worried this meant Dave Meachum would crap out and leave him fighting sleep on his own again, but the man quickly put that concern to rest.

"Lot of people think I'm crazy traveling this way," he went on, "but way back I made a vow to go light and cheap. Trust in good people and the Lord's provision."

"Yeah. I used to hitch myself."

"Did you now? Get around a bit?"

"Not that much. Went to school in Berkeley. Used to travel back and forth from home. Up and down the coast a few times."

"Berserkly. Put in a few years there myself in the Sixties. Quite the scene. Was into it myself at the time. Deeply into it."

Graham glanced to see the man studying him.

"Different times, Graham. Got no car, no bank account, no address now."

"What do you do for a roof?"

"Like I say, the Lord provides. Pretty much live on the road. Meet lots of fine people like yourself, and that keeps me going."

Graham suspected a touch in the works before long. What would it be, a few dollars or a place to crash?

"Say, I wonder if you'd mind rolling up the window, Graham. I've been out in the weather since Sunday. Like to warm up some. If it's all the same with you."

As Graham cranked the window shut, a deer emerged from the woods ahead and considered the road, its eyes reflecting green. Graham eased off the gas to see what the deer had in mind. For a second it seemed inclined to take a leap but then retreated to the trees. The snow blowing into the beams was making Graham dizzy.

"Got critters up here, do you?" the man observed.

"Yep."

"So what do you do, Graham, all the way out here?"

"Teach a course, for the university."

"That so? What university?"

"Northern Michigan University. In Marquette. I come up this way every week to teach an extension course."

"Professor!"

"Sort of. Math. What about you?"

"Like a fireman. Except I attend to the Lord's work, putting out blazes for Him."

"I bet." Graham wondered why he always encountered such weirdoes. A whirl of snow ahead indicated he was catching a log truck.

"Got a family, Graham?"

Graham shook his head, unwilling to make chitchat on that one.

Ignoring Graham's refusal, the man went right on. "Used to have one. Got into a scrape, got myself sent up a few years. Long and short is, my woman took off, and the bank took everything. Like to killed her when I heard. But I came to terms with it when I got the calling. The Lord said he had work for me. From that day I was His."

Graham hung back from the load ahead. The snow and debris the trailer was sweeping up was making the view dicey. He wondered if the man was just a walkaway from Baraga Correctional Camp. He had been standing only a few miles from the M-28 intersection after all.

"You don't have to go into it if you don't want," the man said. *"Your* family."

Graham shrugged, focused on the whiteout ahead. Answering might invite more questions, but the man's remark about his runaway wife irked Graham more than a little. What did he know?

"Don't mean to be nosy."

"I'm trying to get us around this truck without getting killed."

"Sure. Take your time."

"If you must know, I did that myself, cut out, split." Graham kept his eyes on the road. "Wife and a daughter. I haven't seen them since. I'm not proud of it, but it happened." He shut up. The whole scene was not something he wanted to recall.

"Yeah, we had kids." The man seemed unable to abide silence. "A son and a daughter. Well, they were hers. I doubt they even think about me. And your wife? Where's she?"

"Somewhere. Ohio I think. Remarried."

"Ohio," the man noted with sudden interest, "What's she do there?"

"Teach. She used to be a science teacher. Probably still is."

"Oh," Meachum said, then tried another tack. "How do you feel about it?"

"I said, I'm not proud of it."

"I reckon you made a mistake. You can still redeem yourself."

"Redeem myself?"

"Your daughter."

"Forget about it."

"Just a thought. Myself, I wonder about my own family, but I expect the little lady has found someone else for her hot pants now. Men always had the eye for her."

Graham glanced across at this.

"Anyway I'm a soldier of the Lord now. Not a halfway kind of thing. Whatever my own feelings might be, the Lord has His agenda. Like that with you?"

"No."

"People think faith is easy. 'Believe on him, and ye shall be saved' kind of thing, but the Lord wants soldiers. He's not looking for freeloaders."

"So you go around converting people?"

"No sir. I do the Lord's work. I fight His fights."

"What kind of fights are we talking here?"

"Abortion, homos, radicals, any people weaken the Lord's nation, I'm on them. It's a deal I cut with the law. I track them, like a bounty hunter."

Graham sorted all this. "What about being deeply into the scene at Berkeley?"

"We change. The Lord's work is what I'm talking now. America's the Lord's nation, my man, and nobody better fuck with it, if you'll excuse my language. Take a look at this."

When Meachum clicked on the dome light, Graham expected to see a deck of nude women. The man instead opened his jacket to show his tee shirt with gentle, bearded Jesus and a body like Sylvester Stallone's, cradling an M-16. The legend, "…is Coming with a Sword" curved into view around Meachum's belly. Graham snapped off the dome light.

"I sell these at the rallies. People think Jesus is about turning the other cheek, but I say the Lord is no wimp. Somebody who parts the sea does not turn the other cheek, my friend. He smites."

"I thought that was Moses."

"They think I do it to get in the news, but I tell them, 'Hey, smile for the camera. You can stand up here.' Nosiree, you have a message, you don't sit back until people figure it out. These so-called Christians, they say my message is hard, but when there's a wrong, you fix it. Usually I sell these shirts for ten dollars, but I'll give you one when we stop. Got a few in my bag, more on the way."

"Thanks. You can keep it; not my style."

"Ah. You're not saved. That's okay. Come to the Lord when you're ready, I say. I'm no proselytizer; I'm a warrior. Tell you something: Young people don't have any idea what the Sixties were. We stood for things. Not this half-assed maybe so-maybe no like today."

Graham wondered if turning up the radio just enough to compete would seem too rude. Admittedly, this fellow was doing his part to keep anyone from falling asleep. Graham could feel Meachum looking at him again.

"I should have seen it. You looked younger. Vet, aren't you?"

Graham kept his mouth shut and stared into the snow wake ahead, a stab of ice at his heart. He should have realized, all the questions. The guy's onto him.

"Survived it anyway," Meachum said.

"Some did."

"If you served on principle …"

"I didn't."

"We were lied to. You know that, Graham? Lied to. They did wrong to send us elsewhere for an enemy. We had no quarrel with those Vietnamese. No sir, that's not where the enemy was. It was Washington."

Graham made a non-committal sound.

"Believe me. That's how it was. I know; I was involved in national security, if you get my drift, so close to the evil I couldn't miss it."

"Whatever you say."

"Tell you something, Graham: The enemies of the Lord were in power; even I didn't see it all."

Graham rubbed his forehead. The whole discussion rattled his brain. Where was he going with this? He wished he hadn't given the man his name.

Finally at Westwood the road widened to four lanes and the snow stopped. As he zipped through Ishpeming and Negaunee, the last burgs before Marquette, Graham half hoped the man might like them well enough to jump off and spend the night. No such luck.

As they descended the long grade into Marquette, he could see the moon shimmering across Lake Superior. Only a few more miles; he had better start prying this Dave Meachum loose.

"Where would you like to get out in Marquette?"

"Don't really know. Do you live close in?"

He would be putting this guy up if he didn't watch out.

"Actually I'll run through town and let you off by the post office. It's only a short walk from there to the Salvation Army, or there's a hotel I can show you."

Graham turned downtown. Across from the post office, he pulled over to the curb and stopped.

"Here you go."

The man held out his hand.

"Graham, I've enjoyed talking to you."

Graham shook his hand and managed a smile. The man opened the door part way and put one foot on the pavement.

"God loves you."

"I'm sure. Right up there behind the post office is the Salvation Army. And the other way, down there, is the hotel I was telling you about." Graham wanted to be sure Dave Meachum had clear directions to somewhere that was not his house.

"I'm not telling you what to believe. Far from it. The real message I want to leave you is to act, see? Take part."

"Sure, I'll do that."

"You say you will, but you'll settle back in. Take the easy road."

The man was still sitting with the door half open. Winter wind was whipping through the car.

9

"Yeah. I really have to go."

"I have work in your country, Graham. The Lord called me here. You'll read about me. Think about what I said."

"If you could get your bag please."

"I make you uncomfortable."

He extended his hand again. Graham took it but this time kept the shake as brief and formal as possible. He wished again he had never given his last name.

"Whatever."

Half ashamed to be doing it, Graham punched the door lock as soon as Meachum shouldered his bag. He breathed a great sigh of relief as the man walked away up Third Street toward the Salvation Army. Graham made sure Meachum was out of sight before turning the key. As soon as the engine caught, he made a spinning U-turn and sped off the back way to his house.

2

Graham slipped in the back door and stood in the dark, jarred by the encounter on the road and the hitchhiker's remark:

Redeem yourself. Your daughter.

He set his papers on the kitchen table and stepped to the window. Old-fashioned boulevard lamps measured pools of light along the street. Nothing populated them.

By the small fluorescent light over the phone, he found Leila's undialed number where he had stuck it six years ago when he received the notice to cut his support payments. His watch read eight; she might be grading papers, if she even lived there any more.

He drummed the wall, twice put his finger to the "1" and thought better of it, before simply doing it. His breath caught with each ring.

On the fourth ring the breezy familiarity of her voice clutched his heart.

"Helloo?"

"Leila."

Silence. No, breathing, hers: probably deciding what to say. Once that sound had been more precious than life.

"Are you there?" he said.

"It depends."

"This is Graham."

"I recognize that. What?"

Say something.

He picked up a pencil and twiddled it around his fingers to steady them.

"How are you?" he finally managed.

"Oh, *I'm* fine." Her emphasis implied he might not be.

"That's good. Listen, the thing is, I'm calling because— I'm glad you're fine by the way. Really. I mean, I hoped you would be. And I'm glad you are."

"You said that."

"I did. The thing is, I am. Glad. How's Julie?"

He twirled the pencil faster. His hands were sweating.

"Funny you should ask."

"Don't, Leila."

"All right, I won't. Let me ask you something. Are you functioning?"

He switched off the light and stretched the phone cord to the table so he could sit. The pencil rolled back and forth under his palm. He didn't like where this was headed.

"Gainfully employed," she prompted.

11

"Me? You want to know if I— Oh sure. I—"

"Doing what?"

"Teaching mathematics. At a university, Northern Michigan. In—"

"Marquette."

"You know it."

"I know where you are."

He held the handset out waiting for a genie to emerge and illuminate the kitchen.

"Really."

"Omigod. You got my note about the support payments. I need to know your whereabouts in case you manage to get yourself killed or something. Mathematics: So how does that work?"

"It's not Einstein. I'm lucky if I get calculus."

"You've been doing this for how long?"

"Eight years. And I volunteer. Red Cross, the hospital."

"Not in the pharmacy, I hope."

The pencil snapped in two.

"No, and I'm clean, for your information. Absolutely. Totally. Nine years now. It wasn't easy. I needed help."

"Amen. Whatever was going on with you, I certainly hope you're not there any more."

"I'm not. Believe me, I'm not. I'm more like— like I used to be when, at first, you know. Maybe a little smarter, I hope. I'm sure you are, too. Smarter."

"Wised up anyway."

She was probably tapping her teeth with a thumbnail. Her nose would wrinkle.

"Leila, I wish—"

"Don't."

"He's there."

"What do you think?"

"Well. That's great."

"I can tell how great you think that is."

Graham stood, tasting brass, all his buttons pushed. What ever gave him the idea to do this? He was about to replace the handset on the wall when her voice caught him.

"Sorry. That was cold."

He ran his fingertip up and down a wallpaper seam deciding whether to respond or hang up.

"Are you going to tell me about Julie?"

"Depends."

"I wondered if she's okay, for starters, what she's doing, where she is."

"Why do you want to know where she is?"

"I thought I'd send her a card."

"Why don't I give you her phone? You should talk to her."

"I'd rather write. That way, she can ignore me if she wants."

Nearly ten seconds of even breathing followed.

"Whatever. Here's her address."

He switched the light on to jot it down.

"New York!" he said. "What ever—"

"Ask her. She'll surprise you. I still think you should speak to her directly."

"And I don't. She'd hang up on me."

"You don't know her."

She did not sound finished.

"Graham? It'll go okay. Not just with her, with you."

He was so flabbergasted he thanked her for the address without even acknowledging the valediction.

He found the pencil halves in the dark, broke them again, and fired the pieces at the waste basket. Bad aim; they hit the wall and clattered across the floor.

3

Several days passed before Graham faced his computer to begin. He stared at the empty document on the screen.

"Julie," he typed and sat rubbing his hands together.

She'd be 23 now, almost 24, born only a few weeks from today in March, while he was still in southeast Asia, and now a young woman, his own daughter and a stranger.

Leila had thought to take up where they left off before the war, but he was no longer the person he had been. Whether his mother could have salvaged him didn't figure; she was gone. Angry and confused, he had no one to tell what he had survived. Seeking out veterans felt pathetic. What, he was going to sit in a VFW post and trade war stories? When he did run into returnees, it centered around bitching.

He tried. When Leila started teaching in Santa Cruz, he got himself licensed as a paramedic; medical school was beyond him in the state he was in. What followed hardly bore remembering.

He typed, *"Leila gave me your address,"* backed it out, and started again.

"I asked Leila for your address. New York! And you're going to be 24 soon. How much I've missed, so many birthdays between."

That sounded forced. He backed out all but the first sentence and re-typed it to read, *"I asked Leila for your address. All these years I tried to leave behind what I was, what I did. Leila can tell you some of it, if she hasn't."*

Folding his hands over the keyboard, he recalled capsizing in pain and confusion hard to imagine now. Turning down the volume called for new forms of self-destruction—smoking dope behind the hospital, imbibing his secret stash in the garage. He worried he could harm someone. He never told Leila that.

The hospital sprang a drug test on him. He tried to beg off, claiming a kidney infection; there would be cannabis in the works. They all must have known, but he had so pathetically believed in his masquerade that he thought the results would shock the staff. They didn't. Out of work, out of honor, he ran. One day he literally was not there, leaving Leila with a three-year-old. How could he have done that?

"I left you behind, too." he typed. *"That was wrong. It hurts to think how I have failed you, because you are still part of who I am or should be.*

"After this long, if you disdain hearing from me, I understand. I won't try to explain what I was going through; the baggage is no justification. It was inexcusable."

Leaving, he had walked up Kilkare Canyon to his old man's place seeking light from the romantic shopkeeper/poet of his childhood; but the old man's grasp had wandered into the mists of Genesis and Revelations without the anchor of his wife's realism. His sister Tara was staying with the old man, her hands already full trying to keep him from taking off entirely to the realm of navel contemplation. She saved no patience for Graham when she learned of his royal screw-up. He was not welcome.

Eventually Tara had relented enough to tell him when Leila split Santa Cruz for Stockton, where the Manooghian clan had their roots. By the time he got that address, she had already moved on to teach in Cincinnati. Gone. There were no arrangements, no settlement. He sent monthly financial penance, often beyond what he could afford. Leila neither requested nor responded to it until he received a formal divorce notice some nine years later turning his conscience money to an obligation. Then she remarried.

"I can't do it over. All I can do is ask your forgiveness."

He backed out *"your forgiveness"* and typed, *"for this next year to bring you everything you can wish. Believe it or not, I think of you often."*

He paused over the keys. Whether that last was strictly true, she needed to believe it was.

To finish with some nod to accuracy, he typed, *"You may not believe that after this long, and I could not blame you. Anyway, please accept my best wishes."*

He backed that out and retyped, *"Anyway, please accept me if you can."*

The news of Leila's remarriage had killed him. He found it incredible now that he would have expected her to suffer his abandonment. Nonetheless, he had gone into a three-day freefall that finally resulted in trying to go cold turkey before he lost it altogether. It took two years to straighten out, in part because he had such a hard time convincing himself it mattered, afterward drifting to this northern extreme eight years ago to begin anew. As if he could.

Teaching helped; volunteering, even more. Red Cross and the hospital welcomed his first aid and CPR training, and some of the older vets at the VA he practically made into family. Not his peers; them he avoided. Their arrival at such a place unhinged him still.

He folded his hands for a long time over the keyboard before signing himself simply, *"Your father, Graham."*

He printed an envelope, stamped it, and walked it to a drop box so he could not change his mind. Nothing would come back, but he had opened a door, if only in himself.

4

Sunrise at this northern latitude was still hours away when Graham started the day, padding the icy kitchen floor barefoot as the coffee brewed. He had stayed up far too late going over student papers last night. Pouring himself a mug, Graham ran his fingers through his hair. Either he should find a woman or get a cat. Living alone was turning him into a bachelor. While his hair wasn't near the Anchorite length of the old man's, the hitchhiker had definitely given him an aversion to looking ragged. An appointment with Cheryl Maki was in order.

He'd become her customer on the ski hill. Some fellow racers who competed in the Wednesday-evening ski league with Graham had set up a Sunday slalom course at the very end of the season, when a young woman he had seen on the hill a few times skied up to ask if they minded her running the course with them. No one had a problem with this; she was nice to look at. Not only that; when she'd raised her goggles he actually knew her. She'd taken his analytic geometry course, a very bright girl.

Cheryl's ski tails had come two feet off the snow as she dived out of their makeshift start and proceeded to shred the course like a speedboat through cattails. Graham had been waiting when she carved to a stop for her next go.

"How'd you like to be on our team next year?" he had greeted her. "We need a woman and just took a unanimous vote."

After Cheryl had told him she worked at Laborers of Hair Curlers for her day job, Graham stopped wondering how many ways one could work "hair" into a cute business name; that one took the cake. He had to sound it out before he realized: Labors of Hercules. The shop logo of a hand grasping a headful of wild hair should have given him the clue. Obviously tailored to the university crowd with a name like that, her shop—which everyone called LHC—was heavily patronized. On the spot he'd decided to give the place a try; how bad could it be with someone like Cheryl working there?

After years of having men cut his hair in shops sporting red-and-white barberpoles, how would it feel to let a woman, reading *Elle* while he waited instead of *The Sporting News*?

Just fine.

Someone at the shop subscribed to *Rolling Stone*, and Cheryl proved as effusive as she had in class and on the ski hill. The whole time she was snipping, she bantered with everyone in earshot. Only, instead of clubby World Series talk and politics, Cheryl gabbed books and film. Besides being an avid mountain biker and skier, she was enrolled part-time in the university's pre-med program, another area of common interest. Instead of top forty or easy listening, their speakers blared nonstop Janis Joplin and lowdown, funky bluesmen like Big Joe Turner and Lightnin' Hopkins.

•

Graham knew practically everyone who worked there. With one exception—a woman about his own age who worked at the back of the shop by the shampoo sinks. "Linda," Cheryl called her, but Linda rarely participated in the shop chatter beyond a remote smile. The one occasion she did speak up, she didn't have the *Minnesoowta* accent of the locals.

He would have thought her taciturn if he had not seen how she went on with her clients—always women. Sometimes she'd sing to herself between appointments.

Really it was her face. Not quite Botticelli, the dark challenge of Linda's eyes said Modigliani. Her face spelled *fox*. It had focus, with cheekbones that slanted her eyes.

She used no make-up and sported a bob of plain bronze-dark hair.

None of the rings she wore hinted marriage or engagement; neither did she take male customers.

At Graham's age, interesting female opportunities were hardly falling from trees, given that he did not permit himself the coeds or married women who always seemed to insinuate themselves. And this woman simply wasn't available. She acted almost prim about herself, never checking the mirror or pushing a lock into place. Still, he had a hard time not sneaking glances.

She wore a belted smock at work and strappy sandals during the short Upper Peninsula summer. Once during sandal season her smock parted to reveal a heart-stopping thigh before she flapped it down with the back of her hand.

Linda specialized in razor cutting and worked fast and efficiently at it. Her brisk strokes looked like sculpting more than cutting. Sometimes when Linda was doing her thing Graham had to ask Cheryl to repeat herself.

•

Showing up at three for the appointment he'd made, Graham was soon laughing with Cheryl about the ski league race the other evening. On her first run Cheryl had crashed and burned two gates from the finish. She was still limping but assured him she would be ready for Wednesday.

Grace Slick began "I Need Somebody to Love" on the shop speakers. A few stanzas in, Cheryl reached over and turned down the sound. From the back of the shop, the singing continued a few bars in full gravel until the *chanteuse* noticed she was *a capella*.

"You need a band," Cheryl laughed.

Linda turned from her styling and half smiled.

17

Graham tracked her in the mirror when she returned from the cash register after she finished her customer. Back at her station, she arched her back and rotated her head, working the kinks out.

A pair of scissors clanked onto the floor. Linda sighed and crossed an ankle over her knee to let herself down on one leg. Squatting on her heel, she retrieved the scissors and stood in one smooth motion.

Cheryl straightened his head from where he had it angled, watching. Cheryl's eyes were on his in the mirror.

"Bet you can't do that," she confided.

"You'd be right. What is she, a dancer?"

"Frieda says martial arts. Linda showed her some moves." Frieda owned the shop.

Graham asked suddenly, "Can you cut with a razor?"

"Yeah, why?"

"Just asking."

Suddenly Cheryl angled her face around at his. "You have a thing about her, don't you?"

"Please."

"I have eyes, bud," she said. "Anyway, Linda's the pro. Didn't you learn razor cutting on the West Coast or somewhere, Linda?"

Graham shrank when Linda interrupted her sweeping.

"Me?" She spoke to Cheryl, but her look fixed on Graham. "I learned styling in the Big Apple."

Graham was glad Linda could not see his blush when she waved her next customer back. He knew Cheryl could, in the mirror. Uttering the first inanity that entered his head, he asked, "So do you think you'll make it down the hill next week?"

"You do, don't you?" Cheryl's reflection peered at him keenly.

"Do what?"

She leaned in and whispered, "Notice her."

"None of your business."

Midway through his haircut, Graham found himself checking out Linda again and averted his eyes to attend to Cheryl's small talk.

Afterward, taking his money at the register, Cheryl imparted *sotto voce*, "I don't think she's spoken for." She gave him a wicked grin.

18

5

Graham leafed through his program before the lights went down. Scanning the notes took his mind off the empty seat beside him, probably the only one in the theater.

Amid much fanfare, the university's drama department had won an NEA grant to stage a modern adaptation of Sophocles's Oedipus cycle focused on the daughter Antigone. The announcement had set off quite a stir; and Graham had been lucky to snag two tickets the day they went on sale, thinking to invite his friend Gwen from the Art Department.

Gwen had become an older sister who loved stagecraft. After performances they would deconstruct drama and life with friends, and the idea of making Sophocles current would wonderfully engage her. Unfortunately, when he finally got around to asking, Gwen already had plans out of town.

The upshot was that Graham not only departed for the theater alone but also forgot to bring the extra ticket. As he had edged through the crowd at the ticket window, he cursed himself for leaving it home; he would have sold it in a second.

He looked around the small auditorium as the lights began to dim, seeking people to chat with at intermission. Just before the lights went completely down, a woman with sandy hair two rows ahead caught his eye. The woman presented herself in profile just as the auditorium darkened. She reminded him of someone, but then the action on stage captured him.

Several times Graham peered at the woman up front, now that his eyes had adjusted to the darkness. The woman's failure to speak to those on either side of her suggested she had come alone.

The lights went up for a quick break while the stage changed for the next scene. Two rows up, the sandy-haired woman stood in a beige buttoned sweater and removed a pair of reading glasses from her dark eyes to scan the audience behind her. Graham focused; the woman either was Linda from LHC or a pale version of her. Her gaze swept across Graham without recognition.

The lights flashed, and the curtain went up.

Graham wished Gwen could have come to hear her take on it. On re-reading *Antigone* beforehand, he'd found it remarkable that Sophocles placed a woman at the center of the drama as a daring person of action risking even death to bury her rebellious brother Polyneices.

At the main intermission, Graham left his coat on the seat and walked out to the lobby looking for colleagues with whom to compare notes. There, leaning with her ankles crossed by a window, was the sandy-haired woman tracing a finger down her program.

Graham drifted closer. "Linda?"

He left enough space to mumble an apology and fade. For a second the woman failed to react, her head still inclined over the program; then she peered over her reading glasses.

"Hello, Graham."

She knew his name.

"Fancy seeing *you* here!" He wanted to sound nonchalant.

She lowered her program. Up close, she had a crease between her brows, like someone who didn't smile easily. She reminded slightly of old photos of Anaïs Nin, a woman who knew things he ought to know. Graham found it hard to meet her eyes.

"You're surprised," she said.

"I just didn't recognize you."

She twisted her finger into a forelock and tilted her head, studying him.

"Me at the opera you mean." Her lips twitched into a small bow.

"No. I mean I didn't expect... um..."

God! Could he have begun worse?

"That it would interest me?" Her cheek dimpled a smile. "Culture doesn't hurt."

"I didn't mean that. I was just... surprised. So, um, do you like how they're staging it?"

"It works."

"I like the way Sophocles uses women at the center of things. It really comes through in *Antigone*. See, she's going to try burying her brother—"

"The program says."

"Yes, but it's interesting isn't it? We come to see what happens, while the Greeks already knew. They came for the meaning of the event rather than the event itself."

God, why did he do this? She probably had no idea what he was going on about, and he just blabbed away. She flustered him.

She folded her program lengthwise and then again.

"They followed the ripples."

Linda stopped him with this. He had taken her for a Borzoi, all sleek and no brains.

"That's a nice way of putting it. Do you care if I call you Linda? I don't know your last name."

"Linda's fine."

"Um, I noticed you're just a few rows in front of me. I would join you—I mean if there were a vacant seat."

"Yes, unfortunately there isn't."

20

Her "unfortunately" sounded at least receptive enough that Graham asked, "Would you mind joining me? I bought two tickets, and I have an empty seat."

She regarded him with a look one might use to study a bug.

"I see."

The lights dimmed for the next act, so they moved toward the auditorium. As they passed inside, Linda said, "Nice talking with you."

It sounded like a dismissal, and his heart sank further when she reached his row and walked on. He took his seat, disappointed. Then Linda was squeezing her way across to him in the dimming light, trailing her shoulder bag across people's laps and the coat she had retrieved, excusing herself. She draped the coat over the seat beside him in the dark and settled herself.

"I decided I would."

"Thanks. It's much nicer to have company."

"Sometimes."

Graham did not ask if this was one of them. He started to say something more, but she shook her head and put a finger to her lips. The curtain was rising.

Antigone was defying King Creon, and the penalty for her disobedience was public execution. Graham glanced alongside. Linda had pressed her hands together against her lips, following the words as if they were written in a language she hoped to learn.

Later, when the sentries brought Antigone before Creon, she thumbed her nose at his decree and his authority as well.

"Think me a fool, if you like," she defied, "but it may be the fool who convicts me of folly."

Graham liked how the actress handled this, raising herself to deliver the line with a note of brass. She was a willow of a woman, but she made a great Antigone

When Creon said that those who die traitors deserve no honor, she replied, "Ah, Creon, who's to say whether the gods heed such distinctions?"

Linda whispered something, and Graham looked over to see her absolutely riveted, reciting Antigone's lines.

"My blood compels me to love, not to take sides," the actress proclaimed. A tear coursed down Linda's cheek, and she quickly raised a hand to her face.

Abashed, Graham averted his eyes. The chorus was bewailing the loss of Antigone before Graham dared another peek. Linda had buried whatever had overflowed. She looked almost disdainful.

While they walked up the aisle after the play, Graham observed, "You really got into the performance tonight."

"Did I? I suppose I might have."

"You're familiar with *Antigone*. I couldn't help seeing you know the lines."

She knit her brows. "You imagine things."

"You were reciting them."

"You saw me cry, didn't you?"

Her directness stopped him. "You were what?"

"For heaven's sake, I'm not drawing you a picture. Shall we stop pretending with one another?"

"Sorry," Graham apologized. "None of my business."

"No, it isn't, but you didn't know that." Then she shrugged as if her sudden flare was inconsequential. "Yes, I know parts of it. Antigone touches me."

She turned and gave him a thin smile, but her eyes did not take part.

Outside, Graham tried to make amends by asking, "It's only eleven; maybe the Kaffee Haus is still open. Want to see?"

"Another time maybe. It's late now."

"How about a lift home? My truck's up the block. I'd be happy to give you a ride."

"No, thanks. It's not far."

"Are you sure? It's really cold. It wouldn't be any trouble."

"Please don't insist. We'll see each other again, I'm sure."

Graham nodded, and she walked away up Seventh Street. It took Graham a good five minutes to reach his car and get it started in the cold. Nearly ten minutes elapsed before his headlights picked out a woman kicking along at a smart clip as she crossed Hewitt Street. It was Linda, a good half mile from the theater.

6

First thing in the morning, Graham was on the phone to Cheryl to ask who would ski for them the following Wednesday. They discussed the lineup a few minutes, then Graham brought up what was really on his mind. "By the way, the woman at the back of the shop, what's her name?..."

"Linda?"

"Yeah, Linda. I ran into her at Forrest Roberts Theater Friday evening."

"That's nice. And?"

Graham stopped himself from going into detail; if Linda's tears were not his business, they wouldn't be Cheryl's either.

"She looked completely different. Her hair was another color."

"Why not? It's what she does for a living."

"I don't know. She just seems elusive. Don't you think?"

"She's private."

"If you say so. What did you tell me her last name was?"

Cheryl began to laugh. "I didn't. It's Chapman. Professor Bell! I do believe you're hooked."

He paused. "Is she seeing anyone? Married?"

"I told you: She's all yours."

As soon as he hung up, Graham went right to the telephone directory and looked up "Chapman." He found about thirty listings, none of them close to where he had seen her walking. There was no Linda Chapman.

7

The sprightly gavotte of William Boyce's symphony no. 8 sounded a dissonance for the sunset of the baroque. Its musical conflict half registered as Graham steadied ten pounds of stained glass on a stepladder.

A floodlight clamped to the buffet illuminated his work; he should be doing this in daylight but could not tolerate the non-period ceiling fixture he was replacing any longer. Tomorrow would be ski night, and he would have no time then. Thursday he was filling in for one of the EMTs driving ambulance.

Tomorrow would be the last race of the Wednesday ski league, and Cheryl might not even make it. Graham's university team stood within a hair of taking the season, and Cheryl had to get a cold.

He sat atop the stepladder balancing the Tiffany-glass canopy on his thighs and twisted the leads onto the asphalt wire hanging through the ceiling plaster. An electrician had assured him the old wiring could carry any amperage he wanted as long as the insulation remained intact. Still, it had to be a century old.

What would Leila do if he fell off the ladder and broke his neck? Would she really care if he managed to kill himself? Would anyone? Graham turned the canopy to better illuminate his work and began connecting the hot side with a wire nut.

The phone rang. He stopped at the interruption, then decided to let it ring.

If it was Gwen, she could leave a message.

The phone rang again as he attached the common line. He balanced the faux-plaster ceiling medallion on his arm as the phone rang a third time.

He set the half-wired canopy atop the stepladder, balanced the medallion on the whole enterprise, and clambered partway down with a coil of extra wire in his hand. The phone rang a fourth time. One more, and the answering machine would kick in. He steadied the ladder and stepped to the phone.

The fifth ring clicked the answering machine on. His recording said to leave a message. A woman's voice spoke, unfamiliar.

"Could, um, Mr. Bell call me, if he would. The number is two-one-two—"

New York.

Graham snatched up the receiver. "Yes?"

"Six— Oh. May I speak to Graham Bell?"

"Speaking."

"Oh. This is, um, Julie. I got your note."

Julie? Graham's throat constricted. As he floundered for words, she prompted, "Your daughter?"

"I know, I know. I'm just— Wow. How *are* you? *Where* are you?"

24

"Yes, well, I'm fine. I'm in New York."

"Leila said."

"And you're in Michigan. What do you do there?"

"I'm a math instructor. Among other things."

"Really. How long've you been doing that?"

"Seven or eight years. What about you?"

"Columbia School of Journalism. I just got on with the *Times* as an investigative intern."

He was floored. His own daughter.

"Julie, that's... Columbia!"

"Well. I'm free-lancing some, too. I've been writing for the *Voice*. It's New York."

"Are you... married?" he asked.

"No."

He twirled the coil of wire around his finger, waiting for her to elaborate.

"I have other things going right now."

"Like?"

"Other things."

He sensed he might have touched a nerve here and let it drop.

"I'd like to see you." He put it out there and waited for her reaction.

Silence. "Hm. I don't know." She gave a long sigh. "I don't mean to put a damper on your reach-out and all, but... I'm not entirely okay with you."

Graham closed his eyes and clenched his jaw.

"I didn't expect you to be."

"You went off and left me and Mom. People get divorced, but what? You just split. People ask and what do I say? 'He's in jail'? 'Rehab'? 'Crazy'? I don't know."

She wasn't holding back, brushing small talk aside to open the lid, whatever might emerge. Graham twisted the coil of wire in his hand.

"I appreciate you're trying, but really, it feels kind of late. You know what I'm saying? I don't want to say never, but I'm not ready to say yes either."

"You probably don't have a very nice picture of me," he admitted.

"Why would you assume that? Mom was more than fair to you, considering."

"That doesn't surprise me. Leila's too good a person. Actually, she's the best person I've ever known. She deserved better."

"She did."

"I hope— Is the man she married, your stepfather... Mmm." He cleared his throat. "Is she happy?"

"He's devoted to her. He's been a good father, too."

"Ouch."

"Ouch?"

"Never mind. I'm glad she's happy. And you're happy."

Julie took her time on the next move.

"Mom says something happened to you. You came back damaged."

Graham squeezed the wire in his fist tighter. Forbidden territory.

"But you wouldn't talk about it."

"Right."

"Still?"

"Still."

"The war or something else?"

"Not something else."

A long pause ensued, Julie breathing on the other end.

"Are you better now?"

"I'm more the person I was. I've got my brain back. Yeah, I believe so."

"Are you with anyone?"

He shook his head vigorously, even if she couldn't see him. "No. I'm not sitting around. I just… have other things going, to use your phraseology."

"I see. That's good. So I'd better let you go. We'll talk again."

Graham replaced the receiver and leaned on the kitchen table. He looked up at the stained-glass canopy still balanced atop the stepladder with the medallion teetering on top. He closed his eyes, took a deep breath to dispel the flush of emotion he felt, and started back up the ladder.

8

Cheryl came off her sick bed to clinch the evening ski league title for Graham's team. Now he could finally allow himself a haircut. Like Samson, he'd been letting it trail over his ears, fearing to jinx their chances.

At noon the following Monday, when Cheryl penciled him in, Graham slipped his Marquette Mountain Cup tee shirt over his dress shirt and headed for LHC. Cheryl was still with a customer but gave a big laugh to see the tee shirt when he pulled his jacket off. Linda was making change for a client and gave only a glance as he came in. She stopped by Cheryl's chair on her way back to intimate something. Cheryl glanced toward where Graham was sitting, gave a slight nod, and went back to her customer.

"Graham," Cheryl called out. "I'm running behind. Linda can take you unless you want to wait."

"Linda's good," he understated.

Linda crooked a finger at him and clicked smartly back to the shampoo sink in low heels. Graham almost blundered into a chair watching her walk.

"So your team won last week?"

"My team?" Graham floundered for reference. "Oh, oh. Yeah. We did. We came in ten points down, and Cheryl put us over the top."

"How did you do?" she asked, her hands arrested in his hair. Awash in island fruit scent and electrified by the contact, he could not gather his thoughts for a second.

"Me? Um, I did all right. I ended up sixth for the season in points. Pretty good for the old guy, eh?"

Without replying, she grabbed a towel, rubbed his hair vigorously, and then crooked her finger again. He followed to her chair, trying to keep his eyes off her. He glanced up and caught Cheryl's amused "bad boy" look.

Linda swung the chair around at him and said, "Why do you do it?"

When he shrugged, she had to catch the towel before it slipped off.

"The tee shirt. Cheryl's got one."

Linda gave him a look. "Risky way to get a tee shirt."

"No, it's fun. You want to learn?"

"No thanks. Tell me…"

With that, she kept Graham afloat on a stream of questions that had him telling her he grew up in the East Bay area where his mother taught at the local school, learned to ski only in adulthood after coming here, started school at U Cal Berkeley, taught courses at the university, taught first aid and CPR classes for Red Cross and volunteered at the hospital.

27

Only when she got him into such a groove that he mentioned having an ex in Ohio did she interrupt.

"Don't use that term."

"What term?"

"'Ex.' It's dismissive."

Otherwise, she snicked away with her razor and prompted from time to time when he slowed down. Afraid to make sudden moves, he just kept answering her questions—except for deflecting any approaches to the shattering hiatus between taking pre-med and teaching mathematics.

Upon finishing, she handed him a mirror and spun him around. He had to admit the result suited and told her so.

She snapped away the smock and waved him out of the chair.

At the cash register, he handed her a twenty and a five.

Out of earshot of the others, she pressed it back into his hand and closed his fingers over it.

"Give it to Cheryl. And next time ask for her. We don't poach."

"I don't understand."

"Come by at seven after my last customer. We need to talk."

She patted his fist and pushed it away.

•

At the Kaffee Haus, Graham balanced two cups of espresso over from the counter and set one before Linda, feeling a little less flustered than he had with her blonde version at *Antigone*.

With no preamble she said, "You told Cheryl you saw me at the theater."

"I did?"

"Don't act innocent. Did you say how I reacted?"

Graham sighed. "I specifically did not. Why, what did she tell you?"

"She was playing Cupid, that's all. So what did you tell her?"

"What's the difference?"

"The difference is, I'd like to know what you reveal about me."

"Reveal?"

"Wrong word choice. I'd like to know what you said about me, that's all."

"I told her you're elusive. Well, you are." He paused. "The other thing was none of my business; so I figured it wasn't any of hers."

Linda visibly relaxed and sipped at her espresso. She flicked a look at Graham before turning her gaze out the window.

"So you think I'm peculiar—besides elusive."

"Not peculiar. Elusive fits. How come, if you don't mind my asking?"

She cocked her head, getting an angle on her espresso. "You misconstrue me."

"Should I not be interested?"

28

She poked a finger into her espresso and touched it to the tip of her tongue. "It's questionable."

"You're the real Italian, aren't you?"

Her hand stopped in mid-air. "What do you mean?"

"The way you drink that stuff with no sugar."

"Oh." She lowered her eyelids and touched her fingertip back to her tongue. "That's how we drink it in New York."

"What if I were to say I am? Interested."

"In me?" She shook her head.

"Are you kidding? Look at you: smart, beautiful. If anything, you scare me." He clutched his elbows and chattered his teeth to make the point.

Linda burst into laughter—the first time Graham had seen—and revealed her own teeth, remarkably perfect. "Yes, beware."

"Oh I am. And suspicious."

"Of what?" Her smile faded.

"Of the possibility you're being disingenuous."

"Don't drop fifty-cent words on me, Graham. Use English."

"You're hard to read, but I think you're messing with my mind."

"And I think you're imagining things." She glanced at the extravagant Mickey Mouse watch she wore. "I've got to go back and close up."

"What's the hurry? I'm just getting warmed up."

"Walk back with me, if you want. I left my car there."

At the entrance to the shop, she said, "Even if I am elusive, I'm not crazy."

"I think you are, so there's no question but I have to see you again. Purely clinical. Will I?"

"Keep growing hair."

Then she pulled the door shut and waved at him through the glass. It did not surprise Graham to look around the parking lot as he walked out to where he was parked and see no car besides his own.

29

9

Monday the following week, a heart-breaking March blizzard unloaded across the Upper Peninsula. Graham navigated Third Street in near-zero visibility on his way to the university. Just past Ohio Street, he passed a woman in a heavy coat and scarf plunging through the drifts with a large shoulder bag at Linda's no-nonsense pace.

He pulled to the curb and waited until she drew even to roll down the passenger window and call, "Hey. Need a lift?"

Linda shook snow from her scarf and gathered it around her face to squint in at him.

"Sure," she said and hiked her long coat to slide in, hugging the bag into her lap. He pulled out and then had to wait until the light changed at Hewitt.

"So where's your car?" he asked.

"In the shop. I backed it into a light pole."

"You did what?"

"Well, I couldn't see. It was right where that thing by the back window is?"

"I hope you didn't knock the light over."

"It was one of those big cement jobs. I hit the base of it."

"That's going to cost." The light changed, and Graham started across.

"Phh, I wouldn't even bother with it, except I can't get the trunk open. That's all I'm having fixed."

"I take it this is no Mercedes."

"You might say that. It's more like a Citation."

"If you need a taxi in the meantime, give me a call."

They had almost reached her shop, and Graham looked over for a reaction.

She gave him an arch look and said, "What if I told you I get it back today?"

"I'd say, 'How about I take you to dinner tonight?'"

Linda looked across at him, her hand arrested on the door handle. Graham could almost see the wheels going around. He worried he'd put himself out there to be shot down.

"I'll pay for my own, but yes, you can pick me up at 6:30. Here."

As if she were doing him the favor.

•

When Graham pulled up at LHC, Linda came out before he rolled to a stop. He blinked with surprise to see her elaborate French braid. She had even slicked on lip gloss.

30

Halfway across town, Graham could not resist trying to smoke her out on the issues of the day. Obviously she was well informed, so what, if anything, did she believe?

"Did you see the paper today?" he asked. A story about a militant anti-abortion demonstration downstate had him agitated. The photo over the story had shown a man haranguing a crowd with both fists. Graham had instantly recognized him—unidentified in the caption—as the hitchhiker. There had been no mistaking the aviator glasses or tee shirt.

"I don't read the paper," she said. "Fill me in. I've been styling all day."

"Says Operation Rescue may be planning big demonstrations here this summer."

"Hm."

"Some other group, too, calls itself Missionaries to the Pre-Born," he said. "Missionaries to the Pre-Born. Don't you love it?"

"I don't know. Should I?"

"Well, what are they preaching to people who aren't even born?"

Graham looked over, and she shrugged. "It's a figure of speech, Graham."

That bore no fruit. How would Gwen call it? A women's issue that men keep trying to gain control of. Linda had certainly not risen to it.

•

He took her to the Vierling, a local landmark on a downtown corner overlooking Lake Superior and the lower harbor. Inside, they stopped to wait for their table at the restored, turn-of-the-century bar. The bartender interrupted the drink he was pouring to appraise Linda. A couple of men stole looks from tables across the room as they conversed with their companions. She seemed totally oblivious to the attention.

"No woman ends a pregnancy lightly."

Graham turned. For a split second he was caught re-grouping; her dark eyes were so focused on him he could have fallen in. Before he could ask her to repeat herself, the young woman arrived to lead them to the table he had reserved at the back. He had to wait until she was seated across from him.

"Oh I'm sure. It's just the hullabaloo that seems unnecessary."

"To you maybe. No one asks the women having the children. They take this big, brave step, one way or the other; and there's no going back."

While not taking a clear side, she sounded as if she knew something about this.

"Agreed. So why should they face a mob of sign-toting fanatics?"

"Because. When people can't prove something, they argue about it. The more they argue, the hotter they get. Pretty soon they carry signs to make their point. Meantime, who worries about the kids we already have?"

31

"My wife used to liken it to arguing about God," he said, relieved to be converging on common ground. "She called it proof by insistence."

"She sounds wise. Do you keep in touch with her?"

Graham shook his head. "Not really."

"Do you have children, if you don't mind my asking?"

"A grown daughter."

The harbor lights gleamed off Linda's eyes as she gazed out at the ore dock. "That must be nice."

She arranged the napkin on her lap and placed her silverware. Subject closed.

•

Over coffee, Graham asked her how she liked the Vierling's grand Victorian ambience.

"I'm glad we came." Color sparkled as she fingered one of her prism earrings.

"May I ask you something?"

"Depends."

"Is that your music they play in the shop?"

"Sometimes."

"Cheryl says you sing."

"If you want to call it that." She cocked her head slightly and nipped her lower lip in a coy smile. She looked disarmed enough for Graham to ask the next question.

"All right; tell me this: What affected you so much about Antigone?"

There it was, lying between them like unexploded ordnance.

"Why I…" Linda's lips stopped, half open; then she cast her eyes down. "I used to think I could be an actress."

"Oh."

"What do you want? Because I come to dinner, you can interrogate me?"

The air between them turned loaded, and he tried to amend.

"You ask me all kinds of things. I'm not interrogating. You were crying, and I keep thinking about you—about that."

Her narrowed gaze reduced him to total confusion before she replied.

"Don't think I'm some mystery woman. I can dispel that for you right now."

She waved away his protest.

"No, otherwise, you'll go to Cheryl—Yes you will— and bring all this up to her, trying to find out all about me."

"Wait. I didn't mean that. What I intended was—"

She silenced him with a look.

"You want to know, I'll explain. But you're not to ask me about this again; nor do I expect you to speak of it to anyone else, ever. Is that clear?"

Arching her eyebrows until he murmured an assent, Linda looked down at her clasped hands then, as if thinking how to begin. Finally she looked up.

"I'm a twin. I don't tell people. His name was Daniel."

"You speak of him in the past. Is he…?"

She nodded. "We were very different. From the time he was little, Daniel could handle everything. Where I couldn't always manage, he mastered whatever he put his mind to. Maybe he just had a smarter father than I did."

At Graham's look of puzzlement, she explained, "I have none, to be perfectly brutal about it—not of record anyway; neither did he. We were born together, that's all.

"He was so ambitious he finally got into medical school. Can you believe it? No one ever *dreamed* of anything like that where we came from. That's when I learned cosmetology, to help pay his way."

Graham's interest focused. "What medical school?"

"City College. In New York."

"I didn't know City College had a medical school. At least it didn't when I was in med school."

She scarcely missed a beat. "I'm sorry; pre-med. I thought you said under-graduate. You studied medicine?"

"Started. So did he actually go to med school?"

"No, Columbia Medical had accepted him, and he would have made it, too. His grades were perfect 4.0. Then they wouldn't have drafted him."

"I don't need to hear the rest."

She deflected his protest with both hands.

"You asked. He drew a low draft number just before classes were due to start. He didn't want to end up with a rifle, so he signed up and got onto a med evac crew. That was right in the beginning, before we were supposed to be in Cambodia or any of that. You probably wouldn't remember."

"Please, I get the picture."

"Let me finish. I need to say this. We were sending people into Laos and Cambodia already, as it turned out. A Special Forces group got into trouble in Laos, so Dan's unit had to get them out. It was his second mission. One of the men from his unit told us later that Dan's chopper went down in the mountains across the border under heavy fire, and they couldn't recover the crew. They couldn't even admit where they were. He went down knowing he'd never come out."

Graham felt as if his heart would stop. Finally he managed, "Probably so."

"Not probably. I knew. I always knew."

She held herself tightly controlled, her right hand covering her left and gripping it hard enough to whiten the knuckles. He looked away.

"You weren't able to put him to rest, to bury him. Like Antigone."

"Yes, exactly. Like Antigone. Only I went nuts, grieving."

"I know, I know," Graham said, caught in a terrible *déjà vu*.

"No. You can't. I hope to God you will never know what I felt, how much I wanted a re-run where it didn't happen. The people who caused it were looking

33

at some bigger picture where he was just a detail painted out. I got his name on the Memorial. I had to petition for six years, but it's out there, on the end toward the Washington Monument. Don't you tell anyone this. I abhor public grief."

Trying to form the words, Graham reached toward her and asked, "The Corps. How far north was he? Was he flying out of Da Nang or, or… for God's sake, Hué?"

Linda's face froze in shock, and she drew back, leaving her hand spread on the table. A tattoo on the web of her left thumb made two intersecting lines ringed by five short rays—the Pachuco cross of L.A.'s street gangs, not from New York.

Just then her pager tootled, startling him. He had no idea she was carrying one. She sprang up, saying she needed to find a telephone. After the cashier pointed out a pay phone near the restroom, Linda rummaged in her handbag and fed coins into the slot. She spoke twice and then returned to the table looking even more distraught. Before he could stop her, she picked up the check, fished a twenty from her bag, and laid it between them.

"Here. That will cover my tip, too. Would you mind terribly driving me to the emergency room?"

"What's happened?"

She would only shake her head. All the way to the hospital, she clasped her hands tightly in her lap. Once or twice he sneaked a look to see passing lights glance off her eyes as she stared fixedly ahead. Not until they turned into the emergency room entrance did she speak.

"I'm terribly sorry about this," she said as she started to open the door.

"Don't be absurd. Do you want me to wait out here, or shall I come inside?"

She walked around to his window.

"You'd better not. I might be here all night."

At Graham's questioning look, she finally explained. "I do crisis intervention."

Graham's mouth fell open.

"What's so surprising about that?" she said.

"I guess I just didn't picture *you*. I work here myself sometimes, you know."

She leaned closer. "I've seen you. There's a lot about me you wouldn't picture. And Graham…" Her expression became more serious. "Forgive me, okay? I didn't know."

She touched his hand and turned toward the hospital.

10

That fleeting touch still jangled Graham as he tried to divert his thoughts on his way home the next day. Already the ice was melting where the road curved around the foot of Keweenaw Bay. With the beginning of April, the sky would be light all the way home. This early, he could even make it home before the stores closed. He had meant to come up with final exam questions on the way home, but he could not concentrate on mathematics.

Linda stuck in his head like a jingle. Even in her plain smock he couldn't keep his eyes off her. And then looking like she did last night, she threatened wholesale rearrangement of his carefully rebuilt life.

Eight years now he had been functioning again. Cleaning himself up had meant holding every piece of himself in place, had probably been the hardest effort he had put in since learning to speak. He used to think finding a woman would put the icing on the cake. Now he was afraid to take the chance.

Graham tried to erect a mental blind with an inventory of his students' talents. With a supreme effort, he envisioned the Lake Linden construction worker, a fortyish blue collar with Abe Lincoln whiskers who had such knack he could actually be a mathematician. What a thing to learn at that point in life. He conjured the smooth-faced Indian nurse from Keweenaw Bay, the only one who figured out his weird problem about going into free fall. He liked discovering such gifts where no one would look. Strange business.

Strange business indeed. If he had not seen Linda at *Antigone,* she might have remained a passing fancy. Instead, she was keeping him awake at night.

Graham tried to feature Linda in pricey ski clothes, then found himself picturing her in none, remembering that flash of thigh in the shop. She certainly hadn't let herself go in the body department—and that radiant and all-too-rare smile. Either she was extremely lucky, or someone well heeled cared how she looked.

Yesterday kept looping like a mental tape that would not shut off. Graham shook his head. Brain worm. He needed to think mathematics. He saw the Tioga Creek rest stop ploughed open and pulled in. Stretching out of the truck, he tore around it until his heart was racing, then trudged down to the creek.

A splash of ice water did no good. When he pulled back onto the highway, his thoughts went right back to Linda. Tioga Creek's ice water chilled his face, but Graham still cringed to think how presumptuous he had been to ask about the tears.

What he was to forgive he still did not know.

Cresting the rise past the airport, Graham saw Marquette Bay white with ice again. The wind had shifted. This morning there had been nothing but open water, and he had been gullible enough to think spring would come. This could go on for weeks: one day water would sparkle to the horizon; then the wind would drift all the ice back into ridges high as houses. As he cruised into town past the shopping mall, he could see mountains of snow bladed to the edges of the parking lot, sweating glacial runoff that would last into April.

Graham stopped at the house to check his mail and see if anyone had called, then consulted his watch. Five thirty and totally out of anything to eat; he had better take a run to the grocery.

As he drove toward Third Street, yesterday's snow was already disappearing from the walks; people were chopping ice from their driveways and pitching it into the streets to melt. He should see how Linda survived her visit to the hospital. In fact, he would do that first, before LHC closed.

Graham stuck his head inside, but Linda was not there, and Muzak met his ear. The cute, vivacious hairdresser by the door tugged at a fishnet top and asked around her gum if he wanted Linda. Graham's heart sank. Were they the talk of the shop now?

Cheryl interrupted her concentration on a customer's hair to say, "Called in this morning. Guess she was up most of the night with some problem."

"Who's that? Oh. Is that so?"

"'Who's that.'" She rolled her eyes and returned to her work. "Any message?"

"Just call me. Okay?"

Cheryl nodded without looking up as he went out.

Two days passed. No call. Finally Graham, beyond caring who said what, grew concerned enough to pick up the phone and ask if he could speak to Linda directly. The beautician who answered told him to wait, then came back on the line.

"Are you Graham?"

"Yes."

"She's with a customer. She'll call you back."

"Sure. I'll give you the number."

"She knows it."

She did not call. Monday Graham dialed into student records with his computer to see when Cheryl would be on campus and discovered she had a biology lab in West Science. He was waiting when she came out.

"Hey, prof, what's up?"

"Cheryl, what's with your partner? Did you tell her to call?"

"She didn't?"

"No. Is there some piece of etiquette I'm unaware of here?"

Cheryl raised her eyebrows and shrugged.

"She bothers me. There's something about her."

Cheryl laughed. "I see she bothers you. I haven't a clue why she's not calling you back, though. Maybe she doesn't want to talk to you, I don't know."

"How can you hire somebody you know so little about?"

"Frieda apprenticed her, so I think she knows about her. She came into the shop wanting work but couldn't produce a license. Apparently the one she had she left in New York and couldn't go after it. We didn't ask. We could see she knew her stuff.

"I mean, once she proves herself on commission, she rents space from Frieda like any of us. What she does with herself otherwise, that's none of my business—not as long as she does the work and keeps people coming back. And it's not as if we know nothing about her. We know she cares: She brings flowers on our birthdays or lends us money if we're in a jam. And she's good at what she does; she's probably the best in town. Her customers won't let anybody else touch them, so you tell me. In fact, she's the one who came up with the name of the shop."

"She did. Well that's dandy. What if you need to contact her? Do you even know where she lives?"

"Actually no. We do have a phone number, but usually she calls in like she did the other day. I think she does something else in the evenings. I don't know that; it's just a hunch."

"You have a number?"

"At the shop. We're not supposed to use it unless it's really important."

"Oh." He kicked at the ground disappointedly.

"Listen, I'm going there right now. I'll call you in five minutes. Don't say how you got it."

Graham sat on Cheryl's information until he returned from Baraga the following evening with a briefcase of finals to grade. Something was off about Linda—the phony background, the way she looked, having money to lend, the mysterious absences, "doing something else in the evening," the all-night problems, the secrecy about herself, the confidential phone number. He didn't like the implications, but he had to know.

A woman answered after two rings.

"Anchorage."

Graham hesitated. He shouldn't be doing this. Was it her? The voice sounded too formal for Linda's.

"Yes?" the woman said. She sounded tense now.

"Um." He gritted his teeth. "Could I speak with Linda Chapman?"

"You may leave a message. We'll post it."

"But she lives there?"

"We don't give out that information, but I can take a message."

"How do I know she'll see it?"

"You don't. It would depend if she's a client here, and I can't tell you that."

A client?

"Okay. Take a message then. Say to call Graham…"

37

"Oh. It's you. Why are you making your voice that way?"

"Linda?"

"Yes, this is."

"Linda! I'm sorry, is this…" Graham looked for a delicate way to put it. "Is this some kind of business?"

"No, it's not. This is the women's shelter. And please keep that to yourself."

"The women's shelter! Oh!" Graham breathed a huge sigh of relief, then thought of a worse possibility. "Are you—"

"I'm the resident director, not what you're thinking."

"Why haven't you called me?"

There was a long pause. "I really can't talk. We have to keep this line open."

"You're not going to say?"

"If you must know, I've been avoiding you."

"Why? What did I do?"

"It was wrong of me, that's all, letting you close to me. I never should have." Her words hit Graham like a slap; his face even heated.

"What do you mean, you never should have? I'm not going to infect you." Wanting to sound cool, he knew he did not.

"Graham, I'm sorry; it was my mistake."

"Or mine. It's not as if I had any big interest, if that's what you're thinking." Hurt, Graham wanted to hurt back.

"Fine, then I won't think that."

"You're a cold one, you know that?"

"Graham, we could have this out at length another time, but not on this phone."

"Sure. Could be something important."

"You're taking it personally. Don't. It's not you."

"Oh, 'personally'!" His voice rose to a near squeak. "Not a chance. Why would I take it personally?"

He hung up.

11

Graham refocused elsewhere with a vengeance. He began visiting his vets at the VA twice a week. His evenings at the emergency desk soon multiplied, happily without encountering Linda.

No way would Graham go into LHC again; Cheryl would just have to understand. He could just imagine them snickering behind their shears at Linda's latest sucker. He went back to the downtown barbershop for his next haircut. It hurt a lot less than the job Linda had done on him.

He took up running again with Cheryl's boyfriend Kevin, mostly indoors in the new sports dome until the insane Arctic weather let up. For all the time Graham spent with Kevin—and Cheryl when she joined them—he never mentioned Linda, nor did she ever ask him. Neither did she ask why he had stopped patronizing LHC.

Focused on his fitness obsession as he was, Graham found he could go whole days not caring about Linda. He was too strung out most of the time. He began spending more time with his old friend Gwen dissecting the world again, and she was kind enough not to broach the subject of Linda either.

At the end of April a warm snap hit. Once the icebergs in the lake retreated over the horizon for good, Kevin started teaching Graham how to operate the family sailboat. He and Cheryl had it in the water the moment the lake thawed enough to float things. A May Day celebration would follow tomorrow's sailing lesson, however: With the weather so balmy—by Upper Peninsula standards—Cheryl had invited her co-workers, the ski team, and a few other friends to her family's camp along the lake for a Sunday volleyball extravaganza, cookout and sauna.

On his way home from the university, Graham stopped at the Third Street market for a few things to take along to Cheryl's. On his way in, he peered quickly at the newspaper in the vending machine. Another demonstration downstate with a photo of the hitchhiker in his tee shirt again. Graham shook his head and went inside.

He did not bother with a cart and targeted the junk food, chips and drinks first. Rounding the aisle, he literally bumped into Linda. She was walking out of the soup aisle looking the other way with a shopping basket of light bulbs and collided with him. The impact staggered her so that Graham had to catch her by the arms to keep her from pitching into a shelf of pasta.

"Oops. Strange to run into you."

"Mm," she grunted and tried to shrug his grip.

"Well hello to you too."

"Don't make a scene."

"I will if I want. How about telling me what the deal is with you?" He could not summon the aloofness he wanted.

"Stop. People are looking."

"Let them. I don't care."

"Graham, let go of me. Could we continue this conversation outside at least?"

"Absolutely," Graham said good-naturedly and released her. She shook her sweater sleeves back down with a look of exasperation.

"Honestly!"

"Don't forget your light," he added, retrieving a sixty-watt bulb that had dropped when they collided. She took it without comment, and he made a show of strolling nonchalantly off. As soon as he was around the corner and out of sight, however, Graham gathered the rest of his purchases like Charlie Chaplin on roller skates so he could hit the express line before she got away. By the time he was paying, Linda had just stepped into another line, pointedly looking elsewhere.

Outside, Graham wondered what came over him. All he had to do was see her to lose his grip. He was about to walk away when she came out, looking less than pleased to discover him still there.

"You're wasting your time," she said.

"I know. Need a hand?"

"No, thanks. I can manage."

When she started to walk away, he touched her arm.

"Momento: May I pose a hypothesis?"

She shifted the bag to one arm so she could consult her two-inch, neon Mickey Mouse watch.

"I have a customer in a couple of minutes."

"Something happened that night I left you at the hospital."

She hefted the bag like a shield and compressed her lips, as if resisting a smile.

"Maybe. Yes. Look, without getting specific, sometimes I see things that give me an attitude about people. In particular, men. There are things that happen… Well, I can't even get into that; you couldn't understand."

"Why don't you give it a try?"

"Why don't I not?"

"Okay; how's this one: You don't like men, and you thought I was trying to put a move on you."

"Graham…"

She looked around her uncomfortably. Shoppers maneuvering past their mid-sidewalk discussion could not help overhearing this.

"Okay I was; I'll own up. You're an interesting woman. But I don't have to. We could go back to square one, make a non-aggression pact, just do whatever it was—friends, buddies, haircut pals; I don't care. I like seeing you. It doesn't even have to be a man-woman kind of thing. What do you say? The correct answer is 'yes.'"

The corner of her mouth twitched, and she averted her eyes.

"Let me think about it." She shouldered the bag up. "Got to go now."

.

The phone was already ringing when Graham returned from the store. He skidded across the kitchen floor for the receiver and knocked it to the floor.

"Sorry about that! Linda?"

A woman's voice. "Um, no. Is this Graham?"

Graham paused to catch his breath. "Who's this?"

"Julie."

He was so flabbergasted no words would come.

"Your daughter? Or have you forgotten already?"

"Of course not. Julie! My god!"

"Who's Linda?"

"Someone I know, a friend sort of."

"Oh. Listen, the reason I'm calling, I have to be in Minneapolis Monday. I'm interviewing the new senator from Minnesota, Paul Wellstone. Interesting guy, political science professor out of nowhere who sounds as if he's got smarts. So anyway, I know this is short notice and not to put you on the spot, but I was thinking... I could arrange a few days' layover on my way back."

"In Minneapolis?"

"I was thinking of routing myself through Marquette."

Graham could not believe what she just said.

"You still there?" she asked.

"Wow!"

"I'm game if you are," she said.

"Yes, yes! It would be fabulous!"

"Maybe and maybe not. At least we can be adults. It just seems ridiculous not to. You did offer an olive branch. I'll be on the 9 a.m. flight from Minneapolis. Tuesday. That's May third."

"You're already booked?"

"I can back out."

"What I mean is, you might want to stay longer. You could."

"I'd have to pay more."

"I'd cover it. What am I talking about? I'll cover your whole ticket."

"Let's see how it goes. We might disappoint each other. This time it's my ride. I have to be up there anyway, so there's nothing at stake."

"Julie, this is embarrassing: How will I know you?"

"You won't have any problem. I look like Mom, only taller."

41

"Okay. And it's not the world's largest airport; you'll see. Look for a guy with mostly brown hair, about five ten. And I'll wear a yellow, long-sleeved tee shirt. That'll be easy to spot."

"Indeed. Oh, and um, this Linda? She won't be with you, will she? Because it could be… awkward enough. You know what I mean?"

"Just me. You can count on it."

"Perfect. See you in a few days."

Graham lowered the receiver into the cradle, and then leaped into the air and clicked his heels. He pumped his fist into the air, shadow-boxed the wall, did a little jig, and then sat at the kitchen table and rapped out a drum roll with his knuckles. His daughter was coming! Here! In two days! He could not believe it. He jumped up and fetched his address book, licked his thumb and paged through until he found Leila's school number where he had penciled it in at the end.

It was still before lunch, so he called her there. After a little negotiating with the school secretary, he got her on the phone.

"Graham. What is it? You'll have to make it quick; I'm in class."

"Julie is coming to visit!"

"Yes, I thought she should. I'm glad you're excited about it."

"Excited? I'm crazy! And you're okay with it."

"Of course I'm okay with it. She needs to do this. You'll be impressed. Okay? I haven't got time now. Just promise me one thing, Graham: Be good to her. That's all I ask."

"Cross my heart, Leila."

"Okay, got to run."

Graham set all his papers aside and began a wholesale spring cleanup.

•

Trying to find Cheryl's camp the next day, Graham got lost twice. He was supposed to follow Kevin after they docked the boat, but Graham had to swing by his house to pick up the things he had bought, so he waved Kevin on.

Cheryl described a little dirt road fourteen miles out of town. The first one he tried petered out at a marsh with no room to turn around, so he had to back out. Then he found a sand quarry. Finally he spied a balloon on a stake by a dirt lane curving into the woods. Across the road, a highway sign shot full of holes stood by a tilted mailbox reading "Maki."

After a mile of bumping and dragging center, Graham finally saw open sky through the trees ahead and figured he must be near the lake. Another bend in the track, and he saw a dozen cars and half again as many mountain bikes scattered among the trees around a shingled cottage. Cheryl came out on the porch as he coasted to a stop and waved out a spot between two pine trees where he could park.

"About time you got here," she said.

42

Over the dunes, some people obliviously soaked up sun while others cheered the serious volleyball game in progress. Beyond, Lake Superior sparkled invitingly under a cloudless sky. No one was in it. Even in May the water would float ice cubes all day. Far out on the eastern horizon past the Au Train River, Graham could make out beaches and fractured cliffs and then the long boundary against the sky where the lake slipped over the horizon.

Spotting him, Kevin called from the volleyball game, "Get in here, Graham! We're short, and they're kicking our butts."

One of the opposing spikers turned at the mention of his name. It was Linda in a black swimsuit, with yet another head of hair, this time a dark bronze mass of curls that reached her jaw.

Graham lined up across from Linda and gave an appreciative once-over as she retrieved the ball and tossed it back for serve. He should look so good. How did she manage that at her age?

"What are you doing here?" she asked through the net.

"Cheryl invited me."

"She never told me."

"You were supposed to approve it?"

The volleys went back and forth with Graham's side slowly gaining until the score was 14 all, with Linda serving.

"Losers go in the lake," Kevin announced. Linda balked, then put the ball up and curved it over the net like a California beach hand. Eventually, however, Graham's side eked out the victory.

"In the water," Kevin cheered and ducked under the net. A short struggle ensued with one of his opponents, and both of them fell into the lake howling. After general shrieking and running, Graham's side bulldozed the others in one by one until only Linda remained, as if by some mutual consent she had been left for Graham. She dodged behind people, trying to escape as Graham closed in. Eventually he backed her to the lake.

"Are you taking the plunge?" Graham invited.

"I'm not going in that water."

"Take her in, Graham," Kevin called, to general encouragement. By now everyone was waiting to see her dunked.

"Well?"

Linda planted her feet. "Make me."

She beckoned, her dark eyes sparkling with feline focus. She was not small, maybe five seven, 140; but Graham was in condition. This should be a piece of cake.

Graham circled in, faking with his hands. He meant to grab an arm and take her around the waist before she could dodge. Someone booted the volleyball right behind her. When she started at the sound, Graham made his move; but she was not there when he arrived. Instead, he was flicked onto the ground.

She offered a hand up, and he dusted off sand amid general hooting.

"Martial arts. That's what Cheryl thought."

"It's professional. We're supposed to call the police, but there might come a time…"

Before long, Cheryl had the barbecue going, so he cruised over to fill his plate. Linda was in the cottage carving up venison for Cheryl to throw onto the fire, so he shared stories with some of the skiers and caught up on former students until Linda came out to take over the cooking while Cheryl fired up the sauna. A sweet-smoke smell of burning maple drifted through the pines as it grew dark.

As people left for the sauna, Linda sat on the cottage steps with her chin on her fists looking out at the stars over the darkened lake.

"Waiting for the sauna?" he asked.

"I get all sweated up and then I'm supposed to jump in the lake after?"

"That's the idea."

"No thanks. I hate cold water. I'm going to walk down the beach."

She continued sitting, however, and a silence fell between them. After a minute or two she got to her feet. Graham could make out her face in profile still turned to the lake when she spoke.

"Unless you have your heart set on roasting yourself, you could come along."

"Thanks, but I think I'll hang around here."

Graham folded his arms waiting for her to go. She didn't need him to run her roller coaster anymore.

"Hey. I'm sorry. You don't have to be nice or anything; just come with me."

Against his better judgment, Graham fell in beside her. Near the lake, a bonfire crackled where the first round of sauna emergents thawed themselves after their dip in the lake as he and Linda drifted past along the shore. The cooling night offered a riot of stars, Cassiopeia low on the horizon and all but a point of Andromeda plunged into the lake's black void. Ranks of waves lapped the sand. Linda smelled like beer.

"On your suggestion about being friends," Linda began, once they had left the others behind, "I've been thinking about it."

"You have. Like being straight with me?"

"I said I'm thinking about it. I didn't say I'd go that far."

"Oh."

They scuffed farther down the beach until the night engulfed them. She barely showed beside him now. The far-off buzz of a helicopter headed for the hospital.

"Linda?"

She murmured an indistinct response.

"If we're friends, you have to trust me."

He tried to make her face out in the dark but could not. Even so, Linda's presence was intense. He stooped for a rock and sailed it into the lake.

"That's the trouble," she said. "I have a hard time being friends with you."

"I can tell."

"No you can't. What I'm trying to say is this thing could begin steering itself. I can't allow that to happen."

"What thing would steer itself?"

"Me, my feelings, don't you see? I'd let you get too close. That's out of bounds. Especially you. You said to be honest."

Where was this coming from? Graham winged a few more rocks. Actually he wanted to chuck the whole handful straight up in the air and let them rain down on his head. The helicopter's subtext barely registered. In two days his daughter was coming. One thing at a time.

He tried his best to sound as if he were still in control. "Why should I be out of bounds?"

"Because... because of things I'd rather not get into. Let's just leave it at that."

"So where does that put things between us?"

"Strained. If we try to stay friends, we won't."

"We could see how it goes."

"No we can't. We'd get involved, and there are too many reasons why we shouldn't."

"On the other hand, aren't you overreacting to make an enemy of me?"

Linda stopped walking and looked out at the lake, hugging herself against the night wind blowing in from the water.

"What are you thinking?"

She half turned, as if remembering she had company. "The stars. They're so far away. Wouldn't it be nice to have that perspective on the things we do? Sometimes I think, 'If only I could get beyond myself.'"

"You don't know how many times I've wished that," Graham said.

"Because of your wife?"

He wanted to tell her, but this was clearly not the time.

"Other things. How did you know about her?"

"You told me."

"Oh." He had forgotten.

"When you say 'other things,' am I to take it you refer to something specific?"

"You might."

Then she surprised him by guessing.

"You were in Vietnam, weren't you?"

All of a sudden the stakes changed, drastically. The helicopter roared in his ears.

"Where'd you get that idea?"

"When you asked what Corps my brother was in."

"Twenty-five years now: That's a long time. I hardly remember any of it."

"That's untrue, Graham, you remember all of it. Tell me. I need to know."

At his feet, Lake Superior lapped an icy ghost of the South China Sea while the bonfire behind them showered sparks into the night. Graham was trying to sort the storm of images when a DPS helicopter suddenly racketed over the bay, strobe flashing across the stars as it shortcut for Marquette. Time crumbled and gave way.

VIETNAM
1970

The big Huey beats across sharp ranges of jungle, cold rain streaming along the side glass like bullets. It has been ten minutes since they peeled away from the road winding up to the pass, and Witch, the door gunner, tensely scans the unbroken canopy below. Another month and he is out of here. With luck he will be gone before the NVA mount their next offensive. With luck he might even forget this lovely country.

Across from Witch sits Boz, the crew chief, half attending to the pitch of the Huey's turbine as he keeps watch at the other door. Barry, the pilot, peers at the terrain through the rain-streaked windshield up front, checking his flight time and bearing against a sheet of scribbled notes he has taped to his leg while Morgan, the co-pilot, fiddles with the radio again.

"Talk to me, *talk* to me, damn it!" he mutters.

The crew is boring west southwest toward the misted hills along the Laotian border for a ranger patrol they inserted a week ago, 25 nautical miles across the narrowest part of the country from the coastal take-off pad at Hué. This is North Vietnamese Army territory, and they took sporadic fire on the return leg of the drop-off. When Barry had called a hit, Boz scrambled out onto the skid to make a target of himself while he clung to a strut and checked for fuel leaks. Witch remembers the blast of cold air more than he does the anxiety of losing the crew chief or having the craft falter. When Witch thinks about it at all, he imagines going in would be like ditching in the ocean—except the sharks are armed. So far, except for the turbulent arrival of the monsoon, this mission has been blessedly uneventful.

Minutes out from the rendezvous point, they still cannot raise the patrol. Heavier rain drives the pilot in closer to maintain visual contact with a threaded trail below. As sudden pitches of green loom nearer, Witch double-checks the ammo feed to his M-60 and thumbs the safety off.

All at once the trees open, and a settlement appears below, circled by cleared fields glistening with runoff from the surrounding mountains. The land rises in steep ranks from the mist like a Japanese watercolor, striking the Montagnard country with sudden beauty. A small stream to the north winds a broken, silver-gray ribbon from the base of a waterfall off through the glistening canopy toward the coast.

When Witch stepped off the plane at Bien Hoa those long months ago, it seemed exotic: Asia—smells of hot oil in the streets, bananas and water buffalo. Now, he thinks, given time, Americans will make even these mountains their own version of home, strip mine them with bomb craters the way they have the coastal lowlands south of here.

A few people look up from the village as the Huey and its Cobra retinue pass over. A child waves, and Witch cinches his flak jacket and kicks a scrap of salvaged armor plate from a crashed Huey into place under his seat. He does not relish taking a bullet up the ass or, worse, losing a part of his anatomy he's barely had time to enjoy yet.

"Look!" Barry crows with relief. "Can I fly this thing? Two minutes to target."

Witch strains to hear anything like hostile fire and checks his watch. The patrol should have called them into view by now. His stomach begins to knot. Trained as an emergency medic, Witch takes primary responsibility for sustaining casualties on the way to the base hospital. He tells himself not to worry; it's rainy season, slow time, when he gets to see blisters, parasites, and jungle rot instead of men with their guts leaking out and limbs missing.

The radio comes to life up front. One of the Cobra escorts has spotted a faint column of smoke against the storm brewing over the mountains. Strong winds heralding the incoming monsoon are buffeting the Huey now, and its turbine rises and falls in pitch as the pilot drops them toward the minuscule rendezvous where the signal from the smoke grenade is trying to rise. The smoke is not red, but for some reason the patrol has maintained radio silence, and everyone feels edgy about it.

Witch and Boz position their M-60s as the Huey comes in, stirring a reek of jet fuel into the rain gusting through the open doors. When Witch spots the squad leader waving them in at the edge of the small landing site, he relaxes a little. The second Barry bumps a skid against the steep hillside, the waiting ranger appears, his expression wild under green camouflage paint. His jungle fatigues show a red-black spatter that must be blood, and a soaked green bandage makes a headband under his helmet.

"Lost my radio man," he cries over the turbine. "Hit a unit of regulars. Blew him up before they broke contact."

"Let's get the hell out of here then," Boz says. "Where's your patrol?"

"Hurt. You gotta help me. They're out there. Happened yesterday."

"How bad?" Witch demands. "Where are they?"

Witch raises his flight helmet and listens attentively to the extent of the injuries: one man hit in the face and chest and bleeding; the other, a damaged leg from a trip-wire rocket. Witch tries to tell Barry he is going out with the ranger; but it does not transmit, and the pilot shakes his head.

"Get his ass in here," he calls. "We're gonna lift out."

"No, damn it!" The ranger shouts and swings up the muzzle of his AR-15. "We're bringing those men in."

"Jeez Christ, man, easy!" Boz exclaims. Witch grabs his kit and hits the deck. When the ranger nods to follow, Witch sheds his flight helmet and boosts himself off the sill. As Witch falls in behind the ranger, Barry edges the Huey off the landing site to wait.

The ranger moves smartly as a cat along the shower-slick trail, eyeing the ground and the trees on both sides as he keeps his AR-15 at the ready. Rain patters Witch's head and drips off the end of his nose as he keeps a ten-meter safety margin between them in case the sergeant should trip a mine. Feeling terribly exposed outside the Huey, he scans among the glistening trunks of teak and mahogany bordering the trail. Bitter smells of earth and decaying vegetation crowd out the jet fuel of the chopper.

Where the way rises slightly into a bend ahead, the sergeant stops halfway and makes a palm motion near his hip. With no warning, a blast kicks him sideways, his body doubled like a doll's. Before Witch can reach him, an automatic weapon chatters dirt all around the broken ranger. Witch, armed with a .45, drops his kit and wheels for the Huey. Standing off AK-47s with a sidearm is not his idea of heroism. The North Vietnamese, expecting a pickup, must have lain in wait. He has to get the chopper out before they all get caught. This is far too damn real.

As Witch plunges headlong down the trail, he hears Boz's M-60 begin a heavy staccato at the landing area. A clap of thunder almost masks the rip of the rocket, but there is no missing the Huey's crash as it meets the ground. More shots continue until a dull thump erupts as the tanks ignite and light the trees around the clearing ahead.

The Cobra gunships move in to rake the attackers and blast the forest south of the landing area, targeting anything that moves as the Huey goes down. The door gunner knows if he shows himself, either one will cut him down without looking twice.

A lightning strike too close for comfort puts all the ordnance to shame, and the storm breaks into a drenching downpour. The Cobras back into the ceiling and retreat, the racket of their blades fading until the door gunner can no longer hear them through the storm.

He does not stop to wonder if he might have been sighted but simply reacts, every nerve bristling. As the blazing wreckage sizzles behind, he ducks into the brush north of the trail, dumps his vest and flight jacket, and beats a frantic retreat into the steep forest. This is not happening; he flew with those men every day. And wherever the wounded rangers are—if they are still alive—he cannot help them. Any minute he, too, could blunder into one of the North Vietnamese and lie forgotten in these mountains.

Witch carries a topo sheet of the landing area in the balloon pocket of his pants; beyond that, he is on his own. In the rain and high trees he cannot make any reliable bearings but remembers the stream they flew over minutes out from the landing area. If it is the one he thinks, it should lead him east out of the mountains and toward the South China Sea thirty miles away.

He can make that. The storm's cover would give him half a chance of reaching the stream and taking it to the coast by next light, if he did not have to thread through mines and worse. Rather than consider the odds of surviving, Witch tells himself they have dropped half a dozen ranger patrols out here, and this is the first one that has made serious contact. Bad luck, that's all.

Witch lets the steeply forested terrain take him downhill toward where he hopes to meet the water. As he feels for footing he cannot even see, he thinks it would be just his luck to stumble into a cobra. Supposedly tigers roam these mountains, but snakes worry him a hell of a lot more. One soldier bitten in the face died before they could lift him out. Witch thinks they avoid trails, but so must he. Trails will be far deadlier than snakes with enemy troops and booby traps.

After several hours of tiresome bush whacking and picking off leeches, Witch almost forgets how much trouble he is in. Shortly before dark, however, he discovers the stream's water brimming with storm silt, and his fear returns when he sees the trail alongside. Following the bank anxiously for several miles, he halts at every bird call or snapped branch.

When darkness finally falls, Witch muds his skin against bugs and leeches and settles himself among the roots of a tree a short way off the trail. It would be suicide to blunder on into tripwires or mines, not to speak of nighttime patrols. The rain eases off, and he takes a swallow from his canteen. Once he drinks surface water, he'll be racing his gut.

Witch has half dozed for an hour or so amid the incessant whine of blood-sucking insects when he catches a swishing noise and holds his breath. In the dark not ten feet away, six persons with guns travel by at a pace indicating they know the trail. Their equipment clinks rhythmically as they banter in Vietnamese. One laughs gleefully.

Raucous tree frogs reclaim the night. Ten minutes pass, and Witch gets the shakes. His knees crack and scare him anew as he straightens to get a grip. The leaves start rattling under a soft night rain, and he wonders if he might be safer on the trail after all. The soldiers walked with no caution that he could detect. He considers that they might have been proceeding to set an ambush but decides that unlikely. Whom would they expect to ambush this deep in their own territory? He needs to travel slowly enough to keep from catching them, that's all.

Witch weighs the odds and is finally about to make his move onto the trail when some sense warns him not to. He holds his breath, straining his eyes and listening. What is it? A slight brushing sound attracts his attention, and his peripheral vision picks up something darker than the night moving steadily through the trees alongside the trail, directly toward him! His mouth goes dry and metallic.

All at once the sense is gone, and Witch searches the darkness desperately. A patter of water reaches him. Turning toward it, he discerns someone taking a leak against a tree—not three feet away. A gun barrel glints at his shoulder. In another few seconds he will finish, turn around, and walk right into him. He cannot duck out of the way, not this close.

Witch has no choice; he steps out and drives his hand into the soldier's throat when the man turns toward the sound. As the soldier clutches at his throat, Witch seizes his chin and helmet and cracks his neck, then carefully lets him down, the unexpected weight almost getting away. God, what has he done? A human being. He had to. Witch fingers the throat for a pulse and finds none. He flexes his palm, still registering the bristly pressure of the soldier's chin.

The rest of the party could appear any second; he has no time. Witch rifles the dead soldier for ammunition and silently slides the man's weapon from his shoulder. Not until he takes a grip on the shoulder piece does Witch recognize he is holding an AR-15. His mind reels.

Instinct tells him the rest of the patrol is setting an ambush behind him, and he probably surprised the point man. He has no idea how Americans got out here, but they must be tracking the Vietnamese patrol that passed earlier. Witch knows he would have been dead. Even so…

A noise reaches him from up the trail, and the tree frogs go silent. If the ranger's buddies discover him, Witch knows sides will not matter. A ranger patrol this deep into NVA territory will be so keyed up he could never identify himself. And they will drop him anyway if they find him with the AR-15. Witch has seen them on the flights back, eyes haunted with visions he now understands. High on fear and danger, they kill without thinking. His only chance is to move, and fast. He glides onto the trail and sets off into the darkness, no longer caring whether it leads him toward the coast, as long as it takes him away.

After an hour of walking mostly by feel, Witch hears a waterfall gushing. The roar steadily amplifies. Not until the stream suddenly plunges over practically at his feet does Witch realize he must have missed a fork; the trail seems to end here. There are no stars, and a far-off grumble of thunder follows a stitch of lightning over the mountains. Rather than risk backtracking into the ranger patrol, he gropes his way hand-to-hand over the drop along spray-slick rock. He sees false lights in the blackness as the rifle on his back catches every branch and bush.

At the bottom, Witch takes the stream bank until a trail comes alongside again. Here he halts stockstill and listens, his lips slightly parted. He distinctly heard a voice. The Vietnamese patrol must be making camp nearby. No, a woman is speaking—clearly a woman—or a child. It has to be the village they flew

51

over by the waterfall. Hunger goads him to slip in and raid whatever food he can until he thinks of the outcry; the Vietnamese who walked past at nightfall could even be sleeping here. Reluctantly, he descends the stream's winding course away from the village until, hours later, the first gray of pre-dawn enters the sky from the distant South China Sea beyond the miles of still-dark mountains ahead.

Witch begins a numbing routine of traveling by darkness to make another few miles downstream each night. Three nights, and the mountains give way to scrubbed-out bush and open country; the stream swirls into a fringe of palm nodding against the night sky as breezes roll patterns across the moonlit water. Backbones of dikes lead across a pale gleam of flooded paddies where Witch feels like a silhouette with his finger on the AR-15's safety. Keeping his soggy boots on for fear of being surprised, he beds down long before first light. By mid-morning Vietnamese peasants work their fields and balance loads along the dikes as he lies sodden and alive with bugs he dare not swat. Feverish and weak with hunger and diarrhea from the river, Witch is sinking; but each time he drifts toward sleep, that soldier's neck pops in his hands. No amount of denial will erase the memory of him, someone's son who bore his AR-15 into this fruitless war that crossed ally and adversary.

•

One night later, his body raddled with starvation and dysentery, Witch stumbles onto Highway One and sinks to the pavement in disbelief. He has made it! Gone as he is, he still thinks to disarm the AR-15 by pocketing its bolt and firing mechanism before throwing it by the roadside and kicking dirt over it.

By the time he rises unsteadily with the morning sun to flag down an approaching armored cavalry unit, the shooting war has left Witch in its debris. He will need months to shed the hemolytic organisms, fungi, amœbæ and other intestinal parasites he picked up, little eyeless creatures digesting him from the inside. The demons that infect his dreams, however, prove far more resistant.

MICHIGAN
May 1993

"Graham?"

Linda's voice startled him. The helicopter was gone, trailing its faded urgency across the bay. Reflections from the bonfire freckled the water at his feet.

She touched his arm and leaned into his vision.

"Are you all right?"

Shaken, Graham looked away, hoping she could not see his face.

"What is it?"

He turned and found both her hands.

"Ouch. Easy. I break. You're shaking."

"Am I? Sorry. Linda..." He hesitated. Probably he never had a chance anyway. "I need your other self."

"My other self?" Her voice broke, and she pulled free of his grip.

"At the shelter you must hear it all."

"Oh. Very little shocks me any more."

"So how bad? Assault and rape I would assume. Maybe even homicide. What do you do with the things people tell you?"

"Depends. I'm not going into detail, if that's what you're asking. Let me just say this: What I hear stops here. I make no judgments unless I suspect endangerment or criminal activity. Then I have to report it. Otherwise my lips are sealed, and you're not getting anything out of me. I don't care if it's you or whoever."

"I hoped you'd say that."

"I don't understand."

"You want to hear what it was like. I'll tell you, but first I need to... to build the picture. So you wouldn't believe this, but it was actually very beautiful. I remember the beach at Cam Rahn Bay and the South China Sea. It sounds exotic, doesn't it: 'the South China Sea'? It was. A few miles inland, mountains started and then the Central Highlands. We used to fly over waterfalls and little villages surrounded by terraced fields like something out of a picture book. From the air the country could look idyllic: water buffaloes and farmers cutting rice.

"But then you'd see all the bomb craters from the B-52s and the big alleys we bulldozed through the rain forest like firebreaks to expose the VC."

Linda's sudden hand on Graham's arm was electric as he tried to make sense of his impressions.

"The place was swarming with Americans. It was like some kind of strung-out party in battle fatigues, Armed Forces Radio playing Jimi Hendrix and Country Joe and the Fish. Then you'd cruise over one of those picturesque villages, and someone would try to blow your doors off with a rocket grenade.

"You never knew when or where the war would come at you. Guy on R & R might go with some off-limits Vietnamese chick and afterwards claim the sex was so legendary that the VD was worth it. Or he might show up in a ditch with his throat cut.

"It could meet you anywhere. A lieutenant in our outfit got fragged in the john."

"Fragged?" she asked.

"Someone blew him up while he was taking a dump. One of our guys."

"Why?" Linda whispered.

"The lieutenant was going to report him for some infraction. Ed Mather: he's probably on the Wall—Killed in Action. Once going down Highway One we saw a big smoke column ahead. We figured someone was burning farm until we got close and saw an American chopper blazing away in a paddy, no one around. It was just burning. Where had it come from? Where was the crew? The war had that quality, surreal."

"Did you ever tell them these stories?"

"Who?"

"Your family, your wife, your daughter."

"I haven't seen them in twenty years."

He heard her inhale deeply before she spoke.

"Still... you could."

"Tell them? No."

"It might help them understand."

"What's to understand? Things just happened. Random. It wasn't our country."

"It was just the whole experience, is that it?" she said.

"I guess so, the whole experience."

Keep your mouth shut. She won't understand.

"There is more, isn't there?"

He stared out over the lake, torn. She had just told him they might become close; telling her what he had done would end that. But she was also a counselor, and he realized how long he'd needed someone to hear it. He turned them to make their way further along the beach in silence.

"Graham, whatever it is, you don't have to say; but I'd listen. Without judgment."

"The shit that happened. We pulled out these rangers with two VC they'd captured. This one ranger kept bullying them and all of a sudden he pushed one of them out the door just like that. We were a couple of hundred feet up. And nobody looks at anybody. You just sit there with no expression. Inside I'm thinking, 'You sonofabitch!' Excuse me."

"I hear worse."

"The pilot comes on my headset, says 'He's not to do that again! What if he'd gone into the tail? Tell him.' But I don't say anything. Will I go out, too? Or get fragged for it? I mean we're not animals. Maybe they're all thinking the same thing I am. But you don't ask; every one of us was… How can I put it? …potentially lethal? Somebody made a joke after a while. That's the kind of stuff. He didn't push the other guy out. For which I was grateful."

"I'm sure."

Graham took a deep breath and expelled it.

"There's worse. I need you for this."

Compelled finally to unburden himself, he began telling Linda as they drifted down the beach, grateful for the mask of darkness.

"I was on a Huey UH-1 helicopter with three other guys: Barry Weintraub, Hurley Morgan, and Boz Hill. I was a door gunner, but they called me Witch Doctor. See, I was the medical officer, too."

"We took recon patrols out, rangers who'd comb the bush hunting VC for four or five days, and then we'd bring them in. Right at the end of my tour in '70, we got caught in the highlands near the Laotian border. I was trying to bring in some wounded rangers so we could lift them out, when the chopper got hit. Out there on foot, I couldn't help them. All those guys, my buddies, and the only thing I could do was save my own ass. I had to walk to the coast. I almost died."

"Oh god."

"I was crossing NVA territory the whole way, North Vietnamese Army, 25 or 30 miles. I had to hide in the bush during daylight and travel in darkness. Night was the worst. It was the only time I could move, but I couldn't see. There were others out there: patrols, Americans, people like your brother. You never knew."

She said nothing, waiting.

Graham had no saliva.

"I killed one of them. It was dark. He would have shot me if I hadn't. Then I got his rifle and I realized."

"What are you saying, Graham, that he was American?"

"He could have been your brother, out there on foot like me, trying to reach the coast. What if I killed him?"

She let out a long breath. "It wasn't him."

"How do you know? He was someone's brother or son. Whose? I never found out. His name could be on the Wall, for all I know, but which would it be? There are row upon row of names from that time; I've looked. Did anyone find his body, report him missing? I don't know. I was too sick and too afraid to ask. They rotated me home.

"I couldn't forgive myself, went into depression. It was so bad. I was a wreck."

"Did you get counseling?"

"It was too late for my family by the time I got help and pulled myself half together, and I never told anyone. Sometimes I worry it's still too late, for me. I'm sorry."

He stopped. There was no way he could tell her how he tried to deal with it.

"Don't be," she said.

A silence fell between them, and Graham stared into the darkness. He had gone too far. Linda's shoulder brushed his slightly as they walked. A few minutes farther and they would have stumbled into the mouth of a creek carving across their way but for the sudden warning of a bank. Just in front, Graham could hear current gushing past to join the lake and put his hand in. The water felt warm.

"We could probably wade across," he ventured. "Want to try?"

He started to take her hand but released it immediately when she tensed up.

"It might be deep in the middle," she said.

"In that case we might have to take a dip."

"No. I don't want to. I can't see, and what if it took us into the lake? I can't swim. Please don't."

Distressed that he had frightened her, Graham touched a shoulder to steer her away from the bank.

"Hey. I didn't mean to scare you."

"You probably think I'm silly, but I can't help it."

"There's nothing silly about it when you don't swim."

Graham felt around for some flat rocks to skip across the current. He winged a few before she stopped his hand and pulled him around to face her.

"Graham..."

"Yes?"

Shivering, she pressed tightly into him and squeezed him as hard as she could. The smell of her undid him.

"It's all right," she whispered, then raised her face and kissed him, at first almost sisterly; then, as their stifled breathing mixed, she worked her mouth into his with an urgency that set off lights in his eyes.

She tucked her head into his shoulder and murmured, "Sorry, I guess you can tell I'm a little tipsy. I didn't mean to. I just had to gear myself up for this."

Her admission prompted Graham to another confession.

"You were right, Linda; I want you to come home with me."

He knew as soon as it came out he should never have said it.

She drew back to regard him at arm's length.

"And I would, except... we can't."

"Why not?"

"Um… I think Cheryl asked me to stay over."

"I won't touch. Just stay the night. She'll understand."

What was he saying? This was crazy. Now he had put himself out there, he had to insist. The carnal immediacy of her was impairing his sanity.

"No. She brought me out here, so I can't. How would I get to your house?"

Fogged by her as he was, something in what she said did not compute.

"With me," he said. Then it hit him.

"Wait a minute, now where's your car?"

"Graham, haven't you figured out by now I don't have one? It was just something to tell you that was easier than trying to explain why you couldn't know where I live."

Her admission so disarmed him he had to laugh. "Linda, the longer I'm around you, the less I know."

"Probably better. You might not like what you'd see."

"May I give it a try? Look, come with me. It's not about sex; it's about you. I owe you so big time I'll even sleep in another room, and in the morning I'll take you to your shop or wherever you need to go. If it doesn't work, we won't follow up. Okay?"

She withheld an answer until they were almost back to the bonfire. Then she said simply, "Wait by the porch. I have to get my things."

14

For the first ten minutes into town, Graham entertained private second thoughts: In two days his daughter would arrive. This was not the time. And Linda, what was she mulling in her silence beside him? It couldn't be nice after what he'd told her.

Passing through Beaver Grove, five miles from town, she said something so softly that he failed to catch the words.

"I'm sorry, what?"

"It's always someone's brother or son. It makes no difference. Sides don't matter. Either way it's a human being. In the end."

He shifted mental gears.

"I've tried that line of reasoning a million times." He hesitated. "I even tell myself he was the one who pushed the VC out the door. Imagine."

"That would guarantee it wasn't my brother."

He glanced to see her face half lit by the dashboard, fixed on his, unsmiling.

"Listen to me; it was survival. Who cared for allegiances, on either side? Did you?"

"I cared about staying alive."

"Exactly. You had scared boys pushed into each other in the dark with guns and trying to live through it. Some succeeded and some didn't. That's war, at ground level."

"But look what I did."

"Anyone would have. No one blames you, and you shouldn't judge yourself, Graham. It was bad luck. Sometimes the best we do is to make up for the deeds we fall into. Volunteering and teaching are certainly honorable."

"Like the kind of things you do?"

"Things I do. What do you mean?"

"What you said about making up for what happens. I think that's pretty perceptive." As they passed under a highway lamp, Graham saw her staring out the window looking as if she was going to cry. "What's the matter?"

"Nothing."

"Something happened that night we went to dinner, didn't it?"

She averted her face.

"Linda?"

Seconds passed. "Yes, to one of my clients. They brought her to the emergency room. Her husband had attacked her."

"That made you mad at me?"

"How can I put this? I see so many women get run over. Sometimes it gets to me. They're letting people—okay, men—control them. I have to deal with the wreckage. I just reach this point where the only way to convince them is not to get caught up in it myself. It wasn't you; I was coping. Does that make any sense?"

They were passing the great rock bluffs rimming Lake Superior at the edge of town. He thought about that a while. Finally, heading up the last hill before dropping downtown, he said, "Being in control matters a lot to you, doesn't it?"

"Well of course."

"I mean relationships."

"Then you misread me; I'm wary, that's all. I see things that make you seem like a bad idea. Sometimes I think, 'Watch out! Cross the line, and the rules don't apply. Anything goes.' Do you understand? It makes me want to pull back and forget the whole thing. I tell myself I'm doing fine. Why ask for complications?"

"Maybe I think the same thing. It doesn't have to be that way."

"Quite likely it doesn't. I'm just going by my experiences, making a lot of wrongheaded assumptions probably."

Graham let that simmer as he wheeled down the quiet street where he lived and inched into his old garage, built to accommodate a Model A. Things were going to be touch and go.

Linda's hand felt damp when he led her into the house. She blinked when he snapped on the kitchen light and would not meet his eyes as she took in the milk-glass school globe lighting the patterned walls and tile floor. She seemed in no better shape about this overnight than he did. This was looking more and more like an impulse that bore rethinking. Maybe they should call it off.

"Is that the original wallpaper? The faded fruit looks nineteenth century."

"No, but that's the idea; I'm restoring it. You can imagine it never ends."

"I love the faucets." She turned the porcelain tap handles on and off.

"You should see the Tiffany lamp in the dining room."

"Let's have a look."

Feeling as if he were going through some elaborate ritual for which he had lost the liturgy, Graham took Linda farther into the Victorian home he had bought on a shoestring eight years ago after coming up here to start over. It became the refuge he could focus on while he tried to re-make a life in it.

She gratified him by exclaiming over the lamp, which in truth did look pretty spectacular when he switched it on to cast jeweled patterns over the gilt-framed Renaissance reproductions that adorned the room. Best of all, the whole contraption had stayed up. This room was his baby. Her look traveled over the flocked walls and stopped on Botticelli's *Annunziata*. She seemed transfixed by the advancing and receding figures, the composition Chagall-like for the time.

"Classy. Show me more."

In the living room, Linda admired the high ceilings and ornate woodwork he had spent so much time on and pronounced "adorable" his ongoing efforts at restoration. As he showed her what he liked to call the conservatory, Graham turned for a reaction to the far-out chandelier he had found in a junk shop; instead, she was browsing the mismatched array of paperbacks and hardcovers he had lugged down only yesterday and ranked along the bookshelf by the fireplace to impress Julie.

She looked up from her inspection. "Graham, you surprise me."

"The place does have a lot of work in it, but it keeps me out of trouble."

"No, I mean these; I expected technical books, but I don't see any."

"Oh, they're upstairs in my office. I never get to teach that level."

She slipped *Finnegans Wake* off the shelf and started leafing through it. She gave a perplexed look and hefted it at him.

"How's anyone supposed to read this?"

"He's playing with the language."

"Can you read it?"

"I'm on my third try," he said. "One of these days I'll make it."

"Sounds like a pill to me. I'll have to admit *Ulysses* is another take on your Greeks, though."

"That's incautious of you," he said.

"What is?"

"Telling me you've read Joyce."

"I didn't say I read it; I've heard of it."

His question deflected, she moved on to his records and CDs, at which point the hair came down.

"Graham, what is this, the *Fugs?* I didn't think anyone alive had heard of the *Fugs*."

"I used to like them," he said and switched off the radio, which he had only just switched on out of nervousness. "Play it if you want."

"No, wait; I have to see what else you have. God, all this *classical* jazz!"

She started poking around in his tapes and suddenly exclaimed, "Omigod, what's this? The Stones! And Dylan!"

A kid in a candy store, she picked out *Blood on the Tracks*. "Play 'Tangled up in Blue'!"

He turned the selector to "tape" and let her puzzle out the other buttons.

While Dylan sang his tale of love gone awry, Linda hunched onto the couch beside Graham and shut her eyes in rapt attendance. As Graham followed the intricate harmonica and guitar work, the lyrics suddenly arrested him about a woman turning Dylan onto a fifteenth-century Italian poet with words that burned like coal.

Nice, Graham thought, but before he could say so, Linda was holding her nose to accompany the final lines in a nasalised twang startlingly close to Dylan's recounting "carpenter's wahves" and the things they did with their "laahves."

As Dylan and his backup pounded out the bittersweet coda with a pumped-up harmonica-guitar jam, Linda cheered, "Whee, play it again," apparently still a bit tipsy.

Without waiting for assent, she ran the tape back for another go.

Partway into the second playing, Graham got inspired.

"Be right back," he told her and skipped off to rifle under the stairs until he dug out the dented harmonica that had carried him through the Nam. Lovingly, he cradled it to his mouth and began blowing right in with Dylan's melody, the chords tingling his lips.

"Listen to you!" Linda shrieked.

"I used to be really good," he said, "but I'm kind of rusty now."

She snapped off the tape.

"How about Janis Joplin? Play 'Piece of my Heart.'"

"All right, no promises but I'll give it a go."

Graham huffed out a bluesy riff, thumbing off trills while Linda nodded her head in time, getting the hang of it. Closing her eyes, she started piping a reedy Janis Joplin from the back of her throat so unbelievably it sent a thrill up his back and sent him right back to 1968, wailing the war harmonica that had driven Leila up the wall and not improved a bit until he found himself playing alone. Linda threw her head back at the invisible mike grasped in both her hands for the boozy "COME awn COME awn" while he did his best to keep up.

Laughing helplessly, she stopped with tears rolling down her cheeks and laid a hand on his shoulder, her lips inches from his. Graham would have kissed them right then and there if she had not stepped back.

"Oh god, Graham!" She stuck her tongue out like a dog. "That's hard on the pipes. Get me water!" Her eyes and face were shining.

"How about a soda?"

"I don't care, whatever. Something wet."

"Let me take a look."

In the kitchen, Graham poked dill pickles and mayonnaise aside in the refrigerator to find an opened bottle of flavored mineral water on the top shelf.

"How about a Perrier?" he called.

"Bring it on," she said.

Linda had on an oversize pair of reading glasses, scanning the garnet type on a CD case when he returned.

"This might be flat. I don't know how long it's been open."

Taking a swallow, she gave a big "aah" and sighted him shrewdly over the glass.

"You don't drink, do you?"

"I don't."

She raised the glass to him before draining it.

"More power. I need a broom," she said, handing him the glass.

Broom? Graham set the glass in the kitchen sink and returned with one from the back door. Linda set the CD down and laid her glasses on it. Rubbing her hands together, she squared her shoulders and took the broom.

"Now. You're old enough to remember *this.*"

Bringing the handle up to her lips, Linda cleared her throat, took a big breath and launched into Edith Piaf's *Je ne regrette rien*, growling the *r*'s like a tigress. Eyes closed, she cupped her hand out with the words and leaned into the broom to deliver Piaf's vibrato. Her brassy rendition simply riveted him. She was breathtaking.

"Wow! Spectacular. Your French is spot on."

"Is that what it is?" She shrugged. "I just memorized it."

Graham didn't believe her.

Linda looked at the CD she'd set down and fingered her glasses. "How come you got all this baroque music?"

"I like it. You listen to it, too, hey?"

"It's different. You can listen if you want. After all that volleyball and stage-craft, I'd like to clean up, if that's okay with you."

Slinging over her arm the robe Graham offered with a ton of misgivings from the room he had fixed for Julie, she gathered up the overnight bag she'd brought from Cheryl's camp and left Corelli sawing away. Graham tried to settle his nerves by listening but got distracted once the shower began. Linda started singing "Ball and Chain." Finally she let the water blast into her mouth and gargled it. What was she on?

The water cut off and wracked the pipes. Graham forced himself back to the intricacies of Corelli until he remembered the garage. Distracted as he had been by Linda's presence, he had left it wide open. Not that anyone would bother anything, but closing the garage fit his order of things.

The Harmonious Blacksmith was playing on the turntable when he returned, and Linda, draped in the borrowed robe with her head swathed in a towel, stood absorbed at his bookshelf, lip reading a paperback.

"Graham." She looked up in surprise and shoved the book back among its companions. She blinked a couple of times and asked, "Ever try regular soap?"

"What?"

"All your little motel pats in there. Buy a bar sometime. You'll never go back."

"Oh, those. I pick them up on trips."

She leaned back against the shelves as if to distract him further and gave a smile that made his head spin.

"Don't tell me you have tiny bottles of shampoo."

Graham grinned. "One or two."

"Take a load off. Let's talk."

She flounced into the rocker facing him with a leg cross that revealed six inches of thigh. "You make me curious, all these things. I'm not talking about the shower stuff. I mean all this." Linda swept her arm out, hiking the robe another inch in the process. "The period stuff, the music, the books... Is that what it takes?"

"You mean here?"

"I mean is this enough for you."

"Enough?" He shrugged. "Good company. No troubles. That would be okay."

"No hassles. That's it?"

"Well... no."

"What?" She slit her eyes as if to hear more distant music.

He could not tell her about Julie. This was the wrong time to introduce that. He shook his head. "What about you?"

"Forget it, Jack; I asked first. Okay, tell me this; what happened between you and your wife? You can say to mind my own business."

"It's okay. I was nuts. She couldn't put up with it."

"Nuts. How do you mean?"

"Withdrawal, depression. I wasn't always."

"Mm. That's all?"

"I used to arrange, like an addiction. It soothed me. When I couldn't keep it all in place, I'd fly off the handle, break things."

She stopped rocking, sudden attention, and blinked at him amid a frantic counterpoint of strings from Handel. "You'd break things."

He nodded.

"But you didn't used to."

"No. Not until I... not until afterwards."

Narrowing her eyes, she patted at the towel and tucked a stray curl in before asking, "So are you still into this arranging business?"

"I'm getting better."

"Do you feel your wife lacked understanding about it?"

"No; if anything, she was patient to a fault."

"What was her name?"

"Leila."

"And your daughter?"

"Julie. Juliette actually." In two days she would be here, in this room. He really should tell her, but she might walk.

"You don't paint yourself as a good bet, do you?"

"Man of the year."

"You'd like me to feel sorry for you."

Challenging him with a half smile and eyes too dark to let him in, she crossed her legs over a flash of lingerie and smoothed the robe back.

"What do you find so fascinating about me?"

"Your Mickey Mouse watch?"

"Seriously."

"None of your business. What is this, psychoanalysis?"

"Something like that. I'm building a dossier on you."

"Good, we have something in common. Here's what I'm putting in yours: 'Linda's paid dues, but she's come through in good shape. She acts on her convictions. She also likes pretending.' There. How's that?"

"Corny. Sounds more psycho than psychoanalyst."

"Maybe, but I know this: You're not as simple as you put on."

"Oh really? What do you think, I'm a rocket scientist?"

"It's pretty clear you've got a brain in your head. And you're not who you pretend to be."

She rocked forward, looking hugely amused.

"O, mystery woman. Let's hear this one. Who am I supposed to be?"

"For starters, I think you grew up in southern California, maybe Texas. Not New York. I'd guess you're *latina*; and, at some point in your life, I think you were connected with money."

"Bravo!"

"I'm close then?"

"Not even. But let's hear why you think so."

"The tattoo on your left hand: That's a Chicano thing from the Southwest."

"Good eye, Sherlock, but you jump to conclusions. I tried to pass myself off as Hispanic once when I was desperate for a job. Now what makes you think the money?"

"Your teeth are too perfect. Dental work like that costs."

"People are born with good teeth. Did you consider that?"

"I've considered it."

She shifted to adjust her turban. Handel's *Chaconne in G* unraveled from the speakers behind, no competition, as he waited for her to wriggle out of this one.

"Well? That's it?" she said.

Unsatisfied, Graham decided to press further.

"How about the woman at the emergency room? Did you make that up?"

"I did not. Look, Graham, kidding aside, let's drop this now."

"What, am I getting warm?"

"There are times blissful ignorance is preferable. This happens to be one of them."

"So just leave a masquerade between us."

"Maybe we need to examine whether there should be anything between us."

Her eyes fixed on his, impenetrable. She was not smiling. Like a roaring in his ears, Handel recapitulated.

"You're serious, aren't you?".

"Unfortunately. I'm bad medicine."

"Says who?"

"Says me. I've done things you wouldn't appreciate, things I'm not proud of."

"So have I, Linda. All that counts to me is the person you are."

"Yes, and if you knew, I'm afraid it would count. Believe me, it would."

"What is it, the man who paid for the teeth? Big deal."

"Don't even speculate. It's beyond what you can imagine."

"Try me."

"I wish I could."

"So? Go ahead."

"I can't. I'm sorry we brought this up now."

"You want to tell me, don't you? You wouldn't have let it go this far."

"I don't know. I'd have to trust you first. Only then, if ever."

She quieted him with a long look, done talking. In the face of her gaze, he cleared his throat and studied his hands. Where to take this? If he told her about Julie, would she trust him? When he glanced up again, she had settled back and closed her eyes as if the exchange had worn her down. Shaking herself upright all at once, she yawned into her hand and regarded him over the tops of her fingers.

"I'll think about it, okay? Right now I'm crashing, and I have to be up early. What are the arrangements?"

"Sleepwise?"

She raised her eyebrows in a subtle prompt.

"If you want, you can use the guest room upstairs, or..."

Or what? He did not know the music for this. He and Leila never negotiated.

"I think that's best. I promised I'd stay."

"Whatever you're comfortable with. Come on, follow me."

At the top of the stairs, she caught Graham's arm, charged contact like the moment downstairs face to face over his harmonica. Without makeup, the crow's feet and creases only enhanced her.

"You probably think you're harboring a lunatic."

"Takes one to know one."

She touched his shoulder and brushed his lips lightly with hers in what was probably meant as a quick good night.

"You're nice," she said.

When he did not release her, she pushed herself away.

"Friends, remember?"

She waved dismissal and went into the room he had prepared for Julie. The thought of her sleeping where Julie would sleep caused him a twinge of guilt.

Jangled, Graham trudged down the stairs to take his own shower and turn out the lights. Handel was scratching away in the rideout grooves, having failed to reject. He raised the tone arm and slipped the record back into its sleeve. *Dances from Handel:* One curious lady.

Passing the bookshelf after his shower, Graham stopped. It was easy enough to tell which one she had been reading. She had bookmarked it for him, jutting from the others: *Orlando furioso e la poesia di Ludovico Ariosto,* madly erotic fifteenth-century Italian verse from the first summer he had worked with the Italian roofing crew around the Fremont area. He had thought to teach himself; but his first parsing of Lodovico convinced him that this was why men and women had invented language in the first place: not to find food but to find each other.

She had been holding the book open in the middle, lip reading to herself. How? None of it was English. If she were only sounding it out, she would have asked what language. He restored Lodovico to the row of books.

Lying in his own bedroom, he could not sleep. What had come over him this evening? He had not acted like this in years. Linda's impetuosity had caught him up, the way she ran over the edges; and yet he had not a clue about her, really.

After rolling around for perhaps fifteen minutes staring into the dark with thoughts of Linda lying a floor above in next to nothing, he heard a creak from the stairs. A second later, a sharp thump inside the room startled him, followed by a piece of furniture sliding.

"Ow! Ooo, that hurt!"

"Linda! What are you doing?"

"Ah yes, the romantic entrance. The graceful virgin steals discreetly to her lover's bower. Where in the world are you?"

Then her hands were patting the end of the bed, which suddenly registered her presence. She found his foot and hunted along him until she was next to him, her hair brushing his shoulder as she rubbed her shin.

"What's the matter?" Graham asked and pushed himself up on his elbows.

"Bogey men. And I cracked my shin, what do you think? Self-esteem, too. You wouldn't ask, would you?"

"You made me promise."

"Promises! You could have tried."

"We're too knife-edge; I was afraid to."

"Don't be," she said, so close he could feel her breath on his cheek.

For an instant, the unfamiliarity of this strange woman in his bed arrested Graham. With Leila, he'd known the moves, the pleasures and parameters; they could anticipate. Linda was another country. He had no maps, no phrase book.

"Graham?" she said, her knuckle tracing the line of his jaw as she brushed her nails along his neck. A nipple surprised the back of his hand when her mouth found his in the darkness, plushy lips parting that closed over half-truth and evasion, everting themselves to draw him in, afford an opening, the promise of entry.

Save for her silhouette against the window, Linda's presence was tactile, lush convexities and a tangle of hair scented with motel fruit among his fingers. Linda's edges began to yield as Graham confused who she was with his sensation of her. All but lost in her kiss, he registered an artlessness, almost a clumsiness on her part that made her hesitate, and he started to roll her back onto the pillow.

She surprised him. "No, let me do it."

Pushing him back, she began to squirm around until a snap of elastic told Graham she was maneuvering out of her underwear.

"I hope you have a condom," she said.

"In the nightstand." He rolled over and felt for where he kept them, just in case.

"Give it here."

She attacked the wrapper with her fingernails, finally resorting to teeth. Just when he was about to offer a hand opening it, she spat plastic and snapped it free. By this time the wetness of her straddling his thigh had him aroused beyond reason. She bent forward to find him and rolled the condom on in one smooth stroke.

"Slick."

"Practice. I'm forever showing women."

Despite her attempt at levity, Graham could feel how tense she was, almost trembling; her palms pressed damp against his chest. She rose and tried to settle herself, without success.

"Hey," he whispered.

"Sh. I want this."

She swiveled and pushed, gasping as if it hurt, until she had forced herself onto him, the hot squeeze of her almost spasmodic. Breathing raggedly and shaking, she wiped her hands on her thighs and clenched them. Something far too intense was playing itself out in the dark.

"Linda, Jesus!"

Meaning to make things easier, Graham rolled them over in a tangle of legs, but no sooner had he done so than she went rigid and began batting his chest with her hands.

"Stop! Let me go!"

He did, immediately. This was not how it should work. He groped around until he found both her hands and drew her to him.

"Not the best choice, was I?" she said.

"Did I say that?"

"You might not *say* it."

"Is there something I ought to know?"

"It's a woman thing. Let's sleep on it, shall we?"

She pushed him back onto the bed and nestled against his shoulder until she regained enough composure to drift off. Graham lay still, breathing as if he, too, were sleeping, but he was not.

What has this woman been through?

Several minutes after he had lain perfectly still, the bed moved; Linda disengaged herself and eased from the bed. The floor cracked outside the room, and Graham heard her pull the bathroom door shut. He waited a minute, then got up and dropped the condom into the wastebasket. No light showed from the bathroom, but he could hear a muffled rasping that registered as snuffling.

Graham inched the door open and found her sitting naked on the tub, stifling gusty sobs into a towel. He knelt before her and took her in his arms.

"Linda. You've been hurt."

She shook her head and continued sobbing.

"Tell me."

"Tell you what? There's nothing to tell," she said through the towel.

"Okay. Nothing's wrong."

She burst out again. "I can't even begin."

"Try. Tell me now. It's too dark to see each other."

"That's not it. Just forget me. Hate me."

"I could never."

She leaned to hold him back, and Graham rocked her in his arms. Finally she calmed herself enough to whisper, "We'll see."

Graham could not speak. Instead, he raised her and led her back to his room. On the bed beside her in the dark, he smoothed her face until she breathed sleep.

Under Linda's façade lived someone hurt and vulnerable as a broken bird, but she went to such lengths to keep it from showing.

Linda, you keep inventing yourself. Who are you?

15

Precisely at 6:30 the clock radio woke Graham in a fetal tuck on top of the spread, a blanket thrown over him. Beside him, the covers were pulled into place. Graham blinked himself upright and listened. Linda was brushing her teeth. She actually spent the night. He finger-combed his hair and wondered when he fell asleep.

Linda spat and knocked her toothbrush on the sink to emerge in her work smock, ripping at her hair with a brush.

"Up and at 'em," she greeted

Graham sat on the edge of the bed and yawned as he took her in.

"How do you manage, Linda? So early and so beautiful."

"So early and blind as a bat." Turned away to the window, she added, "Forget that business last night. I don't know what came over me. I haven't been getting enough sleep."

"Linda, you grace me coming at all."

"That's nice of you."

"I mean it; sleeping beside you... I could make a habit of it—if you'd let me."

Linda turned herself to him, radiant. She took his face in cool palms and kissed him to the point of intoxication. Then she drew back and held him at arm's length for a moment.

"You're not bad for a college boy."

"As long as I'm good enough for you."

He pulled the rest of the covers into place before seeing what he could scare up in the kitchen. A look in the refrigerator reminded Graham he still had to go shopping before Julie arrived, or they'd have *nada* to eat; and he wanted everything perfect. He made a quick mental list of what they needed as Linda packed her overnight bag. Julie's visit: He would have to deal with that today. Certainly Linda would understand postponing things a few days.

"Hey, you want to go to Babycakes for breakfast?" he called.

"Sure."

In a few more minutes he had a grocery list made and returned to the bedroom to find Linda fishing around under the bed with her foot.

"Lose something?"

"My underpants. Well, I don't want to go rooting for them. You'll find them next time you change the sheets."

"I'll hang them over the fireplace. Want a pair of mine?"

She rolled her eyes. "I brought a change. May I use the phone to check in at the shelter? I always worry. It's hard to find people I can trust."

She shook her hair into a riot of bronze-dark tendrils and pushed here and there with her fingers, his phone shouldered against her neck. She looked immensely appealing, but Graham was not thinking of that.

When she put the phone down after assuring herself about the shelter, Graham asked, "And me, can you trust me yet?"

Overnight bag in hand, she considered. "I'm getting there."

"Well then, for starters, tell me this: Am I seeing the real you?"

"What do you mean by that?"

"Your hair—it's always something different."

She relaxed. "Oh. Well... it's close. This is my natural color, with a little help." She reached up and opened a part at the crown. "See the gray coming in at the roots?"

He peered. "Not really."

"Take my word for it."

"So you dye it different colors every day or what?"

She let out a peal of laughter. "Heavens, no. Haven't you heard of hairpieces? I have tons of them. Some of them might even suit you."

The morning was glorious, so they decided to walk the seven blocks. Linda said she would head on to the shop afterwards for her first customer.

Crossing the intersection where Front Street broke over to downtown two blocks below, Linda remarked on the sunlight glistening off Marquette Mountain in the distance. Still turned half away, gazing at the ridge line, she added, "I could still collect my underpants this evening, couldn't I?"

Now there was no avoiding it. "This evening. There's, um... how shall I say, a conflict."

She turned to him with a look of real distress.

"What do you mean?"

"Didn't put that right. What I mean is, Julie—my daughter?—She got in touch with me. I haven't seen her in twenty years. I told you that, didn't I? She has to be in Minneapolis. In fact, she's there right now. She's coming to visit. Tomorrow. Total surprise. So..."

Graham groped for a diplomatic way to put her off, but Linda made that unnecessary. Her face lit up, and she grabbed his arm.

"But that's *wonderful!* No, truly! I'll stay out of the way. That's too important for the two of you. I mean that. We can postpone things a few days, whenever. You let me know. That's okay, isn't it?"

"Of course it is, and thanks. And I will, I will let you know."

"Your daughter, wow. After all these years. You are so lucky."

Suddenly she clapped her hand to her mouth. "Oh gosh! Make sure she doesn't find my underpants. You don't want her getting the wrong idea. Of you I mean."

70

She bumped him with her hip before ducking the mock roundhouse he aimed at her head. "But you'd look delicious."

They had almost reached the Third Street hill to the post office when she said, "Graham... in regards to that, I know you're still wondering about last night."

Graham froze. Was *this* the other shoe?

She laughed at his reaction. "Oh, I'm sexually attracted; you have no worries there."

He made a show of mopping his brow. "I didn't think so. And I told you it's okay."

"Not if you read something into it. I told you I see a lot of stuff, and I can't talk about it—not to you or anybody else—because of the confidentiality involved. And because of what I see... well, I haven't allowed myself for longer than you can imagine. So if I seem messed up and secretive, it's because of that. Does that clear it up, a little? You'll have to play me by ear for a while. If that's okay."

"You name the tune. We'll play it any way you like."

Graham was elated she had finally let her guard down enough to explain.

An uproar of voices reached them as they started down Washington. When they turned the corner at the post office, a mob bristling with signs shouted and spilled into the street. An under-manned line of harried policemen was simultaneously trying to hold everyone back on the walks and re-route traffic. The excitement centered around the Planned Parenthood office just past the Federal Building.

Police were backing the crowd into two groups, shouting back and forth across the street at each other. One side sprouted gory pictures of fetuses and knives dripping blood with legends like, *"Abortion Kills"* and *"When will the murder stop?"*

People on the other side of the street were urging the picketers to go home.

"Oh god, what is this?" Graham said. "No one does abortions there."

"Women learn options. They don't like that."

"Let's see what's happening."

"Let's not. Let's go to Babycakes. Look after I leave."

"Only for a minute. I want to see if I know anybody."

Shaking her head in disapproval, Linda let him tow her into the jostling crowd across from Planned Parenthood. The closer they got, the more raucous people grew and the more furious the catcalling. The crowd pushed, and the police shoved back. Several times the elbowing bulldozed them into the *Mining Journal* building. Two police cars sat in the middle of Washington Street with lights flashing, and a television crew was panning the crowd. Linda cupped her hands over her face and dragged at his arm.

"Please, I don't like this, Graham. I'm going back."

Suddenly she stopped and rose on her toes. "That woman! See her? Trying to get inside. See?"

"Who? Where?"

Linda pointed at a slight, frightened-looking girl just outside Planned Parenthood, trying to make her way to a door. She did not appear much older than a teen-ager. The sign carriers were calling to her, grasping their hands through the police, trying to reach her. The girl's eyes looked wild as a rabbit's.

"I know her," Linda said, putting her hands to her face again. "They have no right, no idea. You have to do something. Help her!"

"Me? She doesn't even know me."

"I don't care, you have to. I can't. My position, I can't. Please! Get her inside, Graham. I'll go far enough so she sees me with you. Do it!"

Linda was propelling him off the walk ahead of her, and he was about to face his first policeman with no idea what to do. Graham started to appeal to the officer when he caught sight of a man in reflector shades cheerleading the mob on the other side. The thinning hair and half-shaven face looked familiar. Then the man turned and brought the insignia on his tee shirt into view: Christ as Rambo with the legend "Jesus Is Coming with a Sword." Graham stopped dead in his tracks. The pressure of Linda's hand at his back disappeared.

"Linda, I know that guy," he said, turning.

She was gone. He looked around in confusion, trying to find her. At the same time the man in the tee shirt removed his shades. His pale blue eyes fixed on Graham, and he looked pleased.

Meachum. Dave Meachum.

They stood not ten feet apart in the swarm of protesters.

"Graham, my man," he called over the hubbub, "You've come to help."

"Tell your people to quit badgering that girl."

Meachum's face darkened. "Don't you see she's carrying the seed of God? Please, ma'am, don't kill that baby!"

"Move back, sir," the policeman was saying.

Graham searched the crowd again as he retreated but could not spy Linda. The policeman was pushing him harder now. The young woman reached the door of Planned Parenthood and slipped inside. The crowd was turning uglier, and Graham was only too happy to let the officer back him away from it to the other side of the street again. Meachum was working the protesters into a fever now and no longer seemed interested in Graham, who found it remarkable that Meachum had not only recognized him but remembered his name.

Graham continued his retreat all the way to Babycakes, but saw Linda nowhere. If she was still in the middle of that uproar, he had to find her. After craning his neck another fifteen minutes from Babycakes's front window, he decided she must have gone on to the shop.

But when he called LHC from the house, she had not come in. Maybe she'd gone to check on the shelter, wherever that was. He rummaged all over for the shelter's number without finding it. He remembered writing it on the back of a bank slip, which he had probably thrown away. All he could do was go by the shop at ten when she'd said her customer was due.

•

At five after ten, he walked into LHC. No Linda.

"Graham!" the gum-cracking beautician at the front chair greeted. "Where have you been? You haven't come in for ages."

He waved off her question and asked if she'd seen Linda.

"She hasn't come in," she said, "and she's got a customer waiting." She dropped her voice to a whisper. "She's getting pissed, too."

"How about Cheryl? Where's Cheryl?"

"Cheryl's not here Mondays. What do you need?"

"I think maybe Linda went over to the place she stays and ran into a problem." Graham did not offer examples; he was not sure if anyone besides Cheryl knew what Linda did outside the shop. "Why don't you give me her number, and I'll call over there and find out what's up."

"I… really can't do that."

"But—"

"I'm sorry, that's a policy. I just can't. Period."

Finally about noon Cheryl answered at home and counseled calm.

"Don't worry, Graham. She's a big girl. It doesn't hurt her to skip work. She's probably had some deal come up. Did you check the hospital?"

Graham snapped his fingers. "I didn't think of that."

"Did you two hit it off?"

"Tell you later. I've got to call the hospital now."

"Pardon *me*."

When he reached the emergency room, the receptionist assured him Linda Chapman was most definitely not there, and she would know.

That night Graham went to bed deeply concerned. For whatever reason, shame or cold feet, Linda had decided to make herself scarce again. He pushed under the covers and touched his foot to something anomalous. Linda's underpants. He fished them up with his toe and slipped them under the pillow.

In the morning he would meet the 9 a.m. flight from Minneapolis. He reached under the pillow and clenched Linda's underwear in his fist. He should have told her in so many words she had nothing to worry about. Whatever she had done could never come close to what he had to live with.

16

Graham popped awake. He heard the floor crack and held his breath. It cracked again, ever so slightly, and he smiled. It must be Linda. The clock radio said two in the morning.

Suddenly a high-powered flashlight blinded him from the bedroom doorway, and he started to shield his eyes.

"Don't move, mister," a man ordered. "Police. Stay right where you are. Now real slow, roll over on your stomach. Keep your hands where we can see them."

Someone jerked the covers away. Graham senses reeled. At least three men's voices were speaking in the room. Graham started to turn his head toward one of them, but the man commanded him to stay face down.

"She sure as hell ain't here."

"Check the other rooms. She's got to be. There's no way she could get out. We would have seen her."

People trooped through the house now, flinging open closets and scraping back hangers.

"Keep your hands in sight. Now roll over real slow," the man covering him ordered. "Sit up. Don't get adventurous. We've got you covered behind."

Behind the flashlights, two men in black coveralls pointed thoroughly sobering automatic weapons at him. He could feel high-powered projectiles aimed at him, and he had seen what they could do.

"I don't understand. What is this? Do you have a warrant? Whom are you looking for?"

An army invading his house in the middle of the night, and Graham had absurdly used the grammatical *whom*.

"Victoria Damentóva," the man said, "Care to tell us where she is?"

Graham thought he was hearing wrong.

They're looking for a Russian girl? Here?

The man handed Graham a warrant signed by the federal judge for the arrest of one "Vittoria Damantova." He wasn't about to point out that someone had misspelled "Victoria."

"Moscow?" Graham said.

"Lover boy's a joker." The man closest made a slight, impatient motion at the warrant with his assault rifle. "Try harder."

Graham raised both shoulders and shook his head helplessly.

"You have the wrong house. I never even heard of any Victoria..." he consulted the warrant again, and suddenly it hit him: *She's Italian! Victoria from Mantua!* "Oh. Da Mántova."

"That how she says it: 'Damántova'?"

"I wouldn't know, but if she's Italian, I used to work with Italians. That's how they'd say it."

"What's your name, lover boy?"

"Graham."

"Graham what?"

"Bell."

"Graham Bell?" Predictably the man behind him scoffed. He reached over to the chair and shook Graham's pants to make sure he was not packing something deadly and then prodded them across the bed with his foot.

"Here. Get your pants on, Graham Bell. We'll find out what you know."

"Am I under arrest?"

"Depends. Not right now you're not. If you cooperate... we'll see."

Numb with shock, Graham pulled on his pants, took his jacket one of the men handed him from the front closet, and stepped outside. All the lights in the house were ablaze and the place ringed with police cars. Neighbors stood on their porches craning to see as Graham walked to one of the squad cars between two men in black coveralls. He wanted to set everyone straight by shouting, "Hey, everybody, go to bed. This is a mistake. I don't even know what these guys want." Instead, he ducked inside and let them shut the door.

It was three in the morning by now, but they took Graham to a furnished office in the federal building. Lights were on, and people were bustling around.

"No luck, Floyd."

Graham's companion with the automatic weapon greeted a bristle-haired man in a western-style suit with pink, arrow-point piping who was resting his cowboy boots on the desk next to a tall, dark brown Stetson. "She must have got out earlier. All we came up with was lover boy here."

Floyd's jacket parted to expose a gambler's vest and shoulder holster as he indicated a comfortable-looking divan next to his desk, not like the room with a bare bulb in the movies. He laced his hands behind his head.

"Well, let's have a seat, shall we? Have a chat. What can you tell us about her?" Floyd's diction was, if anything, courtly, almost Southern.

"About this Victoria What's-her-name? Not a thing. I don't even know who she is. Look, I'm sure you're making a mistake. I would love to help you, but I really never heard of this person."

"Does this refresh your memory?"

The man leaned forward, suddenly intent, and shot him a photo of a serious young woman in large granny glasses and straight dark hair. She did not look familiar either. Graham made a helpless gesture and handed it back.

"Not really. Is she a student here?"

"Picture's old. Think. You know how she looks now. Where is she?"

Graham sighed. "I told you: I don't know. I don't know anything about this."

75

"We saw you with her at the demonstration this morning. Yesterday morning. She was with you."

"With me? Do you have me confused with someone?"

Someone came in and whispered to Floyd, who frowned at Graham.

"I've got news for you, my friend. Ms. Damantova left her prints all over your place. We found a pair of women's underpants under your pillow that were, let us say, fresh. Don't try to tell me they're yours, either; these were worn by a woman."

A terrible possibility occurred to Graham, addled as he was.

"This person... You say her name is Victoria da Mantova? I was with someone named Linda, Linda Chapman. I thought her name was Linda. If that's who you mean, she was there last night. Linda doesn't stay with me, though; it was just last night."

"So where does she live?"

"I don't know where she lives."

"Come on," the man who brought Graham in said. "This guy's poking her, and he doesn't even know where she lives. Look, lover boy, don't play with us, okay?"

"I'm not 'poking' her, and I don't know where she lives. Honest."

"So how? Did you pick her up in a bar?"

"No, I sort of know her. She runs the women's shelter here in town."

"Okay. Finally. Now where is that?"

"It's what I'm trying to tell you; I don't know. They're not allowed to say."

"Check with the police, Mac; they'll know where it is," Floyd said. He turned back to Graham. "I still don't think you're leveling with us. How do you know her?"

"She works in a place where I get my hair cut."

"Name of it?"

"Laborers of Hair Curlers."

"What? Spell it."

Graham did.

"We'll get on it first thing. Have you got any photos or snapshots of her?"

"I have no camera. Say, who is Victoria, Vittoria da Mantova anyway, and why are you looking for her?"

"When and if we get done with you, why don't you just take a stroll downstairs and read for yourself. Look above the window where you buy your stamps."

They proceeded to grill Graham about every facet of Linda's life. What information he could offer was either sketchy or evasive. Feeling sold out, Graham still could not bring himself to betray her to these men in crew cuts. He told them about the twin brother in Vietnam. He did not tell them about *Antigone*.

76

Neither did he tell them about the woman he had cradled all night. He was tired and confused.

As it got light, they brought him doughnuts and coffee and continued trying to break him. The remarks passing back and forth between them indicated they were debating whether to charge him as an accomplice. Most of the time the only man in the room with Graham besides Mac was Floyd, the FBI agent in the western suit, who kept raising legal issues. Weren't all FBI agents attorneys or something? He thought he'd heard that somewhere.

Parrish seemed to be Floyd's last name. Several times during the interrogation he tipped the Stetson over his eyes to peer at Graham from under the brim. Then he would leave the room to consult with someone outside before returning with a new line of detailed questions about the habits of this woman they still felt more comfortable calling "Victoria."

Only once did Graham lie; he told them she drove a brown Citation with a dented trunk. It seemed harmless enough to say, and it was a two-edged piece of information: It made him seem cooperative, and it might give her at least a little head start on them.

Finally, hours after daylight and half a dozen trips down the hall to the men's room from all the coffee, Graham was told to go home. His interrogators apparently leaned to the opinion he might be giving them the truth after all but told him to stay available in case they needed him for further questioning or to make identification.

Totally disoriented, Graham stopped on his way out by the still-unopened postal clerk's window and looked above it at the FBI's Most Wanted List. Three pictures to the right along the top was the photograph of the studious-looking young woman in granny glasses. "VITTORIA DAMANTOVA," it said. She was 5' 6", 135 lb., and wanted for murder, interstate flight, receipt and transportation of explosives, damage and destruction of government property, sabotage, conspiracy, and suspicion of espionage. She was considered armed and highly dangerous. No attempt should be made to apprehend her unassisted.

Murder.

Graham slid down the wall onto the floor beside the counter where the zip code directory hung and regarded the young woman's picture. Behind the shutter, postal clerks were already moving and talking. He remembered Linda's face when he suggested, "You're not who you pretend to be." Suddenly the lies, the tears, the wildly different looks made a picture. Graham squeezed his jacket around himself, and a tear leaked down his cheek as he remembered her sobbing that she could never have a normal life. He didn't know whether to feel betrayed or what. He studied the large, dark eyes behind the glasses, the longish nose, plush mouth, and pointed chin. Face of a fox. It was her. Then he conked out, wild images running through his brain.

The next thing he knew, a man in a postal uniform was booting him in the foot.

"Get up, pal. Move it. This isn't New York. You don't sleep in here. Go up to the Salvation Army you need a place to sleep."

Graham shook his head, scrambled to his feet, and mumbled an excuse, thankful that the man had not recognized him. He glanced once more at the poster and then the clock caught his eye.

Ten o'clock. Tuesday. Julie! She was arriving at nine on the morning flight from Minneapolis! He ran the six blocks home to call the airport and found his front door standing open. They had not even bothered to close it. Just inside, he almost fell over two suitcases. The place was trashed, drawers and closets open, furniture sideways.

"That better be you, Graham," a woman called from the next room. She sounded hostile.

"Julie? God, I'm sorry. You won't believe what happened to me."

She was standing at the window in the living room, her figure a wand against the morning light. The books were ripped from the shelves and even the rugs rolled back. Hearing his entrance, she turned on him, her dark hair flaring. It squeezed his heart to see how much like Leila she looked, the olive skin, her eyebrows that nearly met. Light glinted from her glasses as she gave her skirt a tug. Great way to start.

"Swell you remembered to come after me. I had to cadge a ride. You're really good at this, aren't you? I came this close to catching the next plane out."

"And I was so scared you would. You won't believe what I've been through."

"It certainly looks like one hell of a party." Distaste was written in the set of her mouth.

Awkwardness tainted the air as they faced one another. Already he had worried if he could handle their meeting, and now this.

Then, faced with the wreckage and the misery she had walked into, she twitched the corner of her mouth and put up a hand to cover it.

"All right, this better be good."

Graham motioned her to the couch and righted the rocker, lying on its side, where Linda had interrogated him. He launched into the long story of Linda the hairdresser, their acquaintance, her disappearance, and the commando raid resulting in Linda's transformation into Vittoria da Mantova and the long grilling session at the district attorney's office that had prevented his meeting her plane.

Julie slipped off her glasses when he finished.

"Wow. Did she stay here last night?"

"What's that have to do with it?"

"I'm trying to get a handle on this thing."

"The night before."

She stood up and pumped his hand. "Graham, you've made a stunning choice. This woman sounds like just the way to enhance your social standing around this burg."

Graham sighed and ran a hand through his hair. He did not know what to say.

"Hey! You're supposed to laugh." Placing her hands on her knees, she leaned down into his field of vision. "Come on; I'll help you clean up."

17

It was nearly three o'clock before Graham and Julie repaired the house, the only real damage a couple of flower pots tipped over and their contents scattered across the carpet. Their back-and-forth cleaning up blunted the initial self-consciousness once bumping elbows gave way to wondering where the hell Graham kept his garbage bags. The books and music she put back on the shelves resonated enough for Julie to volunteer more about her life in New York. Reading between the lines, Graham detected a recent heartbreak and would have put an arm around her if they hadn't been so new.

At three-thirty the paper carrier rattled the mailbox, and Graham went to fish the newspaper out while Julie clattered dishes into the wrong places in the cabinets. The front page flapped open and blared out the headline, *"PROF LINKED TO FUGITIVE BOMBER."* Accompanying the story was an artist's best guess at Linda's cosmetologist persona.

Graham propped the broom he was holding against the mailbox, dropped onto the steps, and started reading.

Federal officials announced that Vittoria "Tori" DaMantova, Vietnam-era radical wanted for murder in a 1970 Ohio bombing, narrowly eluded capture this morning at the home of an Northern Michigan University instructor with whom she had been staying under an assumed name.

Authorities have long sought DaMantova for her part in a midnight explosion that ripped through Ohio's top-secret Mound Laboratory in Miamisburg and killed a guard where DaMantova was employed. Information that came to light after the incident indicated DaMantova and others carried out the bombing as part of an effort directed against the war in Vietnam.

Leading a double life under the name Linda Chapman, DaMantova, now 49, had directed the women's shelter and worked as a local beautician here for the past eight years. While authorities remain unable to pinpoint DaMantova's exact arrival in Marquette, they believe she had lived in the area some ten years.

Acting on anonymous tips, FBI officials and police early this morning surrounded the home of NMU instructor Graham Bell, with whom DaMantova is believed to have been staying. Apparently alerted, DaMantova managed to escape, but police took Bell in for questioning. Bell denied knowledge of DaMantova's identity or whereabouts and was released on his own recognizance. A police spokesperson said, however, law officials may recall Bell for further questioning in the case."

The phone rang inside, and Graham looked up. His neighbor across the street was scrutinizing him through her front window.

"It's for you," Julie called. Still clutching the paper, he took the phone.

"Mr. Bell, this is Grant Gagnon at the *Mining Journal.* We'd like to know…"

"Sorry, I'd rather not," he said and hung up.

At Julie's puzzled expression, he handed her the paper without a word, just as the phone rang again.

Luckily, Graham did not begin by telling the caller to buzz off, because this time it was Stan Kendrzorski, the chairman of the math department. He had heard about the "incident" and wanted a full report. While Graham's explanation placated him somewhat, Dr. Kendrzorski cautioned him that involvements like this did not reflect well on the department or the faculty—news Graham hardly needed to be told—and asked to be kept abreast of all developments. He ended the conversation by trusting there would be no repercussions. Graham's nicely arranged world was coming apart.

Julie was buried in the front page when Graham hung up. She looked up immediately at the sound of the receiver.

"Who was that?"

"The math department. They think I'm bad medicine. I'm putting their reputations on the line."

"How bad? Could it affect your job?"

"Well, they're telling me I better watch it."

"Damn, this really cuts it. That's not fair." She spun the paper onto the table. Ripping off her glasses, she tapped an earpiece against her teeth—exactly what Leila used to do when she was scheming.

"Is there a library around this place?" she asked.

"Why? What do you need?"

"I need to run some things down."

"What kind of things?"

To Graham's questioning look, she said, "Trust me; I do this for a living. Now where's the library? I need one with microfilm."

"Julie, don't get mixed up in this."

"Who's getting mixed up? Great advice, coming from you."

"I'll take you over and grab us something to eat while you're working."

After dropping her off at the library, Graham placed a pickup order for later at the Pasta Shop; Julie ought to be done with whatever she was looking up by then. Back at the house, he surveyed the rest of the mess. The upstairs they had pretty much put away; only the basement remained. But who would see it anyway? That could stay, as far as he was concerned.

The phone rang again. Instead of Julie calling him to pick her up, a gruff voice warned, "You gutless chickenshit. At least I had the balls to go, while assholes like you and Jane Fonda sat around stabbing us in the back and cozying up to Castro. One of these days somebody's gonna blast your blinkin' lights out for you, mister, you and your commie girl friend." Whoever it was hung up before Graham could tell him his history was garbled and to make sure his NRA membership was paid up. A similar call fifteen minutes later imparted a roughly comparable message with exotic variations on Graham's bedfellows.

Just before six the doorbell rang. Graham was on the floor wedging the last pots and pans away under the counter. He let it ring again. What would this one be, a cross burning on the lawn? He realized he was getting paranoid and went to the door on the fourth ring. Cheryl stood there with a paper bag looking worried.

"I knew you had to be home."

"Come on in." He stepped back to admit her. "Have you come to string me up or offer condolences?"

"Excuse me?"

"I'm sorry; people are getting weird."

"Evidently. You look terrible."

"I feel terrible. I haven't slept since about two this morning. Come on back to the kitchen. I'm still cleaning up."

"Have you eaten? I brought you some stuff from Togo's you can heat."

"That's nice of you. I've got something ordered. My daughter showed up."

"Your daughter? Do I know her?"

"We don't even know each other. I miss her plane and she walks into this. It was supposed to be a reconciliation."

"Wait a minute. So... I don't understand. She's here because?"

"She called a few days ago and asked if we could meet. It's too hard to go into. She's at the library seeing what she can find on all this." He held up the paper.

"Graham, some FBI agents were at the shop asking all sorts of questions. They just left."

"You, too? What kind of things did they want?" Graham said. He began rearranging Julie's misplacement of the dishes, half listening. He knew about FBI agents.

"Mostly photos. Anything we might have."

"And did you come up with any?"

"No. Funny thing is, we were forever taking pictures of each other. Except now I realize she was the one always taking them. She said she had a thing about photos. Catch this, though; one time she didn't see me, and I got a really cute snapshot of her wearing a hat."

"You did?" He stepped closer. "Do you still have it?"

"As if. I stuck it on my mirror, and right away she wanted a copy of it, only she would take the negative in herself. Guess what? She lost it."

"Lost it?"

"Uh huh, said she looked everywhere. Oh, but it gets better: The next morning I came in, and the snapshot's gone from my mirror, too. At the time I just chalked it up to general oddness and never asked. After all, she was always doing things for me. But I thought, 'Now that really is a thing about photos.'"

"Maybe not so strange after all. Anything else they want to know?"

"You name it—habits, places, people she ever talked about, clothes she wears, what she drinks. Even what she drives."

Suddenly Graham was listening.

"What did you tell them she drives?"

"Nothing. She doesn't own a car."

"Shit. I told them she has a brown Citation. Now they'll be back."

"A Citation! Why on earth did you say that?"

"She gave me the idea. And probably I hoped... well, never mind."

"Oh, Graham, what's going to happen to her? She's wanted for murder!"

"You tell me."

"Graham..." Cheryl's voice dropped. "If you know where she is, you've got to get her out of here."

Graham made a frantic hand motion and cupped his mouth to her ear.

"Watch your mouth! They've probably bugged the house."

The front door slammed.

"Graham? I'm back."

"We're here in the kitchen, Julie," Graham answered.

Cheryl stood to greet her. "So you're the famous Julie."

Graham marveled at how smoothly Cheryl had picked up on her name to help things along for him.

Julie looked puzzled, and Graham explained, "This is Cheryl Maki. She works with Linda... Vittoria, whoever."

"Cheryl? Oh yes, Graham mentioned you this morning."

Julie plopped a sack and a manila envelope onto the table.

"Here, there was a little shop on the way home. I picked us up something."

"You'll have to help us eat all this stuff. Cheryl brought something, too, and I've ordered at the Pasta Shop. That one maybe I can cancel."

Cheryl raised a hand to decline. "Kevin and I are going out."

"So did you find anything?" Graham asked Julie.

Julie patted the envelope. "Plenty."

"What have you got?" Graham wanted to know.

"First things first. I'm dying; all they had on the plane was peanuts. Then we can look."

Julie dumped out her sandwiches, pulled down some of the dishes Graham had just restacked in the cupboard, and dealt Graham a plate and a sandwich each from hers and from what Cheryl had brought. Then she examined him.

"Not looking so hot, mister." She patted his hand, an unexpected grace. Maybe she was showing off for Cheryl. "How are you feeling?"

"Violated. I must look like an idiot, chasing after a felon." He did not tell her about the calls. There was no sense making things worse.

"Yeah, probably a little." She unwrapped her sandwich. Cheryl ran herself a drink of water, while Julie helped herself to the last soda in the fridge. Graham got on the phone to the Pasta Shop to undo his order.

As Graham was finishing the first sandwich, Julie set down the soda and fetched the manila envelope. She started to reach into it.

"Does she know?"

"She's a good friend. In fact, she just came to tell me there were agents at the shop asking questions."

Julie shook a sheaf of photocopies face down onto the table.

"Here. I've been to the library. Know the enemy, or in this case…" She left the thought unfinished.

Graham flipped over the top sheet. It was a Sunday feature article from the March 23, 1970 *New York Times* .

"Not that one. Start with the first article, at the beginning, or you won't know what it's all about."

But she was too late; Graham had already seen the headline:

CHASING ANTIGONE
Tori DaMantova: The Making of a Radical

PALO ALTO—Stanford University and the Hoover Institute call this affluent community nestled at the foot of California's Coastal Range home. While some residents claim the sprawling collection of estates and mountainside homes only pretends to be a community, Palo Alto does breed a life style in sharp contrast to that of its northern neighbor at the Golden Gate. Palo Alto, some say, spawns institutions rather than revolutions.

But Palo Alto nurtured Vittoria "Tori" DaMantova.

It was allegedly 27-year-old DaMantova who, sometime after midnight last Sunday, unlocked the door to Building T of Mound Laboratories half-way across the country in Miamisburg, Ohio. In her pocket she carried a tiny, battery-powered radio-signaling device designed to set off plastic explosives earlier concealed in a janitor's closet.

Nearly three hours later a woman identifying herself as "Antigone" and now thought to have been DaMantova herself would call Miamisburg police to warn of a bomb in a materials assembly building. Shortly afterward—authorities set the time around 2 a.m.—security guard Arthur Montgomery was making an unscheduled inspection of the building when DaMantova apparently activated the detonator from her home two miles away. The explosion reduced the eastern end of Building T to twisted rubble. Montgomery died instantly.

Graham read the last two sentences again, remembering the lightning impact of mortars, getting the shakes after each one. *Missed.* He would go cold working on the blood-soaked, dismembered aftermath of those who weren't.

Twisted rubble. He conjured up electron-starved compounds of explosive primed to oxidize in an instant, all-or-nothing kiss so exothermic it lit the air, the sudden volume accelerating everything around it into projectiles.

Instantly: walls, bricks, desks, file cabinets, twisted rubble coming at him. Did a wall hit him, reshape him, take him apart, too? A beam?

Graham's hands trembled as he continued reading.

> *This at least is the picture of the Antigone bombing investigators are piecing together from bits of evidence and information provided by an accomplice of DaMantova. Questions remain. Was it actually DaMantova who called to warn of the bomb? Did she carry out the bombing alone? Most of all, residents of this high-tech California valley are asking themselves, 'Why did she do it?'*

> *The answer may lie with those who knew her best. Bernard Maier, professor of physics and a former mentor of DaMantova, pauses outside his Stanford class-room to remember her as a person bound for eminence rather than notoriety.*

> *"Tori was a genius. I used to believe I would read about her making some discovery," he muses, "Never something like this…"*

> *A grand-niece of Continental Savings founder F. L. DaMantova, Tori Da-Mantova was born to all the advantages of Palo Alto. She was also born a twin, a fact which figures into the fatal equation. When her twin, Vicenzo, enrolled at Stanford to study law and embark on what friends predicted would be a rising career in politics, Tori followed suit. Unlike many of her female counterparts, however, she delved into science and technology. Soon Professor Maier and others were characterizing her work in electro-magnetics as "brilliant" and "original."*

> *By 1965 DaMantova had begun graduate studies in gravitational physics and mass acceleration at the University of California in Berkeley. While she excelled academically, DaMantova was said to be increasingly associated with student activists as the war ratcheted up. Some would wield a telling influence over her.*

Electro-magnetics? Brilliant and original? Gravitational physics and mass acceleration? Graham read it again, trying to get his mind around whomever it was Linda inhabited.

Wham. Simple physics. Who would understand that better than she? What was it, C4? Who knew what violently unstable substance she could have laid her hands on? She who had cleansed herself in his shower, slept in his bed.

My god. 1965. I was there.

He tried to remember a student in any of his classes named DaMantova—which seemed to be the official spelling—but she would have been a graduate student. He read on.

DaMantova went on to work as an electronics engineer in the nation's nuclear research program, while the war expanded. Much of what she did remains classified, but Mound officials will confirm top-secret duties eventually led DaMantova to her fateful assignment in the picturesque southern Ohio river town of Miamisburg. There she apparently tried to balance assignments, which according to some sources had a military nature, with what friends remember as her growing concern over the war. It was Vicenzo's enlistment in the Army in late 1968 that would mark the turning point for DaMantova.

She said 1965. What if it was *him?*

He continued reading.

According to fellow lab worker Rachel Gerlach, "In the beginning Tori worried about her brother's assignment to East Asia but didn't oppose it. She came from a really patriotic family and acted proud he volunteered to serve."

Then DaMantova's world came apart. She received word her brother had disappeared in a helicopter crash over Vietnam December 15, only weeks before he was set to return home. Friends say DaMantova became bitter and withdrawn.

Gerlach now remembers, "She started saying it was wrong that she should be working for the government that sent her brother to Asia. She would go days without showing up at work. We would cover, because she was key to what we were doing. And we knew what she was going through."

What Gerlach did not know was that DaMantova was renewing contacts with former acquaintances involved in Berkeley's student radical movement, seeking ways to [Story continues on page 3E.]

Graham flipped through the rest of the sheets, but each one only held a small, headlined story, no continuation.

"Where's the rest?"

"Didn't I copy it?" After leafing through and seeing that indeed she had not, Julie said, "No, I guess not. The rest of it was mostly a buttoned-up critique of California, more digs at Palo Alto and the life style than anything about the bombing. And the DaMantova family wouldn't talk. It did have a little about her getting strange; I guess it was the guy she was involved with."

"What do you mean 'strange'?"

"Not coming to work, not answering the phone, just acting weird. I don't remember. I'll copy it for you. But read the other ones now, in order."

Cheryl had already been sorting through the articles in Julie's stack and was studying one of them. Instead of taking up the first article, however, Graham studied the photos of Tori DaMantova and of the ruined building. Flush with youth and success, she displayed her perfect teeth in a big smile. Only slowly did he remember that Cheryl was waiting to see the article, and he finally handed it over. Julie righted the rest of the photocopies and held them out.

"Here. What you just read was actually my first find in the index. After that I traced it back to the beginning and arranged them chronologically. Start with this one."

She gave him the top sheet, a small story datelined *MIAMISBURG, Ohio* from page 11 of the Monday, March 9, 1970 *New York Times,*

Blast Rocks Ohio Atomic Lab; One Killed

At least one person died when an explosion at Mound Laboratories shattered the early morning hours in this southern Ohio town. Atomic Energy Commission (AEC) officials are sifting through the wreckage of the top-secret atomic research laboratory to determine the cause of the blast. Workers have so far retrieved the body of one victim, believed to be a security guard, and emphasize there is no danger of radiation from nuclear materials stored at the facility, which Monsanto Chemical Company operates under government contract.

Graham passed the article on to Cheryl and turned to the next, dated March 10. The story had now moved up to page 4.

Bomb May Have Caused Ohio A-Lab Blast

MIAMISBURG, Ohio—Law enforcement authorities here now believe that a bomb caused yesterday's fatal atomic lab blast. Today local police revealed a woman calling herself "Antigone" called early Sunday morning, immediately before the explosion, to warn of a bomb. [Greek heroine Antigone defied a state prohibition against burying her brother after he rebelled against the king.]

Monsanto officials stated surprise at Montgomery's presence in the building, normally sealed off at that hour. A source who asked not to be identified said investigators have found articles of clothing on the site belonging to a lab worker and determined the explosive material was located in a storage closet, but declined to elaborate further. It remains unknown whether the person killed in the explosion, now identified as security guard Arthur Montgomery, 43, was involved in the bombing. A spokesman for Monsanto Chemical Company, operator of the facility, indicates that federal officials are following leads that may result in arrests. Authorities continue to emphasize the incident poses no radiation danger to surrounding communities, as damage was confined to a building housing non-nuclear materials.

By March 12, the story had moved to the bottom of page one.

FBI Collars Antigone Bombing Suspect

MIAMISBURG, Ohio—Federal Bureau of Investigation agents here announced that they have arrested a Monsanto Chemical worker as a suspect in the bombing of this top-secret atomic laboratory. A security guard died in the explosion, which ripped through an assembly building at this sprawling hilltop facility early Sunday morning.

Late yesterday afternoon FBI agents brought in an as-yet unidentified Monsanto technician for questioning. While stating the technician worked in the plant, Monsanto officials declined to specify the worker's exact duties there. Atomic Energy Commission spokesman Everett Gordon stated only that the technician had a non-sensitive work clearance that normally would have prevented his access to the destroyed assembly building.

Police remain unable to determine whether the woman who called in and identified herself as "Antigone" was in fact connected with the bombing and continue to follow up leads.

Now unable to stop, his hands sweating, Graham read the remaining story, from the front page of the Friday the 13th edition. This time the photo of Tori DaMantova the police had shown him last night ran beside the story.

Accomplice Fingers Antigone Bomber

MIAMISBURG, Ohio—The man authorities apprehended yesterday as a suspect in the Mound Laboratories bombing pointed to a female accomplice as the instigator of the action. David R. Meachum, 27, said Monsanto electrical engineer Vittoria DaMantova had in fact constructed and placed the explosive device in a janitor's closet. According to Meachum, opposition to the Vietnam War motivated DaMantova to carry out the bombing. Meachum also confirmed to police that DaMantova was in fact the caller who identified herself as Antigone to announce the explosion.

At this time police still have no clues as to the whereabouts of DaMantova, who vanished with two children sometime Monday morning.

Graham read the last sentence word by word.

"She had children," he said, half to himself.

"A boy and a girl," Julie said. "I think the oldest was five. I'll get the rest of that story for you."

Only then did the name hit him.

"Meachum! God, I know this man," he said. "I just saw him yesterday."

"You *know* him?"

"I picked him up hitchhiking about six months ago. Creepy guy. He claims he's a soldier of God and cut some kind of deal with the law. And he's here!"

Now it was clear to Graham how the authorities had zeroed in on him. "We saw you with her at the demonstration," one of them had said. Of course. Meachum was the person they kept consulting with in the other room. And she must have seen him.

18

With Julie's return to New York for her internship at the *New York Times* set for the end of the week, Graham stayed home working on a syllabus for the college algebra course he was to teach in July. While a couple of recriminations flared between them and there were times, like right now, when she felt the need to get out of his presence and explore Marquette, they had done well for a first meeting.

He was particularly inclined to stay home because he did not care to have curious colleagues asking about his adventures, not even his confidante Gwen. Four days after Linda's transformation into Vittoria DaMantova, Graham wanted to focus elsewhere. He wanted to be elsewhere. Julie's clippings finally told him all he wanted to know.

The missing page, when she brought it home the next day, revealed Vittoria DaMantova had married someone named John Park and had a son and a daughter. By now the daughter would be older than her mother was then. At the time the analysis was written, however, no one knew what had become of them or their mother.

The marriage for some reason did not meet the DaMantova family's approval and ended in divorce. The writer, David Eckstein, surmised the real cause lay in Vittoria's involvement with a "charismatic Berkeley radical" named David Meachum, a relationship that apparently intensified after the divorce. After transferring to Mound Laboratories, DaMantova was apparently instrumental in bringing on physics graduate Meachum as a technician there. Eckstein's piece included an interview with a friend of DaMantova's named Rachel Gerlach, who expressed strong distaste for Meachum, claiming Vittoria grew "moody," "distant from old friends" and increasingly "under his influence." Gerlach even suggested Meachum "mistreated" Vittoria, though she did not substantiate this charge.

Graham tried to picture the woman he knew as a high-level electronics whiz doing classified government work. It would not compute. Neither could he imagine her setting off a bomb. Instead of coming from some absent, half-crazy Hell's Kitchen mother in New York, Graham's tortured, razor-wielding beautician had earned advanced degrees from the best schools her prominent California family could afford. And in truth, the photos of the thickly dark-haired young woman looked very little like Linda.

What havoc she had played with his life! Graham sighed and shook his head. He hoped he could chalk it up to experience some day but doubted it. Would he ever be able to look back on this with any equanimity?

The doorbell rang. Graham was still scooting his chair back when the person began rapping on the door—one of those impatient types who assume the bell does not work if they have to stand ten seconds. Graham expected it would be another reporter. Yesterday, he even had to chase away a sleazeball from *The National Enquirer.* Halfway across the living room he thought of a worse possibility: What if it was the FBI, back to put more heat on him about the brown Citation? He had really had his hands full convincing them that he did think she owned one.

Graham opened the door, and Dave Meachum pulled off the reflector shades he had on to polish them on his tee shirt before hanging them on his pocket.

"Graham, my man," he said. A wicked smile crossed his face.

"Sorry, Meachum. You're the last person I care to see right now," Graham said wearily and tried to shut the door.

Meachum wedged a knee into the opening.

"Hold on! Hear me out now. I might have some news for you."

"You have no news I want to hear. I know all about you."

Graham pushed harder, but Meachum's knee kept the door from closing.

"You're wrong, Graham. We have a lot in common now. We need to talk."

"I'll be damned if I have anything in common with you," Graham replied and tried to plant his foot against Meachum's pressure. Suddenly Meachum reached in and threw a pocketful of change in Graham's face. When Graham jumped back, Meachum slipped in and backed the door shut behind him.

"Now that's better. The Lord loves the giving man. Don't you feel better opening your house to friends?"

All the country accent he had affected as a hitchhiker was gone.

Graham collected the coins off the carpet and held them out for Meachum.

"I feel better if you get yourself out. Haven't you done enough damage?"

"Not so simple, my friend. First I need information."

"You heard what I have to say. You were right outside, weren't you?"

"So; she made you brave, did she?"

Without warning, Meachum backhanded Graham in the face. Something cracked, and stars went off. As Graham staggered blindly, Meachum walloped him in the side of the head. Graham buckled and sank to the floor with a nosebleed and his ears ringing. When he tried to regain his feet, Meachum booted him hard in the shin and clicked open a long, evil-looking knife.

"You're a pussy, my friend. I play for keeps, and I've been kissing ass for twenty years to get her, so don't think you're going to scare me off with tough talk. And this is nothing to what I could do to that pretty daughter of yours. See? I'm a mean mother, and I fight dirty. Now let's talk, shall we?"

Graham gingerly pressed his nose to stem the blood leaking onto the carpet. His head spun and about killed him when he shook it to clear his vision. The bastard would hurt Julie.

"What do you want to know?"

"Everything. For starters, where's Tori?"

"I have no idea. She took off right when you said something to me. She probably got a look at you. I have not heard from her since, honest to god."

"You expect me to buy that bullshit?"

Meachum poked the knife against Graham's throat hard enough for the point to pop his skin, and Graham just wished for an axe.

"What good does it do you to kill me?"

"If you don't know anything, I might as well kill you. Oh my goodness, Graham, be sensible. She's not worth it. Just tell me what you know, and I'll be out of here. You don't get hurt. Your daughter doesn't get hurt."

"All right. Let me get some ice."

Graham limped painfully to the kitchen, his shin throbbing, with Meachum right behind him. Putting his head under the tap, he swabbed his face; then he got a couple of ice cubes from the freezer and held them to the bridge of his nose. Already his eyes were swelling.

"Come on, cut the stalling. Give."

Graham plopped down at the kitchen table in a stand-off and painfully worked his way through whatever facts he knew directly about Linda. Such as they were, Graham elaborated on none of them; nor did he even speculate. He figured none of this could do Meachum much good and concluded by asking, "Just what's your big interest, Meachum?" The very act of speaking made his head hurt like a sonofabitch.

"Business. I believe she has something that's supposed to be mine, and I aim to get it. She ever show you blueprints, anything like that?"

"Hardly. She wanted me to think she was a beautician. She's not going to show me something like that."

Meachum scratched his head amiably with his switchblade.

"You know, Graham, one thing you didn't tell me. Maybe slipped your mind."

"I told you everything."

"Naw you didn't. Was she good? She likes it rough, you know."

"God! I wouldn't know."

Meachum grabbed Graham's shirt, ripping it as he stuck the knife to his throat.

"The hell you don't! Never touch her again. Hear? I'll kill you. Tori's mine. You couldn't even use a woman like her. Wouldn't know what to do. You want to hear what she likes?"

Just then the front door opened, and Graham yelled, "Julie, Meachum's got me! Run and get the police! Go!"

There was no reply, only the sound of her feet running back down the walk.

Meachum laughed. "That was pretty good, Graham. What do you think the police are going to do? They owe me. I sniffed her out. I'll tell you what they're going to do. They're going to tell you to stay out of trouble. Don't fool with bad women.

"Remember, my man, if you lied to me, and you know something more, I'll be back; only next time I won't bother with you. Read me loud and clear? You hear from her, you let me know, understand? You can get in touch with me here."

Keeping his knife at the ready, Meachum scribbled his number on a card and poked it into Graham's shirt pocket.

"And don't think you can hide anything. I'll be keeping tabs on you." He shook his head. "Poor Graham. Life used to be so neat." His voice turned hard. "I had principles once, just like you. Can't afford 'em any more, not after you been inside. Your face looks awful. Wash it up."

Then Meachum was out the kitchen door and gone.

Minutes later, Julie returned with the police to find Graham in his torn shirt at the kitchen sink, holding a dripping handful of ice to his face. His head felt like a watermelon.

The officer in charge silently studied the card that Meachum had stuck into Graham's pocket, then handed it back. Just as Meachum had predicted, he then asked with some annoyance why Graham could not stay out of trouble. He did not even offer to fill out a report. Graham stubbornly insisted, however, so he sighed and dragged out his notebook, shaking his head.

•

The next day Graham was waiting in the check-out line at the market when he noticed the latest issue of *Newsweek* in the magazine rack and nearly dropped his groceries. An enhanced video image of Linda adorned the cover with half his own face bled off the side. They must have captured it at the demonstration. He slipped the magazine from the rack and tossed it onto the counter with his groceries. The cashier flipped it over to scan, smiling broadly to herself.

"Yah, it's that woman they're looking for, isn't it? Something, heh? Nothing like this in Marquette since *Anatomy of a Murder.*" The cashier's delight evaporated when she looked up. Even with the bruises, she recognized the other face on the cover and quickly rang his total, mumbling, "Well, anyway."

She fumbled half the change trying to drop it into his hand without touching him. Totally nonplused, she slid Graham's sack all the way to the end of the counter to terminate their transaction.

Outside, Graham hoisted his *Newsweek* from the groceries and paged right to the story. Sure enough, it gave his name as a possible suspect in the Tori DaMantova case. Smashing, just smashing. He stuffed the magazine into the trash receptacle by the entrance and headed home. At least his face was going down, and nothing appeared to be broken, so things could be worse. He would just rather not speculate how.

By afternoon Graham was back at his computer making study sheets when the news carrier clomped onto the porch. Stretching, he shoved back from the screen for a break. Easing his sore leg down the stairs, he fetched the paper and sat on the steps with it. With great interest he read the lead story about the University's Board of Control debate over another tuition increase; then he opened to page three and discovered his name in the police report as the subject of a complaint for instigating assault and battery. Within half an hour Dr. Kendrzorski was on the phone asking Graham to come in for a "little discussion." Full of trepidation, Graham left for the university.

The math secretary had already gone when he arrived, and Stan Kendrzorski pushed back from his desk as if mildly surprised to see Graham so late.

"Come in; sit down," he invited. He propped his hands together and regarded Graham across them. "You look awful. This has been a bad week, hasn't it?"

"You can say that again. I'm getting over it, though."

"Are you really? What I see is the way this thing seems to keep snowballing."

"Yeah, I know it looks that way."

"Let me ask you something. How'd you get mixed up in something like this? I mean, a person like her?"

"Stan, I had no idea who she was."

"Granted, but— How shall I put this? A beautician? What were you thinking?"

"She didn't fit that box, Stan. I met her at *Antigone,* holding forth on Greek drama. Beautician? She reads Italian poetry in the original. For all I know, she sings opera. And now it turns out she was a physicist. I rest my case." Stan had no call waving "beautician" at him.

He rocked back in his office chair, cracked his knuckles, and studied Graham.

"Well, I don't want you in the classroom right now. Just wait—" Stan held up his hand against Graham's protest. "I realize I read you the riot act the other day, but I was upset. It doesn't have to do with scandal in the department or anything like that. I'm thinking of your best interests."

"But, hell, Stan, I'm a teacher; how does it help to ground me?"

"You're a damned good one, too. But right now I just don't think you're going to be effective until you get this behind you. There is too much happening."

"You're getting it all wrong. None of this is my fault. I'm caught in the middle of something here and getting blamed for things I didn't do."

Kendrzorski put his hand up again. "I'll give you the benefit of the doubt on that. No, I really will. I believe you. The thing is, I'm getting calls from administration. You know how hard I've been trying to tenure you, so we don't need problems. I'm going to ask you to lie low for a while. Let it blow over. Get away from here if you have to."

Let it blow over. Graham realized he'd had the very thought that afternoon.

"Stan, this isn't going to work. What am I going to do for an income?"

"I'm not cutting you off salary. You'll only lose the summer course income."

"In other words, I'm suspended with pay."

"Look on it as an opportunity. Spend the summer doing research, and write an article or two. If you came back with work in hand, I'm sure administration would overlook what's happened. I want to see you through this, and it's the best I can do."

"I don't like it. It looks as if I'm being quarantined. As if it's my fault."

"Look here, Graham, I've pretty well made up my mind on this. Bob is willing to take your class, and that's probably the way I should go with it. So I suggest you try taking advantage of it rather than feeling wronged."

"Do I have any choice? Could we talk about the possibilities?"

"Not now. Go home and sleep on it. We can talk later in the week."

By the time he got home, Julie was dumping a pot of spaghetti into the colander. She forked Graham a plateful and let him vent his bitterness over the lay-off. Down on him as she had to be, Graham still could not imagine how he would have made it through this week without Julie's help.

That night as he tried to fall asleep, Graham kept chasing around the bad dream his life had become, wishing he had never heard of Linda Chapman or Tori DaMantova. For the wreck she had made of his life, he ought to hate her. It would not take much. This week could have been the high point of his life, re-uniting with his daughter after all these years. Instead…

The next thing he knew, Julie was shaking him, vigorously.

"Jesus, Graham! What does it take to wake you up!"

"Wha? What do you want?" He shaded his eyes against all the lights she had turned on in her effort and tried to roll away, but she tugged him back.

"Come on! It's the phone, for you. It was ringing and ringing. Didn't you hear it? Finally *I* had to come answer it. Snoring right through it like a chain saw!"

He started to push himself up. "What is it, the emergency room?"

"No, it's—"

He slumped back and slit one eye at the clock radio. It read 12:30. "Good God! Tell whoever to call back in the morning." He rolled onto his stomach. "Say I'm asleep, 'cause I am."

"Graham, answer it."

"Why, who is it this time, Melvin Belli, offering money for my story?"

"It's a Mr. DaMantova."

19

"Mr. Bell?"

"Yes?"

"Mr. Graham Bell?"

"Yes. Speaking. Who is this?"

"This is Rico DaMantova. Vittoria's father. We need to speak."

The hoarse voice on the other end had an Italian lilt to it and sounded weary.

"Do you know what time it is?"

"Yes of course." DaMantova paused. "O! *Maria fa nascere le rane!* So sorry. I have it the wrong way. I thought it was six. When I tried earlier, you were not home."

"It's all right. I'm awake now. How do you know me?"

"I read the newspapers. You have a listing."

"I see. Well, perhaps if you called back in the morning..."

"A moment, please: I need to see you."

"See me? Where are you?"

"Palo Alto. Do you know where that is?"

"I'm afraid that would be a little difficult. I'm in Michigan. Do you know where that is?"

"Of course. You will fly out. Your ticket is prepared."

"My what? No; that's out of the question. Absolutely not."

"It's quite all right. There will be no expense to you."

"You don't understand. I want to forget the whole thing, not be involved."

"Mr. Bell. I have not heard from my daughter for twenty-four years. Every day I ask myself, 'Is she alive?' She is my child. You see. Please."

Suddenly Julie was on the line. "He'll do it, Mr. DaMantova. Don't worry."

Graham had not realized she was listening and reacted sharply.

"Julie, stay out of this."

"Who is speaking? Tori, is it you?"

"No, no; it's my daughter. Pay no attention. She has bad judgment."

"Just send the ticket, Mr. DaMantova. I'll have him on the plane."

Graham ended the conversation with no recourse but to go. Bobbling the receiver back onto the nightstand, he headed for the kitchen and snapped on the light. He found Julie waiting on the barstool by the phone. She shaded her eyes with a hand at the sudden glare and patted a place at the kitchen table with the other, obviously expecting him. She snugged around herself the robe that had covered Linda only a few nights earlier and crossed her legs. Leila's wild, dark curls surrounded her face, a younger, slighter version of her mother. Julie squint-ed myopically under her fingers at him, her face too shaded to read.

"Julie, what the hell," he said.

"Sit."

When he did, it ceded her the commanding position on the barstool.

"You're going to do this, Graham. You can't turn your back on them."

"This is my life, Julie. I don't have to do anything."

She shook her head twice.

"Yes, you do. This isn't only about you."

"I don't even know them. Why should I get mixed up any more than I am?"

"Because. You heard what she means to them."

He shook his head. "I can't."

"Yes you can. What if it were me?"

"It's not."

"You're not turning your back on them the way you did us."

Graham avoided her look, fixed on her mouth, which did not look at all like Leila's. Like whose then? His?

"Well?" she said.

"That's not fair, Julie. It's not the same thing at all."

"Isn't it?" She waited. "Look, what's it going to hurt? Think what they must go through. It would mean a lot to them. It would mean a lot to me."

"Then you'd have to come with me," he said. "I couldn't leave you here with Meachum in town."

"I can't. I figured to leave tomorrow anyway so I could lay over and see Mom."

"Mm."

Julie shaded her eyes with both hands and leaned down to bring her face to his level.

"Then you'll go."

"As if I had a choice."

"Attaboy."

Julie stretched her legs as if she were finished, but Graham was not.

"How is she?"

Julie stopped and arched her back upright.

"She?"

"Leila."

"You talked to her. She's good."

"You know what I mean."

Julie rested her elbows on her thighs and put her face in her hands, bringing herself back to his level.

"What do you want?"

"Is he good for her? I mean, do you think she's happy?"

"You miss her, don't you?"

"That's neither here nor there."

"Are you going to explain all this to me some time? She won't. Or should I say can't?"

"I must look pretty pathetic."

"I wouldn't say that. Actually, you've done rather nicely for yourself. I like it."

"Julie?"

He laid his hands on the table, almost afraid to ask.

"You'll come back, won't you?"

For his reward she almost laughed. "Now what do you think? With all the explaining you have to do... how could I not?"

20

Paint-blue swimming pools winked up from below like nuggets in the greenery, how the other half lives, as Graham's plane banked in toward the Golden Gate. The plane's turn tightened into an uncomfortably steep glide for the runway, nestled between the folds of the coastal range and the glittering expanse of the San Francisco Bay. Just before the DC-10 dropped into its approach, Graham looked down the mountain-cleaving line of lakes and valleys tracing the San Andreas Fault. If he ducked down, he could see Mt. Diablo and Sunol Peak east of the Bay.

He found himself rather looking forward to making the scene again; nearly twenty years had passed since his last visit. If only this were a visit. Maybe he could find a way over to his sister Tara and the old man and mend fence. The skimming marshes bounding the airfield abruptly gave way to a blur of grass, then runway lights and concrete. The pilot squelched down and reversed thrust to reel the big jet's momentum in for its taxi into the terminal; now Graham had to face the other part of his trip. How uncomfortable was this going to be? What would these people want of him, and how much could he really tell them? They were bound to find him disappointing, because he really knew next to nothing about her. The father would probably become sentimental and want to know if she had spoken of them. Graham would have to make up something plausible. He resented that Julie would be back in New York by the time he returned unless he could get this over with and book himself back this evening.

Exiting the passenger ramp, Graham cast about for a white-haired gentleman with a mustache and red-striped shirt, as Mr. DaMantova had instructed. For his part, Graham sported a Northern Michigan University polo shirt. Right away he spotted an elderly man who fit the description. More, he could see where Vittoria got her full lower lip and pointed chin. A sleepy-eyed young man more Polynesian than Italian accompanied him.

Graham repented his coming all over again and might have considered ducking past to hole up in a hotel until the return flight but for the obligation Julie had thrust upon him by accepting the ticket. Too late for that anyway; the old man had already sighted him and beckoned, so Graham threaded through the passengers separating them.

"Mr. DaMantova?" he asked upon reaching the pair.

"So, Mr. Bell," he said and took Graham's hand. "This is my grandson Rob."

Rob returned Graham's stare without offering his hand. Grandson? Was that possible?

"Are you—"

"Do you have a bag?" DaMantova interrupted.

"Just this."

"So I'll take it," Rob said. "We're right outside."

"It's okay. I can handle it."

Rob made a reach, then withdrew his hand indifferently and turned to lead the way through the terminal. At the main entrance he whipped out a ring of keys and walked to a gleaming, ink-blue Lincoln Mark VIII carelessly left in an illegal loading area. When the young man was still ten feet away, some electronic gizmo popped the trunk open to receive Graham's bag, and the doors gave a squeal and unlocked themselves.

As they bent into the car and settled into the back, DaMantova said, "You will stay with us tonight."

Graham's heart sank. "I couldn't impose like that."

"Nonsense. You will sleep at the house. I don't fly you here to stay in a hotel."

Obviously DaMantova did not brook disagreement. After Rob turned the Lincoln south onto the Bayshore, DaMantova made courteous inquiry after Graham's flight and then began pointing out features along the way—the bridges, the hills, directions to distant cities—like a tour guide. Not once did he mention his daughter. Was Graham missing something? Was she not the whole reason for this exercise? In front, Rob sailed past every BMW, Porsche, Mazda, and gleaming eighteen-wheel Peterbilt the San Francisco Peninsula could trot out, apparently quite innocent of the undertaking behind him. He probably was not even born when things like the Weather Underground happened. Graham wondered if he had even heard of them.

Graham mentioned school in the Bay area, which he thought would create a better impression than the fringe world of Sunol would, and DaMantova brightened. His travelogue took on an animated familiarity befitting their shared experience. Before long he was even asking Graham to refresh his memory on certain well-known parks and buildings, but Graham was hard put to recognize any of them now.

Soon, Rob piloted the Mark VIII through a part of Palo Alto lush with Tuscan cypress. Gracious adobe and redwood homes passed by on either side, surrounded by groomed forestry and parks. The road began to wind up into the coastal range until they turned at a high, wrought-iron gate opening through a stone wall curving along the roadway. The gate did not appear to serve any security function; rather it looked built to stand open. Down a short, gravel approach lined with peeling eucalyptus, a lovely, tile-roofed Italianate mansion with carved doors stood demurely in a grove of olive trees. Kilkare Canyon looked more and more Third World here.

The old man broke Graham's silent awe by saying simply, "She was raised well, you know." DaMantova's first reference to his daughter seemed self-evident enough to invite no rejoinder.

At the door a sensationally elegant woman awaited them whom DaMantova introduced as his wife, Chiara. She took Graham's hand and continued to hold it in both of hers through her husband's introduction. Graham could see the daughter all too well. Crinkled in the warmth of her greeting, Mrs. DaMantova's dark eyes stirred him uncomfortably: a fox, like Linda.

Inside, the DaMantova home offered poshness to fit the exterior. The first room they entered looked like a ballroom, with a regular garden of house plants and a glittering crystal chandelier. Nearly as plentiful as the plants were the pieces of dark, baroque furniture. Despite the obvious antiquity, each chair and sofa looked well used, lending the place the patrician gentility of a live-in museum to the Renaissance.

"Let's sit in the garden, Rico," Mrs. DaMantova said. "We can talk there. Would you like something to drink, Mr. Bell? You must be thirsty from the trip." Mrs. DaMantova signaled a Hispanic-looking woman across the room who inspected Graham with suspicion. The woman nodded and disappeared into the back.

The "garden" proved to be a porticoed courtyard in the middle of the rambling mansion, where Rob and a striking, black-haired woman in glasses joined them. The woman's teak skin color and heavy eyebrows lent her a look more Asian than Rob's Pacific Islander. She looked about thirty.

"This is our granddaughter Jen Park," Mrs. DaMantova said. "You've met Rob."

The two acknowledged Graham with curt nods. The way each of them sat with folded arms told him that not everyone here thought this gathering was a good idea. When Graham raised his eyebrows questioningly to DaMantova at their presence, he confirmed Graham's suspicion: "These are her children. They will also wish to hear." His tone seemed almost apologetic.

The young man sat stonefaced. Jen fixed her gaze somewhere across the courtyard. DaMantova explained, "Their father raised them, but we have remained close."

Just then, the woman Mrs. DaMantova had signaled stepped into the courtyard bearing a tray of crystal filled with a burnt-umber libation and slivers of lime. Graham tasted a pleasantly bitter-sweet *aperativo* unlike anything he had ever come across and held up the glass questioningly to DaMantova.

"You have not had this: Cynar. Very Italian. A distillation of artichoke." Before Graham could reply, DaMantova bent forward and said, "Now, please, tell everything."

"Everything. Like...?"

Mrs. DaMantova leaned to her husband with something Graham didn't follow. "Chiedi a lui!" she urged.

DaMantova nodded and turned back to Graham. "She'd like to hear how you came to know her."

Graham rubbed his nose and began the story with his attraction to the razor lady. When he got to the name of her shop, *Laborers of Hair Curlers*, Jen unexpectedly slit her eyes in amusement and clapped her mouth with that endearing quick hand of Linda's. She got it, a literate woman. When Graham added the name was her mother's brainchild, Jen left her arms folded, but narrowed her eyes and pursed her lips in what looked like half-concealed entertainment.

"Oh my god," Rob said, "what do they have for a sign?"

Mrs. DaMantova shook her head when Graham reported hearing her daughter recite *Antigone;* the kinship she professed with the Greek heroine because of her brother made Mr. DaMantova wince. His face otherwise remained impassive.

Graham said, "Of course she was lying to me practically the whole time I knew her, so I don't know about the brother. I gather there was such a person."

"Yes," Mrs. DaMantova said, "there was. What she told you was essentially accurate. They were very close, and..." She shook her head and put a hand to her face. "So she is a... beautician," she said, her mouth twisting slightly.

"She is, and quite proficient at it, although I discovered she also operated a women's shelter and provided counseling services."

"Yes, of course," Jen said. "A women's shelter. It doesn't surprise me."

She said no more, leaving him to wonder what was so unsurprising about this. The soft timbre of her voice charmed him.

"How does she look?" DaMantova asked. "Tell me what she is like now."

"Hard to get a fix on. Physically, she's quite attractive, as you know. Or I guess you wouldn't know," he fumbled. Mrs. DaMantova got a tight look and glanced down.

"Clearly she gets it from you," he added and received an indulgent smile.

"Anyway, she tried to look plain, nothing fancy, no make-up. Still... some things you can't hide. She would wear wigs, maybe just for the fun of it, maybe to keep people from drawing a bead on her, I don't know."

He searched for elaboration. "She keeps herself fit."

Graham stopped, but the daughter and son both looked as if they were holding their breath to see where he would take this.

"How was her mood?" Mrs. DaMantova broke in. "Did she seem happy?"

Graham thought fleetingly of their night together and said, "Sometimes. Most of the time I knew her, no. More like withdrawn. Guarded. In retrospect, of course; but at the time I found it frustrating; she wouldn't let me in."

"You had no idea who she was," Mr. DaMantova concluded.

"I could tell there was something, that's all. Except for the twin brother, nothing was true. She said she grew up in a broken home in New York under hard conditions."

Blinking, Chiara put her hands together and raised them to her nose.

"Did she always sing?" Graham asked, curious himself now.

"Sing?" Mrs. DaMantova blinked.

"Yes, she's astoundingly good."

Graham caught Jen's almost imperceptible nod, more to herself than for anyone to notice. Mrs. DaMantova said, "Well, she certainly listened to them all. But herself?" Mrs. DaMantova looked doubtful. "She was an artist, if that's any help."

"It was mostly in the shop when no one could hear, but with me…" Graham paused at how to depict their encounter.

"You were more than friends. You may speak frankly," Mr. DaMantova assured.

"In a manner of speaking we were, but I also had the distinct impression that she couldn't allow anyone close, if that's what you mean, even if she wanted to. It seemed like more than her situation. Whatever it was, I don't know all the reasons."

Jen drew her eyelids half closed and mouthed, *"I do."*

"Please?" Graham responded. When she shook her head, Graham turned his next question directly to her.

"Let me ask you something: What do you remember about your mother?"

"What do I know? She put us on a plane. Good-bye. Her own children. That's all I know about her."

"Jen!" Mrs. DaMantova seemed stung.

"It's true, Chiara. You know that."

Graham tried to break the sudden tension by asking, "Do either of you by any chance recall a person named David Meachum?"

Jen stiffened and removed her glasses. The DaMantovas glanced at each other. Finally Mrs. DaMantova said, "I think perhaps we've imposed on your patience, Mr. Bell. Perhaps you would like to see your room? Then Rob can show you around before you join us for dinner."

Graham had touched a nerve. He did not press further.

"That would be fine," he replied, "but if it's all the same to you, I think I might take a short run. If there's enough time."

"Certainly. And you will find a shower in your room."

Jen surprised him by asking if he would mind company on his run.

•

She was waiting on the gravel drive in Spandex shorts and an old tee shirt emblazoned, "St. Elizabeth's Benefit Run." The well-used, top-of-the-line running shoes she was wearing hinted she did not jog as casual recreation.

"Want to do the hill?" she asked, indicating the ridge above them. "It's four miles up and back."

"Sure. I'm game if you are."

They turned right at the gate and set off along the shoulder until Jen turned onto a bike path that cut across the road switchbacks at a steeper angle.

"I used to run here every time we came to stay," she said as they moved along. "It's a beautiful trail."

They cut across the road again, and Jen said, "We can't discuss my mother easily, as you probably noticed. I had some misgivings about doing this."

"Yeah, well, it certainly wasn't my idea, either. He sent me a ticket to come."

"You're paying for it with gory details. He put you through all that for our benefit, you know."

"How do you mean?" Graham was starting to get winded from the climb.

"Do you need to slow down?"

"I'm okay; I haven't trained for a couple of weeks, with all that's happened."

"I mean they were hoping she was a saint or something. You seem decent enough. How did you ever get mixed up with someone like her?"

Graham ignored the implication. "Did he bring both of you here, too?"

"Rob stays here. He's in his third year of bio-tech at Stanford. Family tradition, you know. I live in Marin. North of the Golden Gate."

"I know. We used to go hiking up Mt. Tam."

"You lived out here?" she asked in surprise.

"I was born here. I graduated from Berkeley in mathematics."

"No! When?"

"1966." Graham's thighs were burning now. Jen continued loping along at a leggy pace, but her breathing revealed she was pushing herself.

"She was at Berkeley then. Did you know her?"

"No. She must have been a graduate student."

Some time later, the grade evened out as they neared the top of the ridge. Jen directed them to a viewpoint beside the ridgecrest highway and stopped.

"Check that out," she said. "Got anything like that in Michigan?"

The coastal range rolled away before them in ridge after hazy ridge toward the ocean. Sea fog was already mounting the farthest line and brimming into the valley between. Behind, the outskirts of Palo Alto disappeared into a smoggy haze. Years ago, Graham thought, he could have stood here and looked all the way across the bay to the Diablo Range. As it was now, only the distant tops of the range showed where it rose above the smog.

"What do you do in Marin?"

"Live. I work at General. I'm an ER doc."

"Really!"

"Yeah, I interned at UC Medical but somehow got into the emergency side of it."

"I know what you mean; I'm an EMT, or was."

"You know then. Some doctors won't do it any more, especially with AIDS. Everyone's afraid now, but I actually like the urgency. That's when I got into running, to clear my head. There are some great mountain runs around here."

"A doctor! Your mother would be very proud of you."

Jen shot him a look. "None of her doing. Ready?"

Graham nodded, and this time they set off at a crisper cadence. After several minutes of the downhill jolting, Graham knew he was going to feel it later.

"Maybe you're not really being fair to her," he said as they slowed to run in place at one of the road crossings for a break in the traffic.

"Oh sure. As if I shouldn't have any trouble about my so-called mother?"

"You seem like a nice kid. How'd you get mixed up with a mother like that?"

"Don't get smart," she said and fell silent to concentrate on the rest of the run until they arrived at the DaMantova gate soaked and quite winded.

Jen leaned back against the wall, let her head droop and put her hands on her knees. After a minute she managed to say, "You're not bad for an old guy, Mr. Bell."

"Graham, please. I don't really do distance."

They walked along the gravel drive, cooling off as their breathing slowed. Suddenly Jen asked, "Want to see Chiara's garden? She's quite proud of it."

She led him around the house to a spacious grounds lined with cypress along the back. Behind the house were a pool and a separate garage that resembled a carriage house where Rob must have put the car. Beyond the pool was at least an acre of riotous vegetation, all surrounded with formal garden flowers. Graham's mental calculator began to click: There had to be at least five to six acres of land here; at today's prices that alone would be worth millions.

"Look," he said, "I don't know how to ask this, but where does all this come from? He's not some kind of, um… Italian thing, is he, Rico? Don't get me wrong."

Jen gave a wonderfully bell-like laugh. "The mob? Is that what you mean? Come on! You haven't heard of F. L. DaMantova and Continental Savings? These ain't po' folks or gangsters. Rico's a CPA. He runs the biggest accounting firm in California."

Oops. Graham tried to hide his chagrin at having forgotten that, when Jen asked, "Does my mother have a sense of humor, then? That beauty shop name is a trip."

"She has her moments, indeed she does. Your mother's quite a witty lady, if a little elusive."

Jen wove a lock of hair around her fingers. "You said she sings. Like what?"

"Blues, jazz, that kind of thing. And oh my god, you should hear her do Edith Piaf. The French *chanteuse?*"

Jen nodded impatiently. "I know."

He paused. "You didn't seem surprised about that inside. Did she used to sing with you?"

Jen shrugged. "Sometimes." She stirred the ground with her toe. "I don't think I'd care to see her again."

Graham had the impression Jen had brought her mother up again because she wanted to get this off her chest. He gave an ironic laugh and replied, "I know what you mean."

Jen drifted through the rows of flowers with her arms outstretched against them. "My attitude may be hard for you to understand," she said, "but you don't have so much stake in the relationship either."

"You think not? Try getting prodded out of bed in the wee hours by guys looking for your mother with assault rifles. Try crossing paths with people who want your mother bad enough to rearrange my face. I've been laid off merely for associating with her. I must say that relating to your mother has not offered me a completely satisfying experience either. Your brother must feel the same way."

"You won't believe this; for some reason I tried to prevent that. I used to tell him about her when we were little, as if I could keep her in focus, but after a while I realized I was talking to myself. He was too young. It was like telling fairy tales."

"And your father? He re-married?"

She bent to smell a rose.

"Yeah, she's Korean, too. Our dad's Korean; you knew that, didn't you?"

"Well, I guessed something Asian."

"It's what we learned to speak at home. Rob's a lot better than I. According to Rob, I have a real American accent. Probably I was already too old." She gave a self-deprecatory laugh, plucked one of her grandmother's peonies, shook the ants from it and stuck it behind her ear. It looked lovely there.

"I really wish I knew what happened that night," Graham remarked.

"Which night?"

"When all the trouble started, the bomb. Since people have started using my head for a baseball if I don't tell where she is, I can't help wondering."

She toyed with the peony a few seconds before offering, "Actually I recall that night pretty vividly, if you're interested."

"Interested? I'm riveted."

"I don't know how much this will do you any good, but here's whatever I can still remember. Even Rob could recite this for you; it used to be his bedtime story, in fact, when he'd ask about our mother, because it was my last and strongest memory of her."

Jen studied the dent her running shoe made on the garden path.

"It was after dark, and we were staying at Rachel's house—She was a friend of my mother. I'm not sure; I think they worked together. Anyway, Mom came in for us all upset and said something to Rachel I couldn't hear. Then we had to go right away in our van. I remember it—green and white with one of those doors on the side that rolls. It was cold, and she put a blanket around us, said to get some sleep. I lay there until the seat made my cheek all bumpy like a waffle, but I couldn't sleep. Funny I should remember the feel of the seat. It was plastic."

"After a long time we stopped somewhere, and Mom got our bags out of the back. She had all our things, even my reject dolls and Rob's beat-up old blanket, as if we were moving. One of the things she had was a cardboard tube that stood as tall as I did. When we got inside—It seems as if it was a motel somewhere—I remember leaning it against a wall.

"She dumped these big papers out of it that kept rolling back up—I remember it didn't look like writing on them—and kept shaking her head over them."

"What do you think they were?" Graham asked. Jen looked up and blinked.

"No idea really. Rob and I used to make up things, like they were treasure maps or plans for making flying saucers, but you know how something strikes you just because it's not ordinary. She used to draw, so maybe they were nothing more than sketches."

Graham started to ask something more, but she interrupted, "Anyway, here's the part that really sticks with me. One little piece fluttered under the bed when she dumped those papers out, and she didn't see it, so I crawled under and got it for her. She put her glasses on to look at it and then started acting so weird, going, 'Oh, oh, oh!' I thought I did something wrong, but she said, 'No, no, baby' and told me to watch Rob, because she had to make a call right away. When she came back, she was like, shaking and crying. I wanted to know what was the matter, and all she'd say was, 'The shit is gonna hit the fan.' That used to mean we were in trouble, and I was scared the way she said it. Rob started howling, too, just because she was crying."

Jen studied a cypress edging the garden. Graham waited for her to collect herself.

"Then in the morning she told us we were going to see Daddy and drove a long way to an airport somewhere. When we got there, she said she had arranged it so the plane people would take care of us, because she couldn't come right away. I remember she put her arms around us and told us we'd have fun, but I thought she was punishing us. Just before we got on, she gave me an envelope for Dad. On the plane I opened it and found a couple of pieces of paper inside and tried to read them, but I don't know what they said. I couldn't understand handwriting yet. I think one of them was the paper from under the bed."

"Does it bother you what she did, the bombing I mean?" Graham had to ask.

"I'm not sure anyone knows what she did," she responded. "Dad wouldn't talk about it. It was as if she never was. I looked up the news clippings, and once Rob even asked him about it directly; but he wouldn't help on that one. He said it wasn't our worry; she would have to live with it, not us. That's all he would say.

"But to answer your question, if she really did kill someone... you can't wish it away," Jen said, "except I'd still wonder who bore the real responsibility."

"Who else would?"

She shook her head. "She was afraid of him. Or if not afraid, she would always do what he wanted."

"Afraid? Of your father?"

"No, I'm sorry: Dave. That's who we lived with."

"Wait a minute. You do remember him?"

"I didn't want to get into all that with Rico and Chiara. How come you know about Dave Meachum?"

Graham threw out his hands. "Bad luck or fate, take your pick. The first time was pure accident; I picked up this guy hitchhiking who told me he traveled around doing the Lord's work. That was him, if you can feature it. First I thought he was amusing; but then he got creepy on me, telling me he was a bounty hunter and a soldier of god. He said his woman ran out on him while he was doing time, and he wanted to get her back. Frankly he began to scare me; I got this weird feeling he could take charge, even with me driving.

"Looking back on it, he was probably already on your mother's track, and that's what he meant. Next time he saw me, I was with your mother; and he must have passed the word, because that night I got to enjoy Desert Storm right in my bedroom. You know how that ended: my picture on *Newsweek* and a new life of leisure for associating with radical bombers.

"Unfortunately, it wasn't the last of him. A few days after your mother got away, he showed up at my door looking for her or something she's got, and he wasn't subtle about it. He redid my face and threatened my daughter. Does any of that fit the person you remember?"

"I don't know. It's been so long ago. He might have tried to control her, a little. Maybe more than that."

She picked a rose and dissected it petal by petal until the silence between them grew palpable.

"Oh, what's the harm? You may as well know. I was maybe four, but it's such a strong memory. I heard them arguing when we lived in Miamisburg and went to see. I saw him hitting her, using his fists, and she had her hands over her face. He stopped as if he were tired and said she couldn't outsmart him, no matter what she did. Then he walked out. I was scared he'd notice me, but he didn't.

"When she put her hands down, her face was bruised, and she saw me standing there. I had to promise her never to tell, not Rob, not anyone. Later, he acted okay, but I know for a fact it wasn't the only—"

Jen stopped and looked past Graham toward the house. "Rob's coming," she said. "He doesn't know."

Graham turned. Jen's brother was stepping easily across the grass leading a big tuxedo cat with a piece of cord.

"What are you birds doing, Sis?" he said when he reached them. Then he said something Graham did not understand that must have been Korean.

"No, he asked me what I could remember about that night she took us away in the van. I was telling how she put us on the plane," she said.

107

"Oh. Grandma said to tell you dinner will be ready in..." he checked his watch, "about forty-five minutes, so you'd better get stepping."

"Anyway, to make a long story short," she said, "that was the last time either of us saw her. I try to picture her, but I can't any more really, even though both of us used to describe her to each other. We'd make it like a game to see who could remember the most details. I would say she had round glasses and big, dark eyes and a lot of hair, because it would brush me around the face when she got me dressed."

"Get outa here," Rob said, "I'm the one who remembered that. What would she be dressing you for? You were six years old."

"Five. Maybe it was braiding my hair."

"It wasn't. I'm telling you, I'm the one who remembered the hair."

"So if it was; now I can't even remember whether she was big or what her face looked like. Not even the pictures look familiar, do they?"

"I don't know," Rob said. "I never did remember what she looked like."

"You used to draw pictures of her."

"Sure, but I was only going by your descriptions. Except for the hair."

"See, it's what I told you, Graham; I was just whistling in the dark. I forgot her anyway, and he was too young to remember her at all."

It was as if the terrible secret Jen imparted had never passed her lips.

"But what happened when your plane landed?" Graham asked.

"My plane? Oh! Dad was waiting for us."

"Didn't he ask what the deal was or anything?"

"Nnn, I can't remember for sure. I know he didn't ask about Mom, because he hardly ever did when we visited. He was too proud."

"Did she ever call you or anything?"

"When, after that? No."

Rob twirled the cord and got the cat to make a prodigious sidearm snag three feet off the ground. Jen applauded, and the cat modestly licked its shoulder.

"What about the note you gave him?" Graham persisted. "Would your father still have that?"

"Not any more. He died two years ago."

"Oh, I'm sorry."

"He had cancer," Rob said. "We think he was over-exposed to radiation, but who knows? He worked a lot with nuclear medicine. Isn't that why you became a doctor, though, Sis?"

"So I could die of radiation poisoning? No, it was so I could make a pile of money."

"Get outa here!"

"Didn't you go through his papers?" Graham asked, trying to keep them on track.

"Sure we looked, but if he did, we never found it. Of course we can't be sure, because we don't really know what it said; but neither of us ever came across anything that looked like a note she might have sent. For sure there were no letters from her, at least none that he saved."

"So there has been no contact of any sort?"

"Why would there be? The whole country was looking for her, and she'd cut us loose. Maybe she thought she had to, for our sake. I'm sure she has no idea Dad died."

"What do you think those things in the tube were?"

"I told you: I have no idea. She kept that."

"I bet they were plans for blowing up the Pentagon," Rob suggested.

"You're not funny, Rob."

"Jeez, you stink, Sis," Rob replied, consulting his watch, "and you've only got a half hour to do something about it. Better get a move on."

21

As Graham's return flight did not leave for two days, he became a guest of the DaMantovas, granted the use of a family car and free to come and go as he pleased. It would have been like an all-expenses tour, if he were not already on vacation. He wished Julie would still be there when he got back.

The second day he said he was going sightseeing and headed across the San Mateo for Sunol. At the turn from Mission Boulevard into Niles Canyon, his stomach began to clench. At the turn where it happened, he pulled off the road. The hills sloped down a long way to the meager flow rattling down the creek, and his shoes scuffed the drying grass. One or two cars zipped past. So peaceful, this spot where she rear-ended someone in the fog. She always drove too fast. If his mother had worn a seat belt, she probably would have suffered broken bones or lacerations, no more.

It happened six months after he was sent home from Vietnam, before he got up the nerve to tell her. The flamboyant earrings and peasant dresses, her calm reason, no more. The Sunol school where she taught closed for her funeral. If he had not been unhinged enough, her death unhinged the rest, and especially the old man. He sold the grocery and retreated to Kilkare Canyon and his Bible exegeses.

Graham whispered a plea for benediction if any wisp of her fierce intelligence still lingered here in this place where she gave it up. He asked for Tori, despite what she had done. For himself he asked nothing; he would manage.

Sunol remained unchanged, bypassed by the interstates. He might never have left. Even the grocery store remained, gussied up a bit, but still there. He drove by the school and looped across the tracks to Kilkare Road. The house stood empty under the eucalyptus, its redwood siding gray now. It looked so small. He walked around the house and gazed up the slope where he and Tara used to race past the scattered oak. The old man would light up a spliff and read Steinbeck.

Metzger still lived down the road, and he learned the old man lived in Ukiah now with Tara. He got the address and phone and turned around for Palo Alto, overrun with a need for connection.

When he arrived at the DaMantova estate, he made up his mind to have a one-on-one with Mrs. DaMantova. Looking around, he finally encountered her in the garden. Graham stopped beside the row where she was working and traded an observation or two before asking her outright what was really on his mind. He had wondered since reading it in one of Julie's articles, but what Jen had told him raised a whole new issue.

"Excuse me," he said, "there's something I'm curious about. It's the circumstances of your daughter's marriage to John Park, if you don't mind my asking."

Mrs. DaMantova put a hand on her hip and straightened herself for a judicious examination of the question. She looked far too elegant to be pulling weeds in a smock and bonnet.

"That's quite all right," she decided. "Exactly what did you wish to know?"

"I had read that perhaps there was some friction...?"

She pursed her lips and averted her eyes ever so slightly.

"Some of the stories suggested that. John was one of Vittoria's professors, you know, quite respected in his field. Perhaps they did not know each other as well as they could have."

Misreading the friction Graham had meant to ask about, she continued, "When the government recruited Vittoria for the Livermore lab, I seem to recall John did not like having her work there. He was very opposed to the war in Vietnam, and I know that was one thing they did not see eye to eye on.

"We often kept Jen during the week for them, but it was quite hard for Vittoria. You see, she worked in a field that did not welcome women, so she had very little support. The lab almost let her go twice before assigning her that project she was working on when she left him. I can't even tell you what she did, because she couldn't talk about it. I know all that was hard for John to accept. There was a lot of pressure."

Mrs. DaMantova turned away to gather some of the dry stalks she had laid in the rows. Without looking at Graham, she said, as if talking to herself, "I'll be honest with you; Vittoria behaved rather badly. When she asked for a separation, it was the wrong thing to do; but John still went ahead and let her keep the children. It was because he still cared for her, even with the problems they had, that he didn't contest. In fact, it wasn't until she... disappeared that John finalized things. Sometimes I think he only remarried for the children. I really shouldn't tell you all this."

"Did you know she'd sent the children to him?"

"Certainly. John contacted us immediately. He gained legal custody, of course, and changed their first names. We all thought that best under the circumstances. May, his wife, was just adorable about them, too. In all fairness, I think Vittoria still had enough sense to see it was the only place for them until that Meachum went to prison. That character: When they moved in together, that was the end. We were barely on speaking terms after that. I'm so glad he's out of the picture now anyway."

Graham decided not to be the one to disillusion her.

"How did she react when she learned her brother was missing?"

"She refused even to speak of it, but I know she was devastated. But this..." Mrs. DaMantova gestured the stalks helplessly, "this thing she did: Why?"

"Don't you think that's the reason? She told me she went crazy."

Mrs. DaMantova looked at him beseechingly, her brown eyes faded tawny in the sun, and shook her head. "People lose family; they divorce; they have problems, but not this. Everyone looks at us, you know, still. 'How could you let her do this thing?' they think. Did I cause this, some little thing I didn't see that I might have stopped, some way I could have saved her this?"

"You can't blame yourself, Mrs. DaMantova. She was an adult. Whatever she did she certainly never learned from you."

"But think if it were your daughter, Mr. Bell. You would feel responsible."

"I don't know about that. It would depend."

What Graham did know was that he could count his blessings. As far as her children anyway, so could Tori DaMantova.

On the morning Graham was to leave, Rob cut a chem lab to drive him to the airport, along with his grandfather. As they shook hands in parting, Graham had to ask.

"Rico, why did you bring me here? It wasn't necessary."

"Jen wished it, and because you were good to Tori," Rico DaMantova said simply. "For that I am in your debt. Her life has not gone well. Should you hear from her again, I don't know what you must say to her. You will have to be the judge. We still love her."

Jen wished it? This was becoming more and more complex.

22

By the time Graham returned to Marquette, he was feeling surveilled and more than a little used up. He walked over to Gwen's house that evening to call his report to Julie in New York at a number and time they had pre-arranged

"So how did it go?" she wanted to know

"For sure, I got more than I expected," Graham told her, "but it was okay."

"Oh? Why more than you bargained for?"

"They had her children there. I thought no one knew what happened to them."

"You're kidding! That must have been a shocker. How did they find them?"

"They didn't; the son stays with them, and her daughter lives across the Bay. They've been in touch all along. With DaMantovas, I mean. Not their mother."

"So. They came to hear about Mama. What are they like?"

"Like J. D. Salinger people. I guess he's still on the radar, isn't he?"

"Of course."

"So you know: guarded, brittle. Operating in a world where people like me don't figure. The daughter Jen is a doctor at U. C. Medical Center. Her son Rob is about your age and studies bio-tech at Stanford. They're half Korean, because the John Park that Vittoria married was Korean, one of her professors."

"What do they think about having their mother back on the map?"

"Mixed; both feel she abandoned them. At the same time, little things the daughter said gave me the feeling she might make allowances, given time."

"How come DaMantova flew you out there? Is he trying to find her?"

"It may have been the daughter's idea, but no one even suggested making contact. They were just interested in hearing about her. Listen, do you know they keep Linda's room as if she still lived in it?"

"Tori's, you mean."

"Yeah, Tori's. So maybe they didn't say so, but I suspect maybe they did hope to get a line on her by meeting me."

"Sounds likely. What are the parents like?"

"Very wealthy. He owns a big accounting firm. Old F. L., the banker who founded Continental Savings, was his uncle. You should see their place. They have this dynamite estate in the foothills with a tile roof and carved doors. The fireplace is about a mile across with a marble hearth and wrought iron fixtures. She told me she came from a broken home in New York."

"Did I ask about the house?"

"I just wanted to draw you the picture. They're—How should I put this?—very patrician. None of this *mama mia* stuff. On the phone that night was about as emotional as he got."

"They're not going to let you see that."

"I had a one-on with the mother before I left, and she opened up a little more. There were some things she was pretty hurt about, the way it reflected on them."

"Sure. How about your hitchhiker pal Meachum? Anything about him?"

"A little. At first they wouldn't acknowledge him in front of each other, but later the daughter recalled him as kind of abusive. I won't argue with that. The mother admitted she hated him. How did your week go? Good visit with Leila?"

"Good. They wanted to hear all about your misadventure of course. I only told them the nice parts."

"Thanks for that. Did you finish your story about Senator Wellstone?"

"Almost. And I'm working on a new one of my own. I took a little side trip on my way back while you were gone."

"Oh yeah? Where'd you go?"

"I took a drive from Mom's up to Miamisburg."

Graham made a face. "Now there's an exercise in futility. I hope you weren't looking for a memorial."

"Not really. Before I go further, are you calling from the phone in your house?"

"No, we agreed on that. I'm calling from a friend's."

"Good. I interviewed Arthur Montgomery's widow. She still lives there. Wanna hear about it?"

"No! That's not smart."

"Before you get totally bent, I learned some interesting facts. Are you going to foam at the mouth, or would you like to hear?"

"I would like you not to get involved in this. At all."

"You're foaming at the mouth."

"Damn right I am. These people aren't playing around, Julie."

"So you're not interested in knowing how Arthur Montgomery might have been implicated in this thing... or in a trace I picked up on your lady friend."

"Listen, I only went through with her family against my better judgment; but that's the end, as far as I'm concerned. I wash my hands of the whole affair. So should you. Just drop it."

"Ho-kaay!"

Graham stewed in silence for a few seconds while Julie waited. Finally he weakened and asked.

"So, um, what did you think you came up with?"

"Attaboy, Graham. First of all, Mrs. Montgomery was acquainted with your pal Meachum, too. She says her husband used to hang with him. They were tight. You follow the implication?"

"Hmp."

"Also, it seems Montgomery was in a place he wasn't supposed to be the night he died. That's what the feds told her. He was one of the suspects."

"Well, I know, the paper sort of hinted at that."

"But they didn't mention that he knew Meachum."

"So if there were three people in on it: What does all that prove?"

"Just interesting. Could be something was cooking we haven't smelled. Maybe it has to do with whatever Meachum is looking for."

"All the more reason to stay away."

"So you wouldn't be interested in this line on, um, what's-her-name, Tori?"

"No."

"Really?"

"Really." He closed his eyes. "Well... if you've gone to the trouble, what?"

"It happened when I was interviewing Mrs. Montgomery. See, no one ever brings it up any more, and all of a sudden there I was, someone asking. She pretty much unloaded whatever she could think of, including interviews with the feds. Of course they wanted to know anyone she ever talked to, all that happy stuff they ask. You feel pretty safe about this phone?"

"Yes."

"Mrs. Montgomery never remarried. They had two boys she raised herself. It took her a long time to get over it, but people were nice, lots of cards and sympathy. Some of them sent money. No one has cared for so long that she really got to talking and told me how even now someone remembers. Get a load of this: Each month for the past twenty years, she gets an envelope with cash in it. She acted coy when I asked how much but then, since I was so interested, said right now it runs around seven hundred fifty bills—every month. The envelopes come from different places, but the note around the money always says it's for her boys—in the same handwriting."

"And?"

"She thinks it's Meachum, making amends. What do you think?"

Graham set the soda he was drinking down carefully on Gwen's floor.

"Sounds pricey to me, unless the feds have him on a richer diet than I think."

"You're with me so far. And part of that time Meachum was still in prison. Now, what do you figure: Could a good beautician make three grand a month?"

"Oh come on, Julie! That's the most far-fetched thing I ever heard. First off, that would be... a quarter of her income."

"Well, I checked with Cheryl, and that's about what Linda was making, so she could afford it. Remember, she had no housing or car expenses."

"Except the envelopes come from different places. How do you explain that?"

"I'm sure she had ways to manage that. She certainly wouldn't want to pinpoint a location."

"That's so slim."

"Except... Mrs. Montgomery said when each of her sons graduated from high school double the amount came the next month. Of course I had to ask if she's ever mentioned this to anyone, and get this: She hasn't. She probably figures it's between her and Meachum, or else she doesn't want to kill the goose. What I'm saying is, the feds don't know this; neither does Meachum. Only you and I."

"Bizarre. Even if it were so, I can't say it gives much to go on. How do you propose to trace cash?"

"You're not thinking, Graham. How would she know when the boys graduated? Either she still lived around there, which I don't think she did; or she kept in contact with someone there, which also seems too risky; or..." She let the suspense build. "You're really okay about this phone?"

"No one followed me. You can see all around. It's all right."

"Or she was subscribing to the *Miamisburg News*."

Graham snorted, audibly.

"Okay, scoff, but I went to the *Miamisburg News*. I said I was writing a book on circulation patterns among Midwestern weeklies and had selected the *News* as one of my cases. Well, they were just all too happy to help. Wow, the *New York Times!* Guess what? I found Linda Chapman from Marquette on their list, and she had just canceled her subscription."

"Jesus!" Graham kicked over his soda standing up and waved frantic mopping motions at Gwen for a towel. "From where?"

"That would be the obvious question; but they'd probably thrown the card away, and I didn't want to raise red flags. Enough people have read about this thing to ring a bell if I asked. At first it surprised me that she risked that by canceling, but then I figured: She's a smart lady. It would have been more dangerous to have the post office clean out her box and find ten copies of the *Miamisburg News,* wouldn't it?"

"But she's canceled, so what does that leave you? Nothing."

"I don't think so. She's obviously driven about this. I bet if I wait a month and pay another research visit, I could check their new out-of-town subscriptions and get another bead on her. But think about it: We're the only ones who know this, and she doesn't know we know it."

"Okay, genius, but you're not going down there again. What if Meachum is keeping tabs on you? Besides, I'm not interested anyway."

"Oh right. You should have heard yourself trying to explain how she was in the house. You think I can't read between the lines?"

"I don't care," he said. "As far as I'm concerned, if I never hear from that woman again, it will be too soon."

"Get a life. I'm not helping you play turtle another time."

"Julie, listen to me. This isn't the same. You're putting yourself in danger. I can't let you. Anyway, I can't have a relationship with this woman. It's none of my business what happens to her. I'm out of it, for my own skin and yours."

"Sure. Have it your way."

"Julie, I mean it."

"We'll see."

23

Two weeks later Graham received the note.

Resisting the temptation of Julie's information, he had begun spending his unwanted layoff in solitary. No longer working out with Kevin, he had just finished running along the railroad grade by himself and sat slumped at the back yard picnic table, poring over the newspaper. He was considering such weighty matters as whether to cruise down to the lower harbor and pick up a couple of lake trout filets from Thill's for dinner. The mailbox clapped shut on the porch, so he stretched and walked in through the house to avoid the postman. Not until he turned to go in with the mail did the small envelope just inside the door, where someone had slipped it under, catch his attention.

He stooped and turned it over. It was an undersize Hallmark envelope on which was typed,

"For Graham Bell
Please hand deliver
DO NOT OPEN!"

Graham carefully separated the adhesive on the flap and withdrew a small, folded sheet. Inside, a neat script said simply, *"leaflet rack, inside north entrance JXJ. 2 p.m. June 8. on your toes."*

Cryptic. Who had left it? And when? Although he had never seen Tori's handwriting, he would bet it was hers. June 8, day after tomorrow. On your toes: For what? Had she set a bomb to go off in Jamrich? He tore the note and envelope into tiny shreds, walked to the kitchen, and dropped them into the waste can.

On the 8th, Graham drove over to campus after lunch. He had the rest of his lessons to photocopy for Bob at the math office, and then he would box up the last of his books and lug them out to the car from what used to be his office. Stan was putting a graduate assistant there for the summer but had assured Graham he did not need to turn his key in. Yet.

Graham folded down the last box top and looked at his watch. Quarter of two. His window faced John X. Jamrich Hall—JXJ—and he realized he was honest-to-god looking to see if he could spot her. Shaking his head, he toted the last box out and put it into the camper. Now it was 1:55, and he was getting wired.

He strolled over to Jamrich. North entrance would be the one facing the library. He walked in. Leaflet rack. He knit his brow and looked around, seeing no such thing. He drifted farther inside with students on their way to class and then saw the wooden rack on the brick wall across from the stairs. Still two minutes.

He looked the rack up and down and felt inside it. Empty. No note, nothing. He scrutinized the people hurrying to their two o'clocks. *On your toes.* What might he overlook? He scanned every face. Two o'clock and the lobby began quieting as the last students trickled past. Nothing. One minute after two. Had he missed her? His stomach did flip-flops. God, he was losing it. Then he about jumped out of his skin at the sudden jangle of a telephone not two feet away. It was the pay phone on the wall beside him. He hesitated, then snagged the receiver and put it to his ear.

"Graham?" It was Linda! Tori!

"Yes! Oh my god, where—"

"Stop! First answer this. One word: What book did you catch me reading at your house? I know you looked."

"Um." Graham thought furiously.

"Come on, come on, gotta move it."

"Ah shit, Italian guy. Lodovico!"

"Close enough. It's you. Now, are you driving or on foot?"

"Driving."

"Time, exactly."

"Time?"

"Is it now?" she snapped.

"Oh, two three and... thirty seconds."

There was a pause. She was apparently setting her watch. Then she said, "Listen carefully. I'll say this once. Go to Campus Pharmacy. Walk in, precisely 2:20. Got that?"

"Got it."

"Go to the feminine hygiene items. Look confused. Okay?"

"Yes, but—"

"Two twenty," she said and hung up.

Graham turned the receiver around perplexedly. Then what? He walked as casually as a man in a Darth Vader outfit to his truck parked behind West Science, drove the half mile to the University Shopping Center, and pulled up to Campus Pharmacy in a dither of indecision. It was four shops from LHC. She could not be brash enough to come right to where they had been hunting her.

He chewed his thumb until 2:19 and thirty seconds, then heaved himself out of the truck and walked slowly around the back to peel off more time. As his second hand passed the zenith, he walked in. Spotting Tampax along the shelf by the pharmacy counter, he stood looking at it and rubbing his chin. A telephone rang, and the clerk by the cash register picked up. She listened a moment and then called, "Pardon me, are you Mr. Bell? Your daughter's on the phone for you. She has something else you're supposed to pick up."

Graham took the phone. As expected, he heard Tori's voice, again very crisp.

118

"Okay, listen up. If you say anything, call me Julie. Buy some kind of tampons. That's why I called. Then go outside. Stand on the sidewalk on Third as if you're waiting for a ride. Look toward the supermarket. By the entrance you'll see a pay phone. Don't look now; you're listening to me tell you what tampons to buy. Watch the pay phone until two thirty; then walk across the street. At two-thirty it will ring. Got all that so far?"

"Yeah."

"Okay, now... this is essential. If anyone, I mean anyone, uses that phone between now and then or seems to be doing anything to it, let it ring. Don't answer. You got that? And this is all going to break down if the phone company has changed the number. Then I'll have to try something else. So you know what to do: Buy tampons. Stand outside. Walk over and answer the phone at two-thirty, if no one has messed with it."

Graham managed to say, "Got it," before she hung up.

He offered the cashier a sheepish smile and told her, "She says I always get the wrong kind." Then he walked over and picked out a package of O. B. tampons and laid it on the counter. The cashier gave him an understanding smile, while he looked properly embarrassed about it all. Then he walked outside and stationed himself in front of Lutey's Flower Shop before allowing himself to look for the pay phone at the entrance to Jack's IGA across the street. It hung there ominously, like something radioactive, like something about to explode. The minutes passed like hours. At two-twenty-six he started across the street, allowing time for passing traffic. Several people had come into and out of the store, but none had slowed down at the telephone. At two twenty-nine and thirty seconds he reached the entrance and leaned against the corner of the building by the phone. A man was coming along the street counting coins out of his pocket and looking his direction. What if he tried to use the phone just when she called?

Panicked, Graham turned to the phone and put the receiver to his ear while holding the button down and began reciting a litany of nonsense. The man jingled his change disappointedly, paused a second, and then walked on. Almost at once the phone began to ring under his finger, and he let the button up.

"Graham?"

"Yes. Jesus Christ, where—"

"Wait. What color was the underwear I left at your house?"

"Peach. Ask me something harder. They found that."

"Okay, I know it's you." Her voice became less guarded. "Now listen, before you say anything more, you have to follow two rules: Turn toward the entrance when you speak. Anything you say about me, do so in third person, as if you're talking to someone else. They're probably shadowing you, waiting for you to make contact."

His turn to be nervous now, Graham glanced up and down the street. He saw nothing that looked out of the ordinary but could not feel sure now.

"If you're looking, you won't see them," she said. "They're cleverer than that, but if they have a directional mike on you, they can't pick up my voice and very little of yours if you stay turned away, especially if there's traffic."

"Is there a reason for all this cops and robbers?"

"Well, think: If anyone intercepted my note, I had to get you off the first phone before they could get a trace. The next phone would be unmonitored, so I could send you to one they wouldn't have time to bug or you'd see if they tried."

"Wow! You thought of everything."

"Third person please. I have to."

"And the numbers to all these pay phones?"

"I keep them catalogued and updated, in case anything happens."

"Well, where the hell—" He caught himself. "Where the hell is she?"

"Yes, well that's the 64-million-dollar question, isn't it?"

"If she only knew what she set off around here. Pardon the expression."

There was a short silence before she replied.

"You don't need to do that, Graham. I saw *Newsweek.*"

"Really. I didn't see anything in there about the team of FBI commandos who stormed my house the night after she was there and trashed it hunting her. They found her fingerprints and her underpants and dragged me in for an all-night questioning party so I missed picking up my daughter at the airport. I didn't even know what it was about until it hit the papers."

Graham's indignation mounted in the telling.

"And hey, *Newsweek* should have been there to cover it a few days later when her ex showed up at my door and roughed me up trying to get a line on her or something he thinks she has. And I bet *Newsweek* didn't say that she about cost me my job."

"Oh god, I wish you'd never met me! I never should have pulled you into this. I tried not to, but I couldn't help myself. God, I am sorry."

"I just wish she'd leveled with me."

"I was going to. Now you're bitter."

"Bitter? More like burned."

"I hope you managed to catch up with her."

"Who?"

"Your daughter."

Graham scanned the street again. She needed to hear about her family, not his; but her ground rules and his fear of being overheard didn't allow a way.

"Yeah," he said, "she made it to the house on her own."

"How did she take it? I just hope the visit went okay, for both of you."

"Well, considering, I suppose it did. I wish she'd stay out of it, though."

"What do you mean?"

"Journalism; it's what she does. She's on a mission about the whole thing, re-searching her."

"No. I'm radioactive. Make that clear to her."

"Don't worry; if there's one thing I've made abundantly clear…"

"Okay. Okay. I just wish there were something I could do."

"She could turn herself in."

"No, I'm sorry. That I can't. That's not an option. At all."

"Why not? To me, she has to stop running. Her family would—"

"No! You. Are absolutely. *Not*. To go *there*. Do you understand? Don't even touch!"

"Wait, listen to me; there's something—"

He checked the street. If he could at least get her in… He tried another tack.

"Okay, look; with the right lawyer, she could even get off or at least face a reduced sentence. I mean, look at Katherine Power. What's she doing, seven, eight years? With any luck, she'll be back out in three."

"I'm not Katherine Power."

"You mean she didn't kill someone. Is that what you're saying?"

After a silence, Tori said, "If you like."

"Even so…"

"Graham, I have no defense. It's not an option."

"So did she then? I want to know."

Suddenly the line seemed to go dead for about ten seconds; then she was back.

"That was the operator. I have to cut this short. I have no more coins."

"Reverse the charges."

"Right; and you ask the operator where the call originated. You think I'm simple?"

"No, listen. There's something—"

"I'm sorry. I can't trust anyone, not even you."

That cut him to the quick.

"What the hell. After she led me on with her phony persona?"

"I think we need to end this conversation. Before we do, I have to say one thing: I lied to you; I admit it. Now I'll tell you something true: You're the first man I learned to trust. After all these years. Isn't that a laugh."

Graham heard the sudden catch in her voice as she went on.

"I put myself in your hands making this call, because I thought—I don't know what I thought. Life doesn't work that way. Think of me how you will, Graham; it doesn't matter. Just don't blame yourself. I mean that. It wasn't your fault."

She hung up before he could say a word. For several seconds he continued holding the dead receiver to his ear then reluctantly replaced it.

Now what?

Not his fault and she in the dark about her family. Fabulous.

24

For more than a week Graham tried to forget the contact had ever taken place. Still, try as he might, he could not help dwelling on that thread. In the midst of want ads, by his ear when he ran, her voice would remind him, "I put myself in your hands."

Then Julie called to say she was flying up for a short visit. Instead of elation, he felt unease. What if she arrived with more compromising information in hand? Definitely he would have to keep this contact from her. He returned home just after five on the day she was to arrive on the 11 p.m. flight. He was paint-spattered and beat, having emerged from his shell of isolation enough to help a friend paint his house all day. A check of the mailbox showed the postman had left a J. Crew catalogue and one type-addressed envelope with no return and an Iron Mountain postmark that could as easily mean a local mailing. The envelope held two neatly handwritten pages in the same script that had adorned the small note under his door:

Graham, it began,

> *A lifetime ago I should have learned to stop caring what the world thinks of me and get on with whatever my life is. But when you of all people asked if I killed someone, it froze my heart. I may have had a hand in it, but—whatever you think—I did not set off the bomb. At the same time, I'm quite sure if any-one ever finds the detonator—and perhaps someone has—the only fingerprints on it will be mine. I'm out here all alone on this one. You'll be a hero if you turn me in, vindicated. I'm sure you've considered that.*

> *Probably you assume it was a war protest, revenge for my brother. Everyone else did. At this distance I can hardly expect you to entertain any other purpose. Explaining would become too complicated, and you would not believe me any-way. Why should you? What I discovered in motion that night I was too late to stop but gave the proof to my children when I sent them to their father.*

> *Maybe you've learned I had children. I don't know if they or their father kept those things. For their sake, I have never tried contacting them, so I don't know their whereabouts; worse, I don't even know whether they're alive. Another pen-alty exacted.*

> *In the end, only one fact matters: A man died, and his life weighs heavier than any millions in the balance. I carry the burden of him with me every waking hour. Some days I think I won't stand it. Yet I must. You are the one person who can understand that, all too well. Would you believe me if I said letting go once seemed possible with you?*

One more thing: Beware of the man you pointed out at the demonstration when we were last together. I'm guessing he's the one who came after you. If he should <u>ever</u> approach or threaten you again, tell him I will turn myself in. Remind him there is no statute of limitation on treason.

Please take care of yourself. Love is too strong a word for me.

Tori

"Gave the proof to my children." That had to be the envelope Tori had given Jen as she sent her away.

Graham puzzled over her warning to Meachum. Why would he take that as a threat? What would he lose by her being tried for treason? Was he still that hung up on her? The letter cleared up nothing; if anything, it was more opaque than her telephone call. What on earth was this thing she had given her children? When Graham re-read Tori's supposition that he could betray her, her distance felt palpable enough to bring a sting of tears.

Leaving the letter on the table, Graham paced into the living room and stared out the front window, thinking hard. Surely she was not here in Marquette. Someone in town must be passing these to him. It would have to be someone whose loyalty was beyond question, but who? The girl in the demonstration? The woman in the emergency room? Graham did not even know their names. That was the kind of information Tori would never divulge; yet she must have women out there who would cover anything she asked. He was so absorbed he did not hear Julie come in the back door.

"What's this, Graham?"

He whirled around. Julie was standing there holding the letter.

"Oh! Nothing. Gimme that. What're you doing here?"

"I caught an earlier flight. I thought you'd be pleased."

"I am," he said, his eye on the note in her hand.

"Where did you get this?"

"It was in the mailbox. A joke of some kind."

She grabbed him by the arm and led him out to the picnic table.

"Graham. This is no joke. She's contacted you already, hasn't she?"

"Wh-what do you mean?"

"'…when you asked if I killed someone…' '…the man who came after you…' Who was the delivery boy?"

"I don't know. The postmark said 'Iron Mountain,' but it would say that even if it was mailed here."

"In town? You don't suppose—"

"No, I think she's passing them through one of her clients from the women's shelter. Who could link them? No names, nothing ever reported."

"Still, how can you be sure she's not here, Graham?"

"Because I could hear her paying a long distance operator."

"You *talked* to her?"

"Yeah, she set up a contact. It was real cloak and dagger; honest to god, she had me running from one pay phone to another so I couldn't trace her. She even thought I might turn her in. Can you imagine?"

"That had to be pretty gutsy of her, don't you think?"

"Except I accused her of deceiving me."

"Graham, what were you thinking*?*"

"I wasn't. She said something about not being able to trust me, and all of a sudden it was out there. Before I knew it, she just... I don't know... ended the conversation. I didn't even get a chance to mention her family, so she doesn't know. She doesn't trust me. I mean, look at this letter. You can tell. *'You'll be a hero if you turn me in.'* God!"

Graham shook his head unhappily.

"Stay with it, Graham; I don't think so. She's reaching out to you. She wouldn't have risked writing this otherwise."

"Then what is she trying to tell me?" he said. "This hardly explains a thing."

"How about this where she left her children some kind of proof? Was that the thing her daughter told you?"

"It must be, but how can I let her know I've talked to them? I've got to put her in contact with Jen."

Graham took his daughter by the shoulders.

"Julie, I have to locate her."

Insanely, Julie smiled and leaned toward him. Speaking so low she was almost whispering, she told him, "Why do you think I came up here? I have something for you, but I'm not going to show it to you here. What say you and I go to lunch at the Szechuan?"

25

She waited until they sat in the booth before handing him the addresses she'd found.

"Here, the *Miamisburg News* faxed me their last month's subscription changes," she said. "What do you think? Have we caught any live ones?"

Graham studied what she had.

Ed Gebhardt and Tom di Matteo he dismissed out of hand; Tori might be good at disguises, but he did not think she was that good. A male contralto would not fool anyone. That left Rachel Rountree of Troy KS, Alison Schenck in Miamisburg, and an epicene Lesley Alvarado of Flagstaff AZ. The first two were obviously women; the last might or might not be.

"The men are out, and I'd strike Alison: nothing but a local move and too trendy a name for someone of my generation."

"I'm with you so far."

"Rachel," he thought out loud. "We don't know what happened to her friend Rachel Gerlach. Could be her married name. She might have kept in touch with her."

"Too risky," Julie objected. "People would make that connection. Lesley: I like that one; it gives cover from people scanning for women's names. And Alvarado sounds Hispanic or Indian. Going cross-ethnic would give deeper cover yet: People would figure she couldn't pull it off."

"Would she need to speak Spanish?"

"Who says she doesn't? There's a good chance she'd know Spanish, growing up in California. And you said they already seem to speak Italian in her family… so piece of cake."

Julie whipped out the *Newsweek* photo of Vittoria DaMantova and matched it against the early news photos. "Look," she said and began resketching her. "She's got a perfect face. The nose, the mouth, dark hair. Very Latin." Julie joined the eyebrows and gave the result a judicious look. "Kind of like Frieda Kahlo. She could pass. From what you've told me about her, the possibilities would appeal to her; she's a risk taker. I think Lesley is your woman."

•

There was one way to find out. He did not think Tori would bother disguising her voice. All Graham had to do was get each woman's number from directory information. If either proved to be Tori, he would know it, but if this Rachel was in fact her friend, as he suspected, he would have to devise another way to deal with that. Of course, he reminded himself, Julie was also assuming in the first place that Tori would in fact continue subscribing to the *Miamisburg News.*

As soon as Julie left, he began working from a pay phone, now that Tori had him completely paranoid. To see if Rachel fit the bill, Graham quickly obtained the Rountree number in Kansas and dialed it up at half past five. A man answered.

"Good evening. Could I speak with Mrs. Rountree?"

"She's outside in the barn. Who's this?"

This is Tom Clausen of South Central Life. Are you Mr. Rountree? Perhaps I could speak with you. Do you have a few minutes?"

"You selling life insurance?"

"I'm offering an entire range of annuities, benefits and payout plans at prices that frankly we don't feel any of our competitors can match."

"Not interested."

"Can I send you our brochure?"

"Not interested in that either."

"Well thank you for your time. Have a nice day."

He'd answered one question. It wasn't Tori; she would not be staying with a man. Still, it might be Rachel Gerlach, the possibility he had favored in the first place. It bothered him a little that the man had said she was out in the barn. Rachel had been a scientist. Would she give that up to milk cows? Not likely. All right, next.

The Flagstaff operator had no listing for Lesley Alvarado.

"Did you try new listings?"

"Yes, I'm sorry; nothing."

"What about unlisted?"

"No."

"L. Alvarado?"

"All we have under Alvarado is D. J., Juan, Maria, Toby, and Tomás. Could any of those be your party?"

Maria maybe? "No, I don't think so. Thanks anyway."

Graham counted up what little he knew. Three women had added or changed their subscriptions. That did not mean any of them was Tori. Linda had no phone number in Marquette, because she stayed at the women's shelter. The Flagstaff woman had only a box number for an address, the same as Linda had in Marquette. Then he remembered that tiny Pachuco cross on her left hand and found himself going over to Julie's side. How could he have forgotten that? Too many things fit the profile now. But how likely was it? Trying to telephone her was one thing, but physically chasing her to Flagstaff and checking all the beauty shops was quite another. Who even knew if she would do that again? The whole thing was such a long shot.

Yet no matter how Graham tried to slice the idea, he kept hearing her say, "I put myself in your hands," or wailing, "I can never have a normal life. Never."

At least a dozen times he took out her note. Each time the words, "I'm out here all alone on this one," would leap out at him, stabbing his heart. After twenty-odd years all alone with it, she had put herself on the line—to reach him. Whatever she had given her children might amount to nothing, but he had to try giving her that chance.

CHASING ANTIGONE

ARIZONA
July 1994

The minute Graham made Flagstaff, he called Julie to let her know he'd arrived. He had no one else to tell and had driven two straight days with only a brief snooze in an interstate rest stop in the middle of Nebraska. And, in truth, Julie, for all of her undoubted ambivalence about him, was becoming his touchstone. Whether she pulled off her feats of fact-finding from familial loyalty above and beyond the call, professional acumen, *chutzpah*, or just plain brilliance, he owed her, deeply, this undeserved daughter of his.

In Julie he recognized so much of Leila that she set off thoughts of a way back; but that way, he knew, lay futility. Leila stood beyond now, any bridge to her burned by his own hand.

After a couple of unsuccessful tries at the apartment number, Graham reached Julie at her *Times* desk.

"How can I reach you in case anything comes up?" she said.

Traffic whizzed by on Old 66 as Graham flipped through the dog-eared, dilapidated directory in the booth. Miracle: the critical *f* page had not been torn out.

"I know a couple of people here from Berkeley days. One's an attorney, Sarah Fitch. Let me give you her number. And..."

This time he had to consult his pocket address book, since all the *a*'s and half the *b*'s were missing.

"There's also a guy in the forestry department at Northern Arizona University that I know, Joe Argentery. I might crash with him, if he's still here. That number I'll have to confirm with you later."

One thing he did not voice to Julie was his real concern about Dave Meachum's whereabouts and what Meachum might do if he discovered Julie was helping him find Tori DaMantova. He felt pretty sure she had left no tracks.

Graham stepped out of the phone booth into the northern Arizona sunshine. The high mountain air at 7,000 feet was invigorating, and the soaring volcanic peaks north of town made a most dramatic setting. He could live here.

He mulled the most prudent course of action walking to where he had parked his little pickup. Sarah—if she was anything like he remembered her—liked to ask questions, lots of them. It was her profession after all. Joe would be safer.

Finding Joe took a little doing. His place turned out to be a cottage in the Hispanic part of south Flagstaff beyond the Rio de Flag crossing at a little bridge across its dry bed. Graham's Japanese pickup fit right in with the sprung old Rancheros and Bel-Aires languishing along Joe's street.

Graham said he was in town looking for work, and Joe was so delighted to see him that he offered unlimited crash time. For his part, Joe said he was not a bit surprised to see Graham job-hunting. After he had seen Graham's picture on *Newsweek,* he knew Graham would be looking for work. Very funny.

As soon as he had a minute to himself, Graham dashed off a note.

"Am staying with a friend at 320 South O'Leary in south Flag. If you're the sister of Ismene, call me at 774-0021 or drop a note c/o Joe Argentery. Must talk. G."

After putting it into a blue envelope addressed to Lesley Alvarado, P. O. Box 2133, the address Julie had turned up, he cruised around until he found a letter box and mailed it.

The next morning he went by the main post office to mail Julie an innocuous card, then casually drifted along the bank of post office boxes until he passed 2133, a small box in one of the bottom rows. He leaned down quickly and peered through the small window. A blue envelope lay inside. Satisfied, Graham went over to the university to see what if any positions the mathematics department might have. There were none, nor ever likely to be. The secretary did not even offer to keep his resume on file.

He returned to the post office just before closing time, when half a dozen people were retrieving mail from their boxes. He bought some stamps and checked Box 2133. His letter still made a blue diagonal behind the tiny window.

Early the next morning before opening hours, Graham made another pass by the post office. Standing at a counter in the lobby, he wrote out a card to Cheryl, then scanned the boxes on his way to drop it into the mail slot. Someone had picked up the letter in Box 2133. *Bingo.*

Graham spent the next three days checking the job service at Arizona Employment Security and following up every likely lead. Any time he passed a hair salon, he dropped in to ask after Lesley Alvarado, methodically ticking them off in Joe's telephone book until he had covered every listing. No one had heard of her.

Since Joe did not have an answering machine, Graham had no way to know if anyone had tried to call.

"Joe," Graham complained, after he had spent a morning combing beauty shops and job leads, "why the hell don't you get an answering machine?"

"Who are you expecting to hear from, pal?"

"One of these places I've been around to might call with an opening."

"Don't kid yourself. All they have to do is go to the front door and whistle. You're lucky I've even got a phone. Hardly ever use the thing. Buy one yourself if you want; I don't care. Hey, what are you doing with my phone book? You've marked up all the hair places."

"Oh, somebody back in Marquette wanted me to look up a friend but couldn't remember which shop he worked in."

That night he called Julie to bring her up to date. After they got a few pleasantries out of the way and he explained where he was staying, Graham said, "The job hunting here isn't too good. I left your number with some people, in case I go on to Phoenix to look. You didn't get any calls, did you?"

"No, nothing here. You did get a call from Stan at the math department."

"What did he want?"

"He'd like you to come by; he wants to talk. Maybe he's ready to reinstate you."

"I'll do that as soon as I get back. I'm not turning up anything here. I don't think this is the place."

"It was a chance. I heard there were possibilities, but maybe you'll have to try someplace else."

Graham was relieved at how perfectly she picked up his cues. He had forgotten to discuss the need for discretion before leaving, but it all sounded perfectly innocent.

The next day, Graham doped out the phone number for the Flagstaff women's shelter and dialed it up.

"Safe Passage."

The voice sounded like a young girl's, far too young for Tori's.

"I'm returning Ms. Alvarado's call."

"From here?" The girl sounded confused.

"This is the number she gave me."

"Maybe you wrote it down wrong."

"No, I'm sure this is the number. I even read it back to her."

"Hm. Give me your name and number, and I'll post a message."

"But does she live there?"

"I can't give out that information; all I can do is take a message."

Graham sighed and left his name and Joe's number.

Six days passed. Still nothing appeared in Joe's mailbox except bills and magazines, nor did any note show up under his door. By Friday Graham had covered every hair shop, beauty salon, and manicurist he could find from one end of Flagstaff to the other and tried everything short of bribes to learn the location of the Flagstaff women's shelter. Obviously he had made a wrong guess, or Tori was avoiding him. Either way, further effort here was futile, so Graham decided to spend the weekend sightseeing and then head home on Monday.

Joe had a workshop to attend in Phoenix and could not go with him, so Graham left the house about eight on his own, headed for Macy's, where he intended to grab a table on the sidewalk and read the paper with a cappuccino and croissant. As he descended the ditch at Leroux where the storm-filled Rio de Flag would flow later in the summer on its way to South San Francisco Street, a tall black woman with a dog came around a house and started across the other direction. She glanced at him, rather sharply he thought, and angled slightly his way. Just as they drew even, she made a noise to the dog, and it suddenly stood against its leash to lick Graham's face.

"Jody, get down!" the woman cried, pulling back on the leash. "I'm very sorry. I don't know what gets into him. His enthusiasm is over the top sometimes."

"That's okay." Graham brushed at his shirt and wiped the dog spit off his chin with the back of his hand. "No problem."

She looked quickly around.

"Are you Bell?"

"Why yes!" he said, taken by surprise. "How did—"

"Do you know where the Snowbowl Ski Area is? Where they have the Sky Ride?"

"Not exactly. Is it up on the mountain?"

"Ask around. Anybody can tell you. Take the Sky Ride today, about one."

Before he could say anything, the woman smacked her lips, and the dog pulled her smartly away.

Graham scratched his head and turned around to watch her jogging along behind the dog until she turned at the next street. What in the world?

At Macy's he asked a man at the next table for directions to Snowbowl and learned not only how to get there but that he could expect to see the Grand Canyon and half of western Arizona from the top of the mountain.

"Be sure you take a jacket," the man advised. "It's cold up there. See how the clouds are coming down? They get a lot of weather up there."

"The mountain" was an extinct volcano looming nearly 13,000 feet into the sky north of the city. Graham had a good view as he drove north on Highway 180, and indeed a heavy cloud wreathed the top of the San Francisco Peaks, the volcano. The huge, rising mass simply disappeared into it. Seven miles north of town he came upon the road marked "Snowbowl Sky Ride" and turned onto a blacktop road, which became increasingly narrow and serpentine as it rose from the ponderosa into Douglas-fir and flowered mountain meadows. The air still felt warm as he ascended, however. The truck was working hard enough that Graham began keeping a close eye on the temperature gauge, which was steadily climbing as well.

After seven miles of scuffing around one hairpin after another, he passed a large ski lodge with a sign indicating the Sky Ride still lay ahead. The road took another hairpin into a fierce incline, then around another hairpin and into a parking lot with another, older ski lodge at the far end. Beyond the lodge a ski lift ran up the mountain and into the clouds.

Here in the sunshine the air was cooler but still comfortable. He put his jacket on anyway; the man at Macy's had been very definite about that. Graham's watch said a quarter of one. Another car or two labored up the mountain somewhere behind him, the only sound besides the wind. By the time he had walked the short distance to the old lodge, he was totally out of breath. A sign there read

9,500 feet elevation. No wonder. He went inside, but there was only a college-age girl selling tickets, no secret signs or passwords.

"I'd like a Sky Ride ticket," he said.

"You probably want to wait. The conditions are pretty poor up there. The temperature is 34° up top, and there's a 25-knot wind. It's completely socked in. You won't see a thing."

"No, I still want to go." *She said one o'clock.*

"Well, it's your money, but we haven't loaded anyone for almost an hour. Be sure you're dressed warmly. That jacket isn't going to do it. She's got blankets up at the lift; be sure you take some, seriously. The lift takes over twenty minutes, and you can get really hypothermic."

A petite, twentyish woman in a ball cap and long braid was waiting up by the lift's loading ramp, swatting herself to keep warm. As Graham ascended the steps, she stopped her swatting and pulled something from her jacket. She peered at it carefully and then tucked it back away.

"Hi! Taking the ride, eh? The weather's gnarly up top, so take this blanket."

Graham looked dubiously up the mountain into the clouds gathered above. Her warning was a little hard to credit in this pleasant field of sunshine and mountain flowers.

"In fact, take two of them," she said, "and be sure to keep your head covered. Now what you're going to do when I tell you is stand where these two footprints are and just sit down when the chair reaches you. At the top, the person up there will tell you what to do. Basically you'll just step down and walk to the side. Here," she stepped close to hand him the blankets and said, "Graham. You're Graham, aren't you?"

"Why yes." *At last.* "How do you know me? What were you looking at?"

"It's a drawing, so I'd know you."

"May I see it?"

"Sure, have it; I don't need it now." She withdrew it and rolled it into the blanket. She took a look down toward the lodge, where a couple of people barely visible through the window were talking to the girl at the counter inside.

"Now listen carefully before more people come up here. I want to give you a good head start. Halfway up the mountain, about there, there's a midway platform we don't use in the summer. The decking is mostly removed so people don't get off there, but right in the middle is a place where you can step down. You'll have to jump, because the deck will be about a foot below you. Just watch out the chair doesn't hit you. Okay, if you're ready, take this next chair and don't let anyone see you jump off. It could spell trouble for both of us."

She swung the chair slightly to slow it, and he sat down and was off. As soon as he was seated, he remembered to turn and ask the girl, "But then what?"

She trotted to catch up with him and said, "Walk down the ramp. You'll see a ski trail. Follow it to the left. She's waiting for you."

133

27

The lift operator jogged to a stop and fell behind as Graham's chair lifted away from the ramp. He gathered up the blankets in his lap, looked back again to see if she had any more instructions, but she was just standing there with her hands on her hips. At his look, she gave a slight wave. Graham turned forward and settled himself before rummaging through the blankets.

Finding the rolled-up sheet of paper, he took a firm grasp and withdrew it from the blanket. He did not want to drop it. The chair was already a good fifty feet above the meadow grass below. Rising up the face of the mountain and disappearing far above into the belly of a cloud, the lift line made a long cut through high spruce on either side. Beautiful gold and white flowers punctuated the berry shrubs under the lift towers. The sheet unrolled into an ordinary piece of copy paper. Squinting against the sunlight it reflected, Graham found a dashed-off pencil sketch of himself. It might not look exactly like him, he thought, but close enough. There was a certain affection to the rendering, for the likeness seemed on the verge of laughing. How could she do that from memory? If his life depended on it, he could not have come up with even a caricature of Tori without consulting Modigliani. He ran his fingertips lightly over the shading. Rembrandt lighting, isn't that what they called it, the way she'd illuminated his face from the side? The strokes smudged; she might have done it only this morning.

Carefully Graham re-rolled the drawing, placed it inside his jacket to keep it from creasing, and then attended to the view up the mountain. Some distance ahead a small shack stood along the lift line; perhaps that was Midway. Under the cloud's shadow now, the air was rapidly cooling. Below, the flowers and plants kept changing with the ascent up the mountain. Inspired to signal his arrival, Graham reached into his jacket pocket and pulled out his dented harmonica to play "Summertime."

Blowing the final notes into a long, wailing tremolo on the mountain air, Graham wondered how far he had come and twisted to see behind. The ground fell away hundreds of feet and swept out to sunlit plains and distant mountains miles to the west. Even at this distance, the girl standing at the loading area was still visible. Someone was trudging up the steps toward her and briefly looked up as she apparently said something.

Graham suddenly stowed his harmonica and looked closer, squinting hard. It was a man wearing a big western hat and sunglasses. He was showing the girl something and pointing up the lift. She shook her head. The hat: like the one that man Parrish wore who had questioned him in Marquette. Graham pulled his eyelid tight to sharpen the focus. Possibly a second person was standing just at the edge of the trees by the lodge, but Graham could not tell for sure. The cowboy in sunglasses boarded the lift.

Graham panicked. This could be serious. Or was he only imagining things? Two more lift towers remained before he reached the lofty midway ramp. The one he was approaching first bore the usual "Prepare for unloading" sign. "Ski tips up," left over from winter, showed on the next tower, right before the ramp. The deck began a good twenty-five feet above the steep downhill slope, but he was still too far below to see it. Squeegeeing through the sheaves overhead, the lift cable disappeared ahead, where a set of ponderous sheave assemblies drew it down across the brink of the midway ramp. Farther up the slope, it reappeared, a stately line of chairs fading into the misty bottom of a cloud. Already he could hear the squawking complaint of rubber sheave liners as they bore down on the cable passing over the ramp.

Whoever was behind would not be able to see him once his chair passed the next tower and drew downward over the deck. At the last tower the ramp finally came into view, its open timbers framing an uncomfortable drop to the steep rocks underneath where the decking had been pulled off and stacked along the side. Just a narrow catwalk of 2 x 10s had been left where maintenance workers could alight, and the chair would bring him no closer than a foot above it. He could smell damp lumber.

Taking a quick look behind, Graham could still make out the chair far down the line with a man in it, holding onto his hat. In another moment the end of the ramp would pass between them and shield him from view. As he prepared to slide out of the chair, Graham suddenly thought, *What if he has binoculars?* He would see the chair rising empty from the other side when the cable climbed into view again. Unless the cloud closed in by then, the man would know he had jumped off.

You're being paranoid. Get a grip; it's some guy. Just because he's got a cowboy hat. Do it. Now.

Teetering in indecision on the edge of the chair, Graham suddenly scooted himself back. He couldn't risk it. Then the deserted lift shack was behind him and the down ramp dropping away as the cable began to rise to the next tower. Still hidden from anyone coming up, Graham scanned the forested mountainside frantically as he lifted across the ski run sloping off through the dripping evergreens on his left; he saw no one. Just in case she was out there and could see him, Graham pointed behind and made a frantic waving-off motion with both hands. Nothing moved. Fifteen seconds, and he was back in the slot headed up the mountain. The high trees blocking his view on either side no longer bore the ragged cones of Douglas-fir. Other trees, more stunted, had taken over as he approached timberline. Here and there showy, scarlet primrose decorated the steep cut below.

A tower leaning out of the slope above was growing fuzzy edges in the cloud, and the air turned downright chilly. Another minute, and gray vapor closed in around him. Mist droplets stung his face, and Graham pulled the blankets tightly around himself, shivering. Gusts of wind began to whip scraps of condensation overhead and rock the chair back and forth as it climbed farther. A cocoon of fog wrapped him, hushing even the turning sheave wheels at each blurry tower in the condensing cloud. On either side, the ghosts of trees barely showed now.

His vision limited to a hundred yards or less, Graham could no longer make out the midway ramp behind him. A mix of rain and sleet began to drum his back, and he wondered how long he would last if the lift stopped and left him hanging up here. A darker mass began to appear out of the gloom ahead. Gradually it resolved into a small building and what must be the top of the lift. Graham looked behind again but saw only one tower back, and even that was barely visible. Ahead, a treble fan of lift towers signaled the approaching ramp with the same warning about ski tips.

Directly ahead of him, a dim figure was standing, as the last tower raised him high enough to show the decking in front. The person was telling him something that the gusts of wind at Graham's back sailed away.

"...on the footprints and then follow them off to the side," the person, a young man bundled up in a jacket, was saying. A set of large yellow footprints painted on the decking showed where Graham should alight and step, so the passing chair would clear him. He hit at a fast walk and moved smartly aside as the young man maneuvered the chair by him.

The lift attendant, whose nose was daubed with zinc oxide, looked more than comical; he looked perplexed. "Kay must be sleeping. Good thing I looked down the line just then, or I wouldn't have seen you. She didn't say you were coming."

Graham realized why; he was not supposed to have arrived here.

"Any people behind you?" the attendant asked.

"One guy I think. Way back."

"Okay. Him she called about. Hell of a day you picked to come up. It's been socked in since ten. You can wait around to see if it clears. Sometimes it does, but I don't think it will today. Too bad. On good days you can see all over: the Canyon, the South Mountains beyond Phoenix, Hualapai Peak in Kingman, some days all the way to the Music Mountains, and that's a good hundred and fifty miles. But not today. Lucky to see your hand. Go in and warm up if you want." He indicated his lift shack.

"No thanks. Maybe I'll just look around up here anyway."

"Okay, but stay inside the fence. This is an endangered plant area. Check out the bristlecones. They don't look like much, but some of them are a thousand years old."

"Up here? I thought bristlecones grew in the Sierra Nevadas."

136

"No, they used to live all over the Southwest, but they got stranded up here after the Ice Ages. Nothing else can survive this high."

Graham wandered around in the obscurity for a few minutes and came upon a few of the shrubby trees clinging to the rocks, their massive trunks supporting sprigs of life. Eventually he wandered back to the lift, where the attendant was sitting pensively on a rail in the fog smoking a suspicious-smelling, twisty cigarette.

"Do you get a lot of weather like this up here?" Graham asked.

"All kinds. The mountain makes its own, it's so much higher than anything else around. The air cools when it passes over and forms condensation clouds like this. In a week or two, the monsoon will begin and build up clouds below that roll right up the face of the mountain. If the air is carrying enough moisture, we get some wild thunderstorms up here. You don't want to be out in the open then. And it might not hit town or even the rest of the mountain. That's just how it rains out here."

"What do you do about the lift?"

"As soon as lightning shows anywhere in ten miles, we start getting people off and shut down until it's over. We get hit all the time but the lightning goes to the towers and down. You're not grounded on the lift—unless you touch. I've even stood right here and had bolts zing right over my head along the cable. But if you get caught out there," he gestured vaguely up into the gloom, "all you can do is get on your knees and keep your head down, but not right on the ground—unless you want to take it through the noodle."

"Kind of like praying. That's good to know."

"Take my advice, stay inside. Don't try it out."

"Not much sense hanging around up here, is there? How do I get back down?"

"Not really. Step over to the other side and stand at the footprints when I tell you. It's just like when you got on. And put the bar down, because you're pretty far off the ground as soon as you leave the ramp up here."

They waited for the next chair to pass, then stepped across to the downhill loading side. The chair dangled slowly back toward the bull wheel where the cable would take it around and back down.

"Oh, say," Graham advised as the chair came around the wheel, rocking gently toward them from its sharp turn, "I'd put that smoke out before your next customer arrives; he carries a badge."

Just before the chair reached them, the attendant swung it forward toward Graham and then held it a second so he could sit. The ramp moved away under his feet, and then he and the chair sailed out over a vertiginous twenty-foot drop down to the steep slope and began descending.

"Thanks," the attendant called behind him. Graham turned. The attendant high-signed him as he stepped his smoke out on the boards. Graham waved back, then faced forward. A chair with one person on it approached him on the uphill side of the towers. Graham pulled the blanket tighter around his head. When the man came within thirty meters, Graham recognized he was indeed Parrish, the agent who had questioned him in the Marquette district attorney's office.

As they drew even, he pulled the blanket hood around his face and looked away. Then they passed each other. Graham did not look back.

By the time he emerged from the cloud, Graham was almost upon the midway ramp. Once again he looked all around as he passed over the ski trail at the upper end of the ramp but still saw no sign of anyone. A sudden movement far down the trail only marked a ground squirrel scampering across. The ramp did not extend under the cable on the downhill side. There was nothing but air, no way to get off. Nevertheless, Graham kept looking as he passed the ramp until the trees closed in around him on either side to frame the long cut onto sun-dappled western Arizona again. Old cinder cones dotted the high plains, and a Steller's jay shrieked from a fir. Suddenly, like magic, a doe stepped from the trees into the open. Without a sound, spirit-like, she picked her way daintily across to the other side and disappeared into the forest. Graham was spellbound. He could almost forget how close he had come to seeing Tori—and how much closer he had come to getting her caught. Somewhere up there, he hoped she was getting the hell out of here as quietly and as swiftly as that doe.

The girl Kay was waiting for him at the bottom, her arms folded in reproval.

"I thought you were going to jump off. You went on to the top," she accused as Graham alighted.

"Too risky. I was afraid I'd fall through."

The girl gave him a strange look, but Graham only squinted back up the lift line. No one was descending that he could see. The agent was probably still grilling the top attendant up there. Graham peered around, but he and Kay seemed to be alone. He must have imagined the second person. At that distance it would be no surprise. He hesitated and scratched his head.

"Was there another guy down here?" he asked.

"A long time ago. He went on up. You should have passed him on your way down."

"Oh yeah, I did. Was there anyone else?"

"Nobody that got on. I think maybe there was a guy walked out of the shop and started up the steps once, but then he left. Why?"

Graham stood on the top exit step and tugged at his chin nervously. How much could he tell this girl?

"Listen." He stepped closer. "Do you know what's going on here?"

"Jesus, watch the chair!" she shrieked and pushed Graham back just as the cable towed it between them, narrowly missing him. "I'd say a hell of a lot more than you do. Why do you think we have that arrow there?"

"Sorry, I wasn't watching," Graham said. Feeling really stupid, he started backing toward the steps to leave.

"Wait a minute," she called after him. "You asked me a question."

Graham stopped at the second step and turned. She reciprocated his look, sizing him up. Now he understood she did not quite trust him either.

"You told me to jump off at midway," he said finally.

"Well, you seemed to know what I was talking about."

"You said she was waiting. Who was waiting?"

"You know who."

"Lesley?"

She nodded once, no more than the slightest inclination of her head.

"Okay, I'm going to tell you something. Kay, is it?"

"Yes. Who told you?"

"Guy up there; I stayed on, because the man who got on behind me means big trouble for Lesley." Graham appraised Kay carefully. "Will you see her?"

"I don't know."

"Make it your business to. Tell her I was followed. Things are hot. Oh. Let her know I've spoken to Jen."

"Who?"

"Jen. She'll know. Tell her she needs to get in touch with me. Now, can you see if that guy's started back down?"

Kay picked up the handset by the lift controls and rang the top operator.

"Hey, what did you do with Bozo, throw him over the side? I want to go home."

She listened a moment, nodded and then laughed. "Yeah, you, too. You might as well lock up and jump on. No one else is going to ride today. Be sure to let me know which chair you're on."

Kay said, "Get outa here. Your friend started down about ten chairs ago. I'll slow down the lift a few times so you have enough head start to make the highway. Are you going back into town?"

"I planned to, yes."

"Actually, I thought you mentioned heading up to Grand Canyon to meet someone, didn't you? If he asks."

"I believe I did." A mile or so up the cable the darker chair laden with its one distant figure in a broad-brimmed hat inched down the line. Just in case he should be packing binoculars, Graham waved and blew him a kiss.

"What are you doing? Get a move on!"

"I'm on my way. Remember: *followed* and *Jen,*" he said and headed for the parking lot. Whether the agent believed the story about Grand Canyon or not, Graham needed to leave and get him away from Flagstaff in a hurry.

He turned the corner at the lodge, puffing from the altitude, and headed for the parking lot where his Toyota waited. Only one other vehicle was parked in the lot. Graham almost laughed; if it hadn't been for him, the Sky Ride probably wouldn't have had any business today. Graham was ten steps from his truck when the other vehicle's door opened, and Dave Meachum stepped out to block his way.

"You seem to be in a hurry. Why don't you stick around and have a chat?"

"I'd love to, you know, but I'm not really interested. Besides, I've got better things to do. So if you don't mind…"

"Oh, you should be. We find the things you do real interesting. Like coming up here when you can't see anything."

"You know, this would be funny if my taxes weren't paying you to follow me around."

"Let's say we were just curious to see why you came out here all of a sudden."

"I'm trying to find a job, thanks to you. I don't have government underwriting, like some people I know."

"Cry me a river. You could have looked for jobs in Michigan."

"I did, but I came out to see this guy in the forestry department because he thought the university might have something here. I've been looking lots of places. Go to the unemployment office downtown and check, if you're so interested."

"We have."

"Meachum, I don't need you guys trailing me. If you like wasting time so much, why don't you do it at someone else's expense?"

"You know, I find it real interesting you're looking for jobs in beauty parlors."

"I'm not looking for jobs there, you idiot."

"Watch who you call idiot. What are you doing then?"

"The woman who cuts my hair heard a friend of hers was working in one of the shops out here. She asked me to look her up, that's all."

"Her name wouldn't happen to be Lesley Alvarado, would it?"

"Oh, that was hard: Shake a few beauticians down. Sure, that's her friend. You could have asked me and saved yourself a lot of trouble."

Meachum looked over Graham's shoulder toward the lift. "Somehow I fail to persuade you that I mean business, my friend. Let me lay it out for you." He jerked his chin toward the ski lift. "That guy goes by the book. He doesn't break laws, but he doesn't ask what I do. And I'm going to break more than laws. You know where she is, and I told you what would happen if you held out on me."

Meachum shoved his hand into his pocket and stepped closer. Graham backpedaled into the bumper of his car as Meachum grabbed his jacket.

"Just cool it," Graham said. "As far as I know, she's still in Marquette. I haven't seen her."

Meachum drew a knife and flicked it menacingly in Graham's face. Looking right through the blade, Graham tensed. Meachum lacked the element of surprise. A blow to the larynx would drop him. And kill him.

"Don't lie to me, you worthless piece of shit," Meachum threatened. "She's here!"

Don't. It's broad daylight; he knows better than to stick you. Don't do this to yourself again.

Graham then remembered what Tori had advised him to say and slowly released a breath to calm himself.

"Put it away, Meachum! She said if you mess with me or my daughter again, she'll turn herself in."

"Great! I'll make lunch meat of you right here."

"No you won't, because she would also remind you there's no statute of limitation on treason."

This stopped Meachum's game like magic. He let Graham's jacket go and hefted the knife.

"She said that, did she?"

Meachum backed off a step and smiled coldly.

"Well. That changes the rules. It's just me and her. They'll never get to her, because she's coming in feet first. I'll see to that."

"Lay a hand on her, and see who becomes the hunter," Graham warned. "I'd find you; believe me, I would."

Meachum laughed.

28

Shaken by the encounter, Graham sped into Flagstaff, determined to consult his other old friend before leaving town. He needed legal advice, and Sarah Fitch would be the person to have it. They had met during the Free Speech days at Berkeley when she was just starting out, doing *pro bono* work for the ACLU defending people like Mario Savio and Angela Davis. For a year or so, she and Graham even had a thing going; but then he met Leila. Except for the occasional Christmas card or note, they had lost track.

If anyone, she would know whether he could obtain an injunction to keep these characters off his tail. This time the shave had cut too close for comfort; Meachum's partner had come around the corner of the lodge just when Graham was about to get himself either carved or into a world of trouble for assault. Luckily, at Parrish's appearance, Meachum stowed the knife. Graham had released his breath and knocked Meachum's hand from his shirt.

"Get outa here. Get your ass on the road," Meachum had said, playing the bully to what he thought was Graham's fear, "but don't think you've seen the last of us. We're keeping our eyes on you."

Still shaking with adrenaline, Graham needed no second invitation and was behind the wheel fishtailing out of the parking lot before the agent even reached them. He had come that close after swearing never to commit violence on a human being again. So intent was Graham on making tracks that he was halfway down the mountain before it hit him: They had a name to work with, and she did not know.

As soon as he hit the edge of town, Graham wheeled into the shopping center at the top of Humphreys and pulled up by the grocery, where he spotted a public telephone. Finding Sarah's home and office numbers in the plundered directory still chained to it, he dialed her house and got an answering machine.

Rotten luck. Of all the times to be away.

He left an innocuous message that he had been in town and was sorry to miss her. He hammered the phone with the heel of his hand in frustration; then, forgetting it was Sunday, tried her office.

On the first ring, a woman answered with a curt "hello."

"Is this the law office where Sarah Fitch works?"

"It's Sunday. We're not open."

"Oh, hell, that's right. I'm just passing through, and I really had to talk to her."

"Name?"

"Graham Bell. You know, like the phone?"

"Graham! I've been thinking about you. Saw your picture in the news. What in God's name are you doing here? Where've you been hiding yourself all these years?"

"Sarah?"

"The one and only."

"Care to tell me why you're in on Sunday, pretending to be a receptionist?"

"Oh, I just got in from Tuba and needed to write up a few things where it's quiet. You'd be surprised how many people expect me to live here. If I don't tell them we're closed, they'll waltz right in at midnight on the Fourth of July expecting me to defend them on the Fifth. But that's not your problem. Actually I thought it was Ted calling to see if I was back yet."

"Ted?"

"Oh right, you wouldn't know; I'm spoke for now. So my goodness, Graham Bell. How many years has it been?"

"Too many, I'll tell you."

"Yes, it has. I hear life's been exciting out your way."

"Where did you ever hear a rumor like that?"

"I saw your name in connection with that Tori DaMantova thing, and I thought, 'Good for Graham! He's getting political again in his old age.' You dropped out of sight. I always expected—"

"Old age, hell; and there was nothing political about this; the involvement was purely personal. I got caught in over my head. Sheer accident, if you want to know."

"I bet. Well, you're going to tell me the whole sordid story. Where are you?"

When Sarah heard he was standing outside Basha's Market, only blocks from her office, she directed him to drive over that minute.

As he neared the address, Graham took a precaution that was becoming second nature. Turning onto a side street, he parked two blocks away and walked the remainder through the slant shadows of late afternoon. He found her office in a lovely old house that Sarah must have converted for her practice.

She met him at the door with a huge embrace; then they held each other at arm's length. Graham thought time had favored her. Instead of the long-haired Berkeley wild girl, she wore large glasses and her hair at a very professional neck length, belied only by long feather earrings. Faded jeans and sandals evoked the old Sarah, however.

"You look great, Graham," she said, echoing his impression of her. "Get your car. We'll scoot over to the house. You can meet Ted, and then I'll send him on a snipe hunt."

"Ah ah; he might get suspicious. How about we both ride home in your car?"

"Whatever. You can park yours in the lot."

"Actually I think I'll just leave it down the street."

When she drew back and gave him a look, Graham explained, "I'd just rather no one connect us yet."

She frowned but said nothing. Once in her car, however, she got right to the point, "All right, what's this about?"

"Oh, nothing. Just a dead end for anyone following me."

She fingered back a lock of dark-brown hair and arched an eyebrow.

"Come on, you think people are following you?"

"I know they are. I just had a run-in with a couple of them not an hour ago."

Turning onto Aspen, she glanced at him with a look almost like respect. "Just what are you mixed up in? Are you under indictment?"

"No. It's just the FBI thinks I might still lead them to their woman."

"Could you?"

"I came out here to find a job, Sarah. There's a guy in the forestry department we used to know, Joe Argentery?"

"I know Joe."

"Okay, well he thought maybe he could find me something at the university."

"I see. Too much notoriety, and you wanted to make a fresh go. Is that it?"

They pulled up to Sarah's house at the end of Aspen near the city park.

"Something like that."

He stepped out and admired the old two-story, built of Flagstaff's red sandstone by some raw-material baron. The carved front door was set with an oval, cut-glass window and etched transom in true prairie grandeur.

"You must not do charity cases now," he said as she let them in the back.

She stopped with the door and her mouth half open.

"You mean I've sold out. Let me tell you something, Graham. My focus is Indian law. When the government foots the bill, I make sure the partners get paid in full. Do you have a problem with that?"

"Come on, Sarah, I was kidding. I like your house."

"And I still do my share of *pro bono* work."

"You don't have to convince me. This is hardly Mr. Activist you're talking to."

Sarah's look eased slightly, and she led the way inside. "Theodore, an old friend! Open another beer and water down the chili. Come meet Graham."

A big man whose creased face had spent time in the sun met them in the kitchen, still in his Forest Service uniform. He pumped Graham's hand in his huge paw. Graham felt a flash of jealousy at his rugged good looks, but what did he expect?

"Ted Corcoran. So you're Graham. I've been hearing about you for years."

"Should I prepare to defend myself?"

"Hell no; I never believed any of it." Ted plunked two bottles of Dos Equis onto the kitchen table while Sarah dumped her files in the living room.

Graham said, "Why don't you two have those? I'll go for water or whatever."

"Whatever you like. She's kidding about the chili; I just got home. I'm making fajitas, New Mexico style."

Just then, Sarah returned and nabbed two glasses from the cupboard. She started to slide one to Graham, then passed it to Ted and decanted her beer into her glass.

"Is this something new?" She pointed her glass at the water he was drinking.

"Since you saw me."

"Should I ask?"

He shrugged. "Let's just say I got pretty bad after I came back."

"I wondered. You never got in touch." She raised her glass. "Would you rather we didn't—"

"It's okay; you enjoy it. It doesn't bother me. It's not like a moral thing. Some people don't drink coffee."

"It takes more strength to get there than most people ever have, Graham; don't minimize it. And I bet that beast didn't offer you soda or iced tea, did he?"

Ted doled out three plates and a clay warmer full of tortillas onto the table. He winked at Graham as he thumbed his nose at Sarah.

"He's got to ask. Here, make your own mess."

They proceeded to do just that. Sarah sat with one leg curled under her, talking as she ate and dabbing at her mouth every few minutes. Finally she rolled up a tortilla to mop around her plate and sat back with a puckish smile.

"Okay, how'd you get mixed up in this thing?"

"I believe I'll adjourn to the dishes," Ted said.

Graham wiped his fingers one at a time, a little crestfallen Ted didn't consider him competition enough to require a chaperone

"You're going to be disappointed."

"I'll be the judge. Talk."

"Well, first off, you need to understand I hadn't been doing much in the Significant Relationships department."

"You?"

In the pit of his stomach, Graham could feel the old sexual undercurrent between them and hoped Ted did not notice at the sink, where he was cleaning up.

"Yeah, some things happened, and I um… Well, I left Leila. Not her fault. After that I wasn't really looking any more, except for a few on-again off-again things. Decided I was better off away from that scene. Then a year ago, I started getting my hair cut at this place in Michigan where I knew one of the women, somebody I ski raced with."

"In Michigan?"

"We have hills. Anyway, one of the hairdressers was a woman about my age. Picture it: very striking but aloof, and I was like a moth to a lightbulb. Is that nuts? I can only say there was something about her."

"Evidently."

145

As if to justify his attraction in the face of Sarah's amusement, Graham began fleshing out inscrutable Linda Chapman in the entirety for her. He elaborated on her reciting *Antigone,* the martial arts, her volunteer work with women, but most of all the maddening stand-offishness. His reminiscence simply got away from him, and he suddenly saw Sarah knew it.

"Anyway, that was Tori DaMantova; only I didn't know."

Zeroing in on him, Sarah asked about this business of people following him.

"Around the same time—this is eight months ago we're talking now—I picked up this hitchhiker named Dave Meachum. He started telling me how he'd done time and then cut some deal to get out. Said he bounty hunts for the Feds and he's a soldier of Christ or some business like that. Actually, it turned out he used to be DaMantova's boyfriend and has been hunting her ever since. That I found out later. Anyway, he remembered me the next time we met, which, unfortunately happened to be when Linda and I—Linda: That's the hairdresser who turned out to be Tori—walked into the middle of a demonstration in Marquette last month. Whom should I spy leading the cheers for Right to Life but Mr. Meachum? When I saw him spot us, I looked around and she'd split. That night the Feds raided my house and took me in for questioning. They thought I was an accomplice. That's when I learned what was up.

"After they decided I wasn't involved, they turned me loose. A couple of days later, the ex-con boyfriend showed up at my door to threaten me—and my daughter—with dire results if I didn't tell where Tori was hiding. The trouble is, I didn't have a clue. At the same time, so much stuff was appearing in the paper that the university got bent about having such a badass on the payroll and laid me off."

"You have a daughter! How old?"

"Twenty-four. We just reunited after so many years I'm embarrassed to say. She's on an internship researching investigative reports for the *New York Times.* She's a tough, smart cookie. You'd like her."

"I'm sure, but this business you're mixed up in is no laughing matter."

"That's the thing I want to talk to you about: Is there any way to keep this guy off my tail? He's bad news. I think he works undercover for somebody, FBI, Treasury, Defense, CIA, I don't know. One of the agents that questioned me in Marquette is here with him, guy named Parrish. Just what the deal is I don't know."

"Hm. How close were you to this woman?"

"Well…"

"Obviously they think she's going to make contact with you."

Graham sipped some water and rubbed the cool glass against his brow. He turned it in his hands a few times before setting it back onto the table.

"Has she?" Sarah put both feet on the floor and regarded him shrewdly across the table.

When Graham frowned, she said, "You don't have to tell me, but I need to know what the grounds are here. Understand I'm not going to rat on you. You know me better than that. Or you should. Lawyer-client thing aside, I have principles. You see, what they're doing could constitute harassment—unless they have reasonable grounds to believe that you are in contact with her."

Graham gazed into the glass. "We did speak on the phone—but it was only a few minutes; and she wouldn't tell me where she was. She called from a pay phone somewhere."

"And nothing since."

"Well, yes, a note later."

She traced a circle on the table. "What did it say? Just in general."

"On the phone I told her to turn herself in, and we argued about it. The note was a little cryptic but seemed to say the bombing was not what people thought. She didn't explain herself, though. Then she warned me about this Meachum character and said if he ever threatened me again I should tell him she'd turn herself in and there's no statute of limitation on treason, however that was supposed to help. So today, when Meachum was about to perform cosmetic surgery on me, I told him that; and by God he backed off—except he promised to get her then."

"'Get' her? You mean bring her in?"

"He said he'd see to it that she came in feet first."

"I see. Where was the note mailed from? Do you have it?"

"I left it with Julie. That's my daughter. It wasn't mailed; someone slipped it under my door."

Sarah clasped her hands and rested her forehead on them. "So you wanted to get away and came out here looking for a job, is that the idea?"

"That's what I said," Graham agreed.

"But you need this guy off your case. And he has reason to think you'll lead him to Tori DaMantova. Now what about your daughter, Graham? Would he carry through on this threat to harm her?"

"I don't know what he'd do now. I guess I'm concerned."

"You should be very concerned. If this man is really as you describe, I don't think she's safe alone. I'd have her stay with someone until I can find out what your options are. Or, depending what your plans are, she could come here and stay with me. What do you think?"

"She has a job, remember. Let me call her tonight."

"Please do. Meantime, I'll see what contacts I can make about these two men."

"I appreciate it, Sarah. Oh, there's something I meant to ask you, while I'm here.It doesn't concern me, but I remember you used to work on domestic violence cases. Do you still do that?"

Sarah made a face. "Not to that extent any more; it's nasty and heartbreaking, but, yeah, I still do it. I can't walk away."

"There's supposed to be a women's shelter here, isn't there?"

Sarah cocked her head and raised an eyebrow. "Yes?"

"Someone back in Marquette asked me to look up this woman that she thought might work there." Graham made a show of searching through his billfold until he came up with his insurance agent's card and pretended to read from it, "Lesley Alvarado. Ever hear of her?"

"My God, Lesley Alvarado! You think she's *here?*"

Graham's insides did a barrel roll. "You *know* her?"

"Yeah, about fifteen years ago, when I was doing work with Navajo Legal Services. She set up a women's shelter over in Gallup in a vacant rooming house. At first, it was mostly Latinas like her, but I got involved when Navajo women started signing up. She needed backing, so I lined up some non-profit and tribal buy-in. Pretty soon she was offering shelter services and medical exams, steering people into rehab. She even arranged job training for the ladies at the community college, getting them on their feet—all low-key but getting it done."

Graham lost Sarah's words for a second as he suddenly saw why Tori wore the Pachuco cross: It had solidified her cover as Lesley Alvarado.

"You've got to know Gallup isn't exactly progressive, yet she managed to enlist the local constabulary too, as if she needed any protection. One time I saw her face down a guy—way bigger than her—trying to hassle one of her clients. Nothing she said; she just looked like such a bad idea that he actually tipped his hat and apologized. Tough as nails and smart as a whip Lesley was."

"Hm. She sounds like quite a person. What ever happened to her?"

Sarah shook her head. "Some of the city folks over there got the idea to make her Citizen of the Year and hold an award ceremony with her picture in the paper and all. They asked me to help since I worked with her. This was about ten years agto. Anyway, Lesley got word of it and came to me real distressed. 'I don't need recognition,' she said and wanted me to call it off. I said to sleep on it and we'd talk it over.

"When I drove by next morning, no Lesley. All her stuff was gone like she'd never been there. We reported her missing but never turned up a trace. Still, even if she was in some kind of trouble, you'd think she would have contacted me."

Graham shrugged helplessly.

"Who gave you the idea she might be *here?*" Sarah suddenly narrowed her eyes. "Didn't you say DaMantova ran the Marquette women's shelter?"

"Um, yes, that's exactly why I thought of this Alvarado person. I'll be honest; I thought she might know something. See, Linda… that is, Tori… used to talk about her." Graham stopped and scratched his head for a plausible angle. "You know, she… maybe even had a letter from her, now that I think of it."

"Is that so? From here?"

"Oh, I don't know; she never showed it to me. She only mentioned it the once."

Graham wished to hell Sarah would drop this. What a piece of luck! Who'd ever have thought that she would actually know Lesley Alvarado?

"Graham, you're such a bad liar."

"What are you talking about? I just happened to remember the name, so I thought maybe Tori would be in touch with her."

"Then you're not looking for work; you're looking for Tori DaMantova."

"No!"

Graham was thunderstruck. Using cross examination so subtle he hadn't seen it coming, Sarah had led him right to the wall. As he sweated bullets trying to look indignant, she gave him a cool once-over.

"I'll see what I can do about these characters. You should have stuck close to home; they might have lost interest if you had. But that's hindsight, isn't it?

"Tell you something else, Graham, which somehow never struck me until now: Lesley had been begging me to get a cousin onto the new Vietnam Memorial. After she disappeared, I finally carried through on the affidavits to get his name up. I felt like it was the least I could do. I remember thinking it didn't sound exactly Spanish. I'll check my records. Wouldn't it be interesting if it's something like... DaMantova? Wouldn't that be a coincidence?"

•

Graham wheeled up in front of Joe's cottage and turned the headlights out. He just sat for a few minutes, rubbing his forehead, before climbing out. Too many people were getting in on this thing. He walked up to the porch and sank onto the front steps, lost in worry. Somehow he had to let her know they had her name, whether they connected it with her yet or not.

Joe was watching a baseball game and popped the sound off with his remote when Graham came in.

"Hey, there you are. Somebody stuck this note under the door for you."

He handed Graham a folded, taped piece of paper.

Graham unfolded it. *"Who is Jen?"* was all it said.

"What've you got, an offer to work for Gordon Liddy?" Joe said.

"No. I asked some guy to give me this woman's phone number, that's all."

"Oh." Joe dialed the sound back on. "Get yourself something. The Angels are ahead."

"Thanks; I'm already floating."

He plopped onto the other chair and tried to watch the game, but his mind kept wandering. How could she not know who Jen was? Of course. They changed her name when she went to live with the father. First thing in the morning he would mail another note to her.

149

29

Madness.

He shouldn't still be in Flagstaff, but he could not leave Tori unaware that the feds might have drawn a bead on her—especially when he was the cause of it.

Note in hand, Graham had just backed into the last empty spot near the post office, half a block up the street. He was about to open the door when he froze. Coming out the main entrance with a long, white envelope in hand was Parrish, the agent who had questioned him in Marquette. Right beside him and trying to maintain her composure despite the grip he had on her arm was the black woman who had accosted him with her dog. Parrish must have caught her picking up Tori's mail.

Graham slid back into the car and ducked below the window.

Oh shit, what do I do?

Peeping over the dashboard, he saw Parrish hustle the woman over to his car, where he put her in back, then drove off with her. Graham did not see Meachum.

Still down, he consulted his watch. In two hours he was supposed to check in with Julie, but now he had to figure out another way to warn Tori. After a minute on the front seat thinking fast, Graham popped up. The coast was clear. He had to find a telephone.

Up the street, he located one in a hotel, looked up the number, and dialed it.

"Arizona Snowbowl."

"Is Kay working today?"

"Kay. The lift operator?"

"That's the one."

"I believe… Yes, she works Mondays."

"Oh, thank goodness! May I speak with her?"

"She's on the mountain. I could radio her a message, but it might be lunch before she'd reach a phone. Is there a number where she can reach you?"

"Actually, it's rather urgent."

"Let me get the mountain then, and we'll do it over the radio."

"Wait, I don't think that would work. Tell you what; I'll go see her myself."

"If you want, I can radio a message."

"No, it's okay. This is private."

•

Constantly watching the rear-view mirror for anyone following, Graham careened onto the seven-mile drive up the mountain. Soon he was climbing around one hairpin after another, madly rowing between second and third. By inches, he missed taking out a car coming down as he squalled through one turn half sideways, engine revved to the max; then it was gone from his rear view mirror before he even had time to feel lucky. The engine smelled like oven cleaner, and the red coolant light was glaring by the time he skidded to a stop in the top parking lot and puffed up to the lift with his lungs burning from the elevation. He found a lean, red-headed woman manning the controls.

"Kay, where's Kay?" he gasped.

"Left for town a little while ago with some plain clothes cop. I don't know what's up, but I hope it wasn't about her boyfriend again. Guy's a prick."

Graham smacked his fist into his palm. All over. They would sweat Tori's whereabouts out of Kay before noon. That was probably them he had just missed wiping out.

"What's the deal, Mister?"

"Aw, I just drove all the way up here to see her. Something I had to ask her."

"I might know. We work together every day."

Graham shook his head. "There was something she wanted me to find out for a friend of hers, woman named Lesley."

"Lesley? Why don't you go ask her yourself? I just talked to her. Kay said to be sure and let her know she had to go in with the cop. See, Lesley's been helping her out with some problems."

Bingo!

"Where? Where do I find her?"

"Whoa, easy! See the new lodge below the parking lot? Look in the cafeteria."

30

Graham sloughed around the turn-out and jerked to a stop at the big A-frame lodge the lift operator had indicated. Inside, a round, middle-aged Native American woman sat at a table examining a large ledger sheet and sipping a cup of coffee, while several people who looked like tourists were standing at the large window enjoying the view of a distant rainstorm building to the west.

"Lesley around?" he asked the Indian woman.

She pouted her lips toward the kitchen, and Graham hurried back to peer over the counter through the serving window. A man in a white smock was loading cases into a walk-in cooler, so he pushed through the door.

No one seemed to be in the kitchen besides himself and this short, white-coated man with a froth of black hair and Fu Manchu mustache.

"Where's Lesley?" Graham asked.

Surprised, the man put down the crate he was holding and said, "What?"

"Lesley? Where is she?"

"Aroun' somewhere. She was jus' on phone meenute ago. Go try rental shop."

No one in the rental shop had seen her either. For a good fifteen minutes Graham scoured the building from top to bottom and all around outside. No sign of Tori, so he returned to the Indian woman.

"Does Lesley have a car?" he asked her.

"She don't drive," the woman said shortly and returned to her work.

No car, but she must have received the message from the lift operator, so where would she go? Then Graham thought, perhaps when the woman at the lift talked to her, she might have said; so he returned to the top parking lot.

He looked out to the west. Great cloudships sailed over the sunny volcanic landforms under an impossibly blue sky. Miles to the west, a high, saddle-shaped ridge blurred into the far-off storm's gray curtain. Here the sun still bore down, but a billow of white was rising over the peak at his back. A muffled peal of thunder reached him. This could be the monsoon the lift attendant at the top had told him of the day before.

As Graham puffed up to the lift, the red-headed operator interrupted her anxious scan of the weather forming over the mountain.

"Oh, there you are! Did you find Lesley?"

"No. No one seems to know where she is."

"Because right after you left, one of the maintenance cats went up lift line after some workers. It looked like Lesley on the back, but I didn't see her when they came down, unless she was inside. Ask over at maintenance."

"Thanks. Thanks a bunch."

The maintenance shop was a cavernous corrugated building with two truck-sized doors, both open. Out in the equipment yard, four workers were scrambling to cast plastic tarps over the equipment and nail them down with cinder blocks. A man was welding a snow cat just inside the door where the light was good; in the back, a woman torquing down a large wheel in a vise looked entirely too substantial for Tori. The welder noticed Graham blocking his light and snapped off his torch. Raising his hood in the sudden hush, he asked, "Looking for something?"

"Yeah, Lesley. They told me she might be over here."

Before the welder could respond, the woman turned from the bench and said, "Not here; she works in the kitchen."

"I just came from there."

It was only a second, but Graham caught it as he turned his head to nod back at the new lodge: The welder's surprise at the woman's interruption and her quick shake of the head. He was not supposed to see it.

"Please, if you've seen her," Graham said, "there are some people who want to harm her. It could be a matter of life and death."

The welder looked back at the woman for guidance, and she shook her head.

"Seems to me there's a whole lot of you people chasing after her," she said. "If she isn't in the kitchen, that means she's off today. Try tomorrow."

So saying, the woman returned to her work at the bench. The man lowered his helmet and popped his torch back on. End of conversation.

Stonewalled, Graham grew desperate. She must have been over here, and they said other people were looking for her.

Outside, the sky was darkening overhead. A pair of nutcrackers turned against the gray ceiling in acrobatic darts, and sudden gusts bore smells of rain. As he walked back to the lift, a flash of lightning illuminated the overcast, trailed by a crack of thunder much closer than before. Where in hell was Tori? Unless they were hiding her in the shop, she must be up there on the mountain somewhere. The woman at the lift did not seem to be in on the conspiracy of silence. He would try her again.

"How far up was the work crew?" he said.

"Past midway. The second-to-last tower before the fan towers at the top."

"Would you call the top and see if Lesley's up there?"

She looked doubtful but rang it anyway.

"Mark. Have you seen Lesley?"

She nodded, listening.

"Got any more people coming down?"

She looked up the line and then said, "Okay, as soon as they arrive, we'll shut down until this blows over."

She turned back to Graham in wonderment. "She was just there. Mark asked her to send him up a sub for lunch, and she delivered it herself."

Graham clapped his hands. "Fantastic! Where is she now?"

"That's it; he doesn't know, but I bet she's in the patrol shack with this coming."

"Put me on the lift."

"No way. As soon as chair 97 arrives, we're shutting down. This puppy's coming over the mountain, and it's going to hit before you'd ever reach the top. You don't even have a poncho. Just buy a ticket and wait inside; we'll run you up when it passes."

"Could Mark look and see if she's in that patrol shack at least?"

"Not now; he can't leave the lift. After we shut down, I'll raise him on the two-way and get a read on how many people are stuck there. Don't worry."

Light rain started to fall. Up the lift line, tiny packets of loaded chairs descended. The woman cranked up to six hundred feet a minute and kept eyeing the sky. As each chair arrived, she would throttle back, instruct the people to run for cover in the office, then bump the speed back to maximum.

"Damn it, this one's building faster than we expected," she said.

Rain began to pelt harder, and a bolt of lightning dazzled racket down from the ridgeline. One more loaded chair glided in, almost to them now. The minute the occupants stepped off, the operator got on the phone and said curtly, "Shutting down. Everybody's off." Then she popped a fist-sized red button, and the lift ground to a halt.

"Let's get out of here, Mister. This one's too friggin' close."

She hightailed it for the observation room on the second floor of the lodge, not waiting to see if Graham was with her or not.

A crack of thunder split the air when he was halfway to the lodge, and rain began descending in buckets. Graham was drenched before he even reached the door. Inside, he pressed water from his hair and wrung out his jacket. The lift operator was sitting at a table fiddling with her two-way radio.

"Mark, calling Mark. Mark, can you read me? This is Olivia. Over."

Finally the two-way crackled to life.

"Yeah, Olivia. This is Mark." Crackling ensued as they took another lightning strike. "...coming like gangbusters. You ought to see it up here. Over."

"Mark, where are you? Check the patrol room. Over."

"That's where I am. Over."

"How many people up there? Over."

They waited. Finally Mark came back on. "Nine. Three walking. They should be down by now. Over."

Graham plucked at Olivia's sleeve. "Ask him about Lesley."

"Mark. Is Lesley there? Over."

"Negative. Over."

Olivia peered out at the violent thunderstorm with a look of concern.

"Maybe she's coming down with those people," Graham said.

Olivia squeezed the two-way immediately. "Mark. Was Lesley with the people walking? Over."

"Can't tell. Maybe." The two-way gave a long rasp. "Ouch! Just took one right on the lift. You should see it up here. We're getting hailed on big time. Those people show up? Over."

"Negative. Let you know. Over and by."

"Over and by."

Graham rubbed his hands nervously and watched the storm, which seemed, if anything, to be intensifying.

"Did you see the man who came up for Kay?" he asked Olivia.

"He was outside when she asked me to cover for her."

"Was he wearing reflector shades? Can you remember? This is important."

"I think, but I wouldn't swear to it. Like I said, he was outside. I never really got a good look."

"How about what he was wearing or anything? Like his jacket."

Olivia screwed her face up, trying to recall.

"I can't remember. Red maybe?"

"Do you have a phone here?"

"To call out? You have to go to the new lodge where you just were. They have one."

"Do you have a poncho I can use?"

"You're not going out in this!"

"I have to. What's Kay's last name?"

"Eckert."

Once he ventured out, even with the poncho, Graham knew he'd made a mistake. The downpour came on unabated, and the road was awash under an inch of muddy runoff from the mountain. Thunder surrounded him with deafening reports of heavy ordnance; yet a few miles to the west the sun was shining. By the time he ran the fifty yards to his car, his pants and shoes were totally soaked. He had to crawl along the road because his wipers could not keep up and almost missed the turn-off for the lodge in the deluge.

As a starting point, Graham raised the police to see if a Kay Eckert had come in for any reason. When Graham mentioned he was concerned because she had not shown up for a family get-together this morning, the dispatcher said she would check. While she was gone, Graham took off his shoes and poured them out. The line kept crackling with the electrical storm, and he prayed it would not become a lightning rod.

The woman came back on the line. "Sir, we have nothing on her. I also checked the hospital. Do you wish to file a report?"

"Not yet. If anything does come in on her, call this number."

Just as he feared. After giving Sarah Fitch's office phone, Graham went into the men's room to twist his pants at least halfway dry, and decided he might just as well wait out the storm here so he could warm up a little. He tugged his pants back on damp and flapped out to ask the Indian woman if anyone could radio over and find out from Olivia whether the people walking down had shown up yet.

The woman frowned and looked up from the figures she was penciling in.

"If they don't know no better than to hike down in a storm, looks like your friends gonna learn the hard way."

"My friends? I don't even know them. It's Lesley I'm worried about; she might have been helping them down."

"Oh. Let's ask CJ then. He's got a radio. Up this way."

She took him to a mezzanine floor over the cafeteria and indicated an office with "Mountain Manager" printed above the door.

"Ask him," she said.

When Graham explained that he was looking for Lesley and had reason to think she was accompanying some hikers down in the storm, the manager did not hesitate. He slipped a two-way from the charger on his windowsill and snapped it on.

"Olivia. Got your ears on? CJ here. Over."

"Go ahead, CJ. This is Olivia. Over."

"Did the hikers make it down yet? Over."

"Yeah. Just got here, scared and wet, but they're okay. Over."

A new voice crackled on. "Mark here. Got an inch of hail already. Awesome. Over."

"What about Lesley?" Graham said.

"Olivia, was Lesley with them? Over."

"Negative. Over."

"Keep an eye out. Guy here looking for her. CJ over and out."

"I know. Olivia over and by."

CJ made a what-can-you-do shrug and stuck his radio back into its charger.

"Don't worry; she's sitting it out somewhere. Lesley knows the mountain."

"Well thanks."

The Indian woman stepped from an office by the stairs when Graham came out.

"She's not with them people."

Graham nodded and started to move on, but the woman stopped him with a lethal-looking, segmented stainless steel rod. When she thrust it practically in his face, he recognized it as a series of ledger posts screwed together.

"Hang on," she said in a low voice, "I like to know what business you got with Lesley. Seems to me there's a whole lot of interest out of nowhere."

"News to me. I need to see her about something personal, that's all. I'm a friend."

"Yeah?" She lowered her voice still further. "I don't know what's going on here, mister, but I'll tell you this much." She took a quick look to make sure they were alone. "You better be a friend. 'Cause if anything happens, it only takes one time forget to watch behind you. You read me?"

Graham glanced away from the woman's stony gaze to size up her squat, powerful form in the poorly-lit corridor. She looked eminently capable.

"Loud and clear."

"Just watch your step, 'cause me and Lesley go way back."

The Indian woman retracted the rod then and let him pass. When he was halfway down, she said once more from the top of the stairs, "Remember."

Graham blew a long, silent whistle through his teeth as he retrieved his drying shoes from a chair.

Brr. Nice friends.

His socks still squished, but at least the shoes weren't holding visible water, so he laced them up and went over to the window. Outside, the storm raged tree-bending gusts of torrential rain against the glass. Graham stuck his hands in his pockets and shook his head. He couldn't even see his car. What if Tori tried to run and got caught in the open?

31

After the initial fireworks of the storm front's passage overhead, another two hours passed before the deluge let up. Even as blue sky and sunlight skimmed the distant cinder cones out the big west-facing window, the mountain remained swathed in gloomy aftermath as the storm tail-ended into light sprinkle.

Outside, water dripped softly from the spruce, and a balm of washed mountain air suffused the slopes. Wet evergreen tingled with the astringency of a sneeze, and the temperature had plummeted fifteen or twenty degrees. Far to the north, the departing storm sent back faint rumbles of thunder as it rolled out toward the canyon.

Leaving his car parked among the trees beside the new lodge, Graham slogged up to the lift. Ski runs cut through the forest afforded views up to the mist shrouding the summit. Trees at the cloud line rose in stark, wintry splendor, where hail at the higher elevations had turned the mountain white.

Olivia was bundled in a down jacket by the lift controls in an earnest conversation on the telephone when Graham stepped onto the ramp. Nothing was moving.

"What about the safety gate? Check that," she said, then tried the controls again. No soap. "Nope. Ray's on his way. He thinks it's the derail on tower 22."

She noticed Graham and said, "Took some damage in the electrics, I think. Maintenance is going to check it out for us, so we can get those people down."

"How long do you think it will be?" Graham checked his watch; already two.

Even as she shrugged her uncertainty, a diesel cat rolled out of the maintenance shop and began clanking up the mountain.

"They did some line checks and think it's one of the relay boxes where they were working. We'll have to wait until they give us the go-ahead. May as well sit inside."

After an hour of waiting, Graham closed his eyes for a while. When he opened them, the lift was just creeping, so he scooted back out to see how things were looking. Olivia had lined up about a dozen propane bottles along the loading ramp and strung a yellow tape across the steps. Graham halted at the bottom to ask about the outlook.

"Not good," Olivia said. "There's damage in the main, so we fired up the auxiliary. Mark's going to start loading people down as soon as we run our checks."

"What are all the gas bottles for?"

"Top always needs gas, and they'll balance the people coming down so we don't overspeed."

Graham looked up the line. It felt cold enough to ski, but when he turned around, his blood froze, too. Through Olivia's legs, he could just see a familiar head bobbing toward the maintenance building: Dave Meachum, wearing his shades even in the clammy overcast. *Christ, where did he come from?* Graham dropped to all fours and uttered an involuntary, "Jesus!" His only hope was that Meachum had not noticed by the new lodge where Graham had left his car. Meachum might not even be aware he was here.

"What's the matter with you, Mister?"

"That guy! He's after Lesley. Give me some blankets I can cover myself with. I'll jump on the chair while those people are coming down."

She gave a look of disbelief and shook her head. "What are you talking about? We're closed. As soon as I get them down, I'm turning it off. What's the deal?"

"He's going to kill her. You've got to send me up. She's up there, I know it."

"You kidding me? Then what? How do you propose to get back?"

"I'll walk; anyway, I'm not coming back while he's here. Look, you have to run the lift long enough to get them down anyway, and that's long enough to take me up. It'll help your weight going up, too. Hurry, there's no time. He mustn't see me."

Making up her mind, Olivia reached into her pocket and withdrew a ring of keys. Twisting one of them loose, she handed it to him. "Here's the key to the patrol room, in case it gets dark. It's under the lift building; you'll see it. You know how to light a gas heater?"

"I think."

"There are matches and blankets up there. Lesley'll know, if you find her."

The telephone beeped once, and she picked up.

"That's Mark; he put the first ones on. Here, wrap these blankets around yourself. Lie on the chair, and keep your feet up, and I'll start loading bottles behind you. Stay wrapped, because it'll be a half hour to forty minutes on the auxiliary. And try to look like a gas bottle. I'll tell Mark you're coming. Get your feet up!" she said as the chair slowly lifted him away. "He just walked out."

With the lift crawling along at less than half speed, his departure from the ramp seemed interminable. He peeked from under the blankets; a scant hundred meters separated him from Olivia. Meachum was close enough to hit with a rock, walking from the maintenance building in the direction of the old lodge. Graham figured he was still no more than ten meters off the ground when Meachum looked his way. Seeming to notice something, he made for Olivia, and Graham turned to stone.

Meachum crossed behind the lift and beyond Graham's field of vision, but he could see Olivia shake her head as she plunked another bottle onto a passing chair and then pointed to the yellow ribbon. She put her hands on her hips as if listening to a child before reaching down for the next gas bottle. At first she simply raised it and stood swinging it back and forth by her knees; then, saying something heatedly, looked as if she was going to heave it. Finally she set it on the next chair and made a "get outa here" motion as she went for another bottle. Graham loved her. The girl was a brick.

Not until the second tower passed did Graham feel safe enough to take a look around. The open area under the lift crisscrossed with ground squirrels and chipmunks. A deer mouse poked along the edge of the forest. Just before the midway ramp, four deer climbed slowly through an aspen grove on his right. Plants below glistened with jewels of refracting water droplets, trembling in the subdued light, and the bitter smell of wet broadleaf cut through the pine. Birdcalls carried through the trees from far away in the dampness.

There was no sign of life, no footprints, nothing to indicate anyone had visited the midway ramp as he passed over. Cramped from lying on his side so long, Graham finally felt safe to swing his legs down and sit up as he approached the tree line. Hail covered the ground and decked the branches on either side. The Parry primrose was battered to scarlet wreckage. As he rose into the mist, the faint mountains along the horizon behind and the long wandering crack marking the Grand Canyon greyed out and vanished.

Mark was waiting on the top ramp with a backpack slung over his shoulder and a two-way radio in hand when Graham arrived.

"Sure you'll be okay up here?" he said. "You can ride back with me if you want. Just make up your mind, because I'm jumping on as soon as I unload these bottles."

"I'll be fine. Can I ask you a few things about Lesley?"

"Sure." He set down his pack and radio. "What do you want to know?"

"What time was she up here?"

"Before lunch, a little before the storm hit, maybe 11:30. I thought she walked up at first, because she had a backpack, but I guess she caught a ride with Ray. Still, it seemed funny, because she usually just gives it to the bottom when we ask for something, and they send it up on a chair. You know what I mean?"

While he talked, Mark kept moving and stacking propane bottles along the ramp as they arrived.

"Did she seem nervous to you?"

"Now that you mention it. Like really nervous. Kept watching down the lift the whole time we were talking and then said she had to go. When I asked where, she told me she was just going to hang out for a while. I thought that was a little weird."

"Didn't she see the storm?"

"I told her to keep an eye on it."

"Which way do you think she went?"

"She was sitting right there on the rail, and then I got busy watching the weather and rounding people up. She must have left when I wasn't looking. I kind of eyeballed around while I was loading people but never saw her, so I fig-

160

ure she must have walked down. The thing is, if she'd gone up there…" Mark indicated the ridgeline leading to the summit. "I would have spotted her moving through the rocks. Anyway, she wouldn't go climbing with a storm coming."

"You sure?"

"She knows. At least she ought to."

"Would she be easy to spot? What was she wearing?"

"Jeans and a flannel shirt. Green vest. She'd be hard to see if she was sitting. She wasn't really dressed for the cold; that's why I think she went down."

"What color was the backpack?"

"Just army green."

"Did any of the people getting on see her?"

"It wasn't until I'd already sent everyone that Olivia called to ask, so I don't know." He shouldered up his backpack and hefted the two-way. "That's about all the help I can give you. If she doesn't show up by morning, we'll call search and rescue. Do you want me to leave the two-way in case you find her?"

Graham hesitated and then realized that, even if he did locate her, he couldn't broadcast her whereabouts.

"No, I won't need it."

"Okay. Good luck, Mister."

Mark swung into one of the chairs as it crept over the down ramp and said into his two-way, "I'm on chair 57. Over." Then he waved and faced forward.

Graham watched until Mark dissolved into the sun-dazzled cloud and gave it another ten minutes for good measure before he started calling.

"LINDAAA …TOOOREEE! …LESLEEE!"

He paused and listened. The humidity should carry sound quite far, but there was no answer. He tried punctuating her names with long, shrill whistles, until he had covered the compass. Other than a single echo that almost fooled him coming back from the north, no sound returned. Graham knew if he were to stray up the ridge into those vast, shrouded boulder fields looking for her, he would lose himself; so he climbed only until the lift started to fade before giving voice again.

Unanswered, Graham zigzagged back down to the lift and regrouped. Say he were on the run, what would he do? He couldn't get off the mountain the way he'd come, that's for sure. They'd be looking there. Once the storm passed, he'd go on over the mountain. So she must be holed up somewhere, but where? With people in the patrol room, she couldn't have hidden there, could she?

Graham skidded down the slope beside the lift and let himself into the patrol room underneath. With the last afternoon light making it hard to see inside, he decided he had better locate anything he needed for tonight. Two books of matches sat behind the door on a shelf near the small heater, and blankets filled a footlocker along the wall. A couple of wooden bunks against the back made do for an infirmary. The heater required holding a button while lighting the pilot until it heated a thermocouple enough to let the main jet stay open. Cursing, Graham wasted about half a book of matches before the burner stayed lit.

With probably an hour of daylight left, Graham had the sinking feeling he would not find Tori. The lift operator's station was about the size of a big closet; Mark would hardly have missed her there. The patrol room afforded no place to hide; and even if she were up there in the boulders somewhere, his chance of coming across her in this soup was zip. What did that leave?

Outside the door, the lift ramp stood on pilings with chicken wire enclosing the space underneath. Graham peered under. The space contained a jumble of tower pads, extra chairs, stacks of overturned ski patrol toboggans, cable pulleys, fiberglass cordage, and coiled lengths of cable—all blown over with hail. Graham exhaled a cloud of breath at all the iced-over junk shoved under the ramp and noticed an anomaly. Only the patrol toboggans were piled neatly, making two stacks—except one was short a toboggan. It caught his attention because someone had otherwise taken such pains. Working his way farther around the enclosure, he finally located the missing toboggan. Overturned like the others, it lay under the center of the ramp, almost surrounded by piled parts.

"Tori!" he said through the chicken wire. Silence. Seeking a way in, he scrambled on all fours along the steep cinder slope around the enclosure. Finally, after making a complete circuit to the severe detriment of his hands and knees, he found it: A framed-in panel with an unlocked hasp right beside the patrol room that lifted out to give access. Graham removed the panel, and crawled under.

He worked his way through all the equipment over to the lone toboggan and flipped it up. A cocoon of blankets lay under it, surrounded by melting hailstones. Graham turned it over, and the blankets parted from Tori's face.

32

Tori worked an arm free from the damp blankets, flailing to push herself as Graham tugged her through the equipment to the open panel. Outside, he tried to stand with her but toppled back onto the steep slope.

She mumbled and shook her head when they landed back on the cinders. Graham sat back and pulled her against his chest so he could scoot them until he gained his feet. Something she had under the blanket weighed a ton, and the altitude had his heart pounding. He got her arm around his shoulder and struggled to his feet. *Thump.* A backpack dropped from the blanket, and he caught it with a foot to stop it against the enclosure before it rolled away. That's what was so heavy.

Lightheaded from the lack of oxygen, he staggered toward the patrol room while Tori's legs kept giving way, threatening to bring them down again. In the waning, cloud-filtered light, her lips looked blue. She breathed something unintelligible in his ear as he reached the patrol room door and shouldered it open. The heater, having run at most ten minutes, had done no real damage to the cold; but he had to remove her wet packaging, regardless.

Unwrapping her, Graham found her clothing soaked. Gone was the Mickey Mouse watch, and her hair was gray. He knelt for a closer look. She was wearing turquoise earrings delicately carved into birds in flight—so unlike the plain studs she used to wear as Linda.

Graham quickly drew three or four blankets from the footlocker to spread over a bunk. Stepping to where she lay on the floor, he began stripping off her wet clothes and hanging them by the heater. By the time he lifted her to the bunk and bundled her up, her lips were faintly moving but producing no sound. She was going out like a light. Gritting his teeth against the still-cold room, frantic now, Graham tore his own clothes off and slipped into the covers to warm Tori with his own skin before she went into shock.

For what seemed a half hour, he chafed her hands and face while she trembled in gusts before falling still, her breaths finally strong and even. The sky was turning dark before she felt truly warm against him.

•

Graham opened his eyes and shook his head to complete darkness. His watch read almost two o'clock! He'd been sleeping four or five hours. Despite the wind sifting through the windows, Graham eased out of the blankets to find his clothes before freaking Tori out with the monster erection he was sporting. He stepped into his shoes and then blundered over hers finding the door. He really,

really had to go. Outside, he noticed her backpack still leaned against the enclosure, so he hefted it back inside with him when he finished.

He set her pack on the floor and knelt to unzip it. She had everything stuffed
into plastic bags, which he rummaged through until a flashlight came to hand.
He played the beam over a ton of canned goods that she must have grabbed from
the lodge's kitchen shelves. Food! But no can opener. Poking around some more,
he turned up a gallon canteen of water, a folding Sterno stove, and a change of
clothes crammed into a bottom compartment.

A Swiss Army knife in her jeans revealed she was not totally vacant. Setting
up the Sterno on a shelf by the window, Graham ratcheted the knife's opener
around a can of corn, ripped off the label, and set it on the stove to boil. Once
it did, he would set it aside and heat up a can of spaghetti he had found. He
needed to get warm calories into her, and he could stand a few himself. While
Graham waited for the corn, he popped open a tin of cocoa but could not find a
cup or plate. All she had was a spoon.

After setting the spaghetti on, he went through the rest of her pockets. Besides
her knife, there were a set of keys, a pair of bifocals, glacier glasses and a billfold
in her vest with a sheaf of bills and an employee card. He found neither photos,
nor credit cards, nor driver's license. The flashlight showed a sixtyish, bespectacled Lesley Alvarado on the employee card. He rolled the wad of bills and
tucked them back into the vest pocket while he studied her picture.

As the smell of spaghetti sauce began to fill the room, a sneeze erupted from
the bunk. He pocketed the wallet and held his breath. Dead silence followed. He
could not even hear her breathe. Carefully, he set the backpack down.

"Tori?" he said, "Are you all right?"

"Oh god, it is you," she said. "I thought I dreamed it."

"Yes, it's me. We're alone."

"Where are we?"

"The patrol room at the top. Here, eat something."

"Not until I pee; I'm about to burst! Where are my clothes?"

"They're wet. Let me—"

"Never mind; can't wait." She swashed a trail of blankets to the door.

"You can't go out barefoot. The ground's ice cold."

"It's a flood if I don't."

Wind whisked in as she ripped the door open and squatted outside, holding
the blankets up out of the cascade. After a good minute, she hotfooted back in as
if she were walking on thumbtacks.

"Ow, ow! My toes and fingers. Oo, they hurt! Listen, I don't know how you
got me in here, but you're lucky you didn't squeeze me the wrong way."

She stepped over to the bunk and re-wrapped herself in the blankets.

"Look in my jacket. See if there's a pair of glasses."

He handed them to her, and she fitted them on.

"Now I'll take some of that spaghetti."

"Here." He passed her the warm can of spaghetti in the dark. "Got it? There's a spoon, too."

Rhythmic scraping ensued, as she got right to business.

"You must have been lying out there all day."

"S'pose so," she said around a mouthful of spaghetti.

"You came that close to freezing, you know."

"You don't need to tell me."

The spoon clanked more deliberately. "Any more?"

"Yeah, I heated corn, too. You ate the whole thing?"

"Try starving all day." She began on the corn.

Graham knew he'd better fish his own dinner out while there was any left.

"Didn't you hear me calling you?" he asked over his shoulder as he played her flashlight over the labels.

"Not sure. Maybe."

Graham frowned at her response and selected a can of vegetable beef soup. Not his favorite, but she had not left him much to choose from.

"Okay, what do you answer to?"

"You may as well call me Tori. You know who I am."

"Well your pack must weigh fifty pounds, Tori. How'd you plan to lug it?"

"Actually, I never stopped to ponder that. I didn't have time to weigh it. I just grabbed and ran."

"But up here? Where did you think you were going to go?"

"Over the mountain and drop into the crater. From there it's a five-mile hike to the highway. I would have made it, too, if the storm hadn't come."

"So instead, you hid under the ramp, right out in the weather."

He seated himself on the end of her bunk.

"I didn't want to get hit."

"You could have come inside."

"Oh right. I didn't know who there'd be and wasn't about to stick my head out to look. All I could do was grit my teeth. After a while I went goofy. The cold, I guess. I think I halfway heard you calling me; except by that time I was slipping in and out, talking to myself. Like, 'Don't breathe a sound, or he'll show them where you are.' Damn it, why did you come after me? What do you want?"

"Tori. God knows, I didn't mean for them to follow me."

"I almost made it. You should have known."

The vegetable beef was warm, and Graham offered her dibs if she wanted it.

"Have yourself something. Here, take the spoon; I licked it clean. Just hand me the canteen, if you would."

As he traded canteen for spoon, Graham let his hand close around hers. She paused just a beat before withdrawing for a long pull from the canteen. The wind keened at the corners of the building, but a glimpse of stars outside showed the sky clearing. Tori expelled a sigh and nudged him with the canteen.

"Here. I don't know how long I've got. I was sure they'd have a helicopter by now."

"I'm not sure they know you're here."

"Ha! They're all over the place. They know."

"Not unless someone tells them. Like the lift girl."

"God, poor Kay; she's already gone through so much. Now this. When she tipped me off over the intercom, she was coming to pieces."

"I'm afraid our friend Meachum was the one who picked her up, too."

Tori's nails clamped his wrist.

"Or spooks."

"What are you talking, spooks?"

"You don't want to know."

"Well anyway, they don't know for sure you're on the mountain, believe me. No one even saw me."

"What are they doing up here then, sightseeing? It's a matter of time, Graham. They'll get it out of her one way or another."

"That's why we've got to get you down somehow."

"Screw it. They've got me this time. End of the line."

"Tori, listen…"

"No, you listen. You don't know. What kind of life is this? It's wearing me out."

"You do look as if you've put on twenty years, Tori."

Unexpectedly, this drew a laugh.

"Cosmetics, you fool."

"Whatever. You didn't wear glasses before."

"I wore contacts."

"Why did you risk coming back here to the Southwest, of all places?"

"Excuse me, where do you get this 'back here' stuff?"

"This is Lesley's second time around."

Tori edged herself toward him and tilted her head in the dark.

"How do you know that?"

"You'd be surprised what I know. I just don't see why you took such a chance."

"No choice. Linda Chapman was *finita*. I lost my contact for ID years ago. I just hoped enough time had passed. How did you figure it out? I covered every track."

"Almost."

"So how then?" The faint window light reflected from her glasses. All at once she put her hand to her mouth. "Wait, I get it; this Jen person! Is she the one?"

Graham studied her shadowed face and decided not to offer Jen yet. Not until she leveled with him about what she had done. This had to be a *quid pro quo*.

166

"I'll explain who she is, but you have to stop hiding from me. For starters, I want to know exactly what happened."

"I only know what Kay told me, and she wasn't making a whole lot of sense."

"The bombing."

"No. That one you can just forget. I won't talk about it."

"Yes you will. You have to. I need to know exactly what took place, and why. You were going to tell me."

She sat, finally letting a long breath into one fist before pressing both of them to her eyes.

"My miserable life! You have no idea. I can't drive; I can't open a bank account. I might as well be a cockroach."

"Tori, I have to know. It could make all the difference. I think I can help you."

"You can't. If you think I didn't have a hand in the explosive or the detonator, I'm sorry to spoil your fantasy."

"Tell me the facts then, straight."

"My brother? That was true. Not the part about the Memorial. That I couldn't do for him, but someone did get his name up there finally, somehow."

"I've got all night, love."

"Please don't call me that."

"Tori, let me in." He had to get her talking. This might be the only chance she would have, because her time probably was running out.

"You want me to say I didn't set it off. Well I didn't."

"All I want is the truth."

"You read the papers. They reported it as a war protest: One dead brother, one dead building."

All at once a heavy clank sounded outside, followed by a rumble and scrape.

"Oh God!" Tori whispered.

Graham got to his feet, listening. Only the wind wailed. Feeling for the flashlight, he stole toward the door.

"Where are you going?" she said as he eased the door open. "Don't leave me!"

"Gonna look. Sit tight."

Graham flattened himself against the building and peered around. The rising moon shadowed the bleak cinder slope surrounding the upper lift. Below him, treetops riffled in the wind. Graham sidled along the wall to the opening under the ramp. He swept the flashlight beam underneath and saw nothing different from when he dragged Tori out. The wind's rush covered the crunch of his feet as he edged back the other way. At the base of the ramp a gas cylinder was lying over in the cinders. The wind must have toppled it and rolled it down the ramp. Graham scouted around until he was satisfied they were still alone, then returned to the patrol room.

Tori was no longer on the bed. In fact, she was nowhere.

"Tori?"

He trained the flashlight beam around the room and spied a mound of blankets on the floor. Stepping over to the foot locker, he raised the lid and put his hand on the rounded blanket inside. There was a backbone under it.

"Hey, relax." He raised her from the fetal tuck she had packed herself into. "It was a gas bottle. The wind rolled it down the ramp. Why didn't you answer?"

"They could have been making you say it."

"Tori, you're shaking."

"I'm scared. I don't know where they'll put me, but it'll be the end."

Graham wrapped another blanket around her and held her tightly, trying to calm her down.

"I'm not brave about this. What if it's a death sentence?"

She crumbled and covered her head with the blanket, wailing, all her bravado gone. Graham guided her to the bunk and rocked her in his arms.

Inside the blanket her sobbing had subsided into sniffles when, totally out of the blue, she said, "I can't carry this any more, Graham. I have to tell you; you're all I have. Do you remember what we called mutual deterrence?

"Where neither side could start anything because both had nuclear weapons?"

"But not until we developed long-range ballistic missiles," she said.

"Come out of there; I can't hear you."

She tossed her head free.

"I said, it was missiles that let either side retaliate. With them, it didn't matter any more who struck first. You can't take out missiles the way you take out airfields. The funny part was it actually worked. Mutual deterrence created this kind of mad stability, like knives at each other's throats. All we could do was sit tight and keep our fingers crossed."

"I don't get you. What's this got to do with anything?"

"People like me made that insanity possible."

Graham wagged his head. Was she losing it?

"Perhaps. In a manner of speaking, but—"

"No, listen: When I worked at Lawrence Livermore, I designed the electronic guidance systems that made mutual deterrence work. I really thought the capacity to deliver automatic annihilation would hold off World War III. Given that both sides had the technology, you see, stalemate seemed the best we could hope for."

"I don't know; that sounds a bit like rationalizing after the fact to me."

"Of course it was rationalizing. That's all we ever did. It was crazy. No one ever thought to cut the knot and suggest mutual renunciation. In fact, we went the other direction. At the time they transferred me to Mound Laboratories, I was dreaming up a revolutionary system to use as a protective shield, much more sophisticated and a completely new approach. This was late 1968. I won't give the details, because it's best no one knows; but it would have given us a reliable way to stop all missiles. On the face of it, it sounded great. I should have canned the whole idea."

"I still don't—"

"Just listen. Once it filtered up to the Pentagon what I was working on, they called me in to assign my team top priority. Within six months, America's big missile buildup started. I had to wonder what was going on; we already had plenty for the job, so I started asking and had enough clearance to find out: The Pentagon was planning to retrofit my system onto all their new missiles and then go for a first strike. The strategic consequences were alarming, but all the brass saw was an edge. The technology was there, so do it.

"I kept thinking, 'Stay cool. They've taken that into account. Finish the project.' The day after Christmas, 1969, I got news of my brother's disappearance; the next month—Enzo would have been rotated home—a man from his unit came to see me because he thought I should know what had really happened. That was when I finally understood. No one was in control. There were no rules. I couldn't even go in to work. I kept asking myself, 'What are you doing? Open your eyes!'"

Tori stopped. "You don't understand."

Graham, too slack-jawed to speak at her stunning revelation, finally managed to say, "Not really. Was this something like Star Wars?"

"Star Wars! No, that goes at it backwards. I destroyed the concept that would have made a real shield." She wound a coil of hair around and around her finger before deciding, "Okay, I guess I need to explain. Imagine the earth as as giant— Wait; do you understand anything about E8 mathematics?"

"E what? Eight?"

"Never mind. You wouldn't be safe if anyone got an inkling you know any of this."

"You think I'm safe now? Spill."

"Okay. I can't go into the physics of it with you, but the plan was to deliver a first strike on one of the major cities like Moscow, to draw an all-or-nothing retaliation. Only we'd have a massive follow-on already in the air. That was the reason for all the extra ICBMs. The follow-on would target their rising missiles and… This part I can't tell you. Just know it costs millions of lives, but that's not our problem, is it? We made the world safe for democracy. And my design would be responsible. How would you like that on your shoulders?"

Graham was too awed to reply. The woman had been working as a hairdresser.

"Push that button and stability would become a thing of the past. Either we'd use it at once, or the Soviets would develop it and use it on us. Where was the advantage in holding off? Conscience alone would stop anyone, and I saw precious little of that around.

"We were testing the components in Building T at Mound Laboratories. I imagine you've read enough to know about Building T. Nowadays we'd keep a design like that encrypted and distributed over a secure computer network, but in those days we kept hard copy in highly classified sites while we perfected the technology.

"Once I faced what I was creating, I knew I had to deep six it—the whole concept—before it went any further."

"So that's why the bomb."

"Not at first. What happened to my brother finally opened my eyes. That's what it takes: a single life. Suffering humanity won't register. You know how that feels. You want to hear the really funny part? I hadn't even opposed the war; he had but went anyway because he thought he could help. So it fell to me to lay him to rest, like Antigone. I thought I could destroy all the plans and drop off the face of the earth."

She tipped up the canteen to swirl a quick mouthful around. Graham shifted uneasily on the opposite end of the bunk, trying to fit his mind around this thing she was relating. Tori patted the blankets around herself and tucked her feet against him as if she were telling campfire stories.

"All it took was a bomb big enough to wipe out all the work and pieces of my clothing as if I had died in the explosion."

"Christ, Tori, why didn't you just steal the plans and run?"

"Because they would hunt me down; I was the only one who knew how to make it work. This way they wouldn't even look. I'd be dead, blown up."

Tori stretched nervously. The telling seemed to have overcome her sense of their predicament.

"You think it didn't scare hell out of me? You'd better believe it did. I'd never even got a speeding ticket."

She paused for effect, hugging herself.

"I won't pretend I worked alone, and that's the bad part: I was so naive I left myself open to being used. Somewhere along the line, a collaborator arranged for Arthur Montgomery to be in the building, and he died in the explosion. Nothing like that should have happened. You of all people should know what that did to me. Here was a conviction strong enough to make me risk what I did—and I let myself be maneuvered into someone else's agenda. Now that man's life overshadows everything and everyone I meant to save. I'll tell you the truth; I considered killing myself, but then who would repay the hurt? You see where playing God gets you?"

At this, Graham laid one of his trump cards on the table.

"So you thought to make it up to his family by supporting them."

"My god, you have done your homework."

Tori sank back onto the bunk, rubbing her feet.

"But no, not really. I couldn't care for my own children. Maybe I hoped looking out for hers would square things somehow."

"Just putting cash into an envelope, didn't you wonder if it even reached them?"

"Oh sure, always; but it was all I could do. Some months I was too strapped, but usually I made it a rule of thumb to mail a quarter of my income. Always cash; anything else they could trace."

"A fourth."

"I don't exactly live it up."

"Mrs. Montgomery thinks Meachum has been paying her."

"All the better. They don't trace it to me."

"So tell me, how do you make the money arrive from different places?"

"You'd love to know, wouldn't you? When I was waitressing along 66, I'd give the envelopes to truckers and tell them my sister collected postmarks. Depending which way they were going, I'd give some town in the middle of the Panhandle or out beyond West Podunk where they should drop it off. That's one way. I'll be honest; it felt like throwing bottles at the ocean. I'm glad she got them."

Tori had distanced herself enough after the outburst of tears to relate this as if she were telling about someone else. Graham remained unsatisfied about what he was not hearing, like where Meachum fit into this.

"Tori, I understand your reluctance to rat on people who helped you."

"I'm protecting *you*. It's too dangerous for you to know."

Another noise silenced them. It resolved itself into skittering from the corner of the room. The flashlight startled a white-footed mouse with a piece of blanket. Graham's anxiety finally got the best of him.

"All right," Graham said, "What's the plan?"

"There is no plan. Save your own skin, Graham. Clear out before they find you with me. There'll be enough moonlight for you to make it down the Lower Bowl before morning."

"You mean just up and leave you on your own?"

"Don't be an idiot. You have a daughter to think of if you won't consider yourself. Just go. Whatever happens to me happens. It's not your affair."

"I can't walk away from you, Tori, not if it means losing you again."

She stared up at the dark ceiling and rolled her head back and forth against the wall. Graham reached out until his fingertips grazed her cheek. It was wet, and she turned her face away from his touch.

"Tori?"

"Don't."

"Tori, you're not protecting anyone by concealing who worked with you. I know Meachum was your collaborator. Somehow Arthur Montgomery was in on it, too."

Tori remained stubbornly silent.

"Look, if Meachum has any idea what I know, he's already figured out I'm as dangerous as you are. How did you discover he double-crossed you?"

171

She shook her head, and Graham had to play his last card.

"You force me to suppose. It must have something to do with a large tube of drawings and a note that fell out and slipped under the bed in a motel. A little girl crawled under and got it. What did the note tell you?"

Tori gasped. "How do you know that?"

Then it clicked.

"My daughter!"

Half the blankets fell from her as she gripped his arms. *"How?* How did you find her? *Where?* No, don't tell me. Did you see both of them?"

"Hey, hey, it's all right. Yes I did, and your parents, too."

Tori relaxed her hold and heaved a ragged breath. "Thank God! Every time I'm near a big library, I sneak a look in the Palo Alto directory, just to check. I wonder what they must think…" She stopped herself. "Does this connect somehow to the Jen you mentioned? Did she locate them?"

"Jen is your daughter. Your son goes by Rob and lives with Rico and Chiara since his father died."

"John Park died?"

"They suspect radiation poisoning."

"I shouldn't ask," Tori said. "Are they, you know, all right?"

"Jen is a ER doctor at San Francisco General. I'm not sure if she's married, whether you're a grandmother or not. Rob studies bio-tech at Stanford. They have their mother's brains."

She made a choked sound. "God, this changes everything. They have to know."

"Who, your family?"

"My family, my children. I'm not a murderer. You have to tell them."

"Tori, you gave Jen some papers when you put her on the plane to John Park. What were they? She couldn't read yet."

Tori twisted the blanket in her hands, trying to compose herself.

"Promise me first."

"I'll make sure they know."

"All right. This goes way against my better judgment, but you already know too much. I lived with him, with David."

"What's the secret there? Everyone knows that."

"Yes, but as soon as I heard about the retrofitting scheme, I told him. The thing is, he was a brain on military strategy, and I needed to know if I was wrong. But he agreed: What I was developing presented a real threat to any hope for disengagement. When I told him I intended to shred the plans and disappear —because that's all I had in mind at the time, he convinced me it would take more than shredding. I would have to make a *plastique* bomb and remote detonator if I wanted to be sure. At every point during the next month, David insisted I keep him informed on every detail, that we could not stand surprises. Even though I pretty much had access to the building any time I needed it, he said we still needed compliance from security to get everything ready; and that was the part he would work on. But at some point along the way—I don't know when or why—he saw a different opportunity."

"You mean—"

"Let me finish; you wanted to know. When Arthur Montgomery's name came up as his contact, I had no reason to think David had brought him in on it; he even assured me Montgomery knew nothing. Once I decided on two o'clock Monday morning as the safest time, David told me Montgomery would clear the building between midnight and six.

"The explosive was no problem, and I designed a radio controlling device to activate a series of electrical relays. Then I moved all the drawings, plans and formulas to a cabinet right against the closet containing the explosive. David had me detail precisely where everything was—to evaluate the effect of the explosion, he said. He kept pinning me down to make absolutely sure I located everything to do with the project in that cabinet and just where it would be."

"So he would know—"

"Exactly. To give me time to clear out, David said he would activate the detonator. All he had to do was push a button. He could push it right in a crowd without anyone's knowing and have a perfect alibi, while some of my clothes would make it look as if I'd been blown up. Meanwhile, some of his Weather Underground friends got me a phony birth certificate. As it turned out, the clothes didn't fool anyone. In retrospect, I think David knew they wouldn't.

"There was a departmental get-together in town that night that would probably go until three or four o'clock, and David went so everyone would see him. I dropped the children at a friend's house to sleep over and told her I was meeting David at the party. That was the hardest part, acting casual when I knew it might be the last time I would see them. You'll think it's heartless, but I couldn't drag them around with me, hiding out."

"You tried to do the best for them."

Graham's anxiety was growing while she recounted her tale. He desperately wanted to keep her talking, but the minutes were ticking, and they had little time to spare. Outside, the wind had finally subsided to an ominous hush.

"I don't know that, but it's what I did. Anyway, David was to whisk them right off to John before anyone found out. I told myself I could surface a year or so later under another name and get them.

"I was already leaving town, when I realized I hadn't brought the ID with me and had to go back to the house about an hour after David left for the party. I found all his things packed on the bed, as if he were leaving somewhere, too, and I thought, 'Well, maybe he's driving the kids to John.' It seemed reasonable he'd do that in case they connected him, since we stayed together.

"I found my papers on the dresser where I'd left them and put them into my purse. I grabbed the phone book just in case, and that was when I noticed the big cardboard mailing tube next to David's bags. When I picked up an end, it weighed a ton; so I got curious and pulled the cap off. It was solid with papers. I only needed to pull one partway out to recognize all my drawings and formulas. Instead of letting them be destroyed, he had brought them all out, for God knows what reason. Either he was going to sell them back to the government, or he was going to offer them to someone else. To put the most generous construction on it, he may have thought he was doing some good by spreading the technology around without realizing how dangerous the capability was in anyone's hands. That's when I understood the reason for cultivating Arthur Montgomery: David had used him, because he had access to Building T, to bring out all my papers."

"That's what you meant by 'no statute of limitation on treason' then."

"Yes. And I knew then he was walking out on the children, too; so I would have to take them to John myself. I was almost relieved. I lugged the tube to my van. There was no time to check all that was in it; David might walk in and find me. I drove right over to Rachel's place—she was a friend—and told her David and I had a blow-up, and the kids and I were leaving town for a while.

"She didn't find that strange, because he put me through a lot. You don't even want to know. I drove south nearly half the night to the North Carolina border before I looked for a place to stay."

"North Carolina!"

"Some little town in the mountains. Hayter's Gap. Once I was in the motel, I had to know what was in the tube. In among the plans I found that slip of paper Mimi pulled from under the bed. It was a note in David's handwriting telling someone to be in Building T at 2 a.m., so David could meet him with the money. It had to be for Montgomery, and Montgomery must have stuck it into the tube so he wouldn't have anything incriminating on him. If it was Montgomery, then he really had no idea what was up."

"Wait a minute. Hadn't you talked to Montgomery?"

"I scarcely knew him. He was a night guard that I hardly ever saw. Anyway, then I saw why David had been so interested in locating everything: so he could tell Montgomery how to find it. But at 2 a.m. David would set off the bomb. He wanted to eliminate the one person besides me who could link him to the plans.

"It was a quarter of two. I went ballistic. I called the police in Miamisburg to alert them, but the lady kept asking, 'Where are you? Who is this?' I guess I was screaming, and she couldn't understand me. I kept thinking 'Antigone' for some reason and blurted it out, and it stuck.

"So that's what I sent to John with the kids: David's note, along with instructions for John to keep it safe somewhere, that it might clear my name some day, if that mattered to the children. At least I wouldn't be a murderer. I also told him to get custody of the kids and do whatever else necessary to keep them from David. Then I changed my name again."

"Jesus, why don't you tell this to the authorities?"

"Graham, I'm accessory to a murder. I helped blow up a building. You think they'll overlook that?"

"You also prevented a major espionage disaster."

"Who would believe that? David got to them first. It's his story they believe. The whole thing will come down on me. I'm screwed."

"Then we have to get moving. For all we know, Meachum is on his way up now. Which way?"

"We'll never make it to the Inner Basin now, not in the dark with my feet like this; and we'll get lost in the trees if we head south toward Schultz Pass. Damn!"

"Think, Tori. If Meachum catches you, he's going to take you out, and I don't know what these spooks you talk about have in mind. I don't know the mountain. You do, and you can get us out of here."

Tori peered out the window at the sky.

"We have to take an enormous chance. We're going right back down the lift line. That's the last place they'll expect me."

33

Graham's watch read two as he awaited Tori in the dark. Over his objection she had spent half an hour gathering up all the cans and clothing lying about before wasting more precious time on whatever she was doing up there on the lift ramp. Twice the distant clank of metal resounded from above. What was she doing, throwing trash around? Ears cocked for the grate of her shoes, he fretted over the delay.

Finally she returned, out of breath. As Graham shouldered up her pack to start down, she said, "I threw cans up the mountain as far as I could so they'll think I dropped them on my way to the top. I scattered my clothes by the foot of the trail, as if I was trying to save weight."

Graham kept setting off little cinderslides as they picked their way down the first steep pitch. Overhead, the stars beamed a riot of pinpoint beacons through the suspended chairs. At this elevation, they actually looked nearer.

"Have you ever stayed up to watch them move?" Tori whispered, clutching his shoulder for support. The sheer grandeur of the spectacle seemed to hush her.

"Mm, not exactly," he grunted. Whether it was lack of sleep, Graham was only half attending. Tori's hand on his shoulder, the altitude and fatigue, were working an aphrodisiac effect. He found himself growing a monumental desire for her.

"You have to watch for a long time," she said. "Did you know in winter the Big Dipper goes down in the night and returns before morning at this latitude? Alice showed me that."

"Really? Who's Alice?"

"The Indian woman who keeps books for us over in the new lodge."

"Oh yes. I've run into Alice." He tried to re-route his attention to what Tori was saying. "She threatened me if I got crossways with you."

"She would, too. Alice knows me from before. She was one of my clients, and I got her out of a nasty situation."

They had descended three towers into the high, dark trees on either side of the lift, when something heavy crashed into the brush off to the right.

"Deer, probably," Tori whispered as the sound of cracking underbrush receded into the forest. "You have to watch, though; we have mountain lions up here, too."

That got his attention.

"What if you meet one of those?"

"Say 'nice kitty'?"

Her humor didn't encourage him.

"So I wonder if walking straight down like this is a good idea. We're sitting ducks. What if Meachum or someone comes up?"

"Too dark. We'd hear in plenty of time. If we want to get down before light, this is the way. I can do it under thirty minutes in daylight."

A bright moon silhouetted the terrain of northern Arizona's high plateau to the west but no longer lit the narrow cut they were descending. The surrounding darkness only heightened the show overhead.

It was wasted on Graham, so attuned was he to Tori's presence. All he could register was the movement of her hip.

A hunting owl's shivery cry resounded among the trees to shatter Graham's single-minded focus. He swore he heard his heart pounding. Not even crickets sang at this elevation. Dark evergreens towered a hundred feet above them.

"Tori, how did you ever get mixed up with Meachum?"

"Roman Catholicism. We're big on martyrdom."

"Seriously."

"It was basically over the war. I had all these contradictions to deal with. Like Enzo: He volunteered to go but didn't support it. I myself had nothing against the war and scant sympathy with the whole anti-war movement, while John was so opposed he wanted me to stop the work I did.

"I was balancing all that with being a mother, trying for some kind of closeness that probably wasn't even possible. Like I nursed Mimi—Jen—but almost got myself canned for trying it when—what's-his-name now?—Rob came along. Sometimes I thought it was tearing me in two."

"So where did Meachum come into all that?"

"He was a student protest leader who hung out at our place a lot. John was like a mentor to him. What interested me about David was that he could discuss the movement without judging me. He was the only one I ever talked to who could. Sometimes he took the children to give John and me space when we were having problems. And finally, when things became too strained, David advised it was in my best interest to separate. That was a big move for someone like me. In retrospect, it wasn't my interest he was looking out for. Probably that was when he began to manipulate me."

"Jen remembers worse than manipulation."

"She was a child. She imagined things."

"Like hitting you?"

"Absolutely. I wouldn't let someone abuse me. It was control, that's all. He could persuade people to take on his wars. He was manipulative. I don't think anyone recognized that about him. Maybe he didn't even see it."

"He struck you, repeatedly. She saw him."

She removed her hand from his shoulder.

"Graham, believe me; there are things you don't want to know about me."

"How far did it go, what he did to you?"

She started to slide and renewed her grip on his shoulder, but the silence between them grew.

"You think that's why I'm screwed up sexually. Let me set you straight. I got raped at a truck stop when I was on the run. It was so stupid, and he probably would have killed me if I hadn't got away. And I couldn't report it."

"Why?"

"Are you kidding? Me, go to the police?"

"Oh my god, Tori. No wonder you worked in the shelter."

"Yeah, no wonder. I swore I would never let anyone—or anything—gain that kind of hand over me again. I have no excuse for letting that happen. Or David, for that matter."

"Tori, you know better than to blame yourself."

"Easier said. I don't want to talk about this. Don't bring it up again."

She broke off and squeezed Graham's shoulder to stop him as the lift's bottom terminus came into view in the moonlight below.

"There's a catwalk through the woods here. We'd better cut across in case someone's watching for us down there."

About 200 meters along the narrow trail, Tori hissed that blisters were killing her and begged Graham to stop.

Rather than lose any time, he piggybacked her and the pack. Staggering along the best he could, he was happy now she had insisted on leaving her provisions behind. Just when he was about all in, the trail opened onto a wide run cut through the trees; and he let her down to size up the situation.

Below, an open meadow surrounded the lift and lodge. Across the run in a sheltered area no more than a hundred meters from the lift lay the sprawling maintenance shop and yard. It was not yet three o'clock. Her escape plan was working.

"Do you want to see where I live? I need to pick up my kit."

"Hm?" Still processing Tori's revelation, Graham had missed what she asked.

"Cut across this run. We're high enough no one should see us."

Before he could object, she steered him across, one hand firmly on his shoulder, and down along the trees at the far edge of the run. The maintenance building stood just below them, and she picked her way carefully down toward the rear of it. Ten meters from the back entrance, she stumbled over some castoff metal tubing in the dark and raised a clank loud enough to stir the dead.

While the pipe was still rolling to a stop, a dog erupted into a furious commotion and ripped around the corner of the building. Graham froze, but the dog saw Tori when she kept right on walking. Its wild barking turned savage, and it charged. In that heart-stopping moment, the powerful, black-and-white form streaked straight for her, a red bandanna incongruously fluttering from its neck.

Just before it struck, Tori said, "Sammy!" and bent down to offer her face.

Instant recognition turned the dog to a mewling pussycat sidling up for a lick.

178

Before Graham could unfreeze, Tori said, "Don't move; Mr. Samuel here still doesn't know about you."

She led the dog over by the bandanna and told it, "Samu-el, this is Graham. He's good. Come on now. Just move slowly. Nothing sudden."

The dog stiffened warily as Tori approached and stopped a short distance off.

"I need to kiss you so he can see we're pals," she said and planted a *pro forma* smack on Graham that unexpectedly turned ardent when her tongue probed through the center of it, and their teeth hit. Just when they were about to eat each other alive, a nose investigated Graham's leg.

She did not release and tell the dog to get down until he was uncomfortably sniffing at Graham's rear end.

"There, he gets the idea."

By that time Graham had also got his own idea: Tori rampant in his arms.

"That your dog?" He fought down the image, remembering their situation.

"Not really. He just lives up here and thinks he's the one who owns the place. He does guard the shop, though. Come on, he's okayed you now."

Tori produced a set of keys from her pocket and unlocked the back entrance. Ordering Sammy out, she closed and locked it behind them.

In the abrupt darkness, his imagination shifted into overdrive: Tori crying out in ecstasy.

"Are you coming?" she said.

"Almost."

"Hey, are you listening to me?"

"Yeah, yeah, I am."

What was the *matter* with him? Her unexpected kiss had him delirious.

"So come on. Don't track dirt on the rug."

She took his hand and led him through the littered shop floor. Just as Graham was imagining Tori in lingerie—Vittoria's Secret, he ran into her back.

"There's a washroom here. I'm going to use it. Stay put."

Huge shapes loomed in the shop's recesses from the tiny slit of light emanating under the door. He imagined oversized snow machinery and chain hoists sleeping in the shadows around him. He remembered heavy workbenches and wondered how she negotiated it all in the dark. Water ran behind the door. Finally the light went out and plunged everything into blackness as the door opened.

"I washed up; you might want to as well. The switch is on the right. Close the door first and be sure to switch it off before you come out. We don't want to announce ourselves."

When he emerged, he could not see a thing, and she had to shepherd him along by the elbow. She slowed, feeling her way, and he almost knocked them both down when he stepped on her heel.

"Whoa, watch it. There's a ladder here. Feel it?"

He did, a rough ladder of unfinished two-by-fours.

She clambered up and scraped her feet onto a deck. When Graham arrived, her hands met his face and glided to his arms to steer him off the top.

"*Voilà*, my house. Hand me the flashlight; I'll give you a tour."

Graham retrieved the light from the side pocket of her backpack and put it into her hand. She clicked it on at the floor. The beam showed a bare plywood deck.

They stood in a small enclosure walled off with parts bins. In the tiny space was a rolled-up mattress pad, a footlocker, a card table with a hot plate, and a single chair. The faint light illuminated a loft suspended over the shop floor. A reek of degreaser and wood smoke permeated the area.

"This is where you live?"

"Not exactly the Taj Mahal. Saves their paying a caretaker, though."

She moved the beam around the tiny cubicle and stopped it on the footlocker.

"David was here when you got onto the lift?"

"He was here all right."

"Kay must not have told him where I stay. No one has been here."

"How do you know?"

"He would have rifled my footlocker. I always fasten a piece of tape across the end when I leave. If anyone's opened it, I can tell."

In the light, a tiny strip of tape fastened across the seam gave way as she reached in for a plastic tackle box that she stuffed into her back pack. Her "kit."

"That's ingenious."

"I'm an ingenious lady. I wouldn't still be out here if I weren't."

"I see what you mean about how you have to live, though."

"It could be worse. At least I can come and go."

Suddenly her mouth was on his, working, her tongue probing. With her breath whistling intoxicatingly on his face, Tori sagged against him and let the light go out.

"Hey. Let's try again."

He pushed back, not sure he had understood her. "Now?"

"Yes. I may not be alive tomorrow. Or else I'll be where I can never see you again. Give me another chance. We have an hour, give or take."

"We have to get out of here, Tori."

"Please? You have to. You want me, don't you?"

"Of course I do, but—"

What was this, an animal imperative or an emotional one? He hoped the latter, but with her he never knew.

"Don't talk. Undress me."

Nonplused totally, Graham slid Tori's vest away and knelt to unzip her jeans. She pressed on him while he smoothed them over her hips then lifted her knee against his elbow stepping from them. Graham's lips brushed her stomach, a touch of down, as he undid her shirt button by button before parting it off her shoulders and letting it fall to the floor.

180

Murmuring assent, Tori arched her back and unclasped her bra while Graham peeled down underwear so lacy it must be her sole indulgence. Her dark plushness, the woman smell of her, began sounding chords in his head. He couldn't help himself; he tasted her.

She gasped and stopped him with a hand on his face. She was vibrating.

"Graham." She was breathing fast. "I still don't know if I can."

Tori's urgency was catching but not enough to stop him. He was inhaling her, oceanic. He submerged, swimming with whales, beyond breath, his only lifeline her fists in his hair.

He surfaced when she backed away and released his head.

"Get your things off," she said.

Graham was riven with misgiving as Tori shoved things around while he shed his own clothes. This was crazy. They had no time. She couldn't handle it.

Her mattress flopped, sending out a sudden gust.

"Come here."

He reached until their hands linked and touched her fingers to the condom he had carried. "Here. I was an optimist, in case I found you."

Getting it on, however, might be another matter; given their predicament, Graham's antenna would not go up, his fancies notwithstanding.

"Yes, can't take a chance if—" She left her thought unfinished upon discovering Graham's condition. "Oh. I'll say you were an optimist."

"Tori, I can't with all this stuff coming down."

Abruptly, she shoved him back onto the mattress and administered CPR until the reluctant member of her impromptu party came to attention.

"Now where's that thing?" she said, feeling for the condom until she had it.

She fumbled for a second before snapping the condom away into the dark. "Aa, screw it. I'm safe."

"Wait. Slow down."

He tried to stay her with his hands, but she gripped his wrists and removed them.

"Ssh. Don't worry."

Straddling him, she rose on her knees—murmuring incitements not to him— and adjusted herself for the exquisite feat that he could just see going awry again.

"Tori, you don't need to do this."

But in the breathtaking rush of entry, her need became the order of the night.

Primed as he was, Graham knew he would not withstand her and held her hips for dear life; but she was somewhere else, and her brakes had gone on the fritz.

"Hey, hey," he said.

"Hm-mm." She shook off the slowdown until Graham thought the top of his head would come off.

When it did, she stiffened as if he had hurt her and then returned to the fray with renewed force before Graham's part in the act wilted.

"Yes! Yes! Yes!" She underlined each one with her pelvis. A drop of sweat or a tear—he could not tell which— pinked him in the chest.

"Easy! Tori! Easy!"

He might as well have been speaking Navajo. She did not even seem aware he was no longer taking part when a series of spasms wracked her to a shuddering largo. Gripping his shoulders to steer herself while the storm passed, she demurred.

"D'amore si rari i frutti; gioirli si breve il tempo."

34

The moon passed from view, leaving the mountain in obscurity as Graham
and Tori shadowed the dirt lane to the parking lot and down to the new lodge.
Sammy trotted along the berm as they made for Graham's car, concealed under
the aspens there. Graham massaged the nail dents she'd made in the back of his
shoulder. She had fallen so silent that he began to wonder what she was rethinking when she took his arm.

"What was that Italian thing you said?"

She shook her head. "It was just… something I found. You can look. You'll
know where."

"You're going dark on me again, Tori."

"Graham, there are normal women in the world. Find one."

"Listen, I only came out here to let you know what your daughter told me.
God knows, I never intended to fall in love with you."

Tori tightened her grip on his arm. She said nothing more until the bend just
above the new lodge, then took his sleeve to stop him. He turned, thinking she
had seen something. Her face was hidden in deep shadow.

"Don't. I'm not worth it." Her voice broke, and the words came out bitter.

"Afraid I decided otherwise."

She put her head down, hugging herself. "What time is it?"

"Just after four-thirty."

"It's only twenty minutes to the highway. Maybe you can still pull this off."

She escorted him down the dark road until the new lodge loomed into view. At
the truck, Graham shoved her pack into the camper and then jumped in to crank
the engine. It would not start. After several tries, he popped the hood and walked
around to peer in. The spark plug wires were missing.

Tori leaned on her fists beside him. Graham wanted to sit and pound the
ground.

"We'd better start hoofing it."

"No. It's seven miles down the mountain and seven more to town, and by then
they'll be watching all the roads. We need wheels. When the lift crew arrives, I'll
take the carry-all. They usually leave the keys in it. We can be gone before they
notice."

"What time do you look for them?"

"Around seven-thirty."

He bent dejectedly over the disabled engine.

"What if you could produce Meachum's note to Montgomery? Wouldn't they
have to believe you then?"

"No. Anyway, I can't. I don't even know if it exists any more."

"Jen could."

"She was too young; she wouldn't remember."

"On the contrary. Talk to her. Is there a phone here?"

"Forget that! I'm not dragging her into this."

"Listen, with that note and a good lawyer you could have a fighting chance, and I know just the one. She used to help with the women's center in Gallup. She told me not a day ago that she would go the limit for Lesley Alvarado any time."

"Sarah Fitch? You know Sarah Fitch?"

"From Berkeley. She got your brother's name on the Wall."

"Sarah. Does she have any idea who I am?"

"I think she suspects."

"Then the time has come." Fishing out her keys, she walked toward the lodge.

"For what?"

"What I should have done a long time ago. Jen Park you said?"

Letting them in, she pointed the way up to the manager's office with her flashlight. Seating herself at the desk, she slid up to his phone and balanced the receiver on her fingertips thoughtfully.

"We can dial out on this one. Was it San Francisco?"

"Marin, she said."

"I bet still the 415 area code." She dialed.

"Marin County. Jen Park." A moment passed. "The regular way: P-A-R-K. ... No, I don't. ...That's probably it." She groped in the drawer, found a ball-point, and wrote the number onto the back of her hand.

"Got it. J. Park in Mill Valley. It has to be her; it's the only one."

She tapped the ball-point twice on its head and dialed the number.

"Quick," she said, "there's an extension in the bookkeeping office at the head of the stairs. Get on in case I need any facts."

Graham raced down to the office Alice had stepped from to issue her steely warning and crashed into a desk in the dark. Cursing softly to himself, he saw a tiny light glowing and grabbed at it until he sorted out a receiver to put to his ear. The phone on the other end was still ringing.

Finally a woman answered. "Yes?"

Tori's voice said, "Mimi?"

"I believe you have the wrong number."

"Wait, are you Dr. Park?"

"Yes I am." She sounded frosty.

"I see..." A pause, then Tori's whispered plea: "Graham, I can't do this. Please help me!"

Someone clicked off, and Graham said, "Jen! Are you still on the line? This is Graham Bell. Remember me?"

"Of course I remember you. What's going on?"

"We need to talk."

"Now? Do you realize what time it is?"

"I know, but it's urgent. Could you hold the line just a second?"

"I suppose."

"Stay on the line. I'll be right with you."

Graham ran to the manager's office. Tori was tipped back in the chair, hugging herself in the dark and weeping.

"Pick up the phone, Tori."

She shook her head stubbornly. "I can't. You do it. Please."

"Not unless you stay on the line." He picked up her receiver. "Jen? Graham here again. Hang in there. I'm getting this sorted out."

He handed it to Tori with his hand on the mouthpiece. "Now stay on the line," he whispered. "I might need input. You don't have to say who you are."

He jogged down the hall and took up the phone he had left on the desk there.

"Okay, Jen, still with me?"

"If this is some kind of prank, it's not amusing. I didn't get home until eleven."

"It's no joke. I apologize for the time, but it can't be helped. To— Lesley, are you on the line? Lesley?"

A barely audible "yes" returned.

"Jen, when we talked at Rico's place, you told me about papers your mother gave you the last time you saw her. Remember?"

"Yes, of course."

"It's crucial you locate them."

"That's her with you, isn't it?"

"Do you think you could find them?"

"If we still have them. They were in a small envelope that said 'John,' two half sheets of yellow paper. 'John' was the one thing I could read, because she printed it."

"One of the notes should be white," Tori said.

"Whoa. Who might this be?" Without waiting for a reply, Jen said, "I know it's you; you called me Mimi."

"Please, I—"

"What do you need?" Jen's voice turned wary.

"Your help."

"After twenty-four years, my help. Interesting."

"Jen," Graham said, "please. Everything's coming down. We don't have any time. Your mother's in a hell of a jam."

"Tch! My mother's in Sausalito. Tori DaMantova abandoned me."

"If you could just—"

Jen cut him off. "Excuse me, Mr. Bell. I'd like to hear what she has to say."

"I know how you must feel," Tori said. "It wasn't abandonment. I got you to your father."

"While you ran."

"How could you understand?"

"Oh, I understand perfectly. We would have been in the way."

"No. Not in the way. That's not it. You must never think that."

"What am I to think?"

Please, Tori, don't fold.

"You're a doctor. Think how you'd feel if you couldn't start a practice because you wouldn't want anyone asking questions, if you couldn't drive a car because you might get stopped, if you felt like running every time someone looked at you twice, if you couldn't even sign your own name. How could I condemn you or your brother to that kind of life?"

"So just to put us on a plane, that was right?"

"It wasn't a question of right. I had to. Do you realize where you'd be today if I hadn't? I can guarantee you wouldn't be a doctor. How would you have gone to medical school?"

"I assume you've heard of scholarships."

"Excuse me, after getting jerked from one school after another, you'd have been lucky to finish at all. I sent you to your father because I wanted you to have a life. I won't say I haven't wondered how things turned out for you."

"Gee, somewhere along the line you might have devised a way to find out."

"I couldn't allow myself to; it wouldn't have been good for either of us."

Graham wanted to say something at this but kept his mouth shut. What would it cost Tori simply to tell her daughter she loved her? Not even twenty-four years should erase that.

"Oo, you're a real piece of work, aren't you? Just shut it off."

"I made such nice work of my own life I didn't need to screw up yours by reminding people your mother could go to prison, or worse. How would you look anyone in the face after that?"

Jen said nothing for a moment. When she did, something subtly shifted in her voice. "I wouldn't have a problem letting people know you're my mother."

"You have no idea what you'd be letting yourself in for."

"Maybe, but I'll tell you something: Rob thinks I'm luckier than he is because I can remember you."

"As I was."

"As you are. Graham told me about your work to protect women. That takes a strong person, a good person."

"There's nothing admirable about it. It just seems the least I can do."

"I understand. I come into contact with battered women, too. It's wrenching; they're so quick to blame themselves. Aren't they? I know what went on."

"I have no idea what you're talking about."

"Oh you do. And it's not your fault. You were strong enough to get away."

"It was the other thing I was running from."

"Listen, he may have damaged you, but he didn't break you."

"Find the notes I gave your father to keep."

"But that's the thing. I told Graham: We already went through his papers, and I don't think he kept them. He died, you know."

"Yes, Graham told me, and I'm sure he would have kept them. Believe me, he would."

"All right, I'll try again. Tell me what I'm looking for."

"As nearly as I remember, there was a note on yellow, lined paper and one on plain, white paper, each about a half sheet. The yellow paper was a message to your father in black ink. I think it said, 'Keep this note safe. It may clear my name some day, if that matters to the kids.'"

"You remember the *ink color?*"

"My life rides on those notes. It's the other one I need, the one written in blue ball-point. All it says is, 'Building T at 2. Cash.' Something like that. I'm not sure, but it may have had, "Art," written on it somewhere, too."

"Yes! On the back! Yes! I came across it in a safe deposit box at the bank and asked May about it. There was nothing else with it, no other note, and May claimed not to know what it was."

"And?"

"I don't know. She took a few things; whether she took the note I didn't see. She might have tossed it, too. What if I do find it?"

"Hang on to it. Something might break today. If I come in alive."

There was a second's pause, and then Jen chose her words carefully, keeping her tone authoritative but controlled. "Graham, are you two sitting together?"

"I'm down the hall from her. We're using—"

"I want you to go to her. Now. Tori, Mother, whatever you have, put it on the desk. Right now. Talk to me."

Before Graham could move, Tori's voice came back, almost amused for the first time tonight.

"Jen, I like breathing as much as the next person. This isn't in my hands. If it's a matter of finishing me off, someone else will have to do the honors, not me. Unfortunately, that's a very real possibility; everything depends on who gets to me first."

"How much danger are you in?"

"You don't want to know."

"Is there a place you can sit tight until I can reach you?"

"Out of the question. Right now I'm even afraid of your phone; as soon as I find another way to contact you, I will. In the meantime, locate those notes. And keep tabs on the news."

Tori drew a deep breath and dropped her voice to a ragged whisper. "Jen, whatever happens, I'm sorry I wasn't a mother to you and Rob. For my sake. I wish I could tell both of you, but you tell him for me. Graham says you're beautiful. I always knew you would be. I love you both so much it hurts. Cutting you off was the only way I could protect you."

Finally. Finally. No hedging.

Then he heard a tiny click and Jen's voice pleading, "For God's sake, Graham! Mother! Isn't there some way you can get here?"

Tori must have disconnected.

"That would be difficult, Jen. We're walking, and it's like six hundred miles. I wouldn't worry, though. Your mother's a brick at this stuff."

"Please, tell me where you are."

"Too risky. Just find that note and be ready to come forward with it. If anyone traces this call, it was only me. Got it? You and I spoke; no one else."

"Understood, but how will I know what to do with it?"

"Okay. In case you don't hear anything, I'll give you my daughter's number. Call her if you come up with anything. She'll know what to do. And Jen, thanks for what you said. Tori's lucky to have a daughter like you."

With that, Graham himself hung up, hoping that nothing would keep him from seeing his own daughter again.

35

Tori stepped from the manager's office right into Graham, as he gingerly traced his way along the cedar paneling of the dark corridor. She started as he put a hand to her, orienting himself.

"What?"

"Nothing. You startled me."

"If it makes any difference to you, that conversation was overdue. For both of you, believe me."

His watch glowed five-thirty. Through the windows behind Tori, twilight had already washed out the stars above the peaks.

Tori's head shook disagreement against the half-light.

"I never should have done it; that was pure self indulgence."

She wiped at her eyes; but for that, only the break in her voice would have given her away.

"To you. She's waited a long time for that contact."

"Ha. I'm sure: Daughter hears from outlaw mother. And then all over page one when I get caught? 'Oh, is that your mother? You poor thing!'"

"I'm not going to argue with you." Graham steered her toward the stairs. "It's still two hours before your people show up. Maybe we should just walk it."

Tori balked. The entry light cast the tables and upturned chairs at the bottom of the steps into relief and highlit the hand rail.

"Then what? Stand on the highway and flag a ride? We need the carry-all. And while we're at it, we need to do something about you." Tori flicked her light toward the foot of the stairs. "The ladies' room window faces away, in case anyone's around."

In the rest room with Graham, Tori snapped on the light to shattering effect. Once he squinted himself up in the mirror, he was all red eyes and stubble. Tori looked just as bad. At least her glasses hid some of it.

The narrow bathroom contained three stalls, a row of sinks, and a wall-length mirror. The place smelled of Lysol rather than the camphorous urinal pucks Graham was used to.

Tori pushed Graham onto a john and delved into her backpack for the tackle box she had salvaged from her footlocker. She opened out an array of brushes, combs, razors and cosmetics and selected a pair of scissors to tap on her lip while she pondered him a second.

"This won't be a work of art, but it should get you out of here in one piece."

"What about you?"

"Let's worry about this first." Her back was to him as she cupped a handful of water from the sink. She patted it into his hair and went to work. Right in the middle of littering the floor with clippings, she could not resist observing, "You're getting thin back here."

"Thanks for noticing."

She stuck out her lower lip and puffed a hair from the end of her nose, then used one of her straight razors to scrape the top of his head until Graham's hair, which usually grew halfway over his ears, lay all around his feet.

When Tori lifted her shirt to towel his head after shaping the edges, Graham hardly registered her touch on his wrist as she consulted his watch. Her breasts were practically in his face.

"Ah. Still time. Let's do your face."

She stuck the razor in her pocket and squatted before him, bracing an elbow on her knee to steady her hand. Her gaze bewitched him as she penciled eyeliner between his eyebrows and patted his cheeks and chin with make-up. That finished, she grabbed a handful of clippings and pasted them under his nose with an ethery concoction that about knocked him out before she trimmed them with her scissors.

"*Voilà!* Have a look."

When his eyes stopped watering, Graham beheld how Tori had salt-and-peppered the stubble on his cheeks, joined his eyebrows, given him a bushy mustache, and topped it all off with a bald pate and fringe that lent him ten years.

She clucked her tongue. "Groucho Marx. You need a cigar."

Tori rested her hands on his shoulders. "Graham." She took a breath. "I'm taking the carry-all. You can walk out scot free. No one will be the wiser."

"What are you saying? No."

"Graham, listen; I've ruined your life enough. Whatever happens to me, I don't want it happening to you. Think about your daughter."

"You have children."

"They've learned to live without me. But your daughter—"

All at once, against the pre-dawn peace came a sound etched forever in Graham's memory: the rhythmic slap of helicopter blades. Tori caught it, too, stopped in mid-sentence.

"Oh Lord," she said, "They're here. Sweep this mess into the john and flush it. We have to douse the light before anyone sees."

Graham scooped up gobs of hair in his hands and brushed them into the toilet while Tori stuffed her things into the pack. The beat of the helicopter amplified until its blades passed overhead, then dropped in pitch as the craft slanted in for a landing somewhere up by the ski lift.

The two of them were still cleaning up when the chopper's turbine abruptly shut down. Tori glanced around, snapped off all the lights—even the one over the entry—and tugged Graham into the dark cafeteria toward the kitchen and back entrance. From outside came a scuff of gravel, people running. Before Graham and Tori could grope their way through the jumble of tables, someone was hammering the entrance. Tori shrank to the wall as the pounding gave way to scraping and tinkering.

"No!" Tori hissed, "they're coming in!" She cupped her hands around his ear. "They'll know me. Here, use my glasses."

She thrust them into his hand as she whispered frantic instructions: "Stay cool turn on a light like it's okay say you're the caretaker or something so you can get yourself out of here!"

She propelled him toward the door and skated away along the wall. Graham shuffled across the room with clammy palms wondering how on earth to buy enough time for her. The rattling at the entrance grew more systematic. Praying he could pull something off, Graham switched on the light over the entrance.

Two men in jumpsuits bent over the latch outside jerked up in the sudden pool of light. One shone a flashlight in his face as Graham peered through Tori's glasses.

"Can I help you folks?" he shouted through the glass in a hoarse voice.

"Yeah, open up!" said the taller of the two. The shorter man was coarse and beefy, his full lips almost pretty.

"You mind not shining that thing in my eyes? It hurts when you do that."

The tall man dropped the beam slightly.

"We don't open for a couple of hours. You'll have to wait. Nobody gets in till eight. Orders."

"You've got new orders: let us in," the taller man said, reflecting a badge at Graham through the glass. "We're federal agents. We're not screwing around here."

These two looked nothing like the crew-cuts in suits and shoulder holsters who grilled Graham in Marquette. The taller man seemed haunted and ascetic, while his partner exuded florid, dissolute menace.

"Get outa here! You think I'm stupid? You got no business here."

Graham was not sure how far he could go with this. The answer came in a hurry. The short, burly man produced a gun.

"Look, Mister, open the door. You had lights on. There's something going on."

Graham stood his ground, hoping they were not prepared to shoot him to gain entry.

"Course there is. I'm cleaning up, you damn fool and about to go home. Now you get on outa here, you phonies. You was trying to break in."

The tall one finally got a purchase on the lock and forced the door. Graham tugged back on the crash bar, but the burly partner had wedged a flat metal bar into the opening.

"Nice work, Fosdick! You set off the alarm. We're wired into the sheriff's office, so you're gonna be looking at the law in about two shakes."

"Shut up, man! We are the law."

The shorter man with the gun thrust a card at him, and Graham pushed Tori's glasses down to read it: Imre Gyorgy, Defense Intelligence Agency, Office of Internal Security. Were these Tori's spooks?

"Defense, eh? Got a grandson in the Army. Was over in Eye-rack with that Desert Storm. Either of you boys over there?"

"We don't have time for this, Imre," the taller man said. "We need to take a look around."

Ice clutched Graham's heart.

"Now look here, I just got the place all cleaned up. If this is some kind of inspection, it can just hold till the manager shows up, because I sure don't feature hanging around to keep you two out of trouble."

"You let us worry about that," Gyorgy said and brushed past. He found the main switches with his flashlight and turned on the overheads. Graham thought his legs would fail as the man made straight for the kitchen, where he and his partner began checking closets and behind doors.

Graham shadowed them, unsure what he would do if they came upon Tori. More than likely, he would get himself arrested or shot.

The two agents talked back and forth to each other as they looked.

"She's got to be around here, Kirk," Gyorgy said to the tall man, "Meachum's been up here twice since, you know, and Parrish wasn't with him either time. He's onto something."

Graham's ears pricked up at the mention of Meachum.

"He would have said."

"Bullshit he would have. And who knows where he is after that fiasco with the girl? The guy's unstable."

"Oh he's around. He won't take off with her this close. We've just got to get to her first."

This was interesting. They had people following Meachum as he trailed Graham, in what began to look like an overlapping effort to catch up with Tori.

Quick and thorough, Gyorgy and Kirk poked through bathroom stalls, upstairs offices, and even the roll-around waste bin until Graham himself wondered what had become of Tori. The chain was still in place on the back door to the kitchen; somehow, she had vanished. Gyorgy scratched his head, stymied.

"What are you guys hunting anyway?"

Kirk reached into his jumpsuit pocket and produced the sharpened video shot of Tori at the demonstration that had run on *Newsweek's* cover.

"This one. You wouldn't happen to have seen her, would you?" Kirk said, his look boring right into Graham's.

Graham poked Tori's spectacles down again to examine the photo, calculating what these men might be onto that had brought them up here.

"Hm. Lesley was talking about some woman yesterday," Graham said and held his breath.

"Who's Lesley?"

Graham almost cheered when neither jumped on the name. If Meachum knew, he had not told them.

"Lesley, works in the kitchen. She was setting here yesterday morning having coffee describing some woman that sounded kind of like this." Graham gestured at the photo and said, "Seemed like the woman aimed to hike over the top and Lesley planned on going with her. She's a game one, Lesley is. Real big on the outdoors."

"Where's this Lesley? We need to talk to her."

"She went up that way to the Inner Basin yesterday, what I heard, with that woman. Big storm came in, she didn't come back. Lot of people looking for her."

"And you think it was this woman she was talking about?"

"Sounded like her, way Lesley described her. She in some kind of trouble?"

Gyorgy said, "What Inner Basin? Can you show us?"

That one Graham would have to fly by the seat of his pants. He did not have a clue beyond Tori's mention of it during the night.

"Over the mountain. Ask the pilot."

"Up there, you mean?"

"Yep, and you walk to the highway. They probably figured to catch a ride back."

The two men looked at each other, and Gyorgy slammed his hand on a table.

"Can you believe? If that woman makes it to a highway, she's gone."

"Damnation! If she gives us the slip again... Let's move."

"Wait a minute," Graham said, "what about Lesley?"

"I'm afraid your friend Lesley's in a fix, pal. This woman's bad news."

Without further ado, the two men huffed up the grade to the waiting helicopter. In minutes, its turbine cranked up and its blades began to slap. The instant the chopper lifted off, Graham made for the kitchen, where he had last seen Tori.

"Now what? They're gone, but so's she," he said aloud.

At the sound of his voice, the top of the waste bin popped off, and Tori emerged like a rabbit from a hat in a reek of soured milk, hoisting a trash bag onto the floor as she blinked and shed Styrofoam cups, hair, and paper napkins. Graham sagged with relief.

"They looked in there. Where were you?"

"Under the trash bag, afraid to breathe. Tore a hole pulling it in after me. Give me my glasses."

She shook her head and finger combed bits of egg shell and stale bread from her hair before putting them on.

"It sounded like two of them. They show any ID?"

"One. Defense Intelligence or something like that."

She stepped closer, her dark eyes intent. "Did you notice the name?"

"Yeah, Imre something." He spelled "Gyorgy" for her.

Tori's expression froze. "It's pronounced *George*. He's Hungarian, got asylum here after the '56 uprising. The other one would be Roland Kirk."

"Yep, I heard Gyorgy call him that. You know them?"

"Omigod!" She beat on her head. "This is a disaster."

"I overheard them talking about Meachum. Does he work with them?"

"You better believe. They've been using him to run me down. This is beyond bad; it's off the scale. If they break me, I'm screwed. The *world's* screwed. How much time do we have?"

A hint of jet fuel left by the helicopter drifted through the door as Graham checked his watch.

"Twenty after seven," he said.

She grimaced. "Damn! The crew should be here."

Tori gnawed her lip and gazed toward the emerging summit, where the sound of blades faded into the distance.

36

Tori paced in the dark as they waited, while Graham watched the time and kept an ear out for the helicopter that had vanished over the top of the mountain. Twenty before eight came the sound of a motor grinding toward them.

Tori said, "That has to be them."

The minute a battered, gray Suburban nosed into view, Tori unlocked the rear door with Graham in tow and ducked into the scattered aspen behind the lodge.

The carry-all pulled up in a crunch of gravel, and the doors creaked open and chunked shut behind the small crew of lift operators and lodge workers who climbed out. A man and woman carried on some back-and-forth about not paying attention, while they stumped across the deck to the entrance.

Someone whistled. "Look at this! Somebody left the place wide open all night." The talk faded inside.

Tori pulled him around the lodge to the carry-all, where it sat ticking off heat from the climb up the mountain. Huddled against the van, they couldn't be seen from the lodge. Tori tried the driver's door and felt all around the seat and steering column.

"They took the key," Tori whispered. "Get Alice out here. Don't let anybody see you."

Too nervous to swallow, he slipped around to where Gyorgy and his partner had forced the door only an hour ago and peered in. Half a dozen workers, including Alice, were gathered around the welder Graham had tried to interrogate in the equipment building. Whatever he was saying held the others spellbound. The welder swung around to point up the mountain, and Graham ducked back to keep from being seen.

As he watched, Alice separated from the others and made for the ladies room. Graham raced around the lodge, waving Tori back to the kitchen as he passed the carry-all. Light showed from a small window about seven feet up that had to be the women's room.

Graham chinned himself on the sill and angled his head at the slight opening. Water splashed inside. In a harsh whisper, he called, "Alice!"

The water cut off abruptly, followed by long silence.

"Alice," he said again, "Lesley's with me. She needs to see you."

Another second of silence passed before Alice said, "I don't know who you are, you pervert, but you better make tracks."

By now Graham's arms were shaking from the exertion of hanging from the sill. "Alice, she's in trouble. She's out back by the kitchen. Don't tell the others!"

He dropped from the window and trotted back to Tori.

"Be ready to run in case she didn't believe me."

Graham waited at the kitchen door. Anxious seconds passed until the entry cracked and brought up against its chain. Alice's face, outlined in the opening, squinted him up.

"You! What'd you do to yourself?" she said.

He put a finger to his lips. "Lesley needs to talk to you. You didn't say anything, did you?"

Alice appraised him. "Where is she?"

When he nodded over his shoulder, Tori stepped from the trees to show herself. Alice's eyes widened, and she released the chain to shove Graham aside.

"Lesley, where you been? We called Forest Service, search and rescue, everybody. Heard one of their choppers already this morning." She breathed relief. "I'll go call 'em in."

Tori grabbed her sleeve. "Don't!"

Alice stepped back from her friend as if she saw something askew. "Kay's in the hospital 'cause of you, you know that?"

Tori covered her face, avoiding Alice's eyes. "Oh, god, no!"

"That man picked her up yesterday told Olivia he wanted some woman supposed to be dangerous. Now two guys stop by Ray's four o'clock this morning asking questions. What's going on?"

"Dangerous?"

Alice frowned. "Lesley, that man told Olivia he was looking for you."

At this point, a helicopter rose into view over the mountain. Descending slowly down the lift line, it made zigzag sweeps as it came. Tori seized Alice's wrist.

"Alice, you have to get me out of here. If those people see me, I'm dead."

The searching helicopter continued its steady approach.

Alice studied Tori's eyes. "Get in the carry-all. I'll tell them I have to pick up something in town."

As soon as she went inside, they hotfooted to the carry-all. Crouched on the front seat, Graham kept an eye on the helicopter. It came to a hover, level with the trees near the upper lodge, when Tori slid in beside him and threw her bag in back only seconds before Alice herself hopped in the driver's side.

"Keep down! Nobody seen you yet," she said and cranked at the engine. "Stupid thing don't want to go when it's hot."

Finally the engine coughed once, gave a pop, and spluttered to life. Alice did not even wait for it to catch hold; she released the clutch and let the Suburban buck around the lower side of the lodge and onto the road down the mountain. The helicopter's turbine was idling; it must have landed.

"Still don't see nobody," she said and killed the engine shifting to second gear.

"Piece of junk. Ray gotta take a look at this." She depressed the clutch and let the vehicle coast down the road, gathering momentum.

Graham looked across at her from where he was hunched by the door. "What do we do now?"

"Keep down. Some guy on the road."

She popped the clutch, and the engine gave a couple of lurches and fired up. Graham was about to sit up, but Alice pushed him back down.

"After the gate."

The vehicle swerved.

Graham peeked over the dashboard. An image flashed by: the wooden sign for the Snowbowl and a seriously disheveled Dave Meachum looking right at him, windmilling his arms in front of a huge, gnarled tree leaning away from the road.

"Stupid try to wave me down!" she said.

Graham looked out the back window. Up the road, Meachum shook his fist.

The Suburban lurched one way and the other. Alice was flogging it down the mountain faster than he ever would have dared. Graham pressed his foot to the firewall as she blasted into the next turn without even touching the brakes.

"What's going on, Lesley?" she said, never taking her eyes from the road.

"I'm in trouble."

"Looks like it. Something to do with Kay?"

Barely audible over the din in the carry-all, the words hung between them like a breach of faith.

"Alice, you know better."

Wheeling the carry-all headlong out of the next bend, Alice worked her jaw.

"Well, people been saying things, but I didn't think so."

She brought the rear end halfway around through a curve and bumped onto a dirt section of road under repair. The carry-all began to slough and slide, as a cloud of dust rose behind and sifted through the floor. Graham remembered what the lift operator had said about storms out here. Obviously yesterday's had missed this part of the mountain.

Alice pressed on, undaunted. The woman could drive.

Something amiss came into view off the road ahead, what looked like a vehicle overturned in the brush.

Graham said, "Hey, there's a wreck in there on the left. See it?"

Alice acknowledged it without slackening.

As they passed, Tori craned around for a better look. Then Graham saw fresh skid marks. That did it.

"Stop!" he yelled.

"Graham…" Tori started to object.

He shook his head. "It just happened. Somebody could be hurt. Let me out."

"Fine! Go!" Alice said and slammed on the brakes, jerking him into the seat belt as the carry-all skidded past the wreck to a sideways halt. She dropped the Suburban into low and wheeled it around.

Dust still billowed over the hard gravel curve Alice had just negotiated. The pavement ended just uphill where the bend rimmed a small meadow ringed with aspen. Ranks of evergreen rose on the other side. A swath of aspen saplings sheared straight into the meadow ended at a red Blazer on its right side some twenty yards off the road.

Pulling to a stop opposite the upset vehicle, Alice waved at it dismissively.

"Git. Do whatever you gonna do. We're not waitin'."

A smell of earth and pine needles from the previous night's rain tickled the air as Graham climbed down. Feathery signs of the approaching day decorated the sky. His hand still on the door, Graham hesitated. Why play hero? Someone else would come along.

The skid marks showed where the Blazer had gone off the road and over the bank to rip through the aspen before hitting a stump and tipping over. People might not even see it coming up from below. It was up to him. He left the Suburban and half slid down the embankment into a stink of heat and fuel. Someone groaned, and he peered through what was left of the Blazer's windshield. A man with a pepper-gray crew cut curled around the steering wheel clutching his leg. The smell of gasoline dizzied Graham: volatile and high-octane rather than the smoky burn of jet fuel. A movement in his peripheral vision startled him, and Tori was standing beside him.

"What are you doing?"

Ignoring him, she rapped on the roof, "Hey! You all right? We'll get you out."

The man turned his face up in surprise. It was Parrish, the agent who had been tailing Graham. He gave no sign of recognition.

"My leg's caught." His voice was muffled inside.

"We need to get the weight off that door," Tori said. "I'll see if there's any rope in the carry all."

Up at the carry-all, Tori rattled the end of a log chain from the back and hooked it to the carry-all's front end. When she dragged the other end toward the Blazer, it stopped five feet short. Graham forced the Blazer's back hatch open to see what he could find. Inside was a disaster zone and smelled of char. Metalwork was crushed, and everything including the seats were loose and thrown around. Graham spotted a skein of heavy climbing rope under the back seat and drew it out the hatch.

As he backed out, Parrish raised his head over the back of the driver's seat. "Look out," he warned.

"Say what?"

Parrish shook his head in obvious pain.

Whatever that was supposed to mean, the gasoline was giving him a headache. The rope was just long enough for Graham to take several loops around the passenger-side doorpost and tie it off to the log chain.

"I'll get inside and stabilize him," Tori said.

"Don't." Too late. She had already squirmed through the passenger window. As Graham turned, he heard her saying, "Sir, I'm a first responder."

One more thing he didn't know.

Alice backed the slack from the chain, and Graham rapped on the Blazer. He could hear Tori talking inside. She called, "Okay, we're set."

Through the windshield, he could see she had positioned herself behind Parrish with his head clamped in her forearms.

He signaled Alice, and she inched back, tightening the chain. Graham watched his rope nervously, but it held as the Blazer slowly creaked upright. The driver's door was unlatched, and Graham began jerking at it in the shadow of the tipped vehicle. The top had jammed into the frame when the vehicle went over, and the door refused to yield.

"Can't move his leg yet." Tori's voice came from inside. "We have to force that door somehow."

Graham waved Alice to inch off a little more, and the log chain went slack as the Blazer bounced and settled onto its wheels with a massive thud. Parrish cried out at the violent repositioning. Graham jerked and pried at the door with a tire iron from the Suburban, but it remained stuck.

"Everything is dumped around in here," Tori complained.

All at once Graham noticed a wisp of smoke rising from the hood.

"Hey! It's starting to smoke." She began booting from the inside. "Did you hear me? Tori!"

"I heard you. Keep working on the door."

Graham resumed prying while the smoke rose. All at once it gave, and Tori yelled, "Support him!"

Parrish yelped in pain as his leg came free, and then Graham had him.

"I'm going to skooch him out," Tori said. "You know what to do."

Tori edged out underneath with Parrish's head still clamped in her forearms.

"What've we got?" Graham said.

"AO4. Left knee pain eight. Sternum five."

Graham clanked the tire iron onto the hood and did an extremity check and finger-walked Parrish's spine before letting Tori release. Her shirt hung out, and her face was smudged. The two of them looped Parrish's arms over their shoulders and walked him to where they could let him down.

He used Tori's knife to slit Parrish's trouser leg. Rather than the trauma he feared, Parrish's knee was merely turning black and blue. He could move his toes and exhibited no obvious deformation. Graham fashioned a splint from a carton flattened on the floor of the Suburban.

"How's that feel?" He was all bedside manner now he had the leg immobilized.

Parrish winced. "Better."

"It'll hurt soon enough. Let's have a look at that chest. Right side or left?" he asked as he slipped a hand under Parrish's shirt. Parrish's buck gave him the answer as he touched a point right of the sternum. "Okay, let's be careful of that. Tell me the minute you have any trouble breathing."

"Hang on, Floyd," Tori said. "We're going to plan some help."

She nudged Graham up to the road where Alice was looping the chain back into the Suburban.

"Graham, we need a word."

"Tori, this guy is the law."

"I know that, but he doesn't know who I am. Listen, he says David ambushed him and made him drive up here. When they came to the dirt, Floyd hit the brakes to get the gun and lost control. He tried to jump. When David saw he couldn't get out, he started the back seat on fire."

"Jesus! Is that cold or what?"

"Yeah, lucky for Floyd it went out. But David's got his gun and could be anywhere."

"He's at the lodge. I saw him when Alice swerved. You need to get out of here. I'll stay with Parrish."

Tori started for the road and then looked over her shoulder.

"Graham... Take care of yourself."

Turning for the Suburban before Graham could make a response, she was halfway up the berm when Parrish propped himself on an elbow and called after her, "Tori. Wait."

Tori stopped without turning, and Graham froze.

"My name's Lesley."

"He called you 'Tori.'"

"I have to go." She took another step.

"You can't keep running, Tori."

"Watch me."

"Please listen. I can cut you some slack."

"Get going, Lesley. We need help." Graham hoped to cover his earlier slip.

"You don't know what's at stake," she said to Parrish.

"Don't I? Tell me what."

Parrish pushed himself to a sitting position and gripped his knee to extend the injured leg.

Tori half turned to study Parrish. She shook her head warily. "I can't."

"What's going on?" Alice said. "What's she done?"

"You can trust me," Parrish said. "I need to know who it is and how far they'll go."

She shook her head.

"I'm offering you a chance, Tori. Think of your family, your children."

Tori came fully around, her eyes ablaze. "Have you no decency?"

By this time Alice had come around the carry-all to follow the exchange.

"Lesley, come on. Let's go. Don't listen to him."

Smoke coiled from the front of the wreck as Graham followed their wary exchange. The thin line of trees hid all but the stretch of road where Alice waited; Tori faced them from the embankment, sizing up Parrish across the fifteen or twenty feet separating them. She needed three steps to reach the carry-all.

"Damn it, Tori, talk to me." Parrish gritted through the pain he had to be feeling now. "You don't have a lot of time. Tell me what they want with you."

"It won't do any good."

"I can put you in protective custody."

"Right where they want me."

"Who?"

"Never mind. You can't help."

"Tori, listen to me; I can arrange witness protection where they can't find you."

"You don't know these people."

Poised to bolt, Tori searched Parrish's face. "It was only supposed to be the design. You have to believe that."

"I'm listening."

"David wanted the plans, and he didn't want the guard to tell." She shook her head miserably. "I had no idea."

"What plans?"

"I've said too much. He doesn't have them."

Parrish grimaced and pressed his temples. "Who does?"

"Nobody does. It's what they want. David wants me, because I found out."

"Who are these people you're protecting?"

"I'm not protecting them. You'd never believe me."

"Do these people have names?"

"Imre Gyorgy, Roland Kirk," Graham said.

"Graham, are you insane?"

"Meachum worked a deal with some intelligence types to get out of prison. He told me so. We think it was DIA."

"Stop! You want to make the list, too?" Tori said.

Parrish's frown deepened, and he sat up in an attitude of strained attention. "Kirk and Gyorgy?" he said. It seemed Parrish did not believe him.

"They want what's in her head," Graham said

"Shut UP!"

Parrish mopped his brow and unbuttoned his torn, sweat-stained dress shirt to offer the understatement of the year: "You have interesting people on your tail."

Graham took a step to wave Tori away, when Parrish said, "I can stop this, but only with your help. I'll keep them off, guaranteed. Once we go public, they won't dare touch you."

"You can't promise her that."

Graham glanced over his shoulder. The Blazer was still fuming.

"If I go with you, it's our best chance," Parrish said. "There's a roadblock, but we'll get through if I show them you're in custody."

"Forget him," Alice said. "I know another way."

"Please believe me," Parrish said.

Tori hugged herself in indecision and stepped back.

"Here, damn it." Parrish took a pair of handcuffs from his belt. "Put them on yourself. Hold the key if you like, but it has to look like you're in custody."

He extended the cuffs to Graham with the key.

"Give them to me," Tori said.

"Lesley, don't," Alice said, but she had already taken the handcuffs and key. As she clicked them onto herself, her eyes widened, tracking something over Graham's shoulder. Glass shattered behind him.

A huge blast blew both of them to the ground as the Blazer ignited. The tire iron whistled past his head and stuck in the ground not ten feet away as pieces of metal clattered around them. He shook his head in the wall of heat and pulled Tori to her feet.

"Graham! I dropped the key," she said.

"Go, go! I'll bring Parrish."

"We don't need him," Alice said from where she had ducked behind the carry-all. "If you think I'm hauling Lesley off to the pokey, you got another think coming."

The jeep was sending up a spectacular fireball, and he had to close his eyes against the blast as he ran for Parrish. Graham met him hobbling from the flames and looped Parrish's arm over his shoulder. Head down, he was dragging Parrish away as fast as he could manage, when Tori screamed.

Graham jerked his head up. Tori was clambering awkwardly for the carry-all with her hands manacled—just ahead of Dave Meachum. Graham slipped and stumbled as he bolted from under Parrish's arm. Alice kicked open the Suburban's door from inside, but Meachum had already brought Tori down and put a pistol to her jaw. Graham held back uncertainly as she began to whimper under his grip with the side of her face pressed into the dirt and her glasses knocked off and broken. Her eyes widened with shock and fear.

"Stay back," Meachum said, "I've got her."

"Give me the gun, Dave."

Through the crackle and roar of the gasoline fire, a helicopter clattered. When Meachum took a nervous glance at the sky, Graham stepped up until Meachum waved his gun. He looked terrible; his clothes were torn and disheveled, and his face was marked with cuts and bruises.

"Keep back. She's a federal prisoner. You'll get her hurt if you interfere."

"Let me handle this," Parrish said.

Graham looked back and forth between the two men. What was this, some elaborate scheme they had worked out? Meachum shook his head as he wrenched Tori's manacled hands above her head and wrestled her to her feet.

"Forget it, Floyd. She's mine."

"Graham, help me!"

"Stand up, damn it."

Meachum tightened his grip on the cuffs and shoved the pistol up under her chin as he dragged her backwards up the slope.

Parrish made it to his feet.

"Dave, you're making a big mistake. You can't get away."

Somewhere above the pall of smoke, helicopter blades beat downward toward them. Graham angled toward the embankment where Meachum held her halfway between him and the carry-all. Parrish was hobbling on one leg to Graham's right, a few steps from the embankment

"Stay away, asshole; I'm warning you," Meachum said.

"Use your head, Dave. No one needs this. Give me my gun."

Parrish stumped toward the embankment, his determination apparent.

Meachum looked desperately back and forth. Whatever the hell was going on here, he was unraveling. Graham moved forward.

"She'll be the one who gets it if you come any closer. Her and then me. You get to clean up. She's better off dead than having them get their hands on her. I know."

"Of course you do, Dave. I know how it went. Just give me the gun, and I'll take it from here. You'll be okay."

Meachum shook his head. "She's mine, and I'm taking her."

Tori stifled a sob, and he wrenched her wrists back farther, twisting them as he thrust the gun into her cheek.

"Not in this," Alice called down from the road. "I'll throw the key in the woods."

She reached for the ignition, and Meachum said, "Get away! I'll shoot her."

Alice froze, and Meachum turned to make sure the key remained in the ignition. As he did, Graham shot up the embankment; but Meachum heard him coming and spun around with the pistol.

Graham, terrified for Tori, stopped short as Parrish stretched a hand out. Meachum turned the gun at Parrish, his hand shaking.

"No!" Tori screamed.

She stomped on Meachum's instep and shoved her hip back hard enough to knock him halfway around as he fired. Parrish grunted and twisted face-down onto the ground. The report shocked Graham's eyes shut. When he blinked open, Alice was backed against the carry-all, and Parrish was hit. Meachum yanked Tori to her feet to clout her face with the gun. Squeezing red from her lips, she raised her cuffed hands against another blow.

"Dumb cunt!"

He walloped her again, as she tried to squirm away.

She sagged, blood drooling from her split mouth, and Graham went ballistic. Before Meachum could react, Graham ploughed into him and flattened them both. The gun discharged by his ear, and he hesitated just enough when Meachum shoved her damaged face in the way of his fist for Meachum to knee him in the stomach. Graham doubled over, sank to his knees, and slid down the embankment, unable to stand and sobbing for breath.

Through a fog of pain he heard her cry out and Meachum say, "As far as you're concerned, asshole, I already killed her. But you first."

Graham tried helplessly to draw a breath as Meachum elbowed Tori aside and used both hands to level the gun on him.

Suddenly Tori erupted behind his hands and drove both his arms up with her shoulders. He cracked off two gunshots in the air as she raised her wrists and hammered the cuffs down on his face. He cried out and brought the gun toward her head when she kneed him in the crotch and drove her thumbs into his eyes. Just as he got a grip on the handcuff chain, she pivoted free. Backed against him, she locked both hands on the wrist of his gun hand and popped his elbow over her shoulder.

When the gun fell from his grip, he never had time to yell before Tori brought her hands down and drove her left elbow into his gut. Her lip was split and one eye swelled shut as she fumbled her pocket with her manacled hands and withdrew the straight razor.

"Call *me* cunt. I'll cut you one." She snicked open the blade.

Meachum was doubled over in agony, flailing around in front of himself with his good arm, trying to find her. Graham was still gasping to intervene as she dropped into a crouch and lashed out. A ripping sound opened a rent in the front of his pants. He groaned in fear and, perhaps mercifully, backed into Alice's two-fisted swing with the tire iron that caught him at the base of the skull before Tori could complete her surgery.

Doubled over as he was, he toppled into Tori and took her down with him. With her hands manacled in front, she had no way to break her fall. As she came down hard underneath, Graham stretched to catch her head and drove a rock into the back of his hand taking the impact.

Tori lay unmoving under Meachum. Her face had gone slack. Graham agonized with her head cradled on his mashed hand. A terrible moment passed as Graham knelt to shoulder Meachum off. The helicopter slatted nearer.

Then Tori took a breath. Keening, she dragged Graham's hand across the rock twisting herself free. She pedaled halfway to her feet to spit a gout of blood before dropping onto all fours in the handcuffs. Meachum's hand fell from her.

Alice stepped around Meachum and belted the gun away with the tire iron. When Tori moaned, Alice clanked the iron down and knelt by her.

Too late he saw the handcuff key, lying right where the gun had stopped. Alice snapped it up before he could move. Tori shook her head unsteadily, spit more blood, and collapsed face first into the dirt. Alice got an arm around her and hauled her up.

Pushing himself upright with the tire iron, he stood transfixed in an exquisite, sparkly rhapsody of pain. His gut ached like sin, and his hand felt as if a truck had run over it. Alice's sharp rebuke broke the spell.

"You happy now? What he done to Lesley?"

Bereft of further words, she hefted Tori to the carry-all and bundled her in.

He gripped the tire iron and stared down at Meachum's still-open eyes. Life faded from them as Alice cranked away at the carry-all to get it started. Grass crackled into flames all around, and the surrounding pines began to flare as the downdraft of the big chopper circling above fed the blaze into ferocity. Hot creosote and grass smudge burned Graham's lungs and stung his eyes until he was aware of nothing but time running out. He used a foot to nudge Meachum over. His shirt bore the bloody imprint of Tori's face. Tori's straight razor lay open by his foot. Retrieving it, Graham closed it against his leg.

Close by lay a revolver with four cartridges fired and the man one of those cartridges had turned into a coroner's report. And here he was, holding the razor that might have reconfigured Meachum and the tire iron that killed him.

The carry-all coughed into life, and Graham looked up to see Alice pulling away. The wail of the circling Huey drowned out the departing Suburban as Alice deployed for Indian country with one door still half unlatched, breaking contact before she took enemy fire.

She did not even turn to look as the carry-all roared off down the road, Tori's head lolling against her shoulder.

"Wait!" Graham called after them. When the carry-all vanished around the bend, he spun the straight razor across the road and into the brush. Caught on the Laotian border again, char and branches rained down like tracers from the torching crowns overhead. Behind him, the conflagration crackled off a steady gunfire of snapped limbs and flaring needles.

37

The unit's in trouble. Call in air support.

But he couldn't move. The war was on again. He was stranded.

Someone made a low moan. Parrish was crawling to the foot of the embankment just ahead of the flames, dragging his splinted leg as best he could. Another few seconds, and the fire would take him.

Graham could run. Or not.

Abandoning a comrade in arms: not a choice. He skidded down the bank and into the heat. There was no time to worry about delicacies; oblivious to his throbbing hand, he heaved Parrish aboard and humped him through the grass blaze. The thick boil of smoke choked and all but blinded him as he blundered his way through scattered aspen for the road.

Graham emerged from the acrid pall and plodded a few more paces before sliding Parrish off. Back in the combat zone, he prepared his casualty for medevac. He had to get this guy out alive. He blinked to see and tried to wave in whatever chopper was circling around up there.

He waved both arms frantically until the chopper pilot seemed to spot him. Graham pointed at Parrish and made a lifting motion. The chopper banked to approach. The descending gray craft bore a Department of Public Safety emblem. Graham bent to Parrish.

"You hear me?"

Parrish managed a nod.

"Tell me where you're hit."

"I'm not. I played dead. She saved my life. Oowee!" He paused to suck in a breath. "Never saw anything like that. She flat took him apart."

Graham was thunderstruck. He could have pushed that questionable rib into Parrish's lung humping him out. How many times had he humped wounded rangers out the same way? Battlefield triage: See who's breathing.

As it rocked onto the ground at a clearing down the road, the helicopter radiated a blast of air that blew back the approaching grass fire. A crewman reached them, and Graham cupped his hands around his mouth.

"Injured knee. Broken rib."

The man shouted, "Let's move!" and pointed to the fire.

They scooped Parrish into a fireman's carry that about killed Graham's wounded hand and ran him to the waiting chopper. While the crewman was arranging Parrish inside the craft, Graham shouted to the pilot, "There's another one. I'll get him."

Before the pilot could answer, Graham ran toward the smoke. He was wading through low flame, slapping his pants legs out, before he stumbled onto Meachum still lying beside the road. He heaved his dead weight aboard and slogged him along the road itself to escape the fire.

Graham veered through the aspen and smoke with his burden and emerged once again, eyes smarting, where the chopper waited. The pilot powered up the turbine as the crewman dashed out to meet him again.

At the helicopter, Graham and the crewman rolled Meachum's body into a tarp and lashed him to a skid as the pilot monitored their progress over his shoulder. Then the crewman seated himself beside the pilot, and Graham clambered into the back with Parrish. They were already in the air before Graham could buckle himself in.

Graham rested against the transmission box looking out the open door of a chopper again. Smoke drifted through, and the familiar bench cushion lifted him up, up to the shrieking turbine and *whup whup whup* of the blades. He shivered. It all comes back.

Still, he saved a life. That counted. He'd saved others, but this felt different; he could have run. Even Meachum he would have brought in alive. St. Graham to the rescue.

He examined his left hand. It was beginning to swell and hurt like hell when he tried to move his fingers. Parrish nudged him, startling him back. He was trying to say something. Graham leaned in closer.

"When she was... in the Blazer. With me."

It obviously hurt him to speak. The rib could be a problem then. Graham frowned and nodded that he had heard, and Parrish went on.

"Did she know?"

Graham gave him a questioning look.

"Who I was?" Parrish explained.

Graham blinked and drew back, processing. What?

Then he figured it out and nodded. "I think so."

Parrish squeezed his eyes shut, then opened them a second to say, "Thanks, both of you."

The road snaked down the mountain below, appearing and disappearing in stitches through the ponderosa and aspen. As the bottom parking lot appeared, a faint cloud of dust boiled from the trees east of the road. A gray vehicle flashed into view speeding through the forest; then it was gone.

Graham put his right hand to his hip to scoot himself sideways so he could see better and felt the object in his hip pocket. My god, he still had her wallet! He withdrew it and fingered it. He had better toss it out. Inhaling to steel himself, he opened it for one last look at Tori when he noticed Parrish watching.

"What's that?" Parrish mouthed, beckoning with his fingers.

Oh what the hell; they already had him.

"Her billfold."

"Give it here."

Graham handed it over. There seemed little point in getting rid of it now. Parrish thumbed through it, pausing for a long look at the photo, before slipping it into his jacket pocket, apparently satisfied.

Graham carefully dared another look at the road below. A fire truck headed up the mountain, nothing else. Where had they gone? He glanced down at his throbbing hand, which was starting to look like an inflated rubber glove.

The chopper descended below the ponderosa tops onto the tarmac of the lower lot, where a half dozen Coconino Sheriff's Department and U.S. Government cars waited.

As they settled toward the lot, Parrish beckoned him close again.

"You're a suspect. No lawyer. Say nothing. I talk. Hear?"

The pilot touched down and let the craft settle. He idled the turbine and said over his shoulder, "Radioed for an ambulance. Ought to get here any minute."

Kirk and Imre Gyorgy trotted up to the chopper ahead of the sheriff's deputies. Seeing Graham, Gyorgy beamed and greeted Parrish, "Ah, you picked him up. We were going to, but then—" His face fell as he saw the bundle tied to the skid.

"That's her?"

Parrish pushed himself straighter on the bench, drew a breath and exhaled it slowly to gather himself. He studied Gyorgy as he unbuckled himself before saying anything.

"Your boy Meachum went rogue. Got my gun. Tried to kill me."

"What are you talking, 'our boy'? We got nothing to do with that crazy bastard. Guy's a loco. What was he trying to do?"

"Outfox you. Told me. You hoped he'd smoke out DaMantova. He did."

Graham steeled himself to hear Parrish tell what happened. It would never end.

"Got to her first then." Kirk said.

He stared at the rolled tarp that the crewman was now unlashing from the skid.

"Yep. Already. Killed her. What he said."

What?

Graham had to put his head down and hang onto the shoulder harness to keep his surprise from showing.

"Caught her along Highway 89 or somewhere. Would have done me, too. Except for this good man."

Parrish smiled amiably at them. Graham knew his rib had to be hurting badly.

Kirk said, "So you found her?"

He indicated the bundle.

"No, sorry. That's Meachum."

208

Kirk looked stung. Graham thought he had better release himself and climb out before anyone remembered him. The minute he alighted, he edged over to where two deputies were watching the crewman and pilot unlash the bundle.

Gyorgy blurted, "He wouldn't kill her. We had—" He stopped himself.

"Better believe it. Her blood's all over him. See… Here's her billfold." He held it up so they could see. "We found it on him. He killed her all right."

Kirk and Gyorgy stared at the billfold and then at each other.

"Stupid idiot!" Gyorgy said. "We have to find her."

"Good luck figuring out where. Lot of country over there. Could've dumped her in a lava vent. Happy hunting."

The ambulance arrived, and two paramedics helped Parrish to their rig. Once he was settled, they returned to load the bundle containing Meachum in as well. Graham backed in among the deputies, watching for his moment to turn scarce while everyone focused on the ambulance. One of the paramedics climbed out and latched the back. Then he turned, looked around until he saw Graham, and beckoned.

"Come on. Yes, you. Up front. We need you for the report."

Graham climbed in and peered out the side window at Kirk and Gyorgy as the driver turned on his light and siren to squeal out of the lot and onto the highway. Kirk looked as if he were chewing aspirin.

38

Once the EMTs got a look at Graham's hand, they took him to ER as well. During his examination, the doctor changed focus to possible spleen damage when Graham mentioned the knee to his gut. The doctor wanted him back immediately if he should experience rigidity in the area, and Graham had enough background to know he wasn't kidding.

By the time the doctor finished splinting Graham's hand, it was nearly noon, and he hadn't seen Parrish since arriving at the hospital. He started out the emergency room door only to meet an Arizona highway cop who wanted his own report about the incident. Graham repeated what he had told the ambulance driver: that he had been driving down from the Snowbowl when he came upon the accident. After he pulled a man from the overturned vehicle, another man had appeared on the scene waving a gun. At that point in the original report, Graham had begun to sweat, painted into a corner. Given what Parrish had already told the DIA agents, Graham had little choice but to say he himself had struck the second man down when he tried to shoot Parrish. Parrish's story left no one else to do it. This time around, however, he implicated himself with the ease of being too tired to care any more.

Even as he signed that report, Jordan Reno, the Coconino County sheriff, introduced himself and took Graham to the courthouse so he could go over the whole thing again—in detail and on tape this time.

Reno's boyish face and straw-blonde hair made him an unlikely sheriff. Barely forty, slight, and no more than five eight or nine, he presented the antithesis of frontier justice offered by Hollywood. Here was a man who looked more natural in button-down Madras than ten-gallon and holster. Even his questions showed sensitivity and intelligence. When Graham inquired about the need for all the multiple reports, Reno freely leveled with him that there was going to be some dispute over authority because of the locale and personalities involved.

From this, Graham gathered that Reno wanted a major say in handling the case while other agencies jockeyed for jurisdiction.

Reno's office recalled an old schoolroom, with a ceiling fan turning slowly overhead to a slight hum, even though the morning was nowhere near warm yet. Graham slouched down exhausted in the chair Reno offered. The muffled horn of a Santa Fe freight locomotive sounded through the window, and the slant of the Peaks appeared through the tangle of wires and trees outside.

Reno returned with a tape recorder and a spit-and-polish Hispanic woman about Graham's own age he introduced as Rosario Castellanas, his investigator.

This was interesting: An educated sheriff with a female investigator? Changes had come to this part of the west anyway.

From their questions, it quickly became apparent that Reno and Castellanas had already brought themselves well up to speed on the DaMantova case, and Graham found himself skirting issues until Reno finally had to say, "Look, we know about your involvement. You had a relationship with the DaMantova woman. You must have come out here to meet her."

"No, I came out here to find her. I had reason to believe she was here, but I didn't know that."

"Oh? And what reason would that be?"

Graham thought about that one a second before replying.

"I'd rather not say at this point. If it becomes significant to the case, I may. There are people who helped that I really shouldn't expose."

He was thinking, of course, of Julie; but he was also protecting the link she had used. Castellanas gave a perceptible start when he connected Tori to Lesley Alvarado.

Reno then asked him point-blank if he had met with DaMantova after reaching Flagstaff. Since the only available person who could know had just provided him cover, the answer was obvious: He tried but missed. She had, he conceded, spent time with him in Marquette. More to the point, she had confided information the sheriff ought to know. It took Castellanas another full cassette to record Tori's patrol-shack revelations about the strategic fallout of her rocket guidance system. When he finished, Reno sat nodding in silence with his eyes closed. Graham waited.

"So as far as you know, then, she hiked over the ridge to the east and out the Inner Basin. And this would be sometime in the afternoon, you said. Before you got there."

By this time, it was already mid-afternoon, and Graham had reached zombie status. He had neither slept nor eaten for a day and a half. What the hell, they would need Alice or Tori to refute his account, and he did not think that was on. It was all too problematic. He needed sleep. From the chaos rampant in his brain, two precepts emerged:

They can't have what she knows.

Like it or not, I have to cover her.

"That's correct."

"All right, it looks as if we're done then."

Reno stood, then gave Graham the bad news: "You'll need to remain available, so don't leave town. Make sure you give Officer Castellanas an address and number where we can reach you."

Castellanas came out with Graham to collect the information needed and then, to his surprise, offered him a lift.

Outside, in the patrol car, she inserted the key without turning it, as if she were making up her mind about something. Studying the steering wheel as if someone had written on it in tiny print, she said, "You were well acquainted with this Da-Mantova woman."

It was an observation, not a question. She looked up at him for corroboration, so he nodded, wondering what she was leading up to.

"Would you say she was about my age?"

Graham shifted uncomfortably. "I don't know. I mean, how old you are. I'm not asking."

"I'm the same age as you are."

"Then I would say yes."

Castellanas nodded and focused on him. "Let me ask you this: Could she sing?"

"Sing?" Graham stared back at her.

"You heard me. Did you ever hear her? You know, stuff like Grace Slick, or Blondie, or…" She appeared to search. "Bluesy stuff, say… Janis Joplin?"

Graham's breath caught. Did *everyone* know this woman?

"I don't know. Maybe."

Castellanas pursed her lips and started the car. As they were rolling out of the sheriff's lot, she tapped the rim of the steering wheel with one fingernail a second before saying to the windshield, "You spoke of some kind of evidence that could exonerate her. It would be nice to get our hands on that."

Graham studied her warily.

"Please: This is personal."

"One of her children may have it."

Castellanas gave him an sidwise look. "Children? You're kidding! There must be a way to trace them."

"I have her daughter's address and phone number."

Castellanas squealed to the curb so hard that Graham lurched into her shoulder. She unpinned her badge and set it on the console between them.

"Give it to me! I'm not asking as a law enforcement officer. As a friend. She turned my life around."

"I doubt she'd appreciate that."

"What if she could prove her mother's innocent?" Castellanas insisted.

"It's complicated. She'd prefer no one know who or where she is. Anyway, she'd never talk to you. She doesn't know you." Graham looked at the badge set between them like a pledge. "You'd have to work it out with Sarah Fitch. Not even Sarah knows this, but she has Sarah's name. And it couldn't go beyond you."

"You have my word."

Graham bit his lower lip, considering. "Let me think about it."

After letting him out a block from Joe Argentery's place, Castellanas sped off without so much as a wave. He worried he should have kept his mouth shut. Graham walked down to the Rio de Flag, where a skin of water seeped along the arroyo. Graham forded from old tire to broken cinder block across the remnants of yesterday's storm, barely an inch of water that he could just as well have waded.

Graham imagined how the Rio must have looked at the height of things two days ago and thought of Joe's story about a local river runner who kayaked the Rio from north of town during a brimming summer rain. Things apparently grew hairy when the flow poured into block-long storm sewers under the bars and cafes of south Flag before bursting forth again just upstream of where he was standing.

Graham tried to picture a gush of storm runoff dragging him against the ceilings of pitch-dark tunnels beset with bedsprings, sunken tires, and flotsam he wouldn't care to name. Still, a person had a chance if he could hold his breath long enough; nothing about the current situation promised such an outcome.

39

Joe arrived home just as Graham had already consumed just about everything readily edible from the refrigerator.

"Hey, man, where you been?" he greeted. "Everybody's calling: the lawyer lady, your daughter. Your daughter says to check in with her."

When Graham straightened and turned, Joe stood speechless for a second.

"Jesus, what did you do to your hand? And what's with the haircut, man?" He shook his head as Graham took a long pull of Joe's last soda. "If this is your hairdresser, you should have got a second opinion. Did she roll you, too?"

Graham just managed a smile. "Long story. I should call Julie before I crash."

Graham stifled a tremendous yawn and dialed her. No answer.

About ten minutes later the phone rang, and it was her. She sounded immensely relieved to hear his voice.

"What is up, Graham? You were supposed to call."

Graham made sure Joe had strayed into the other room.

"I ran into a little excitement."

"Meaning what? You didn't find a job, did you?" Her voice practically dripped with implication.

"Sort of. Things didn't exactly pan out."

"Oh? Anything you can talk about?"

"No."

"That's okay. Hey, listen, I'm in California. I pitched a profile on DaMantova to *Rolling Stone*, and they want it. Can you believe? They want it."

"Drop it."

"Too late. I'm in Livermore right now getting more background. This is a huge break for me. I have most of the story already, and no one else does. You can bet they're digging like crazy. You just can't believe the way this thing's taking off."

Graham made a sound of dismay.

"Are you all right?"

"Things could be better."

"Can't be that bad. Look for me in a week or so, depending what I turn up."

He collapsed on Joe's couch in broad daylight; but, even then, little sounds, Joe's comings and goings, kept half rousing him. At one point, Joe was listening to the radio. As if in a dream, a report about a person killed in a car crash on Snowbowl Road brought him to consciousness. A story followed on the possible death of fugitive Tori DaMantova near Sunset Crater. He sat up rubbing his eyes. Perfect. His story worked... except for her family. Hearing a rattle of paper, he made his way to the doorway where Joe was surrounded by assignments listening to the radio.

"Hey, I need something at the university library. Could you run me over?"

"Here, run yourself over." He tossed Graham his keys. "Can you drive with that hand?"

•

After some aimless driving around in Joe's old Ranchero—never asking anyone, of course—Graham finally located the university library on north campus, where he dug up a hefty Italian dictionary, summoned all the Italian he could remember, and sat down to write himself a script.

With the news already out there, he needed to sweeten somehow what the DaMantova family would hear. He owed them that, but state of mind and the cloak-and-dagger of the past months instilled such thorough caution in him that he felt the need to encode his sugar coating.

Once his efforts satisfied him, he looked for a phone where no one would overhear but quiet enough that he could hear himself think. Finally he found one in town and dialed the DaMantovas' number.

Mrs. DaMantova answered.

"Signora," he greeted, "This is Campanello."

"Who? I don't know you. We're not talking to anyone. Please."

Her voice sounded as if she had been crying.

"*Aspetti!* Campanello, you know, like in church?"

In case she did not link *campanello* with *bell*, he spelled it out for her: "*Sono visitato da lui.*" He had visited them; that could be anyone, but he hoped his terrible Italian would give him away.

"*Senti!* I just want you to know the paper isn't right. La mortadalla Mantova it talks about? You know? The one you wanted?"

Graham prayed his discourteous "*senti*" telling her to listen would tip her off to what his malaprop sausage actually was.

"*A si, Campanello! Allora.*"

Her exaggerated precision showed she knew his command of the language was a joke.

"*Cosa vuol' dire 'mortadella?'*"

Graham breathed relief that she wanted to know what he was trying to say about bologna.

"*Senta,*" he said, formally this time. "*La morta dalla Mantova.*" He pronounced the Italian for "the dead lady from Mantua" carefully.

"*Capisc'?* I just want you to know that particular item is still available if you're interested. Not to worry, the notice is incorrect. But only for you. *Capisc'?* Good customers."

"*Ooo! Va benissimo! Grazie! Tante grazie, Campanello! Ci verrò oggi. Ne vendrò.*"

She played it perfectly, telling him she would step right over today and buy some.

"Ci vediamo."

Graham hung up before anyone listening managed to figure out his news about bologna actually carried a message quite different—that the dead lady from Mantua was still available. He stepped away from the phone and looked up and down Aspen Street before heading back to Joe's. She had him completely paranoid.

40

Graham felt loose and edgy as a cat, rising from sleep sometime before dawn to steal out to Joe's front step. He hunched there watching the bright line in the east become dawn, remembering a distant Asian morning where a soldier washed up along the coastal highway, the war's jetsam. To all the sun comes.

He stood and gingerly fingered where Meachum had kneed him. Relieved to feel less sensitive, he padded back into the house to take a leak. In the shower, he drank gallons of water to ease his parched throat but resisted Tori's insane musical gargling. Joe was still snoring in his bedroom when he emerged.

He considered his sorry head in the mirror and stuck his tongue out. At least his hand was more hand-sized again. After a quick shave, he kicked into his shoes and headed for Macy's to wire himself on coffee before consulting Sarah.

From the north arrived the trickle of the Rio de Flag. Dawn bathed the San Francisco Peaks in bright relief. Flagstaff yawned and stretched itself around him in the early hour. A sharp snap attracted Graham's attention as a buxom young woman in a house dress flapped a sheet in the mountain air from a second-story bedroom, then reeled it inside. A growl of locomotives pulling a long freight up the grade from Winslow broke the tranquility when their air horns blatted reveille. Several blocks away, crossing bells began to clang.

He turned over every aspect of his last night with Tori as he walked. Could things have turned out differently? That was what tormented him. For that matter, she would probably still be fixing hair if he had not dragged her into that demonstration. Perhaps everything followed like a Greek tragedy from the first time he saw her, like *Antigone*.

Because of him, Meachum got drawn in. He had brought this calamity on, and Tori had all but put Meachum's lights out. He turned up his bandaged hand; she'd have taken that rock in the head if he hadn't caught her. The whole thing was too fraught to contemplate, but he could contemplate nothing else.

The train clanked auto carrier after auto carrier across the Beaver Street crossing by the time he reached Macy's. He expected to wait until they opened to get his coffee, but the crew-cut waitress with the chains and tattoos had already switched on the lights and wiped down the picnic tables out front. Graham ordered a cappuccino and took it outside to warm his good hand while the street came to life in a wash of early sun.

Two cappuccinos later, a group of veggies were playing hacky sack in the parking lot across the street; the scuff of sandals and quick laughter punctuated their balletic saves. Hints of patchouli made scented notes over the smell of fresh-roast coffee. New customers arrived, a few joining him outside at the tables. A bearded

217

man in hiking boots and cut-offs lounged in dark sunglasses at a nearby table reading Edward Abbey. Across from him a woman in heavy Navajo jewelry and a long tail of gathered, decidedly non-Indian silver hair shaded pages of D.H. Lawrence from the bright mountain light. Neither looked up. They seemed oblivious, beyond sampling their croissants, to the gifts lavished about them. Graham was totally buzzed on the day by now.

He regarded the Fujiyama rise of Mt. Agassiz and, but for his splinted hand and the wispy smoke still curling against the limpid sky, would never have believed what a hellish night he survived up there. Shipwrecked on the reef of Tori's cosmic outing, Graham knew he would never steer his safely plotted course again. She had sunk that boat. He tipped up his latest cappuccino until it drained froth into his nose and made him sneeze. His tablemates never looked up, and the kids went on playing their innocent hacky-sack across the street.

Soon it would be eight, still early to start for Sarah's office. He had nothing settled, nothing figured out.

A great-looking girl in Spandex pedaled by on a mountain bike. Graham was still admiring her when an all-too-familiar voice startled him.

"My my, if it isn't our caretaker, on the street again."

Graham turned his head back to discover Imre Gyorgy leaning his hands on the rail around the tables. Gyorgy's heavy eyebrows rose as his full lips curled in menace. The bearded man in the cutoffs at the next table glanced up briefly but went back to his book when he saw the remark was aimed elsewhere. The woman with the jewelry seemed not to have noticed.

Although Graham knew he would never carry off the act a second time—especially without the mustache—he tried anyway.

"Mr. Agent! Sorry things didn't pan out on that woman you was lookin' for."

Gyorgy squinted him up more closely.

"You're that guy they picked up in Michigan."

Graham stroked his bare lip. "You think?"

"You're playing with fire, my friend. Drop the act. You were in cahoots with her. If I blow the whistle, you go to the slammer. You read me?"

The bearded man's sunglasses showed over the top of his book. He carefully closed his book and eased away from the table to leave. The woman with the Navajo jewelry suspended her own reading and looked around for the shortest way to the sidewalk. Very deliberately, Graham slid his cup aside. Obviously Gyorgy wanted to make breakfast of him.

"Listen to me." Gyorgy leaned in closer and lowered his voice. "You're over your head here, pal. We know what DaMantova had, and we'll get it. You can save yourself a world of hurt by telling us where it is."

"I really can't do that."

"Don't play with me, pal. We'll grind you up. It's only a matter of time, and you haven't got much of it."

"It never was her you needed, was it? It was her idea."

"Sherlock!"

Adrenaline kicked in. He was walking on the edge again, where things got iffy. Tori's patrol-shack revelations were not going to suit Mr. Gyorgy.

"The way I see it," he said, "you have a few problems."

"I'm not the one with the problems, pal."

"Let's see about that."

Graham put up his wounded hand and began with the little finger.

"First, the technology is banned under SALT II, so it does you no good."

He moved to the splinted ring finger.

"Second, we agreed under START to deconstruct such items. That's a problem."

Graham went to the next digit to tick off his third point and hoped it was not lost on Gyorgy which finger he was using, even if he couldn't raise it alone.

"Both of which bring into question just what you could actually do with her design."

Before Gyorgy could voice an objection, Graham ticked off on his index finger the final point, which he formulated as he went.

"Finally the whole idea becomes strategically worthless anyway, because—"

Gyorgy leaned across the table and got right in Graham's face.

"You don't seem to understand the gravity of the situation here, smartass. If she's told you how it works, we won't hesitate to disappear you. Nobody will say a thing."

"That wouldn't do you any good either."

Gyorgy jabbed a finger in Graham's chest, and Graham flinched at the pressure.

"Believe me, you'll talk. Before we're through with you, you'll wish you'd never been born."

Graham's tablemates had disappeared. Across the street the hacky-sack players had called time out to watch. To push one more button, Graham threw a final monkey wrench into the works, totally making it up as he went.

"I might talk. She knew that."

Graham let that register a second.

"You think she wouldn't take account of that? It's all arranged: If you get her secret, well-placed individuals will make the whole design public. All of it: how to build it—and how to defeat it. Think about it; who could better undo the design than the designer? The moment you get it, it's obsolete."

Graham automatically brushed his hands together and then wished he hadn't. Ouch.

"Just like that. *Finito*," he managed.

"Oh, really. How would they know?"

"Interesting problem, isn't it? You have no idea who's watching. Neither do I, but I know she worked it out."

"There's no way she could do that. She wasn't that smart, and she's dead."

"Smarter even."

Graham slid his sunglasses down and peered over them.

"Disappear me. But I tell you this: Once the plans change hands, you hold the big zero, my man."

Gyorgy awarded him a look of disgust. "You're dead meat, friend."

"People are watching."

Graham rose from the table and walked around Gyorgy with a space prickling between his shoulder blades where he expected a small missile to enter and either kill him or render him unconscious. The guy truly scared him.

From behind, Gyorgy said, "Don't say I didn't warn you."

41

"Did you hear about this?" Joe said. "Look at the headline."

Joe was still squirming on a tee shirt, paper in hand, when Graham hurried past with his ball cap tugged so far down he risked running into things. He didn't want to explain his shaved head again.

"Any chance I can use your car?"

"I've got class at ten," Joe objected.

"No problem, I'll have it back," Graham snagged Joe's keys from the hook by the door. He needed to talk to Sarah pronto. Outside, he slid into the Ranchero and cranked away until Joe appeared at the car window.

"You flooded it, man. Hold it to the floor."

Carburetors. Half the gauges didn't work either.

Graham held the accelerator down and cranked some more until the engine finally caught in a stinking cloud of blue smoke. Another car jerked to a stop behind, and a Volvo appeared in the mirror. Speak of the devil.

High heels emerged, and the mirror framed Sarah Fitch approaching in a tailored dress. A dark froth of gathered hair outlined her face, and turquoise decorated the hand she slapped onto the door.

"Where do you think you're headed?"

Graham gawked. "Look at you!"

"I asked you a question."

"Over to see my lawyer?"

When she ducked to peer in at him, her big, round eyeglasses framed mascara and eyeliner. Even Joe shifted his attention. She made an arresting package dressed up.

"What'd you do to your hand?"

"Hurt it."

"Hm. I guess when your car's impounded, you borrow." She was practically in his ear.

"Say what?" Joe reacted.

Sarah looked over her shoulder. "They found his car at Snowbowl." She turned back to Graham. "Hey, how about turning this tractor off? The fumes are giving me a headache."

Graham switched off the ignition.

"Thank you. And take the hat off so I can talk to you."

She reached in to remove it, but Graham jerked back and peered from under the bill, the pitcher sizing up the call.

"Uh-uh, new look. You like?"

"What's the matter with you?"

The matter. How to start?

"Nothing. Just speechless to see you."

"Stop that! I'm serious. What's up?"

Graham sighed. "Okay, that trouble we talked about the other day? It just got worse."

"Why am I not surprised? Tell me about the car. What took you up Agassiz this time?"

"Tell me you weren't mixed up in this," Joe said.

Graham took the paper Joe was brandishing and scanned the lead story:

Man Killed on Snowbowl Road

FLAGSTAFF: An out-of-town man was killed and another injured in a rollover yesterday that ignited a brush fire along Snowbowl Road. A Forest Service fire crew contained the blaze by day's end.

He skipped down the page:

The accident occurred against a flurry of rumors that federal fugitive Vittoria "Tori" DaMantova has been hiding in the Flagstaff area. … DaMantova has eluded arrest for over twenty years following an Ohio nuclear plant bombing in 1970.

The story finished with a note about Lesley Alvarado:

In connection with DaMantova's apparent escape, the fate of missing Snowbowl employee Lesley Alvarado remains unknown. Alvarado was reported missing two days ago, and authorities fear DaMantova may have abducted her while trying to flee.

Graham offered Sarah the paper, but she shook it off.

"I've read it."

"What is this?" Joe said. "Is this the woman you've been chasing? Don't tell me; you're some kind of secret agent."

"What are you talking about?" Graham objected.

"You were in the war, man. You came back all hush-hush."

Graham sighed, climbed out, and dangled the keys out to his friend.

"Here. Guess I've got a ride."

Joe took the keys, blinking at him.

42

"Since when the glasses?"

Sarah handed them to him without taking her eyes from driving. Graham held them up to look through plain glass.

"Image." With that curt explanation, she got right to the point. "Look, it's a matter of time before everyone and his dog figures out what happened to Lesley. You already knew who she was when you came out here. That's how you hurt your hand, isn't it?"

Graham laid the glasses on the console between them and mumbled a weak acknowledgment.

"Buckle your seat belt. Talk to me! Yes or no?"

He buckled. "Okay. Yes."

"That's better. You may as well know I've listened to your interview with Jordan Reno. When did you hear all that from her?"

"The last time we talked."

"In Michigan then."

Taking Graham's silence for assent, she went on, "She still committed a crime; that's the bottom line, especially for you." She arched her eyebrows and took a quick look at him. "I see potential for obstructing justice, possibly aiding and abetting. You were trying to help her escape. On the plus side, you put yourself at risk for Agent Parrish. According to his report anyway."

"He said that? How do you find out all this stuff?"

"How do you think?"

Years and all, the Berkeley girl was still there. She worried her lower lip the way she did when provoked. Suddenly aware of his scrutiny, Sarah turned and frowned.

"What?"

"You could get the plans for the atom bomb."

They locked eyes, and she gave a slight shake of her head. "Back off. I'm cleaned up for court."

She was still fixed on him when a motion in Graham's peripheral vision caught his attention.

"Watch it!" Graham exclaimed, pressing his feet to the floorboard.

"Oh my god!"

Too distracted to register the bell, Sarah nearly put them into the windshield as the railroad-crossing gate missed dropping on the hood by inches at the San Francisco Street crossing. Shortly, four locomotives rumbled past towing a mile of freight cars. She pressed her hands to her cheeks and faced the passing train.

After a second she collected herself to place her hands back on the steering wheel.

"Smooth. Get us killed." She had to shout to make herself heard.

"Sorry. I shouldn't—"

"Really." She turned and looked at him for several long seconds before adding, just enough to hear, "That was a long time ago."

She averted her eyes back to the train. Another dozen cars passed before she shifted gears, as if nothing had happened.

"She left upper Agassiz in the afternoon?"

"Who? Where?"

"Who? The woman you're after. I'm asking if she left the ski lift. At the top."

"Oh. Yeah. The guy up there saw her before the storm started."

Sarah let about five freight cars roll by. "And?"

"I hung around but never saw her."

"You didn't. So what did you do?"

A string of GATX tankers jounced over the crossing while Graham formulated. "Stayed up there and walked down to the lodge in the morning. I didn't know what else to do. No one was around the lodge, so I started for town. It was on the way down I saw the accident."

Sarah let another tanker pass. "And Parrish had been tailing you."

Graham nodded.

"You didn't identify David Meachum."

The gate rose, but Sarah waited for him to explain.

"No one asked me to."

Someone honked, and she jolted across the tracks.

"Okay, help me understand something: Where was Meachum at the accident?"

"Lying in wait?" he tried. It sounded questionable even to him.

"Lying in wait. For what?"

"For somebody to come along."

Sarah drove a block processing this before asking, "Did he say anything about this woman, DaMantova?"

"Didn't Parrish cover that?"

"You tell me."

They arrived at Sarah's office, and she pulled around back to park. The engine ticked off heat as she waited.

"Well ... he said he killed her, Meachum. Must have already caught up with her somewhere. He did have blood on him."

"That could have been his own. He'd just been in a rollover."

"I suppose, but I bet if they check—"

"This is bothering me why Meachum was waiting around the accident."

Sarah pushed her door open. She was ambling head down toward her office with her hands clasped behind her when Graham caught up.

"The gun they recovered had been emptied," she said. "Parrish was only hit once. What was he shooting at?"

"Tori. Before."

"Hm. It was Parrish's gun, though. He had another gun on him, you know."

"I didn't know," Graham said as they went inside. Sarah's receptionist gave him a smile; without thinking, he removed his cap and hung it on the coat tree by the entrance. Sarah glanced over and did a double take.

"Yes, they— What did you do?"

"Oh. Um, yeah. That." Graham passed a hand across his scalp.

"Yes, that. What happened to your hair?"

"Well, she, um I... you know, cut it off. Looks different, doesn't it?"

"Yes... She?"

"The hairdresser. I had her shave it."

"Ah. When did this happen?"

"After I saw you last."

She picked up the *Arizona Republic* lying on the receptionist's desk and took it into her office with them, where she motioned him to a beat-up Morris chair.

"Not that you'd want to alter your appearance. Or wear a hat to hide it."

Frowning, she scanned the paper before handing it to him.

"The latest," she said. "It comes a little closer to your story."

The phone rang, and Sarah swiveled away to pick up. Her voice faded to background as Graham scanned this story.

Fugitive Missing in Flagstaff

FLAGSTAFF: A ski area employee missing and first thought abducted from Flagstaff's Snowbowl by bombing suspect Vittoria "Tori" DaMantova yesterday may actually have been DaMantova herself.

The Republic has learned preliminary results of ongoing investigations conducted by the Coconino Sheriff's Office and U. S. Justice Department into the injury of one federal agent and death of another, as yet unidentified person. Early findings indicate that the ski area employee identified as Lesley Alvarado, 50, and missing since July 19, was actually DaMantova, sought since 1970 for her role in a fatal Ohio nuclear plant bombing.

Wednesday, the day before a fatal automobile accident on Snowbowl Road, ski area workers reported seeing DaMantova near the summit of the 13,000-foot San Francisco Peaks as a storm approached. While she has not been seen since, a source who declined to be identified stated that DaMantova may in fact have been intercepted on Thursday morning and killed in a gun battle near Sunset Crater north of Flagstaff while attempting to escape. Other officials remain guarded about this account.

Graham looked up. Sarah had swiveled back at him behind the distressed mission-oak library table she used as a desk. It had all the marks of a thrift store buy.

"So what was the purpose?"

"Of what?"

"The hair."

He hoped she'd forgotten. She hadn't.

"I was scared. There were all these people running around with guns."

"They weren't hunting you."

"Meachum was."

Sarah tented her fingers under her chin and studied him.

"You're holding out. What are you not telling me? If I'm going to help you, I need to know what's going on."

"I'm telling you everything. You have to trust me on that."

She picked up a pen and rapped it endwise on the dark wood table, considering.

"Trust you. I'll think about it. Now, you were on your way to see me?"

"I had a run-in with one of the government agents this morning. There's a prelude to it, too…"

Graham gave her the expurgated, Tori-free version of his confrontation with Kirk and Gyorgy at the Snowbowl before going into the one with Gyorgy that morning. When he finished, Sarah whistled a long breath through her fingers.

"You have a knack for trouble, don't you? You need to think twice before launching stunts like that."

She focused on him before adding, "I won't even ask what you were doing in the lodge, lest we add breaking and entering to the charges. And how about not antagonizing anyone else? You don't need that. Meantime, I'll see what if anything I can do about what you've already stirred up. Check in with me, here, toward six."

•

By five-thirty, the slant light of afternoon flushed the peaks with sun and gilded the last snow from Wednesday's storm. Tomorrow he would beg a ride to Snowbowl before anyone else got to Alice. Maybe he could learn where she'd stashed Tori.

Sarah's car still sat in the parking lot behind. Inside, no one appeared to be around, so he called her name.

"Back here."

He discovered her in a room at the rear, paging a legal tome at a card table that fit right in with the impromptu look of her office. She poked her glasses down to see him.

"So. I gathered a few pieces for you. Which do you want, good news or bad?"

"Good?"

226

"Sucker."

Graham sighed and sat down to hear.

"The federal prosecutor wants a grand jury to indict you for obstructing justice and possibly more. Your undercover chums claim you deliberately stalled them so DaMantova could get away. Some kind of wild goose chase searching the lodge."

"That was their idea."

"I'm just telling you. You initiated contact with a fugitive. You should have reported it and didn't; they see conspiracy. And it hasn't escaped their notice that you managed to enter the lodge somehow."

"Conspiracy? I don't know what happened to her any more than they do."

"I'm afraid they're fairly certain what happened to her. The blood on Meachum's clothes could confirm it. They've determined it's not all his; whether some of it is hers would depend on a sample of her DNA, which they haven't got.

"This is going to sound heartless," she continued, "but we need to lay our hands on some of her tissue, fluid, saliva, anything like that." She narrowed her eyes at him. "Do you have anything?"

If only, but nothing came to mind. Her glasses were toast. If he wanted souvenirs, there weren't any. Except...

"The FBI has her underwear."

At Sarah's astonished look, he said, "They seized it from my bedroom as evidence. Parrish ought to know."

She arched an eyebrow. "Underwear. Okay. I'll work on that. Oh. Here's another item I picked up, whether it has any bearing: Snowbowl actually lost two employees yesterday. Their bookkeeper went missing, too—a Navajo woman named Alice Mendoza. She took one of their vehicles to town and didn't come back. This morning they found the vehicle in the lower lot with the key in the ignition."

"And no bookkeeper."

"Yep. She did call in, around nine. Said she picked up a drunk hitchhiker on the way into town, and he threw up in the front seat. She had to clean it up, so that was why."

"I'll talk to her. They were friends; she'd know something."

More importantly, he could warn her to keep quiet.

"You might, except she told them she was leaving for a funeral on the reservation and never showed up."

Graham's insides turned over.

"A funeral?"

"That's what she said."

"I should go."

"Go? For what? To stick your oar where it doesn't belong again?"

"I just thought maybe—"

"You thought maybe she knows something. Forget it. All we have is her Flagstaff address, and no one's there. I checked. The place has been cleared out. And the rez, you wouldn't know where to start; it's bigger than New Jersey."

"What do we do?" Graham asked.

"*We* do nothing. It's you I'm worried about. You need legal help to keep your butt out of the slammer."

"Would you? Assuming you'd even think about it, I'd need to figure how to pay."

"Oh don't worry; you'll pay, one way or another. For time being we'll chalk it up to… whatever, evening scores; I don't know. It's not exactly my field, and it would depend on your being straight with me. Especially that."

Sarah tented her fingers and regarded him. He regarded her back. Sarah sighed with resignation.

"Think about it, Graham. I'm on the rez until Friday taking care of business, so I'll be pretty much out of touch. Can you stay out of trouble until then?"

"Believe me, nothing'd suit me better."

"Atta boy, just sit tight until I get back." Her expression softened slightly. "I know the rez. I'll see what people have heard about Alice."

43

The day Sarah left for Navajo country, Graham set off on foot to explore Flagstaff. The sheriff had his car impounded—probably, Graham suspected, to keep him from leaving town. His wanderings finally led him up McMillan Mesa, an ancient lava flow bisecting Flagstaff. Here above the traffic and houses, dry grass scented the breeze. Wildflowers nodded in the sun. Just off the northern edge stood the massive volcanic rise of Mt. Elden.

Far below the southern end of the mesa, a railroad train blared at the crossings as it snaked through town; beyond, traffic bucketed along I-40 for Albuquerque and LA. Somewhere, Tori was still out there. Her past almost caught up with her this time. Driven back underground and out of his life, he just hoped she'd survived.

She'd ripped his reordered life apart, that's for sure; he should be relieved to have it over. He wasn't. Something about her charisma with all these women and the way her advocacy for them closed their ranks around her wouldn't let him. All those years she had supported Art Montgomery's family at the risk of being discovered, a quarter of her meager income.

Still, it wasn't the merit badges he missed; it was her presence: the whimsy of her Edith Piaf impression, the sand scent of her hair, that Modigliani face. Tori had blown a hole through him. Touching her, at whatever cost, had rearranged him.

In the end, he would have to make something from the pieces. Once this was resolved and his car released, he would return to Marquette, where notoriety might even lend him a certain cachet: the man who hung out with Tori DaMantova. Graham pictured himself Marquette's desperado. Students would whisper about him and queue up for his classes. Some recompense.

In the meantime, when Julie called, he'd say to keep her head down. Further involvement at this point would spell trouble for both of them.

It was almost four when Graham shortcut across the swale of the Rio. Halfway over, a tiger cat was hunkered on the next stone. It regarded him amiably, but the debris trickling past offered more interest. Finally the cat deigned a silent "meow" as Graham balanced onto an alternate rock. Unable to resist, he squatted to stroke it, and the cat slit its eyes and nudged into his knuckles. When Graham rose and tottered to the other side, he saw the cat abandon its pursuit to prowl along.

Turning onto O'Leary, Graham spied a police car parked in front of Joe's house. He didn't have a good feeling about this, and started back toward the Rio with the cat in tow. When he looked over his shoulder, two officers had stepped from the car to beckon him. Running didn't seem an option, so he turned to see what they wanted. As they walked up to intercept him, one of the officers was an intense, dark-haired young woman who did not invite trifling; the other, a linebacker with a moustache and boot-camp buzzcut. The cat situated itself at the edge of the grass to watch the proceedings.

"Alexander Bell?" the man asked.

"That's me, but people call me 'Graham.'"

"Whatever. You need to come with us."

"What's this about?"

"You have a warrant for illegal entry, criminal trespass, and obstructing justice."

44

Everyone else had been taken away to pay their fines or serve their time. Graham faced the blank TV monitor that dominated the roomful of classroom seats. A few minutes ago, he and three other arrestees who'd joined him during the night had been brought in to confront a tired, balding man on the screen who arraigned them one by one. Except for one, the other two got a few hundred dollars for disorderly conduct or public intoxication; when it came his turn Graham got charged with manslaughter, conspiracy, obstruction of justice, trespass, breaking and entering, aiding and abetting and ordered to remain in custody. No mention of bail. The others sneaked looks at him as they filed out.

Graham nodded, half asleep. His night in the holding cell had been a stint in an asylum. Sleep proved impossible on the hard fold-down that served as a bed with all the lights on. At first only he and some skinny, disreputable dude too whacked out to say anything coherent shared the space. His teeth were occasional at best, and his eyes didn't track. During the night, the police hustled in two more with attendant commotion, the larger of them a black man the size of a phone booth and still combative enough for Graham to guard his face against random impact.

It wasn't the frustration and dark thoughts; he could lie on his stomach only so long to escape the lights overhead before having to roll over and cover his eyes with an arm. The others snored and mumbled; he could neither ignore the racket nor turn it into background noise. The choice was to cover his eyes or his ears as he lay awake. A sourness of skin, alcohol-sweet exhalations, and the ammoniac reek of urine added to the delights.

When he was brought in, the booking officer couldn't have been more matter-of-fact: "Empty your pockets. Everything on the counter. Belt, shoelaces, rings, jewelry." She swept it all into a plastic bag and swiveled a form for him to sign. The rest followed like clockwork: the routine he remembered too well from his post-war misadventures. The telephone on the holding-cell wall worked only for collect calls, and the receptionist at Sarah's office wouldn't accept.

But no bail: decidedly not routine. Graham studied the blank TV, trying to make sense of it.

He was dozing off again when the door bolt slid back. He raised his head and shook it. Sheriff Reno was closing the door behind him, looking preppy as ever in his crisp tan uniform. Graham sat up and folded his arms, blinking hard to clear his vision. Wordlessly, Reno scraped a chair around and sat with his arms on the back facing Graham.

"You don't look so good. Need that hand looked at?"

Graham shook his head. "Guess what, I don't feel so good. What's going on?"

Reno interlocked his fingers and studied him. "I didn't have you brought in."

"So who did? Why no bail?"

"The federal magistrate says word came down from DOJ. Department of Justice. Washington," he explained. "Word has it more charges are coming down the line. You're in a world of trouble. I'd say someone's squeezing you. They think you're withholding information."

Graham said nothing for a minute, considering.

"Why are you telling me this?"

"Just FYI. So are you?"

"Am I what?"

"Withholding information."

"Um, I'm not sure what you mean."

Reno studied his face. "That you might have something to give up if your prospects become bleak enough. Which they will. I hear they're considering treason. Then you go to federal lockup. Not in your favor. Is there anything I should know that's germane to your situation, beyond what you already told us?"

Germane. Graham was so struck that someone like Reno would use the word that he almost laughed. The impulse died under Reno's dead-serious gaze and his warning of treason.

"We're off the record here," Reno assured. "Trust me."

"I don't know, maybe. Why?"

"There's something funny going on. I'd like to know what it is."

Graham considered. He studied a blot on the concrete-slab floor—dried blood?—uncomfortable with the whole discussion. Finally he looked up. "I don't think so. Not without understanding the ramifications."

Ramifications. There, Mr. Germane.

Reno waited a few seconds, then shrugged.

"Suit yourself. Just understand I'm not the enemy. I'll try to help, but I'm no longer in charge of what happens. It's been taken out of my hands."

Reno studied him a second longer. "I have to ask you: the coroner's report. What did you use, a ball bat?"

"Whatever I could get my hands on, "Graham said. "It was him or me."

More like a moutain lion, he thought.

Reno shook his head, then unfolded his arms and pushed away from the chair. "I'd appreciate it if you don't tell anyone we spoke. I will mention it to Ms. Fitch. She is representing you, I take it."

"Certainly hope so."

"For your sake, so do I."

Official now, Graham was given jail duds and taken to a block of cells farther along his escort called a "pod." The cells opened upon a common area with a listing picnic table and a worn bench against one wall where the inmates ignored the nattering TV hung well beyond reach. Two heads gave back and forth on a screen specked with what Graham hoped was food. He recognized the black man palming out fierce rhythm on the end of the bench as the one who'd routed his sleep last night. In the daylight he resembled a commercial refrigerator. One inmate stared at the wall, methodically scratching his crotch. In one of the cells a man on the crapper with his pants around his ankles studied Graham with inter-est.

The guard delivered his final admonition with a jerk of the chin toward the ceiling before letting him in. "Behave yourself. We monitor."

The heavy clank of the door drew the sidelong interest of a wild-west saloon sizing up the new hombre. The holding tank had amounted to bad weather: keep your head down until it's over. Here, Graham could look forward to extended acquaintance. It was not lost on him that his was the only white face present.

45

"Got Jesus?"

Graham had just stashed his towel and bedding in the assigned cell and taken up a vacant seat among three or four others in the pod following what turned out to be a Diamondbacks game the talking heads had interrupted. The query cut through the racket of the bench-slapper like neon.

The prior occupant of the holding tank yesterday, the slight Indian man with occasional teeth, awaited an answer. An hour ago, the remote-control judge had set him a $10,000 bail for armed robbery. Graham had trouble matching this sorry specimen to such derring-do. Graham remembered him as Morgan something. Begay?

Graham weighed how hard the man might take his denial; he had, after all, the balls to perform armed robbery.

"Nope."

The man mouthed something but Graham couldn't hear it over the bench beater keeping time with some hard-edged rap about pigs and bitches.

Graham cupped his ear. "What?"

The skinny Indian mumbled something with a direct stare.

When Graham shrugged helplessly, the man leaned closer and intimated, "God gave his only begotten Son. John 3:16. Gonna save you."

The reek from the inmate on the crapper was beginning to arrive. This guy was in here for armed robbery telling Graham to get Jesus?

"Don't bet on it."

The man shrugged and turned to the TV.

Ridin' in the squad car, cruisin' through the 'hood

See a ugly bitch think she lookin' mighty good," racketed from the end of the bench beyond the defeated evangelist.

The pod door clanged shut again, and Graham turned to see a burly, half-shaven Hispanic with a heavy moustache arrive. Paying as much attention to all present as someone headed across a motel lobby, the man dropped his bundle in the cell where Graham had just put his. He exited the cell and stood under the TV.

"Who the hell's in my bunk?" he bellowed.

Graham, inspired by the surroundings, put up his middle finger. The man squinted at him. Graham kept his attention on the TV as the man maneuvered into his line of sight.

"Hey, asshole, I can't see," an inmate on the other side of Graham from the Indian Jesus freak complained.

"Then take yer head outa your ass," the burly Hispanic growled without taking his eyes from Graham.

"What are you, a smartass?" he said at length.

Graham finally deigned to acknowledge him. He shrugged. "I'm the bunk."

The racket at the bench did not let up.

Pigs pick me up 'cause the bitch set me up

Gonna put the ho down when I get back on the town.

The mustachioed man looked over his shoulder. "Shut the hell up!"

The black rapper stood and put fist to his crotch. He gave a couple of tugs in the Hispanic's direction. "Bite me."

With the other hand he hamboned his thigh to a new verse.

Wetback dude got a cob up his butt

Can't keep his motherfuckin' loudmouth shut.

Whackatawhackatawhackatawhack.

The PA over the door crackled. "Hey! Knock it off or go to segregation."

The poesy cut off as the black rapper faced the Hispanic expectantly. The Hispanic shook his head and arched a fist in Graham's direction without taking his eyes from the rapper.

"Enjoy the bunk. Pleased t'meetcha."

What the hell, Graham bumped fists. "Yep."

The rapper sized them up and returned to his scabrous rhyming until a solo opportunity should present itself.

The Hispanic turned his attention from the renewed racket to his expedient ally. "Zat?"

"Said I plan to."

Graham had earned enough stints in the slammer after the war not to be a pussy. His new friend obviously had, too.

The Hispanic considered him. "Rough mother. Break that hand on somebody?"

Graham nodded. "Yep."

"Good. Who do I want when I need ass kicked?" the Hispanic asked.

"Graham, like the cracker."

The Hispanic estimated Graham some more. "Machado. Hector. Kinda mean mother you be, Graham Cracker? I gotta keep an eye open or what?" He sucked his teeth under the moustache and squinted.

"Not really. I shouldn't be here in the first place."

The picnic table took an alarming lurch as Machado plopped himself across from Graham.

"You too. Some dude starts it with me, and it's assault."

Graham's alarm went off. This wasn't his first rodeo in the slammer; no one volunteers why he's in. To see how it would play, he decided to reciprocate.

"Me they got on some trumped-up conspiracy deal."

"Conspiracy?" Machado narrowed his eyes. "What's yer name again, Cracker?"

"Graham."

Machado snapped his fingers. "Yeah! You and some woman, like Bonnie and Clyde. It was on TV."

Just as he thought. No news had connected Tori DaMantova with him. The last time anyone drew that connection was when she escaped from Marquette. The guy was a snitch.

If he was right, Graham could manufacture some luck here. If he was wrong, things wouldn't get any worse. What Sheriff Reno intimated had him worried. He had a pretty good idea who was behind his arrest, and it didn't bode well. Maybe he could delay the train wreck anyway.

Waiting until the evangelist had Machado's ear, Graham asked a guard if he could use the phone. Since he couldn't leave word with Sarah, he tried Joe. Sarah wouldn't do for this anyway. Relieved to catch him home, Graham snapped his fingers over his shoulder and motioned at the guard for a pencil and paper. Graham scribbled away while he told Joe he was in jail and needed a visit ASAP.

Graham crumpled his notes into a fist and rejoined the fray in the cell block. He fidgeted forever before the wall speaker crackled through the din that he had a visitor.

Down a narrow passageway lined with steel doors, a guard admitted him to the second one and locked him in. Graham found himself in a closet-sized chamber with a heavy glass window and stool. A telephone handset hung on the wall. Joe appeared on the other side of the window, looking as if he were facing a tsunami.

"Jesus, man," he said when Graham picked up the phone, "what kind of shit you got yourself into?"

"It'll blow over. They want information on Tori DaMantova, that's all. If my daughter calls, tell her I'm fine."

Graham leaned to the glass. "Meantime, though, you could do me a favor."

Joe looked at him warily. "Is it legal?"

Graham pointed to his ears and the phone before setting it aside to smooth out the paper he had torn into quarters. Hesitating a beat, Joe set his own phone down. Graham showed him the first paper. On it he had written, *"You're too late. We have it. Fidel."*

Below that, Graham had written and circled, "Write this big in Spanish on a sheet of paper."

He'd had to write so small to make it fit that Joe had to pull on his eyelid. Making it out, Joe rummaged his pockets until he came up with a ballpoint and scrap of paper to write on and scribbled it down.

When he looked up, Graham held up the next quarter sheet.

"Get a big cardboard mailing tube and put the paper inside."

Joe jotted another note. Graham waited for his eyes to show him the next piece.

"Top of the road: Big Snowbowl sign, below the first parking lot. Know it?"

As soon as Joe nodded, Graham held up the last piece he'd written on. Here was where he asked Joe to enter questionable territory.

"Toward dark tonight after everyone's gone. BIG leaning tree by sign. You'll see it. Hide tube there under dirt."

Graham waited for his acknowledgment before wadding the paper in his fist and taking up the phone again.

"Will you?"

Graham scanned his friend's face nervously. He would be perfectly justified in refusing. To his relief, Joe's lips curved. "Know that tree; it's an old limber pine. I take my classes to see it. How deep?"

Graham breathed again.

"Don't knock yourself out. Tonight?"

Joe looked at his watch and nodded, getting to his feet. "You'll owe me."

"You bet. One more thing."

Joe frowned and sat back down.

"You ever see a yellow tiger cat around your place? Maybe down along the Rio?"

"Sometimes," Joe ventured. "What about it?"

"Could you take him in? You know, unless he lives somewhere. Until I get out?"

Joe relaxed and flashed him a lopsided grin. "You're kidding."

"Would you?"

Joe shrugged. "I'll consult him. If he's cool, you're on."

"Fair enough."

They bumped fists on the glass, and Graham knocked for the guard.

46

That night, the first in his new quarters, Graham lay on his back staring at the ceiling with his arms crossed behind his head. He thought it would be nice if they ever turned out the lights around here and put a damper on the ongoing cell-to-cell trash talk and laughter. It had to be near midnight, but he wasn't sleepy. He was waiting.

Graham had no idea how this worked, whether Machado would begin or was waiting for him to say something. Finally, just to show he was awake, he ventured as if to himself, "Anybody ever sleep in here?"

"Whazzit sound like?" Machado laughed, too quickly. He'd been waiting, too. Probably hadn't wanted to go first lest Graham think him nosy.

Okay, Graham would toss him something to work with.

"Know a good jailhouse shark? I need my ass out of this place."

Machado snorted. "You and me both, bro. Shoulda thought of that before."

"What's that supposed to mean?"

"What do you think, jackass, they build jails for model citizens?"

Graham smiled to himself; Machado was fishing. Now it would take finesse. Twitch the hook.

"That's bullshit. I know why they picked me up. It's harassment."

"Who you jiving, Cracker? They don't like your ugly ass so they throw you in jail. C'mon!" Machado gave a snort.

"They think they can break me."

"Break you? Like you some big gangsta?"

"Forget it. Nothing." Graham rolled toward the wall and waited.

"Hey, I got news for you, sweetness: Boo hoo. What I heard, that was big shit you were in, FBI."

"You don't know jack," Graham said to the wall.

"Well enlighten me you're so all-fired innocent."

"Piss off."

Jive from the other cells continued as Graham waited for Machado's move. After a minute it came.

"Okay, say I buy your story. How do you explain the *chica?"*

"What chica?"

"Bonnie."

"You wouldn't understand."

"Just sayin'. Don't look good, mixin' with somebody like her. How's that go?"

Graham grinned self-congratulation to the wall and re-baited his hook.

"How's I supposed to know what was up? I didn't even know who she was."

Little by little, Machado's questions became more pointed without being provocative. Graham suspected the coroner's report had earned him points there: Machado didn't want to piss him off enough for a repeat performance of what happened to Meachum.

Machado asked what Tori was like and what kinds of things she talked about with Graham. Just what had gone down with her?

Graham obliged him with all kinds of stories. Several minutes of silence passed while Machado digested the news that Tori had Cuban contacts in the Mexican police. Graham worried he might have overdone it until Machado observed from the other bunk that she must have been pretty smart to keep from getting caught this long.

"Smart ain't even close. I could tell you things."

"Bullshit. You're pulling my leg."

Graham made fists and clenched his teeth. Only Machado's breathing broke the absolute silence from the other bunk. He wished he'd been able to see Machado to read how that malarkey was going over.

Finally Machado whispered, "Try me. I'm not gonna believe you."

Graham let out a breath of relief. "Eat shit."

"So you got nothing. You had me going there."

Machado wanted a rise. Graham gave it.

"She said I couldn't tell. Anyone."

"She said. You big pussy, why the hell should you care?"

"Because. Okay, just between you and me: This woman?"

"Yeah?"

"She had spy stuff."

Graham held his breath.

After a long time, Machado ventured, "I heard. That's kinda what the TV said. She was carrying it around with her then?"

Chomp.

"No, she hid it," Graham said.

"Figures. And you don't know where."

Graham said nothing and waited.

"Do you?"

"Maybe."

"C'mon! If she had stuff like that, she'd never tell *you* about it."

Graham reacted to Machado's scoff like the patsy he was supposed to be.

"Don't bet on it. We were like *that.*"

"Get outa here!"

"She did. She rolled up all this secret stuff in a tube and buried it next to a big limber pine, by the sign going into the Snowbowl. Didn't believe me, did you?"

"Good story."

"Whatever." Graham crossed his fingers and pulled his blanket up.

47

The day before Sarah was to return from the rez, Graham got the visit he expected.

This time the monkish and balding Roland Kirk scowled through the heavy glass visitation window. When the gaunt DIA agent signaled him to pick up the phone, Graham shook his head. Kirk had to gesture more urgently before Graham would put the phone to his ear. The agent wasted no time in chitchat.

"Real joker, aren't you?"

Graham drew back, wounded.

"You know what I'm talking about," Kirk said.

Graham knit his brow and shook his head.

"I suppose you want me to think you had nothing to do with that tube by the Snowbowl sign."

Graham shrugged helplessly. "I shouldn't even be talking to you."

Graham replaced the handset in the cradle and stood. Kirk beckoned furiously on the other side of the glass for him to sit back down.

They locked eyes through the glass. Kirk might believe Graham was stringing him along but couldn't discount the alternative after what Graham had told his partner—that Cubans might have Tori's guidance system. Trusting that Kirk couldn't afford to be wrong on this, Graham held his gaze.

Nothing he knew would give Kirk what Tori had designed—except for approaching the problem from the wrong end and her cryptic remark about E8 mathematics, whatever that was. He'd never encountered the term in his own mathematics studies, and he doubted any of them would know either.

He had no idea what means of interrogation they might use on him, but he'd seen what they'd done to Meachum. If they could pry out of him what actually happened up there on the Peaks, they'd hunt her down. If there was half a chance Tori was telling the truth about what she was carrying, he couldn't risk that. He couldn't risk her.

In the end, whether she'd told him the truth didn't really matter. Beaten nearly senseless, she'd still saved their lives, admitted, but it was the memory of her in that dark, makeshift loft above the ski area's equipment building that wouldn't let him.

He wouldn't, couldn't give her up, even if she'd lied. To delay that eventuality, the best he could do was to buy time and hope it was enough for her.

Looking more confident than he felt, Graham turned and signaled the guard to let him out. He never looked back; Kirk would surely read his face.

Back in the block, Graham found Machado gone, transferred out, according to another inmate. Whether Kirk thought Machado had fulfilled his mission or not, he had outlived his usefulness here. Graham sat against the wall rubbing his shoulder as he reflected on the encounter. He had crossed a line, and it scared him. These people were calling the shots, and he worried what they could do to him. He hoped he could devise a way to jam the gears before they ground him up. Would they really use the coercion Gyorgy had threatened?

48

"I'm right outside, ma'am, if you need me."

"We'll be fine," Sarah assured the guard, and he shut them into a small interrogation room that offered a pair of cheap plastic chairs for parking oneself, a shaky card table, and little else.

"I was about to give up," Graham greeted.

When Sarah slid her chair up and touched knees, he jumped as if he'd been burned. A Saturday, she had on jeans, sneakers, and a knit top—the decorum he was used to. Gray flecked her dark-brown hair, tamed in haste; she hadn't bothered with the eyeglasses.

"There was a note on my desk when I got in last night. Your friend Joe left word about you."

"Listen, this sucks. I hope you can get me out."

"Right now, that doesn't look promising." She leaned forward and gave his leg a pat. "I'll give you the unvarnished. People higher up are floating treason charges. Frankly, I was surprised to find you here. I thought they'd have you in federal."

"I know. Sheriff Reno warned me. Is that serious about treason?"

"Afraid so. I might have kept you out when they first arrested you. Honestly, it seems too well timed. Somebody knew I was out of town and moved on you. Now they've had time to generate this other stuff. They want more on DaMantova; that's what Jordan thinks.

"Jordan?"

"Reno, the sheriff. I called him last night."

"Then you know I was denied bail."

"Because of the treason thing. Reno says they didn't file the paperwork yesterday. Some kind of temporary hold. Maybe it'll buy time; I don't know." She raised an index finger. "I did ask around the rez, and no one's seen Alice. For whatever that's worth."

She searched his face until he grew uncomfortable enough to look away.

"I know you were hoping she had something. Want to tell me what?"

Graham folded his arms and scanned the spartan room. The only window was the reinforced square in the steel door, and no one seemed to be watching.

"Can we talk openly here?" he said.

She shrugged. "We're under video surveillance." She indicated a small glass eye in a corner of the ceiling. "No one is listening, if that's what you mean. They have to respect lawyer-client confidentiality."

Graham put his fist under his chin, making up his mind.

"Remember I told you about running into Imre Gyorgy at Macy's? How he wanted to get his hands on the process Tori had created? And I told him it would be made public if anything happened to us?"

Sarah sighed. "I remember that little adventure. I doubt he took you seriously."

"Maybe not, but yesterday Roland Kirk, the other DIA guy, came to see me."

She leaned to poke his chest. "You should not be talking to him, Graham."

"I arranged it."

She jerked back as if he'd slapped her. "You *what?*"

Graham leaned toward her and imparted in whispered tones his suspicions about Hector Machado and the buried tube with its fake note from Fidel Castro. He did not mention Joe's part in the caper.

"Gaah!" Sarah put her hands to her head. She drew them over her eyes and peered through her fingers. "Did you stop to think what that could have set off?"

"I needed to know if he was a plant."

"What was his name?"

"Hector Machado."

She dropped her hands. "Probably made up."

"I thought. They moved him yesterday, so I was probably right."

"You can't do stuff like this, Graham. You're in a world of hurt."

Graham offered his palms as if the justification was self-evident. "Yeah, but the treason charge is on hold."

"Don't count on it. Once nothing happens, they'll file. They're not giving up that easy."

"We need the time. Some things about this whole fiasco they mustn't find out."

For starters, he didn't want to unravel the construction Parrish had spun for the authorities. Not only would he make a liar of Parrish; he would give up Tori.

Sarah worked her mouth, absorbing that.

"So *do* you know where her stuff is?"

Graham shook his head.

"What are you afraid of giving up then?"

He studied the floor, trying to think how to do this. He squared his shoulders and met her look. "Okay, here's the thing: This is a shady procedure to say the least. Why did they bring Meachum into it? I think it's some kind of free-lance operation."

"What makes you suspect anything irregular?"

"I overheard Kirk and Gyorgy talking the morning Meachum got killed. Beforehand. How they were using Meachum but worried about him."

Sarah teetered her palm down. "Or it sounded like that to you."

"No, there's more. I think the feds or maybe just these two guys enlisted Meachum, even knowing what he did, because they wanted to find DaMantova to get what she'd developed. At the same time, Meachum was hoping to get to her first, either to sell the system to the highest bidder or to shut her up; I don't know which. Somebody's complicit in a cover-up."

"What?" She got in his face. "That would implicate the Defense Intelligence Agency. Holy cow, what have you got yourself into? Do you have anything to back this up?"

"Gyorgy admitted as much. He threatened to 'disappear' me so they could break me down. I'm pretty sure that's what they did to Meachum."

"You're reading more into this than it warrants."

"Meachum was explicit about it: They made some kind of coercive arrangement when he was in prison, and they were paying him."

"When did he say this?"

Well. Meachum had been holding a gun to Tori's head when he said it.

"It was— He implied it when I first met him, that he was like a bounty hunter for the feds, and he said it openly when he assaulted me in my house."

Sarah sat blinking. "Wow." She tented her hands under her chin and gnawed her lip, thinking. "If you could prove any of that..."

"Check it. See where Meachum was imprisoned and who came to visit. Find out if he has any financials. What if you could connect Kirk and Gyorgy in a conspiracy with Meachum?"

She ran a hand through her hair. "That's big. I can't promise it, given the time we have. Meantime, do not—I repeat, do not—speak to anyone about this. Refuse any meetings with Kirk or the other one, what's his name?"

"Gyorgy."

"Gyorgy. Do not speak with them."

"Okay, but I bet if you track down Meachum's prison and his contacts, you'll find both of them."

Sarah whistled out a long breath. "I don't know if we can get that kind of information. That was so long ago, and I have to tell you: It seems out there."

Graham dropped his voice to a whisper. "Get hold of Julie, my daughter. She's doing an investigative piece and may already have come across some of it."

"You don't want her involved. This is dangerous."

"She knows it. You need to contact her before Kirk finds out what I know."

"Like what?"

"Tori DaMantova got blamed for what Dave Meachum did."

"How can you be so sure?"

"Read the deposition I gave Sheriff Reno again. There's proof of it."

Sarah crossed her arms and sat back in her chair to regard him skeptically. "I'd have to see it."

"Has Rosario Castellanas approached you?"

Sarah rocked forward. "Rosie? About what?"

"Go see her; she knows why."

49

Sarah blissfully returned early enough next morning to get him out of the evangelist's Sunday Bible study. His cheer turned defensive when she abruptly stopped in mid-pace to face him with her hands fisted on her hips as he came in.

"Jesus," she charged, "You didn't tell me she had kids."

"Has," he corrected. He avoided her eyes. "I didn't think it was relevant."

She glared at him for a second. "At the risk of sounding like a broken record, I'd love to know what else you find irrelevant. So what's this you told Rosie that the daughter might have? And don't mess with me; Ted's waiting."

Daring her wrath, Graham put up his hands and stepped closer. "Tori discovered a note among the documents Meachum removed from the research lab. She wasn't supposed to know he took them, but she found out. It was a note Meachum had written to the night guard who smuggled out the documents for him. It said to meet in the lab."

Sarah shifted her weight, hugging herself and looking unsatisfied. "So?"

"It said to be there when Meachum was going to activate the explosive."

She dropped her hands to her hips and leaned in toward him with a look of disbelief. "You're saying he set him up? To eliminate him?"

"Exactly. And by the time Tori found the note, she had less than an hour. She tried to warn them, but it was the middle of the night."

Sarah put her hands to her cheeks. "Holy cow!"

"Holy cow is right. She packed her kids on an airplane to California and went underground. She's been bankrolling the guard's family ever since to atone."

"They know this for sure?"

"Nobody knows it. The widow thinks Meachum has been sending the money."

Sarah sank onto one of the plastic chairs, still holding her face. "I'd give my arm to see that note."

"She gave it to her daughter when she put her on the plane."

Sarah jumped to her feet and grabbed his arm. "She still has it?"

Graham put up a cautionary hand. "Could. She remembers it, but she was only a kid. She was going to look for it."

"Going to... you've *spoken* with her? Jesus, Graham, *tell* me things. *That's* why Rosie wants me to see you."

"Her name is Jen Park, *Dr.* Jen Park, and I have her phone and address in my billfold if you can get it from whoever keeps stuff here. And go easy. She has your name, but she's not going to trust you. The deputy wouldn't have made first base with her."

Sarah drove a hand through her hair. "I don't know how to manage this. I'm busting my butt now. It might have to wait until we get you out."

"It can't. This is the key. Trust me; we show it was Meachum, and the rest falls into place. If it's the expense, I'll find a way."

She sighed and shook her head, staring at the floor. "It's not expense; it's time." She glanced at her watch. "I gotta run. I'll let you know."

Back in the pod, enveloped in raucous profanity and man sweat, he saw why Sarah's presence rattled him: Being female, her design was slicker, and she smelled a whole lot better.

•

The man thrashed in panic, unable to make a sound or draw a breath. His chin stubble pricked Graham's palm as he wrenched. Something popped, and the man became dead weight with his gear. Graham had all he could do to keep him from dropping. The others were lurking in the dark. He sank slowly to his knees embracing the man, and made out his face. It was Dave Meachum.

Someone bumped him. He recoiled and opened his eyes to darkness, pressed against concrete and panting.

"You okay, guy?"

All Graham could manage was a low moan.

"Hey, you need help? I can call the guard." His new cellmate's voice took on a tone of alarm.

"No. I'm okay."

"You don't sound okay."

"Get dreams. Thought they were gone."

"Flashbacks?"

Graham hugged himself. "Mm-hm."

"Seen a shrink?"

"No."

"You oughta."

"I'll be okay."

He heard the cellmate ease himself back onto his bunk, and Graham listened for his breathing to slow as he lay awake staring into the dark.

•

"Graham! This is unimaginable!" Julie cried.

He'd just come in from potting at the lone basket with a couple of fellow inmates in the exercise area. The area made a beggar's atrium with no view but up; windowless concrete walls too high to see over surrounded it. Except for the basketball, the equipment looked like the stuff in a budget motel: a couple of treadmills that didn't work until someone complained, a four-station exercise machine with three broken stations, and a chinning bar. The pods had daily access for an hour; they looked forward to it like going to the movies just to see sky through the overhead fencing. He'd hurried off from the sweat and jiving at the news he had a call. Hearing Julie's voice on the other end was like music.

"Well imagine it. Where are you?" he asked.

"Still California. I was about to check in with you when I heard."

"Who told you?"

"Your lawyer friend. I can be there tomorrow or the day after."

"Wait. Are you still on this 'project'?"

"Yeah."

"I don't like it. Be careful."

"Don't worry; I know what I'm doing." After a beat, she added, "I met with the family."

Graham's heart tripped. "All of them?"

"Yep."

Graham worked his jaw. "What did the girl say?"

"Not much. Frankly, I got more out of the parents. She's really guarded, but I expected that. I guess the lawyer had been here the day before, and it made her wary."

"What lawyer? Sarah Fitch?"

"Yeah, her."

"What did they talk about?"

"You'd have to ask them. So can I come see you?"

"No. When the time is right maybe. Listen, watch your back, Julie. If any of these people hear…"

"Don't *worry*. And just FYI, Mom thinks you're getting railroaded."

Excellent. As if having Leila on his side did him any good.

•

The following week, Graham and the evangelist hefted warm armloads of towels from the dryer, where he'd got himself assigned to the correctional laundry after the prison nurse unwrapped his hand. The steamy, noisy work kept him from thinking too much about the forced inertia while Tori's disappearance grew to finality. He comforted himself with the thought that being free wouldn't bring her back either. The smell of hot laundry tickled his nose.

Graham folded and stacked clean bedding, trying not to dwell on the silence from Sarah. Four days now: It made a worrisome break in her pattern. The longer he was in here, the more he looked forward to her visits. After confinement with men, huddling with a female was water in the desert.

Up to this week, Sarah had been checking in every few days to report her maddening lack of progress. Freedom of Information requests, she said, were like watching trees grow. On the plus side, she confirmed touching bases with Julie in California. Julie had somehow uncovered a bank account that Meachum used but could not disclose her source. That concerned him. Still, Sarah said it was proving useful. Nothing had yet come back on the DNA, which apparently the feds wanted before proceeding with his prosecution. If nothing else, the delay offered a glimmer of hope to come up with something.

He'd spent three weeks in here, mid-August already. He should have been on his way back to Michigan by now to see if he still had a job—or a life. Instead, he might be looking at life in prison. Each day he passed in here was steadily shrinking his horizons until he could see them ending at the walls. Incarceration was like an endless bathroom break, biding time in the company of *Reader's Digest*. If he had to look at another year-old *Sports Illustrated* he would tear his eyes out.

His life was becoming way too basic: grub, exercise, shower, the crapper. Always on view; there was no privacy. When the chance to work the laundry presented itself, he jumped at it. Except for Sarah, his most stimulating activity was folding sheets.

If Kirk had waited a week or two to offer him a chance at snitching, he might have taken him up on it to break the monotony.

Julie had called several more times, but he still forbade her to visit. She should never acquire this image of him; if she considered that distancing, she would just have to think so. Now he saw why Tori had cut off contact with her children.

Sarah's last visit she'd been dressed for court. She tried explaining strategy, and all that registered were her knees.

Through the rumble of laundry equipment, someone called his name.

"Bell!" A guard beckoned from the door. "Hey! You got a visitor."

When he was taken to the interrogation room, he prayed it would be Sarah with news. It was, finally. She stood to greet him, too hastily he thought, and then sat back down, crossing and recrossing her legs as she riffled through a folder she'd brought, finally looking up to engage him. She was gnawing her lip, always a bad sign. Her demeanor got him edgy.

When she drew a long breath and touched his knee, he flinched. "Looks as if we're on, Graham," she began. "The DNA results came back Monday. It's sooner than I wanted. The lab must have put everything else on hold."

"You didn't let me know."

She ignored his accusation. "It's a match. Some of the blood was hers."

He relaxed that much. His story would hold up at least.

"For sure?"

"Definitely. The same person as the underpants."

"Search and rescue gave up," she continued. "They'd been all up and down Agassiz. At first they thought she fell or got hit by lightning, but all they found were a couple of empty tin cans above the lift with her prints on them. They combed the Inner Basin and even covered the forest along Snowbowl Road. Nothing.

"Sorry I left you hanging this long," she finished. "I've been putting in so much time on this the partners are about to run me out. But… we might have some payoff. Reno's kind of bent about the jurisdiction matter and helped me run down a few things. Now we may have something even better."

"Which is?"

Sarah hefted the folder. "Your daughter. This morning someone left a box off at the house. I'm still going through it, but it looks like records of Meachum's incarceration, including logs of his visits and written correspondence. I saw financial transactions as well. This could buy us some luck."

"Julie brought it?"

Sarah shook her head. "Some lady I didn't know, but it has to be from her." She put her face close enough to kiss. "I told your daughter what we're up against and what I need. I told her to stay under the radar, so she did.

"I'm still sorting out what I can use. I really need your eyes for this, but that's neither here nor there; I'll have to fly with what you've told me." She gave him a pointed look.

"How much time do we have?"

"Well. We face an evidentiary hearing in judge's chambers to go over what we have. Either we go to trial or we make deals. The feds thought I wouldn't be ready and wanted to go for it like yesterday. We're just lucky the DNA held them off this long. And maybe your little scam, too," she conceded.

She gave him a few seconds. "We're set to go day after tomorrow."

Graham swallowed. "Two days?"

She stuck her chin out. "Pressure focuses the mind wonderfully, Graham. You have no idea how good I am." She gave him a look and clarified, "At law."

Sarah waved the folder and rearranged her face to a patronizing smile.

"After Tori DaMantova, I'd be too tame for you. Good thing I don't have to defend *her*."

Graham blinked. Was she feeling resentful? "Why's that?"

She regarded him conspiratorially. "Conflict of interest. For her I'd lie if I had to and probably get myself disbarred."

He felt reprimanded. The implication was she wouldn't do that for him. Had he thought Sarah wouldn't defend Tori because of the connection? And whether Sarah knew it or not, he might have her lying for him anyway.

Then she dropped the bomb. "One more thing you should know. It'll be in Prescott. They're adding treason and plan to put you in federal detention afterward."

Treason. Federal penitentiary. Life. He had become Tori's stand-in. Dial it back to twenty years, and he'd be seventy.

50

D-Day: High heels clacked normalcy on granite. Graham heard laughter, a keyboard. People completed forms, rode the elevator, transacted business and went home. None of that world for him; he had come up a ramp at the back of the Prescott federal building in shackles with two federal marshals. At least Sarah had arranged regular clothes for him to travel in.

They arrived from Flagstaff with his belongings in the front of the van, a bleak sign that federal custody would continue after the evidentiary hearing. From the window of the van the high forest of Flagstaff had given way to scatters of piñon and juniper as the highway wound down toward the sleepy town of Ash Fork and their turn south toward his fate in Prescott.

Just past Prescott's old Courthouse Square they'd pulled in behind the stone Beaux-Arts structure housing the federal district court. He couldn't help registering the contrast with the New Deal Gothic where Parrish had interrogated him after Tori fled Marquette.

To his surprise, Julie was waiting when the elevator let them out on the second floor; Sarah must have let her know. When she approached him, the escort shook his head and warned her away, making it all the worse. She was blinking back tears, and he could do nothing.

"Thanks," he whispered as she backed away from the marshals stationed on either side of him. She must have dropped everything to be here. Sarah was to meet them at a quarter of nine. The clock on the facing wall inched around to 8:50. Where was she?

The elevator opened, and Sarah stepped out in a pants suit with an armload of paper. She had her hair up and the big round glasses, going for broke. Behind her followed Rosario Castellanas, Jordan Reno and a distracted Jen Park in sunglasses, dark suit, and heels. She gnawed a strand of black hair in the corner of her mouth and barely tipped her head at Graham. She did not acknowledge Julie.

"Sorry, she got delayed," Sarah explained. "We can go in."

Julie trailed the marshals leading Graham into the wood-paneled courtroom; a jury enclosure stood empty along the wall. At the front of the room waited a small, bespectacled woman with a red pixie cut that he assumed to be a court reporter. Neither acknowledging their entry nor their very presence, she seemed suspended, like the clockwork fortuneteller in a gumball machine.

Nonetheless, Castellanas broke out a tape recorder as she and Reno seated themselves with Jen, while the marshals steered Graham to a table near the front where Sarah waited. Even at this far remove from the centers of power, the small chamber with its bas-relief seal above the judicial altar held something like the majesty of church. Graham wasn't feeling worshipful. The marshals removed his shackles and took seats in the first row near Julie, who opened a notebook and began writing. When she looked up at him, Graham managed a cheery look he did not feel.

Graham sat in nervous silence while Sarah arranged her folders and envelopes into piles. Reno coughed once. Sarah leaned toward him and confided, "The feds expect this to be a formality. Well guess what?" She gave a wolfish grin.

He avoided her eyes, still feeling wounded from their last meeting. She fanned through a folder and pointed her lips toward Julie.

"Some of this stuff is so old," Sarah intimated, "I wonder how she got her hands on it."

Graham drew a long breath to calm himself; the thought of really old documents didn't. Sarah must have noticed his anxiety and inclined her head to impart, "Hey, this is preliminary. We don't decide anything. All we're doing is sharing evidence. Still… it's going to be interesting."

He recoiled in disbelief. Interesting? She arched her eyebrows without smiling.

At two minutes before nine, District Attorney Joshua Netherby breezed in. Lanky and long-faced, Netherby acknowledged Sarah with a curt nod and leaned upon the prosecutor's table, tracing a finger along his notes. Noticing the marshals seated behind him, he spoke briefly with them, probably going over the logistics of Graham's transfer to federal detention.

By nine, Graham's palms began to sweat. Suddenly the side door opened, and Ken Castle, the district judge, entered in a black judicial robe, the high priest. The court recorder's head came up for the first time.

Netherby remained standing while the others rose as Castle swept up to his bench at the front of the courtroom and took his place. He was so small his shoulders hunched when he propped his elbows on the dais to wave everyone to their seats.

After a double take at all the people present, Castle rubbed his hands and said, "Let's get started. Ms. Castellanas, we have a reporter; you won't need that."

Sheriff Reno explained, "If you don't mind, your honor, because of the jurisdictional issue—"

Castle shrugged. "Suit yourself. You're welcome to share the reporter's table here so you don't have to work it in your lap."

So invited, Castellanas took the recorder and seated herself in front facing the reporter, who merely pulled her machine closer to make room.

"Your honor," Netherby began, "The FBI and two interested citizens would also like to sit in on this session if that's agreeable."

Castle, chin in hands, surveyed the crowd already present.

"We seem to be more or less public." He turned to Sarah. "Any objections, Ms. Fitch?"

"Is there a compelling reason for the interested citizens?"

Castle raised his eyebrows at Netherby, who explained, "They have an interest in monitoring certain confidential matters that might come up. Regarding the FBI, we have not settled the jurisdictional issue, so they have cause."

Castle nodded and addressed his reply to Sarah. "Given the throng in attendance already, it's hard to say no. Ask them to join us, Mr. Netherby."

The language seemed clear; Graham was going down.

His eyelid twitched when he turned to see Floyd Parrish enter the room on crutches and a walking cast. With his burnt eyebrows and buzz cut still growing in, he looked like a slightly sinister Daddy Warbucks. Imre Gyorgy and Roland Kirk followed him. Like the recorder, none of them acknowledged the presence of anyone in the room.

"This is preliminary, so we won't stand on ceremony," Castle began. "The whole truth so help you God, okay?" He nodded to the room. "All right, whom do we have here?" Castle asked.

Castellanas ticked off the people in the room for him. When she finally came to Jen, Castle ignored the rest for a moment to address Jen directly.

"So you are the daughter of Vittoria daMantova, Ms. Park. Interesting."

"Dr. Park. I am a physician."

"I see. And where are you a physician, Dr. Park?"

"At San Francisco General Hospital. Sir, your honor, I hope my name can be kept out of this. In the interest of—"

Castle propped his fingers together, all but hiding a condescending half smile. "That would depend on your involvement. Mr. Netherby, would you proceed?"

Netherby began, "The United States as plaintiff is prepared to enter criminal charges against Alexander Bell on several counts. Beginning with the most serious, we will show that he was involved in acts against the United States Government. Further, he has admitted causing the wrongful death of an agent of the United States Government. We submit his recorded interview into evidence. We further submit the testimony of Agent Floyd Parrish of the FBI to that effect."

Graham turned to Sarah, who just smiled at him. Then he noticed Castle watching, so he tried to keep his chagrin from showing.

She leaned toward him and whispered, "You knew that was coming."

As if that made it any better, hearing it aloud in front of his daughter. Castle kept glancing at him, so he stayed deadpan.

"Second," Netherby continued, "we would charge him with conspiracy against the United States Government. For this, we have again his own testimony that he knowingly consulted with Ms. DaMantova regarding the disposition of secret documents related to national security. This additionally constitutes at the very least aiding and abetting and could rise to the level of treason.

"Further, as to the involvement of Ms. Park," Netherby said, "we are entering a record of her telephone calls for the month of July."

252

Graham's leaky canoe was headed for Angel Falls, no paddle, and it now looked as if Jen was going over with him.

Netherby explained, "These records show Dr. Park received a call the morning of July 19 from an office phone at Arizona Snowbowl. We'll enter that as evidence of communication with Mr. Bell, we would assume about her mother."

Castle interrupted, "Is this true, Ms. Park, that you were conferring about your mother?"

Sarah answered, "Dr. Park has not seen her mother since she was six years old. She was speaking to my client, Mr. Bell here, about a piece of evidence I will be introducing."

Netherby turned and looked hard at Jen before asking, "Let me then ask this, Dr. Park: Was Mr. Bell alone when he made this call to you?"

Jen paused no more than a heartbeat to consider his question, but to Graham it seemed an hour.

"At the phone he was using... Yes, it was only Mr. Bell I spoke to."

Netherby said, "Did you discuss your mother's personal situation, anything related to the crimes she committed?"

"Excuse me, Mr. Netherby," Sarah said. "You mean 'charged with.' Whether she actually committed a crime—"

"I believe that's moot now, isn't it?" Castle cut in.

"It's hardly moot to her daughter," Sarah replied.

"All right, 'charged with,'" Netherby conceded. "I'm trying to determine whether she became party to the events, that's all."

Netherby turned back to address Castle, apparently satisfied for the moment.

"Third, we would charge Mr. Bell with obstructing justice and impeding the capture of a dangerous felon, Ms. DaMantova. For that we have the testimony of Messrs. Roland Kirk and Imre Gyorgy, who encountered him at Arizona Snowbowl the morning of July 19. I enter their testimony into evidence.

"In connection with that, we would also charge him with breaking and entering, since the record makes it quite clear Mr. Bell is neither an employee of Snowbowl, nor does he have access rights to any of their buildings. In connection with this, Mr. Bell made unauthorized use of one of their telephones, which constitutes either theft or fraud, depending on how we decide to construct it."

Netherby stopped and riffled through his papers before looking up to Castle.

"Is that all, Mr. Netherby?" Castle asked.

Is that all? Murder, treason, conspiracy, obstructing justice, aiding and abetting, breaking and entering, fraud? Is that all?

"For now. If more evidence becomes available, we may add to the charges."

"Very good. Ms. Fitch?"

The court reporter's fingers fluttered and stopped, taking it all down. Graham was in denial. He'd won the devil's lottery: Through no fault of his own, except for buying the ticket, he was going straight to hell, no get out of jail cards allowed.

Sarah began, "I am going to demonstrate that Mr. Bell's actions were quite honorable, admirable in fact. As to the death of Mr. David Meachum, the so-called federal agent Mr. Netherby raised, I would rely on the same testimony of my client and that of Agent Parrish he has already introduced to argue that in fact my client was acting both in self defense and in protection of another. He saved Mr. Parrish's life by striking Mr. Meachum down.

"On these intimations of treason and conspiracy, we have a very different story."

Sarah placed her first envelope on the table.

"Tori DaMantova sent Dr. Park away as a child to her biological father, John Park, when she was six. She carried with her an item her mother gave her, for safekeeping. As a child, Dr. Park followed her mother's instructions. While she did not understand the meaning of it, this is what she carried."

Graham came to attention.

Sarah fingered on a pair of white archivist's gloves and slid a folded scrap of yellowed paper from the manila envelope and began describing it verbally for the reporter and Castellanas's tape recorder while Netherby, looking surprised, rose speechless. Graham divided his attention between the paper and the court reporter. She was uncanny. She would look around watching whoever was speaking, her fingers moving in a silent blur whenever speech happened, sinking into suspension when it stopped, like a voice-activated robot. How could she do that?

"I am holding a slip of unlined, white paper, folded over and doubled again into quarters. On the outside appears the word 'ART', handwritten in blue, all caps."

The word *ART* appeared a second before Sarah's finger obscured it, teasing the note open as she continued her description.

"Unfolded, the slip seems to be about... four inches wide, vertically perhaps five. It appears to be torn from a larger sheet; the edges are uneven. The paper shows noticeable age.

"On the inside, the sheet fully opened now, I find written in the same ink and handwriting the following words: '*Meet me 2 am. Building T. Cash. D. M.*'"

Graham scanned the room as Netherby returned to his seat. Julie was scribbling wildly at her notebook while one of the marshals paged what looked like a manual. Jordan Reno propped his chin on both hands, eyes narrowed in rapt attention to what Sarah was saying. At the front, Castellanas pressed a tight smile into her knuckles. The court reporter waited, fingers poised. Across the courtroom, Parrish stroked his chin. Kirk and Gyorgy revealed nothing, while Netherby rubbed his nose. The marshal who had been reading closed his eyes; the other examined his watch. Jen he could not see without turning.

Netherby was first to speak. Running a hand through his thinning hair, he knit his brow and looked to Sarah for an explanation. "This proves what?"

"'*ART*' is Arthur Montgomery, the guard killed in the 1970 explosion. '*D. M.*' is David Meachum. Meachum was telling Montgomery to be in Building T at 2 a.m. That's when he set the bomb off. He set Montgomery up."

"You allege," Netherby said.

"Vittoria DaMantova told Mr. Bell to that effect."

Castle, Netherby, and the two DIA agents looked at Graham for the first time, as if he had suddenly coalesced.

As soon as she said it, Graham realized how implausible it sounded.

"Oh, *she* told him," Netherby said.

"At 1:45 she was 250 miles away in North Carolina calling the Miamisburg police to warn them. Her call is a matter of record. She had discovered this note and tried to prevent what happened. She tried to save Montgomery."

Castle asked for the paper and turned it over several times up at the bench with the gloves Sarah handed him.

"You're telling me this thing is that old."

"The forensic lab has already determined the degree of oxidation indicates at least twenty years have passed since its initial exposure to air," Sarah said.

Netherby leaned back in his chair and smiled broadly. "Why should we believe Meachum wrote that thing? D. M. could be DaMantova."

"Your honor," Graham spoke up. "I think I can show who wrote it."

Sarah along with everyone else turned to him in surprise, and Graham told her the marshals had the proof.

He snatched his wallet from the bag of belongings they handed over to her and fingered through it, praying nothing had been removed, until he found the card onto which Meachum had scribbled his address and phone number in Marquette. He held it up like the ticket to glory.

"Meachum wrote this and gave it to me in May. Match the handwriting."

He gave it to Sarah, who looked as if she could kiss him. "Thank you," she whispered. While she took the card to Castle, Graham caught a look at Jen. She was beaming. Up in front, Castle held both pieces of paper and squinted at them. He beckoned Netherby to make his own examination. When he finished, Castle raised his eyebrows and shared a look. Netherby seemed to concede the possibility.

"I admit similarities," Netherby acknowledged. "Even so, what are we supposed to see here?"

"Meachum's motive for killing Vittoria DaMantova," Sarah explained. "According to what she told Mr. Bell, her guess was that Meachum planned to sell the design. She discovered that, and he was hunting her down to get the design back as well as to keep her from talking."

"So what happened to this design?" Netherby asked.

"She found it in their apartment and took it with her when she went into hiding in 1970. That much Meachum knew, and it's part of the reason he wanted to find her. Based on what I've learned of him, he was set to take out anyone who stood in his way—Kay Eckert, Mr. Bell, even Mr. Parrish here."

"I'll vouch for that," Parrish spoke up.

Netherby looked impatient. "Okay, but Mr. Bell was helping to conceal classified government documents. That's still conspiracy, at the very least."

"If there were any documents to conceal. We don't know that. But you're absolutely right, Mr. Netherby; we are talking about conspiracy," Sarah said. "I'd even like to introduce further evidence in that regard. If you'll permit…"

She slid out her second envelope.

Graham gaped. Further evidence? He thought she was defending him. He tried to catch her eye, but she was intent on the contents of her envelope.

"Mr. Meachum was not alone in his interest. This is a copy of the sign-out for the motor-pool vehicle that Meachum drove July 15 and 17 up to Snowbowl. The first occasion is when he picked up and allegedly assaulted Kay Eckert; the second, we're not sure about. Mr. Roland Kirk, who I believe is the 'private citizen'"—she fingered quotes—"seated behind Mr. Netherby, signed this federal motor pool vehicle out. We assume it to be the same vehicle Meachum was using when he murdered Vittoria DaMantova."

Without pausing, Sarah produced her third envelope. "A .38-caliber handgun found on Meachum's body has been entered into evidence by the sheriff. The gun used to shoot Agent Parrish, also entered, was Parrish's own gun; but the sheriff has determined that the aforementioned .38-caliber handgun was registered to a Mr. Imre Gyorgy, also present I believe. Would you raise your hand? No? I would remind you that a clear condition of Meachum's parole prohibited the possession or use of firearms. If Mr. Gyorgy is the private citizen he claims to be, he is subject to prosecution for this violation. If in fact he represents a federal agency—as I think some of us in this room know he does—that agency would be well advised to provide some answers about the intent here."

As Gyorgy started to object, Sarah slid another envelope from her stack.

"Here I enter a copy of Mr. Meachum's parole agreement."

"Moving right along," she said as she slid one more envelope onto the table. "A record of Mr. Meachum's visitors while incarcerated in federal penitentiary lists twenty-one visits from Mr. Kirk between 1971 and 1978. The record is silent as to his whereabouts between 1978 and 1980, the date of his release. You might speculate whether private citizens Kirk and Gyorgy work for the same agency that we shall not identify. Is a connection taking shape?"

Kirk stood and leaned over Netherby's shoulder to whisper something as Sarah laid her final envelope out.

"Finally, we obtained Mr. Meachum's financial records, such as they were. These show he was a paid informant for the FBI and acted as a sort of consultant for them. Nothing surprising here; most of us knew this. Imagine our surprise, however, to discover notes about cash payments due from Mr. Kirk, sometimes quite handsome ones. Additionally—"

"Could you excuse us a moment, your honor?" Netherby said.

Kirk and Gyorgy got to their feet and preceded Netherby into the corridor.

Ten minutes passed while Castle scratched on a pad. Voices became audible outside the door, wrangling. As if on signal the room hushed. Castle even put a finger to his lips.

"Under no circumstances. Absolutely not." That was Netherby.

Gyorgy's voice uttered something menacing but indecipherable.

"You've got to be kidding me. You can't do that." Netherby's voice again.

The court reporter's fingers, flicking silently, seemed to be catching all of it.

Lowered voices haggled for several minutes more. Finally the door swung open and Netherby returned alone, grim. He brushed his hands together.

"We can't use any of that evidence. It's all classified, top secret for national security reasons. Turn it over to us, including the recorder's notes and her tape, and we drop the case. In addition, what happened in this hearing does not leave the room. It has to go away."

Here Jen stood. "Sir. Your honor. That note is my property. They can't have it."

"Your honor," Sarah said, "I am willing to suppress my evidence in return for their dropping the proceedings against my client, but everything I presented is public information. They cannot classify it after the fact. The court retains all evidence, and I'll agree not to reveal it—unless subsequent charges should arise."

"We would be willing to add the tape to that," Reno added.

"What say you?" Castle asked Netherby.

Netherby sighed, obviously exasperated. "Let me talk to them."

More discussion ensued outside the hearing room until Netherby returned.

"They want the evidence, the reporter's record. And the tape."

Castle tented his hands and studied Netherby across them.

"I find myself in agreement with Ms. Fitch. This court retains all evidence presented and the recordings thereof. Nor shall it be subject to seizure. The court agrees that these proceedings shall remain confidential. This much, however, is public: Ms. Fitch, I hereby dismiss the charges against your client for lack of evidence."

He banged his gavel.

Graham did not know whether he was supposed to jump up, run in circles, sign papers, or take a bow; so he just sat there, stunned.

As Castle made to stand, Jen asked, "Your honor, what about my mother's note?"

Castle regarded her a second.

"It remains your property; however, this court is retaining it for safekeeping. Only you and Ms. Fitch shall have access to it until such time as it no longer serves the material interest of her client or your mother. All agreed?"

Netherby turned up his hands. "No objection, your honor." He glanced at Sarah and addressed Castle again. "I apologize."

Castle gave him an avuncular smile. "Not your fault, Mr. Netherby. I could cite them for contempt."

Netherby pursed his lips, considering it, and then shook his head.

Parrish added, "When this reaches Justice, I expect they face more than contempt."

While Sarah collected her things and Netherby stacked his papers to shove into his briefcase, Graham looked questioningly at Castle, as he pushed back and stood.

"We have no further business with you, Mr. Bell," Castle said. "You may go."

Then he, Netherby, and the two marshals departed the chambers, each by their own doors. The next thing he knew, Julie had his shoulders, laughing through tears. In front, Castellanas looked quite smug as she popped out the tape she had just made. When she noticed Graham watching, she gave a quick wink before returning her attention to the recorder. Jordan Reno reached up and patted his shoulder as he got up to leave. Across the room, Parrish rose to walk out with Reno.

Sarah stacked her materials, while Jen stood on the other side of her, trying to signal something. Sarah glanced up at the vacant judge's bench before looking over her shoulder at him.

"That went well," she said.

Graham knocked Sarah's glasses askew as he took her into a bear hug with Julie. It was then he noticed Parrish had left and released the two of them.

"Don't run off. I have to see Parrish."

"Graham," Jen called, but he had to catch Parrish.

"Dad?" Julie said.

He dashed out but saw him nowhere. Graham clattered down the stairs three at a time and skidded to a stop just as the elevator opened on the ground floor to release Parrish and Reno.

"Mr. Parrish, could we have a word?"

Parrish tipped his head and turned to Reno.

"If you'll excuse us," he said and motioned Graham aside. He placed both hands on the crutch as if to forestall physical contact.

"What's on your mind?"

"Listen," Graham lowered his voice. "I don't know why you did it, but I just want to tell you how much I appreciate it."

"Oh? Did what?"

"Left her out of it."

"I have no idea what you're talking about."

Graham did not know what to say.

"Look, Bell, I am truly sorry about DaMantova. She seemed like a person I could have admired in other circumstances. To look at it in a certain light, you could say she risked her life for her country. Is that integrity? At the least she should have had a proper burial. She had a point, you know, about people who focus on ways to aim rockets. The Cold War is over.

"Just between you and me, I need to get out of this game. I'm no good for it any more; haven't got the heart. Maybe my allegiance is compromised, I don't know. Anyway, the wife's been after me for years to get back to New Mexico."

He paused. "You know we still would have had to charge her with transporting explosives and destroying federal property."

"I guess you would have."

"Of course; that's the law. So if it's any consolation, she's just as well off."

Parrish reached out and patted Graham's arm.

"Good luck, Bell. Maybe you can find... some peace for yourself now. I hope so anyway."

He walked back to Reno, who was waiting for him by the entrance, clapped on his hat, and together they left.

Graham ran back upstairs to find Jen and Sarah, but the corridor was empty. He was about to stick his head into the courtroom when Jen appeared around the door to the women's room and beckoned.

"I told your daughter and Ms. Fitch I had to go to the bathroom and I'd meet them outside." She began to whisper. "You called Chiara. What do you know?"

"You spoke to both of us the morning of the accident. What does that tell you?"

"She was with you. I knew I couldn't mention that, because if David already killed her somewhere else, how is that possible?"

"It isn't. She saved both of us, Parrish and me."

"Parrish. I see. But the blood—"

"Meachum hit her in the face. It got on his shirt."

"Is she hurt? Can I go to her?"

"She got away. That's all I know. She could be hurt. I haven't heard from her."

"Do you expect to?"

"No. You might."

"Should I contact you?"

Graham thought about that. Tori definitely ran a thrill ride at her funhouse, but the price of admission was out of sight, and his stomach was telling him he needed off. Quit while you're ahead. He had a prison in his future if he kept this up.

"Not about her. I think that would be best all around."

51

The road climbed into cloud cover and entered a world of silent evergreen looming from the mist and fading away. The headlights probed diffuse cones into the obscurity; dark boulders and cut banks appeared like magic, warning of the road's coming surprises. Clouds had shrouded the upper reaches of the Peaks since sunup. Graham would have preferred to show Julie the mountain on a better day, but her flight was leaving tomorrow. They would just have to see what they could.

She'd broken the news that *Rolling Stone* was buying the piece, so she needed to see where everything had happened.

Graham wondered how he would feel to return. Maybe revisiting the scene would lend a different perspective, one where he could wax philosophic if not exactly appreciative about all the fun that had come at him. Even if Tori Da-Mantova was no longer a factor in his life, banishing her altogether was another matter.

Icy drizzle wet their faces and plastered Julie's hair by the time they arrived at the lift. Chairs slowly coasted by, ascending into the gray ceiling; there was no view and the elevation had them gasping. At least Olivia was running the lift. As they debated the options, Graham could not resist directing Julie's attention to a thicket of mountain raspberry just visible upslope that they could pick.

"Later. Show me where she was last seen. Raspberries we can get any time."

Graham wiped his face, reluctant now. The place did not offer the epiphany he had hoped for; nothing about it felt right, in fact.

"I don't know. We're wet and it's cold. If you could stay tomorrow; maybe it'll clear."

"I can't. You have to show me. I need it for the story."

Relenting against his better judgment, he started toward the lift. At the top of the crossties mounting the way to the boarding platform, he saw Olivia and his mood improved. Olivia's wry smile of recognition brightened when Graham managed to catch his breath enough to gasp out what Julie had come for. She liked the idea. After answering Julie's questions, she warned them of temperatures in the thirties and the possibility of getting stuck if real rain developed, then loaded them with army blankets and a trash-bag poncho each.

"You don't pick good days, do you? Stay dry," she said, and the next chair scooped them away. Bundled in layers of wool to their feet, their blanketed heads emerged from holes poked through the weeping bags.

Julie's garbage bag moved as she scribbled blind notes to herself under the makeshift poncho when Graham filled her in on how he had come looking. Four towers before the partially dismantled midway ramp, he decided to tell her about the aborted rendezvous attempt that Parrish spoiled when he came up the lift behind. As the cable bumped through the massive sheave assemblies drawing them over the narrow plankway of the midway station, she left off writing to study the approaching ramp.

"You're supposed to jump onto that?"

"Yeah. Want to try? It's not supposed to be as bad as it looks."

Gaps dropped twenty feet on either side to steep cinder below. Julie considered it and declined. To their left, a grassy skiway curved off through the trees, and Julie bent forward for a better look.

"I wonder if she saw you wave her off."

"I'm sure she did."

"You assume so anyway."

Julie took one last look down the skiway and then sat back as the ascending cable swept them off. She turned once, and Graham followed her look along the line of chairs that rose and swayed from the mist on their way to the summit. Ahead, a set of lift towers emerged one after another from the clouds; they were approaching the top.

The cable rode over the fan towers and curved down to the top station, where Mark's familiar figure resolved itself, motioning them toward the pairs of painted footprints that told where to alight.

"Step to the side," he said as they approached, then recognized Graham. When Mark heard what Julie was writing, he left no doubts about his sentiments on the subject.

"Listen, you can quote me on this: Lesley was awesome; I don't care what they say she did. Ask anybody; we all feel that way. It's too damn bad all this other stuff happened, that's all." He spread his hands helplessly.

Mark's eulogy depressed Graham, and seeing the place he had spent that awful night did little to improve his mood. While Julie grilled Mark for any further details he could give her on Lesley, Graham snapped the water from his poncho and shrugged the army blankets around himself before drifting across the observation platform to mark the scatter of blooms proving life could be wrung from cold, wet cinders. He did not know how long he had been staring at the tough little plants, lulled by the brush of wind through the lift's rubbery squawk, when a low rumble emanated from the saturated clouds that enveloped the mountaintop.

He started. Julie was still absorbed in her conversation with Mark, their breath turning to vapor as they spoke. Graham headed toward them, but Julie met him halfway, her face actually gleeful.

"Graham, they're shutting down the lift. Did you hear the thunder?"

"Of course I heard. Can we get down?"

"Why? This is what Tori faced. Just the ticket."

Stuck here again? Not at all what he had in mind. Nothing about this adventure was turning out.

"He says to wait it out in the patrol shack and go down after. Do what you want. I'm staying."

Her bravado recalled Leila at her best: dauntless, this girl.

"You win. Come on; I'll show you where I bet she hid."

They were scrambling around among the stacked patrol sleds under the ramp when the cable ground to abrupt silence. Mark stumped around overhead gathering his things as Graham held the wire mesh open so Julie could stoop her way out. She stood to gasp for breath when a sizzle of electricity shot up the lift cable with an attention-grabbing crackle.

Silence. The air turned ominous, and they fled for the patrol shack. When Graham paused at the door to call Mark, his hair rose just before a flash and simultaneous blast of thunder flattened him to the wall; with no transition, rain was bucketing waterfalls off the roof.

Julie jerked him inside and put her mouth to his ear. "Awesome! This is monumental."

Mark burst in, totally soaked.

"What is it with you and weather?" he accused Graham.

The storm passed an hour later; incredibly, the overcast gave way to sun, dappling the land to the west: a typical monsoon gullywasher. Julie would get her view after all. Soon Olivia tooted on the two-way, and Mark wrapped in one of Graham's blankets to trudge up and restart the lift.

Outside, Julie gazed up the glistening boulder field another thousand feet to the summit of Agassiz. Her breath steamed in the evergreen and ozone lighting the air.

"Up there, that's where she went? Where's that go?"

"There's a caldera on the other side where the crater used to be. I guess you slide down a few thousand feet and walk out to the highway. I haven't been there."

"She didn't even leave a note?"

"She left word with Olivia, that was all."

A creak above signaled the lift had begun to move. Graham looked down the line to see a chair ease into view from the trees downslope.

"You know, I wonder if you could walk down. In the dark."

"Hardly. Myself, I'd never have found my way down without…"

She turned. "What?"

"Light. I waited until daybreak." No one, not even Julie, could know about Tori.

•

At the bottom, they returned the blankets minus one, still wrapped around Mark. When Olivia hoped they had weathered the storm, Julie assured they would not have missed it for anything.

As they walked away, a mad impulse to show off overrode Graham's prudence. To give Julie something completely exclusive, he asked if she wanted to see Tori's hideout. No one else could show her that.

Sammy the dog sidled up in his bandana, far more amiable about receiving his guests in daylight. He greeted Graham like a bosom buddy and accompanied them all the way into the repair shop. Only the Amazon who stonewalled him last time seemed to be around, muscling a sheave assembly from the back of a snow cat. She clanked it onto a workbench and noticed them when she reached for a wrench.

The woman raised her safety glasses and knuckled back a shock of brown hair. "Need something?"

"I don't know if you remember me. My daughter here is writing a story for *Rolling Stone* about what happened to Lesley. I just wanted to show her where she stayed."

The woman planted her feet and looked from one to the other, scratching her neck with the wrench.

"She never stayed here."

"It's okay. Alice showed me."

Julie added, "He got arrested because she was with him. When the police almost caught her in Michigan? And he just spent a month in the slammer here because he wouldn't give her up. The thing is, people have to know there's more than this Tori DaMantova stuff. They should hear about Lesley, don't you think?"

The woman twiddled the wrench through her fingers and back before pursing her lips and motioning her head at the ladder.

"All right, but I come with you. We keep parts up there, and I don't want you bothering anything."

As they emerged onto the loft at the head of the ladder, the space under the roof felt, if possible, more confined than it had in the dark with Tori. And then he saw the condom, still lying where Tori had snapped it..

"Eew. Looks as if somebody used the place as a rec room," Julie said..

The lift mechanic made a face and handed Graham a grimy shop rag from her back pocket. "Get that out of here."

The lift mechanic cast a sidelong glance at him and put a fist to her mouth as if to stifle a gag.

"Go ahead and look around." She stepped to the top rung and disappeared down the ladder.

After performing the housekeeping, Graham led Julie back to where Tori had stayed, the mattress, the foot locker where she stored her things.

When they climbed back down to the shop floor, Julie whispered, "Wait outside. I'm going to talk to her a few minutes."

Graham had time to chat up Olivia for another fifteen or twenty minutes before Julie emerged from the equipment shop, blinking in the sudden sunlight as she looked for him. He excused himself and fell in beside her on the way to his truck. When they got there, Graham suddenly remembered what Julie had done for him.

"Jules, I didn't thank you for that box of documents you got to Sarah. I'll never be able to thank you enough. I don't know how you managed to pull all that together, but it saved my butt."

Julie raised her sunglasses and faced him across the windshield.

"What documents?"

He placed both hands on the door to support himself.

Julie put a hand over her mouth and then slowly removed it, narrowing her eyes. "You know what, Graham? Dad?"

Graham caught his breath. She had not called him that before.

"Alice didn't show you that place. You're not telling me what happened here. What I'm going to say will never appear. I'm not asking you to confirm any of it."

She leaned her arms on the cab and continued, "Dr. Park actually opened up more than I let on. I told you Sarah Fitch had visited her."

"But you didn't say why."

"The note you mentioned. Dr. Park wasn't about to let it out of her possession, so the sheriff was threatening to subpoena it. What she told me, she agreed to provide it only if she could do so in person."

"Thank goodness she had it. I never thought—"

"That's not why I'm bringing this up. I asked her about Tori and told her some of the things I won't put in the story—like the subscription to the *Miamisburg News*— because… Well, you know why. That's when she volunteered about the note and why she was so upset over this subpoena: You'd told her to contact me first. And until I showed up on her doorstep she couldn't."

Julie rested her chin on her arms and studied him across the truck.

"You called Dr. Park from Snowbowl before light on the morning of the 20th. Tori was with you." She angled up a hand from the cab. "Just saying."

"An hour or so later, you encounter a car wreck down the road. It doesn't take Inspector Clouseau to figure it out: She wasn't on the other side of the mountain; she was here." Julie touched her finger to the roof. "I'm guessing she let you into the lodge to make the call. She probably shaved your head so you could get away. If you hadn't stopped to be a Good Samaritan—which I totally approve, by the way—it might have worked."

She waved away any protest.

"I said no confirming or denying, just a hypothesis. So. She was with you. I'm thinking she was with you at the accident. What I can't figure is what happened to her. I have this gut feeling the missing bookkeeper figures into it somehow. I wouldn't like to think Meachum intercepted her over here." Julie spread her hands. "I just don't know."

She put up both hands when he started to say something and shook her head in wonder.

"But you were prepared to take the heat for her." She traced the roof with a fingertip before looking up. "That's for real, Dad. And so are you."

CHASING ANTIGONE

CALIFORNIA
January 1995

Like distant surf, the rush of I-680 reached Graham high on the ridge. In the wee hours the pitch would drop to an undertow of commercial haulers speeding produce and machinery from San Jose to Concord, relentless. The big deal used to be watching taillights glide along Vallecitos Road past the Japanese camp, people headed for Livermore.

Livermore: Thirty years ago Tori worked there. She would have come up Niles Canyon, driven the very roads. Their paths had crossed.

The cold ridgetop sapped the heat of Graham's slog up after work. Down where Sinbad Creek purled winter runoff into Sunol, he could see the lamp left on in the house on Kilkare Road.

Lights glinted from surrounding hills that once raised only silhouettes against the stars. Christmas bulbs still winked in town. Some families left them up for months; the old man would not take them down at all if Mom didn't make him.

In summer Graham would climb the ridge behind the house to watch fog leak over the Santa Cruz Mountains and bank up against the Contra Costa Range, absorbing the day's heat while evening came on. Laurel and eucalyptus would scent the night. On clear nights Mom called out the constellations, ever the teacher; but tonight the overcast's diffuse light from the East Bay and the city beyond blanked them out.

They would lie on their backs and pick out the great Square of Pegasus or Andromeda in her chair as they traced majesty through the sprinkled heavens around Arcturus. Mom would direct them to the paths of Jupiter and Mars through the surrounding stars. Other nights he would solo up here like this to terrify himself imagining infinity. The earth and its pinpoint life turned in a universe so immense it trivialized the very notion of God.

Raw gusts off the Pacific, heralding rain, scoured the grass and whistled through the oak. Coconino the Cat came to attention when Graham turned up his collar and hawked into the gathering darkness. Cattle backed into the wind, chewing and drowsing. One could walk into them without a flashlight. Long familiar with these hills, he never carried one, which pretty much guaranteed he squashed his share of cow patties. At least the cat could see them.

A Western Pacific freight blatted at the crossings as it rumbled through town. Graham watched its light play over the tracks ahead, then fished out his har-

267

monica to try a few riffs on the Goldberg Variations. Unsatisfied, he put it away and lay back in the grass, re-running his encounter today. He could have called attention to himself, said something maybe, but there'd been no time. And to what end? She'd noticed.

•

It hadn't taken Graham two months in Michigan to realize what a mistake he'd made. Tori had laid him bare in Marquette, and his return tasted only of the exposure. Rather than lining up for his classes, people seemed afraid of him. He'd become the town badass all right, but not the way he'd pictured.

When reporters started calling after Julie's article appeared, that was the tipping point. Graham put the house on the market and began a cache of keepers: Skis, harmonica, and a dozen essential books joined it. The rest he gave away or ferried to storage to follow at some later date. Or not. The poetry of Ludovico Ariosto made the keepers first, the book she'd fished from his shelf.

"You'll know where to look," she'd said, and he did. A dog-eared page still held the fingernailed underline below the stanza that prompted her verdict on their mad coupling in the shop loft:

"Ah, why the fruits of love so sweet, but the time for savoring so fleet?"

•

He grew a moustache and left without forwarding. Whether Graham forsook Marquette knowing his wings would eventually bring him here he wasn't prepared to advertise. Perhaps he'd already recognized the destination when he begged his mother's blessing in Niles Canyon a year and a half ago. That seemed a lifetime now.

His sister Tara met him with the key to help him move in. He demurred when she tried to adopt the cat: It wasn't happening after what he and Coconino the Cat had lived through. As soon as the Marquette home sale went through, he talked his way into courses at Berkeley that would restore his physician's assistant license, feeling as if he had leapfrogged 25 years. By that time he sported a ponytail and introduced himself as Al Bell. It went without saying he scrupulously avoided contact with the DaMantovas; Tori's whereabouts no longer concerned him. Whether he remained on habitual lookout in the city didn't count.

Back in his element as an EMT, he joined an ambulance service out of Pleasanton and volunteered for Alameda County Search and Rescue. That was how he met Grace Royal: hanging from a helicopter on a search and rescue mission. Now they drove an ambulance, and he couldn't team with anyone better. Amazing Grace they called her. An unflappable EMT who could pull off the toughest rescues with aplomb, the woman had a head on her shoulders that she'd never dream of adorning. Earth woman, she never wore earrings or jewelry of any type. When you were Grace you didn't need to. So how to read her lack of a ring? That she didn't offer. Whatever her relationship story was, it would never do to bring up his own. Their partnership on the rig was too valuable and worked too smoothly to risk turning it awkward, so he took it a day at a time. On days they mountain biked, she focused on the ride while he tended to fix on keeping up.

•

Coconino the Cat leaned over Graham's forehead and tested his face with a paw. Graham had been lying motionless so long that checking for life seemed in order. He reached back to assure the cat he was still sentient as he reviewed this morning's rescue. Long-forgotten chopper missions had come along for the ride, and then to see Jen rocked his keel even further.

Early this morning a hunter called 911 to report his partner had managed to shoot himself about two miles from the nearest road. At the search and rescue pad minutes later, Graham went through the checklist with Grace and the pilot. While Grace inventoried supplies before liftoff, the base alerted San Francisco General in case they had to fly him there.

Once the pilot located a place to set down, they found the hunter sprawled against a tree with the shocky look of a combat casualty. His partner was pressing a soaked sweatshirt to his thigh. Both their rifles lay nearby.

Graham had Grace secure their weapons while he got permission to treat. While Grace was unloading the artillery, the hunter managed to identify himself as Elmer Frye. His partner explained Frye had been climbing into their tree stand when his rifle slipped and went off when it struck the ground. Graham took it all down, making no comment about climbing trees with loaded guns. The partner offered that Frye probably fell ten feet. Graham glanced up and spied a fresh divot in the tree trunk just below their jerry-built tree stand. Ten feet looked about right.

Frye's hand and foot responses suggested his spine had survived the fall, but Graham had Grace C-collar him anyway and immobilize him with their jackets the best she could while he cut away Frye's trouser leg to examine the injury.

The entry wound looked bigger than usual, and he couldn't find an exit wound. Graham asked if they were using lead ammunition, hoping they weren't but no such luck. The shell must have deformed ricocheting off that divot to introduce debris along with all the other damage it was doing in there. The leg was puffy and distending already. Graham had no way to tell how far up the bullet had lodged, but it had somehow missed the femoral artery or Frye would have bled out already.

When they tried easing him onto a stretcher, Frye immediately complained of severe breathing difficulties. Broken ribs from a fall like that wouldn't be a surprise; Graham opted for San Francisco pronto. They secured Frye on board with his legs elevated. He still had enough blood pressure for Graham to raise a vein and insert a catheter to start a slow drip.

"We'll take it from here," Grace told the partner, once they had Frye on the chopper. "Let his family know we took him to San Francisco General."

As they lifted off, Graham donned his flight helmet and had the pilot patch him through to the hospital. Grace started Frye on oxygen as they gained altitude, and the pilot explained they were Alameda Search and Rescue with a gunshot victim aboard. Once they had clearance, the pilot gave Graham a woman at San Francisco General.

"Dr. Park here. What's the situation?"

The name hadn't registered as the chopper beat across the ridges for the Bay. Graham had the pilot keep the flight as low as allowable. It felt too much like Vietnam, bearing a casualty to base camp on the kerosene tang of jet fuel, even if it was a Bell Ranger and not a Huey. At least he didn't have to worry about an RPG up the ass. As the bay appeared below, Frye's muffled responses through the oxygen mask became confused and his systolic blood pressure dropped below 100, so Graham increased the drip rate to maintain his pressure and monitored for renewed bleedout.

Among the medical personnel waiting by the rooftop pad he spotted a black-haired woman in green scrubs. Then it registered: *That* Dr. Park. As soon as Graham and Grace scooted out to extract the patient, Jen was at his shoulder for the particulars. He'd shouted them in her ear over the chopper racket without removing his helmet. Then he'd handed her the SOAP report and swung back aboard. As they lifted off, he'd seen her in the elevator looking back at the chopper before the doors closed.

The dispatcher had stopped him when he signed out just after seven this evening.

"Nice work, Al; you rate an attaboy. Here." She handed him a note that said Dr. Park had just called search and rescue from San Francisco to commend "EMT Bell" for saving the hunter's life. That was all.

Graham roused himself from the grass thoroughly chilled now. He stuck the harmonica back in his pocket and checked his watch. Grace would be coming by for her bike in the morning. He'd been too rattled to work on it when he got home, and it still lay in pieces on the kitchen floor. After she complained of her shifting on their last ride, he'd volunteered to install a set of Teflon cables and then taken her bike apart for a complete tune-up, showing off.

Coconino the Cat stretched and fell in as Graham picked his way back down the ridge in the dark to let himself in the back door. Instead of addressing the bike, he stepped over the parts in the dark and went to his bookshelf for the issue of *Rolling Stone*.

•

Julie's profile had appeared almost a year ago now, and he'd allowed her to identify him without realizing what it would entail. He figured *Newsweek* had already named him: How much harm could it do?

He snapped on the light and propped his elbows on the dining room table to read. An unfocused woman with an empty question mark superimposed splashed across the front page. *"Chasing Antigone: The Hunt for Tori DaMantova"* ran above the blurred figure, and the lead paragraph read across the illustration in large type. How many times had he read this?

Inside were the obligatory post-office mug shot and family photos. While she revealed Tori had children and the exonerating evidence one of them produced, Julie had given no actual names or whereabouts for them.

She estimated Tori had probably contributed $150,000 of personal restitution to the Montgomery family over 24 years, allowing both sons to earn university degrees.

Kirk and Gyorgy, Julie noted ironically, seemed to have "decorporealized."

Ending the Cold War changed the stakes. Last January, President Clinton and Russian Prime Minister Yeltsin inked an agreement to stop targeting missiles on each other. And just in time for publication, the Russians and Chinese made a similar agreement. Julie asked readers to speculate whether the threat of Tori's design had persuaded them.

She quoted people who firmly believed Tori to be the Unabomber. Others suggested she'd used convicted spy Aldrich Ames to pass her technology to the Soviets. Speculation was all over the map.

Julie's what-if angle lit the fireworks, though. Graham flipped to the end to read again what she'd written.

She detailed Tori's disappearance with extensive quotes from Jordan Reno and members of the search-and-rescue teams. Floyd Parrish resigned from the FBI shortly after, and one of his colleagues suggested he'd fallen on his sword for failing to apprehend her. Parrish himself declined comment for the story.

But... Tori herself never turned up, and Julie chose to end the piece on that note:

> *Tori DaMantova lies somewhere under the cinders of northern Arizona. Still, no trace of her has ever been found.*
>
> *With her languages and penchant for disguise, someone like DaMantova could blend anywhere from Texas to Tierra del Fuego, go local from Sicily to the Alps, or disappear into vast Pacifica. Her classical Greek would get her by on some scattered Mediterranean isle.*
>
> *She could be the cashier ringing up your groceries.*

No one, least of all Julie, could have anticipated the frenzy those five sentences would unleash. Before long someone got the bright idea of marketing a line of

Tori-Tees, featuring a blow-up of her mug shot on the chest under the legend, *Where's Tori?* A producer contacted Julie to option the screenplay, and negotiations were under way to make a film starring Meryl Streep.

Several Marquette colleagues asked him about it after the article appeared, and he gained his own fifteen-minute celebrity status—until notoriety upended his world when the newspapers came calling. That was when he folded his tent and left.

Fortunately, the Sunol filling station did not carry *Rolling Stone*; so no one in Sunol would ever connect him. It also helped when Tori's wanted poster came down at the post office. She became officially, if not yet emotionally, a non-person.

Only the tabloids wouldn't let it die, front-paging their blurry Tori sightings week after week behind dark glasses like Greta Garbo in his face at the checkout until the O.J. trial finally upstaged them.

The digital readout by the bed read almost one o'clock by the time Graham snapped off the light. Coconino the Cat was already flaked at the foot of the bed.

53

Graham had no idea how long Grace had knocked before she let herself in, creaking the kitchen floor as she inspected her bike. He pulled the covers over his head.

"Hey."

She nudged his foot, and he rolled over to look. She was clad in spandex tights and a sweatshirt with her hair tied back.

"God, what time is it?" he said.

"What do you think? Late enough for me to run over here."

"Good for you." He pulled the covers back.

"No you don't. Rise and shine. I'll make breakfast. I'm starving. I already fed Coco and let him out. It looks as if you've got some work to do on my bike."

As soon as she headed for the kitchen, Graham rolled out for the bathroom. He didn't bother shaving and pulled on some clothes. He emerged to find Grace leaning on the dining room table over the *Rolling Stone* he'd left on the table last night.

She looked up, raising an eyebrow. "When were you going to tell me about this?"

"What?"

"What. This." She held up the magazine. "This is you, isn't it?"

That she would expect him to say left him flatfooted, as if he owed her an explanation.

"Um, what makes you think?"

She continued looking at him and pursed her lips judiciously. "Who's this Juliette Manoogian? You know her?"

"You met her: my daughter."

"Oh. *She* wrote this?"

Graham nodded reluctantly.

She flexed her shoulders, never taking her eyes off him. "Hm. What am I supposed to call you?"

"Alexander's my first name; and I'm not related that I know of, in case you're wondering."

"I see."

"Grace. It takes too long to explain. Don't say anything to anybody. You don't know what it's been like."

"I bet. What else do I not know?"

"Isn't that enough?" There was no way he'd tell her the rest of it. When Julie asked, he crossed a line he wouldn't again. Tori knew of course; but who had a clue where *she* was?

"Well I said I'd make breakfast." Grace pulled his for-show apron down from the kitchen wall, flapped it, and began pawing through his refrigerator for raw materials, sliding out bins and clinking jars before she emerged with four eggs balanced in her hand.

She spooned some coffee into the maker and backed against the table to watch him sheepishly fit the bearings back into her pedals. Taking the pedals apart, that was really overdoing it. She saw his harmonica where he had dropped it on the counter last night and picked it up to blow a few notes, trying to lighten the mood while she waited for the skillet to heat.

"Are you good on this?"

He shrugged, intent on keeping track of the pieces he was picking from the solvent.

"You never play it."

"I play it."

The smell of coffee was making him hungry. Grace flicked water into the skillet for the sizzle before sluicing in the eggs.

"Oranges?" she asked.

"Here." He flipped her a couple from the bread bin, and she snagged them on the fly, one in each hand.

Without comment she elbowed the magazine aside to set down her breakfast. They ate in silence, although once she looked up and suppressed a smirk. He hoped she'd begun to see the absurdity.

"I'll wash. Do the bike," she said, gathering the dishes when they finished.

She watched him work until he bowed and presented the finished product with a flourish to which she didn't respond. Instead, she wheeled the bike out the front door and spun the crank back to sit for a second.

"I need to get my head around this," she said and shoved off down Kilkare Road.

•

Volunteering Vietnam to Julie hadn't been on his agenda.

When she came for Christmas, they could spend enough easy time for Julie to reveal her fun side. Leila had clearly done well with her. They visited his old places, including a day when they borrowed Grace's spare mountain bike to climb Mt. Diablo. Grace had been Grace on that one: girlishly conspiratorial with Julie but clear once they were on the trail that she could kick both their butts.

The day she was to leave, they'd decided to cruise around the city before her evening flight, seeing where it was at when he was her age. The sun had come out as they made their way up Columbus and turned the afternoon almost tolerable for December in San Francisco. On the way, Graham painted for her how North Beach became the headquarters of a cultural avant-garde whose flag bearers—people like Kerouac, Ginsberg, Ferlinghetti, and Corso—drew up their manifestoes in New York and then found their way by whatever questionable vehicle, freight car, or thumb to this Pacific Mecca. By 1960, Kerouac had offhandedly dubbed what they started "The Beat Generation." The postwar doldrums may have had them beat, but they'd also caught the beat of a new song.

Just in time, the proliferation of paperback books put their pamphlets, poems, novels, and screeds into the hands of a generation, as the Internet was promising to do with information now. Graham remembered how cool it felt to pack one of the new Vintage or Penguin paperbacks. Nowadays for granted, but then they offered the world in one's hand like maps.

At Broadway, Graham had steered them into City Lights, Ferlinghetti's literary and cultural touchstone where all the poets, writers, artists, and musicians of the day who aspired to be anybody gathered. He recounted how one could edge through the toppling shelves of the 1960s to bump into Burroughs, Dylan or Kesey. Twenty years on, the revolution decamped to Haight-Ashbury; but City Lights, where it began, remained.

At Molinari's, they'd split a sub and turned up their collars to finish it on the street before ducking into an espresso bar for double shots and a shared gelato.

Afterward, they'd returned to the truck and made for Golden Gate Park, where so many rallies and demonstrations erupted as rage and protest drowned out the humanism of the 1960s. He was pointing out where war protesters had gathered when Julie had taken his arm.

"Dad, may I ask you something?"

"Shoot."

"Back in Marquette I wondered what happened to you in Vietnam. Mom says you came back damaged."

"That's what she calls it?"

Julie nodded. "You wouldn't talk about it. Was it just being there? Or did something else happen?"

What could he say? After the way she'd stood with him through this whole misadventure, Julie had a right to know.

He'd told her everything: What it did to him ending a man's life that way, stumbling through darkness in strange country to freeze in terror at the slightest rustle, the hopeless miles he had to cover undetected, loneliness and fear goading every step. He'd described the spiders and leeches, the snake that crawled over him, how every second he'd expected to die in gunfire.

The thread ran out where he fell to his knees, half dead, in front of a convoy near Hué. He'd finished almost surprised to find himself in San Francisco. A tear traced the side of Julie's nose.

"Sorry. I've never let all that out before. It wasn't fair to lay on you."

"All these years you never told anyone?"

"Not really."

He hadn't been prepared for her reaction.

"You've gone all these miles, and you're still carrying him."

He'd looked at her, taken aback. Where had that come from? She'd held his gaze.

"I know. You can't leave him. It's not settled."

That hit him right between the eyes. If he'd expected throwaway sympathy, *There, there, nobody blames you,* it wasn't her coin. She got it.

"There's a balance involved," she'd said. "It has to add up. One of these days it will."

"Do you think so?"

"I know so. Maybe my accounting's not as strict, but yes." She waited a beat. "The thing with Tori connected, you know. Saving her tipped the balance in your favor."

"I don't know that I thought of it that way."

"You must have told her about it."

"Some of it."

"Mom should know. It would explain a lot. I gather you didn't do so well after you came home."

"It would just sound as if I'm justifying myself."

"I'll tell her if you won't."

"That's probably a good idea. She'd take it better from you."

Heading back to the truck, since she'd brought it up, he'd elaborated on Haight-Ashbury and the years of return. This he told in haste, partly from shame and partly because they had to make the airport.

He'd summed up the whole sorry period on the freeway.

"I was conflicted; it all seemed so sweet, the Summer of Love, as long as no one knew. Turn on and tune out was the order of the day, and I joined with both feet. Then the street turned hard, and we got the Manson family. Bad things happened, and I was out on a limb. I couldn't face her. Or you." He'd reached across and squeezed Julie's shoulder. "I'm sorry."

She'd waved his apology off. "That's under the bridge. Look where you are now."

Parting at the gate, she'd left him on a high note. "Next time I am bringing the boyfriend for your approval. I wanted him to come this time, but he seemed daunted. I think he's in awe."

"Of what, me?"

"Who else? You better live up to the billing. I have him convinced you're one of a kind. Don't let me down."

Whatever else it offered, Julie's table didn't serve sympathy.

•

After Grace left with her bike, Graham picked up the *Rolling Stone* and paged through it again, studying each photo before dropping it back onto the table. *Grace* needed to get her head around this?

Making up his mind, Graham pulled on his jacket and gassed up at the store for the drive into the city. At San Francisco General, he shoved through the emergency receiving doors and made for the intake window.

"Is Dr. Park on the floor? I'm an EMT she works with. Tell her Mr. Bell needs to see her."

The receiving nurse spent a few seconds on the phone, then tilted her head in response to someone on the other end. She beckoned Graham.

"She's with somebody. Sit tight. She'll see you as soon as she's free."

Ten minutes later, Jen popped into the waiting area, stripped off her scrub cap, and shook her hair free to gander around. Even with the glossy hair she evoked all too uncomfortably her mother. When he got to his feet, she blinked and pressed her cheeks in astonishment.

"You!"

"Of course. Who did you think?"

"I had no idea; the name on the SOAP was *Al* Bell."

"But you contacted search and rescue…"

"To thank you. I was just going by the name. I didn't know it was *you.*"

"Yep; Alexander. My father had a strange sense of humor. My sister's lucky he didn't name her Tinker. Hey, what about Frye? How's he doing?"

She wagged her head. "Not out of the woods, but he'll make it. Thanks to you."

He shook his head. "We all had a hand, you far more than me I'm sure."

"Listen, we have to talk."

"That's why I'm here."

"Is there any chance tomorrow? Because I'd be off call, and right now I'm really jammed."

"Tomorrow could work. I have a class in Berkeley, but I could come over early."

"No need; I can meet you there. When's your class?"

"Six."

"So how about four at Caffe Strada? Know where it is? Right off campus?"

•

Certain Jen wanted to tell him about Tori, Graham parked his truck and double-timed it to Caffe Strada fifteen minutes early. Across College he could see her already standing outside hugging herself in a hip-length blue jacket and jeans, craning her neck to spot him.

She waited at the corner when she spied him, visoring her sunglasses onto her head when he joined her. "What's the class?" she said.

"Organic. I'm getting my P.A. back."

She had to catch her sunglasses when she slapped her forehead. "What? That is too perfect."

"Oh? How so?"

"I'll explain." She shepherded him to the entrance. "We'd about written you off."

"'We'?"

"The family. You didn't let us know, no forwarding address, nothing."

"I wasn't sure you'd want to hear from me."

"You kidding?"

"Julie could have told you. You still have her number don't you?"

"How long have you been out here? And *Al;* what's that about?"

"Under cover." He cupped his mouth as if he were a spy. "I've been here a year at my family's place in Sunol, driving ambulance out of Pleasanton. The search and rescue's a volunteer thing."

"Really? Under cover?" She sized him up and wrinkled her nose. "The mustache suits you; I don't know about the ponytail. Here, get me a cappuccino and whatever you want. I'll grab a table out here." She handed him a ten and waved off his protest.

Graham brought her cappuccino and a double-shot espresso for himself from the counter and saw she'd commandeered a table up against the building.

"We don't have to sit out here. There's room inside."

"This is good; it's private. I turned up the heater."

A welcome orange glow reflected off the brushed aluminum hood of the stand-up propane heater. *Just like her mother: Do it yourself.*

Jen rubbed her hands together. "Okay, here's the deal." Graham leaned in expectantly. "I'm starting a community clinic in Oakland, kind of a Doctors Without Borders thing. I'm getting too wrapped in crisis medicine. You're an EMT; you know what I mean. I'm quitting ER to get a life before I lose sight of normalcy."

Graham knit his brow. This wasn't the direction he expected.

"So that's the reason I wanted to meet: when I discovered you're an EMT. Now I find you're going for a P.A. Plus the way you handled that situation... The long and short is I could use you. And I could even give you a bye on the ponytail, what with your combat experience."

Suddenly she had Graham's attention. *"She* told you that."

She looked at him as if he'd just farted. "Your daughter, when we were still speaking. Don't you think I found out everything I could about you?

"Anyway, the clinic: I've got foundation backing, along with some other funding, so I could pay you..." She hesitated. "Competitively, kind of. In all honesty, you'd make more in a regular practice, but this would suit you, I know it would. What do you think?"

What Graham thought was he'd been cheated. This wasn't about Tori. He downed the espresso and tongued a *frisson* of ground coffee against his teeth. "I'm only a year into the program."

"No problem. Start part time if you want." She took a sip of her cappuccino and a residue of foam appeared on her upper lip. "Hiding out, are you? Because of the *Rolling Stone* article?"

Now we're talking.

He shrugged. "I suppose."

She worked her fists a moment. "I know she's your daughter, but—"

"Yeah, I understand. It did stir things up."

"She could have ditched the speculation. Let sleeping dogs lie. What was the sense in that?"

The barista called out an order inside. Graham closed his eyes, savoring the remnant dark roast in his demitasse as he figured how to blunt her resentment.

"Actually she feels the same way now. The reaction took her by surprise. She only meant to use the disappearance for a story hook. You should forgive her."

"Hm. At least she didn't identify Rob or me. Still, it's been bad enough."

Jen stirred a fingertip in her cappuccino and raised an eyebrow at him as she licked the foam from it. Graham focused.

"Your mother did that."

"What?"

"That coffee thing." He mimicked licking his finger.

She gave him a squinty smile. "Like mother like daughter."

He hesitated. Let sleeping dogs lie, but this one wouldn't. He leaned toward her and dropped his voice. "Are you in contact?"

She tilted her head and frowned. "You told me not to let you know. Remember?"

"Are you?"

"No."

"That surprises me."

"It shouldn't. Wouldn't I say that even if I were?"

"Even to me?"

"Especially."

"You're protecting her."

"I'm protecting *you*. She's done enough damage. You're better off."

"Is that you speaking or her?"

"Who's it look like?"

"So I take your word for it."

Jen stirred a finger for more foam and avoided his eyes.

Graham sighed. "All right; let's put it this way: If she *were* to contact you, you could tell her she has nothing to apologize for. If it weren't for her, I'd still be in prison."

"If it weren't for her, you wouldn't have been there in the first place."

Graham propped his fists together and expelled a long breath. He and Jen locked eyes.

"Whatever you think, it isn't happening," Jen said. "She couldn't face you."

"So you do see her."

"No, I just know."

"You just know. Yet you can't tell me where she is."

Jen gave him a stumped look.

"Has her face healed?"

Jen focused. "Her face?"

He showed her the scar on the back of his hand. "This finally did. It took months."

"What are you talking about? What happened to your hand?"

Graham leaned closer and imparted how he crushed it cushioning Tori's head after she took Meachum apart.

"She was pretty messed up. Nothing compared to what she did to him, but still…"

Jen carefully stacked and rearranged her cup and saucer. "Her face is okay."

"Ah." He waited. "That's it?"

She compressed her lips and nodded.

"Thanks for that anyway." He stood. "I need to get to class."

"Graham." She stood with him. "I'm serious about my offer. I really do need someone like you."

He folded his arms and studied her a moment. "I don't know; I'll have to think about it."

"Please do."

Jen fell silent walking to the corner with him. Just as the walk light came on, she caught his sleeve. "The Haight, *sub rosa.*"

He turned, but she was already walking away.

•

Wind surged across Golden Gate Park as he turned up Haight two days later. After he got into the heart of the district past Shrader, he saw how the place had changed. When he returned from Asia, the Haight ran barefoot riot in batik and beads. Everywhere cannabis scented the street, and he'd inhaled aplenty.

Driving up Haight twenty years on, he imagined people would be too busy making a buck on Internet startups for anything like that. The emporia probably smelled more of patchouli than pot now.

As Graham tried to make out what looked like "Wasteland" across the Art Deco façade of the old market on Haight, a woman in cargo pants and pea coat crossed Cole in his peripheral vision on the other side of the street clutching a packet the size of a movie poster under her arm. It was the dimension of what she was trying to keep from sailing off that caught his eye—and then riveted it. She had an oversize cabbie pulled over her eyes, but the brisk march—as if she were booting a can down the walk—the bronze curls peeking from the cabbie, the very shape and size: It was *her!* He couldn't get his window down fast enough and tried tooting his horn, but the woman didn't seem to notice.

Looking back, he came inches from rear-ending a delivery truck. Shooting around it, he squealed a right onto Belvedere and jerked to a stop across someone's garageway and threw the blinkers on.

By the time he ran back, she was gone. He scanned all around and then darted into the nearest place, the Goodwill shop on Cole. He approached the first person who looked as if he worked there, an owlish, full-bearded man in suspenders who looked like Santa Claus.

Right away he disregarded Jen's admonition to be on the QT. "Did you see a woman with a big posterboard? Black hat with a bill, curly dark hair, oval face?" He shaped her face with his hands.

The man shrugged one shoulder in a nervous tic. "Whoa fella, slow down. What's the issue?"

"There was a woman, crossing the street, did she come in here?" He repeated the description with elaboration.

The man gave his tic again. "Sub Rosa."

"What?"

"I say that sounds like Sub Rosa."

"That's a name?"

He shrugged. "It's what she goes by. Maybe Rosa's her last name, I don't know."

"Who is she?"

"Street artist. Red Vic's got some of her stuff up. One time at the theater sang like one of them French *shantoozies* for something the Vic was showing. Pretty good too. Who'd think?"

Graham felt as if someone had smacked him. When Jen said "sub rosa," *this* was what she meant.

"Omigod! Any idea where she lives?"

"In the park for all I know. Lemme ask; maybe somebody else knows."

"Okay, do that, I've got to move my car. I'll be right back."

Graham found a place to park on Waller and trotted back to the Goodwill store. This time a fireplug of a woman about his age looking every inch the Irish washerwoman was stacking new drop-offs onto the counter, her skin as red as if she'd just emerged from a steam room. She looked up unsurprised when he came in, as if she were expecting him.

"You the guy asking about somebody?"

"Yeah, I was just talking to the bearded man that was up here. He called her Sub Rosa. Can you tell me anything about her?"

The woman stopped folding and squinted him up and down like Popeye. *"Sub Rosa?* What kind of name is that? You kidding me?"

"But he said—"

"He must've been pulling your chain. I've worked here ten years. Never heard of anybody like that."

"A street artist? Dark curly hair, about so tall?"

"Nope. Sorry. 'Fraid I can't help you on that one. Sub Rosa! That's a good one." She gave a hearty chuckle.

He spotted the man making himself scarce in the back of the store. "But he told me. Can I talk to him?"

"What for? You don't believe me?" Her posture made it clear his investigation here was over.

"Well, please, if any of you see her, tell her I'm looking for her." He wrote his name and address down and handed it to the woman, who regarded it like an offense and stuck it under the counter.

Graham had run into the Tori stonewall enough times to know he was licked here. The woman no doubt figured he meant trouble. He drew a total blank at a coffee shop down the street before he remembered Santa Claus's mention of Red Vic. Up the street he sighted a three-story red emporium: *"The Red Victorian."* That had to be it.

The front windows advertised *"CAFE"* over big peace signs, so he walked in to look around. He saw the pictures right away, four charcoal drawings signed *"sub rosa"* resembling Goya sketches.

One depicted a young woman in running shorts, her face tipped down as she leaned on a trash bin wiping her shoe on the curb with a look of distaste.

Another portrayed two women on a wall facing the wind, their hair whipped across their faces. One gazed into some distance beyond the frame. The other seemed on the point of looking down, about to discover a large spider on her thigh.

The third frame showed a policeman squatting on one heel. He was extending his nightstick to prod an inert form blanketed in newspaper.

The final drawing was a couple in business garb, the woman in heels and a handbag on her wrist. She brushed something from her skirt with the flat of her hand. Her hair looked ever so mussed, and the artist had smudged an unmistakable flush on her cheek. The man waved a briefcase in the air as if hailing a cab. His raised suit jacket exposed an unzipped fly leaking a tip of shirttail. A sign over the suggestion of an entrance behind read "HOT" before ending at the frame.

Graham looked them over again. They were beautifully rendered, each unsettling with the tension of something unresolved. The viewer couldn't ignore them; they were that compelling.

"Where'd you get those drawings?" he asked the woman at the coffee counter.

She pointed out the window at a storefront across the street. The sign painted on its window read *"sub rosa."* He'd run right past it chasing the woman he'd seen.

"It's not open today, though. I'd try later in the week."

"Do you know anything about the artist?"

The woman studied him a second. "No, I sure don't."

•

Graham returned on Thursday morning and found the little gallery open.

A small handbell attached to the door jingled when he entered, but no one appeared, and he turned his attention to the artwork. The room displayed a painting on each wall, three altogether. If he found the charcoal drawings arresting, these were completely beyond them: exquisite, poster-sized watercolors of city scenes with a use of light and form evoking Edward Hopper. They simply begged closer inspection. When he stepped closer, he discovered figures overlooked on an initial viewing. Once noticed, however, the figures drew the eye back and forth, creating irresistible tension between figure and ground.

The painting on the left wall depicted early dawn spreading over the bay viewed through a gap in the buildings atop one of the city's hills. The structures emerged from twilight blue where a man leaned on the top of his car, door half open, gazing at the lightening bay. Or was he? In his field of vision a woman was doing her level best to restrain a dog ferociously barking at a raccoon emerging from a trash can an arm's length away. The painstakingly rendered figures occupied no more than inches of the big watercolor and yet managed to jar its serenity. The plate beside the painting read, *"Morning Russian Hill. sub rosa $2,500."*

On the right wall, the southern entry of the Golden Gate Bridge emerged from fog. Car lights blurred to points in the gloom. The impression was quite ethereal until he noticed a cyclist cross-legged on the walkway with a wheel in his lap, his bike upturned against the rail. His tiny predicament made an irresistible counterpoint to the ghostly expanse, figure and ground. The tag read, *"Golden Gate. sub rosa $2,000."*

When he turned to the third painting, a short man with a Van Dyke and wire-rim glasses who put Graham in mind of Lenin appeared in the doorway from the back of the shop. Graham nodded to him and examined the watercolor on the back wall. This one pictured Grace Cathedral in striking sidelight. Figures cast long, notched shadows across the steps. Nothing seemed off-kilter until he discerned a cat crouched on the top step, intent on a girl keeping pace with a Slinky halfway down the steps. The pending encounter of cat with Slinky animated the painting with tension. The tag read, *"Grace. sub rosa $2,500."*

Graham blinked himself away from the painting and turned to the man in the doorway. "People pay that much?"

"You'd better believe they do."

"You're not the artist, are you?"

"Oh no. I run the gallery and handle the money."

"So who's sub rosa?"

"The artist."

"Is she around?"

"We only display the paintings here."

"She must come in sometimes. What does she look like?"

"I can't honestly tell you sub rosa *is* a woman. Supposedly it's someone who worked at Vic's theater a while, but that's hearsay. Whoever it is leaves new pieces in the back once or twice a month. Usually they'll be there Wednesdays when I open. People in Red Vic tell me they've seen a woman in here, so it probably is."

"How does she get her money then?"

"I send the proceeds to a bank account after I take my cut. That's our arrangement through an agency. I'm bonded."

"Wow, that's strange."

He shrugged. "Stranger than J.D. Salinger? I don't ask; things move. Who knows? The mystery probably enhances the demand." He smiled. "Maybe that's the purpose."

"So they do sell."

"Faster than she can paint them. These two are already spoken for unless you want to bid up on them."

"No thanks; a little rich for my taste. Enjoyed seeing them though."

"Any time."

Graham walked back to his truck figuring. He'd seen the woman on Monday, hadn't he? His day off, when the gallery was closed. And who would likely be carrying a posterboard but an artist? He should come back Monday. People in Red Vic had seen a woman in there.

He drove off filled with misgivings about the sighting. Had it been his imagination? He hadn't expected the visceral reaction, not wanted it. He thought he was over her.

54

Rain shimmied down the window as Graham wrapped his palms around a mug of coffee, inhaling the bracing scent as he kept an eye on the shuttered gallery across the street. It was a Sumatra roast; he loved the smell of it. A woman passed in front clutching a threadbare parka to her face as she bent into the raw gusts. Not her. He turned a page in the book he wasn't reading and cast an eye back to the gallery. As long as Graham went through the motions, no one in Red Vic seemed to mind how long he stayed.

San Francisco was doing its January worst, gusting winter rain up the street. Haight was practically deserted; at times he could barely make out the accordion gate across sub rosa.

He'd left a bowl of food for Coconino the Cat and pushed the traffic to get here, same time same place as a week ago. At first, bundled in a jacket and watch cap, he'd paced for blocks up and down Haight in the bluster until he decided it made no sense. He'd do better to watch the gallery, even if the woman had been on the street when he saw her. The weather had been better then for one thing.

He would have ended Julie's visit here if they hadn't run out of time after his catharsis in the park several weeks ago. Instead, they'd had to go like sixty even to make the airport. Even if he had brought her— say *she'd* even seen the woman—would it have proved anything? Julie had never laid eyes on Tori, wouldn't have known her from Adam. Still, had Julie been with him, she could have affirmed he'd seen *some*one.

Outside, the rain let up a bit. Graham stowed the paperback and carried his cup over to the bus tray. His watch showed another hour before dark. This wasn't working out. Even if the gallery had a back door, he would have seen a light, wouldn't he? The weather wasn't helping, and the area covered too many blocks; she could be one place while he was another. Or no place. Buttoning up his coat, he headed back into the fading afternoon.

Indecisive, he stood for a moment before fisting his hands in his pockets and walking up the street to Booksmith. Rain pelted his back. Jimi Hendrix filtered into the street when a girl left a store as he passed. Not her. Inside Booksmith, he chafed his hands and selected a book from a rack near the window where he could see the street. He knew he was violating the first lesson of search and rescue: Stay put. She could be on the move even while he was looking for her. Which of them was lost? That was ignoring of course what he was loth to admit: that she wasn't to be found.

Wasn't that after all for the best? Jen said it: She'd done enough damage. He was better off. Except he wasn't; he shouldn't have noticed her, whoever she was.

He glanced down at the book he'd blindly plucked from the rack: *Women Who Run with the Wolves.*

Women Who *What?* Graham started to put it back lest someone think him a deviate. He stopped himself, curious, and opened it to leaf pages describing daring, edgy women who sounded like Tori. Before he knew it, he'd spent ten minutes on wolf women and failed to keep an eye on the street. Shaking his head, he put it back and went out.

On the street, the rain dwindled to mist as darkness came on. Graham made up his mind and walked to the corner. This was insane. Maybe he could patch things with Grace. Tori wasn't to be had.

He put his head down against the drizzle and headed for his truck. No doubt he'd have a ticket; he hadn't moved it all afternoon lest he miss her while he was gone: another souvenir of this fruitless quest.

The truck came into view when he rounded the corner at Page, parked in front of the little gingerbread place that made his landmark. The truck would already have signaled his presence if she was looking. He cast around as he approached but saw no one. He didn't really expect to.

Two houses away he spotted the parking ticket under a wiper. Cursing, he stepped to the truck to retrieve it and found a folded scrap of Kraft paper pinned underneath. He opened it to read, *"Quit while you're ahead"*: Tori's handwriting wicking into the limp paper.

Graham wadded the note in his fist and beat his head. She had been here.

He punched the cab and instantly regretted it. *Stupid.* The pain brought tears.

He nursed his knuckles and shook his fingers to ease the burn as a car crossed the intersection up the block at Cole. The car's headlights inched toward him. The driver must be hunting a place to park, so Graham hiked his jacket to fish out his key.

In the gathering gloom, he scanned the houses along Page one more time. Across the street, two triplets of columns framed an arched entryway over steps leading into a darkened vestibule. As the car neared Graham, it illuminated a woman hugging her knees there on the top step, peering under a black cap at him. She shrugged her navy pea coat tighter before the dark reclaimed her.

The text is set in **Calisto MT**, an old style typeface designed by British typographer Ron Carpenter in 1986 for the Monotype foundry (MT stands for Monotype). Calisto's minimal stroke contrast maintains even color and high legibility.

Old style type dates to Gutenberg and draws on period calligraphy, using low line contrast and angled serifs connecting in curves.

Callisto (from Greek Καλλίστη, "most beautiful") was a hunting nymph who unfortunately caught the eye of Zeus. He came to her disguised as Artemis, and the young huntress let down her guard. Bad move.

Impregnated, Callisto wandered off to have her child Arcas alone. Hera exacted revenge for Zeus's dalliance by transforming her into a bear, which definitely altered her appeal as a sex partner.

Zeus took pity and placed her in the sky as Ursa Major with Arcas nearby as Ursa Minor, but Hera had the last word; she made them circle forever without dipping below the horizon (at Mediterranean latitudes) for a refreshing bath or cool drink.

There: What you need to know about Calisto.

COMPILED AND EDITED BY STEPHEN HIRST

2015

2021

Eyes slit to crescents, Lauren Napier watches a jet draw contrail across an opening in the overcast and imagines people gazing out at the canyon as they pass over. From 35,000 feet, what chance would they have to spot a woman huddled under a juniper on this nameless knoll in these miles of rim country? The snow, pending all morning, already trails a curtain across the sky. She lifts her sheepskin parka against the chill and tucks the hair that whips her face. What if she miscalculated and Bowman can't find her?

The dozen tips of blue mountains break the horizon, one here, one there, broken teeth against the sky. She does not know their names. Chasms she cannot find separate her from that ragged line. He said cliffs would stop her, but she never came to any.

The terrain below the knoll folds into a wash. Dry agave marks crazy surveys across the low hills. Remnants of sagebrush poke from the snow-patched slopes, and juniper clusters the ridges. Across the dips and rises nothing but these brittle plants spells life.

She pulls a tatter of bark from the juniper and shreds it. If the sheer scale were not enough, somewhere the canyons she did not find gash further impossibilities through the dead landscape. Beyond the miles, a peak fades into snow. She can actually see where the distant storm begins and ends. Out here somewhere, if he even spoke the truth about that, the place may still remain; but she has no way to know. What on earth was she thinking when she undertook this?

She should have known not to venture out here. She should have known, in fact, to turn her back on this whole quest.

An edge of the sky lightens, which she takes for west but wishes she could cast a shadow to be sure. Even then, who would know the time? It must be after noon by now.

A jackrabbit draws her attention across the wash: A warm-blooded creature, alive on the snow. Eyeing around, it nibbles brush. Not a stir escapes notice; its head cocks when she shifts position a hundred yards off. Flakes light on it; its ears flick.

Motion registers on her periphery; she angles her head slightly and freezes. From the very knoll where she watches, a mountain lion inches, fixed on the small animal below. Its shoulder twitches. The rabbit bolts, and the cougar streaks after it. Out in the open, its speed and size shock her.

Lauren shrinks against the tree, petrified, when the cougar mounts the knoll with the rabbit in its jaws. If cats hunt by motion and contrast, she prays her dark skin will blend into the juniper enough to escape this one's notice. All lanky and shoulders, the big creature passes so near she sees its nostrils steam and swears the breeze carries its leathery scent. Near enough to show snowflakes on its coat, the cat pads up the ridge and into the brush.

She releases her breath to see where its prints converge with her own, faded by squalls of snow, and begins to shake. She could have retraced herself, perhaps found the way, but no longer. Silently as possible, she steals to where the rabbit had sat, hoping to find a recess or an overhang along the wash where she can take cover. The juniper affords no protection; anything is better.

At the line of tracks, she kneels where the rabbit bolted and makes out what must be the imprint of his tail right where the tracks lengthen into splashes. So that's how flight looks.

And how does her own look? A set of tentative footprints leading away from the cabins, turning every so often and leading finally over the ridges. Every step lengthens that chain. More than a mile she walked over the ridges and across the stony wash to this knoll and its twisted tree, as if to some recognized end point.

Who is she kidding? The cabins mark but a way station on a flight begun a world away so remote it figures as hearsay, so far removed she can no longer find her way back.

A jumble of tracks marks the rabbit's end; a drop of blood shows on the snow. She studies the cougar's prints to etch them in memory before hastening on down the shallow canyon.

Farther along, she spies something manmade. Picking her way down the dry wash to where it opens into a swale, she walks across to investigate a shock of heavy, unbarked logs leaning together there.

Brush and sticks weave a cover around them. The walls might have been tighter once; now they have mostly fallen in or blown away to open gaps to the weather. An entrance of sorts faces back up the wash, but any door is long since gone.

Small as she is, she still must duck to get inside. After her eyes adjust to the muted light, she notices a gunny sack hanging from a nail. In it she discovers a can of Chase & Sanborn. She can barely remember coffee tins like this one. A can of corn and two cans of beans come to hand; then the last of a quart of vodka swings reflections around as she brings it out. Deeper in the sack she feels small cylinders—cartridges, each brass shell marked "Remington center-fire 30-30." Wooden matches carefully wrapped in plastic follow, and she presses out the wrap to read, "Ohio Blue Tip."

Ohio. She shakes her head and fishes up a length of rope and a fat-slicked knife from the bottom of the sack. Grating her thumbprint across the icy blade surprises her it still holds an edge. Feeling nothing more, she stuffs everything back into the sack and hangs it up again.

Hanging against another timber she sees a strange object on a handle—what appears to be a painted gourd the size of a pumpkin. Cobwebs trail from it, and she hesitates to disturb its permanence.

Looking further around the timber shelter, she finds names and dates carved everywhere. The earliest dated entry, "November 26, 1918," follows the name "Greasewater," the letters etched in an ornate hand seemingly old as the log. The last dated entry records a visit in 1969. Has no one come this way for that long? This worries her even more.

Some of the names—"Johnson," "Bob," "Mark Hanna"—sound commonplace. Others have a stranger ring: "Tahotta," "Waskwivma," and Greasewater of 1918.

Near the foot of the timbers framing the entrance she notices a series of symbols resembling humans and lizards clustered together in groups. Some have little tent-shaped roofs marked above them. Two sets were carved so long ago they look like the wood's own fissuring.

As she looks from group to group, dates appear among the figures. The first she encounters reads "1891," far earlier than the 1918 entry above. The dated figures apparently end with a 1912 roofed human until she finds set by itself on the other side of the entrance one more roofed human dated 1942, the year of her own birth. She wonders about that one a long time before going back and counting up: 42 figures in all, 14 of them dated, 9 of them roofed. What happened here?

Powdery ash from countless dead fires smudges the dirt floor. If she had some wood, she might start one of her own. She kicks around in the debris, bringing a few tarnished forks and tin plates to light but nothing combustible. The logs and brush of the old structure itself would burn, of course, but that strikes her as self-defeating. Besides, she feels something sacred in the crude shelter and its long chronicle of comings and goings.

Another snow squall begins sifting through the dilapidated thatch. Low trees along the ridge fade into the flakes. Christmas: only weeks away and farfetched as those mountains. The snow's damp begins to invade her parka, and she paces and swats to stay warm. Somewhere above the overcast and snow, the drone of a small plane brings no solace. Grand Canyon Airport would lie at least forty miles away, and she can only guess what barriers intervene.

Outside the shelter, a pair of birds plump their feathers among the junipers—more life—barely shielded by the wash's dip. She stands on Bowman's ground now and realizes how off balance that puts her. Thrusting her hands deeper into her pockets, she wonders again about the time. He should have come looking by now. Making fists, she closes her eyes and tells herself she is not afraid.

As the afternoon wears on with no sign, she now sees how easily this hard landscape can do her in and grows more disheartened with the passing time.

Warm rooms with fireplaces creep into her longing, and the winter light penetrating the shelter becomes sun slanting through windows. If only.

She digs the knife from the sack again and shoves it into her pocket. Ducking out, she winces at the glare from the snow and hesitates for a second. She works the knife grip in her left hand and wonders if it would be wiser to try retracing her steps or to stay in the shelter she has found. Though Bowman could most easily spot her in the open, she elects the shelter. The cougar sighting decides her. She can watch through the door for any approach. She thinks the cabins lie somewhere in that direction, too.

He was good enough to track her down in what had to be a far more alien setting after all these years; surely he can manage this.

She waits, her breath measuring the ebb of body heat. Through the shelter's gaps, the still summits show along the horizon.

Movement a quarter mile or so away along the ridge catches her attention, and she brings the knife out, ready, as a shape emerges over the crest. Tensely she watches until the shape resolves itself into a human on horseback, head bent down to study the snow. The horse plods and stops as its rider searches the whitened ground.

Framed by the doorway, the horse and rider descend into the wash, clattering here and there over stony outcroppings. Once or twice they pause as the rider inspects the ground, then raises his head to scan. His gaze appears to sweep across the hut where she waits. His ability to detect any trace of her passage after the wind and snow astonishes her. Bowman has come far enough for her to recognize him. This time he hunts on home ground, she the stranger.

Lauren traces the trail that led here as he approaches, back to the cabins and far beyond to another world across a looking glass. She releases a haze of breath into the cold afternoon, remembering.

www.ingramcontent.com/pod-product-compliance
Lightning Source LLC
Chambersburg PA
CBHW050924030726
47503CB00007BB/2454